"You're aboard the F

Dr.

"The captain just told me he's coming down from the bridge to speak with you. Our senior diplomatic officer will accompany him."

"*Tie-tan,*" S'syrixx said, doing his best to pronounce the strange syllables as he heard them.

S'syrixx carefully pushed himself the rest of the way up into a sitting position and allowed his bare, scale-covered feet to swing over the side of the surprisingly sturdy little infirmary bed. He was determined to make a good first impression with this vessel's captain, as well as to demonstrate his gratitude to the person who was ultimately responsible for his rescue.

"My name," he said, "is S'syrixx."

Ree displayed an impressive assemblage of long, sharp teeth. "Welcome aboard, S'syrixx."

S'syrixx heard a brief pneumatic hiss, which drew his attention to an open doorway that hadn't been in his line of sight before.

A pair of uniformed humanoids entered the chamber and slowly approached the bed. S'syrixx suddenly felt unsteady. Had something gone wrong with the ship's environmental systems, or its artificial gravity generators? His claws tore into the bed's edges as he hung on, suddenly desperate to steady himself.

The room spun, and he felt long, scale-covered fingers and forelimbs pushing him gently back onto the bed.

"Mammals," he muttered as darkness made another bid for him. "Why did it have to be mammals?"

STAR TREK®
TYPHON PACT

SEIZE THE FIRE

MICHAEL A. MARTIN

Based upon *Star Trek* and
Star Trek: The Next Generation®
created by Gene Roddenberry

POCKET BOOKS
New York London Toronto Sydney Hranrar

Pocket Books
A Division of Simon & Schuster, Inc.
1230 Avenue of the Americas
New York, NY 10020

This book is a work of fiction. Names, characters, places, and incidents either are products of the author's imagination or are used fictitiously. Any resemblance to actual events or locales or persons, living or dead, is entirely coincidental.

This book is published by Pocket Books, a division of Simon & Schuster, Inc., under exclusive license from CBS Studios Inc.

First Pocket Books paperback edition December 2010

Cover art and design by Alan Dingman

Manufactured in the United States of America

10 9 8 7 6 5 4 3

ISBN 978-1-4391-6782-3
ISBN 978-1-4391-6796-0 (ebook)

For Marco Palmieri,
who first handed me the keys to Titan,
and for Margaret Clark,
who invited me back aboard
for the current mission.

Historian's Note

This story begins in early 2381, during the time of the mass Borg assault recounted in the *Destiny* trilogy, and concludes in late August 2382, more than a year later (roughly coinciding with the principal time frame of *Star Trek: Typhon Pact—Zero Sum Game*).

Lost causes are the only ones worth fighting for.

—Clarence Darrow

In what distant deeps or skies
Burnt the fire of thine eyes?
On what wings dare he aspire?
What the hand dare seize the fire?

—William Blake, "The Tiger,"
Songs of Experience

Prologue

WARRIOR-CASTE HATCHERY CRÈCHE P152, SAZSSGRERRN, GORN HEGEMONY

First Myrmidon Gog'resssh stood upon the observation footbridge that overlooked the enclosed vastness of the incubation chamber. His claws encircling the railings, Gog'resssh recalled the first time he'd looked upon the room from this high, deceptively solid perch; he'd found the sight almost overwhelming. Apart from the immensity of the starlit nights that blanketed the three Gorn worlds where he'd dwelled throughout his span of twenty-eight Gornar suncircuits, he had never before experienced such sheer *hugeness.* The great translucent roof that soared overhead had created an irresistible urge to crane his head in every direction, leaving his thick neck pained afterward by several strained muscles.

Far beneath the dome, which admitted only the most benign frequencies of light from Sazssgrerrn's yellow-white star, stood legions of eggs—the leathery husks that held the developing offspring of the Gorn Hegemony's warrior caste. Row upon row of ovoid shapes, each roughly the size of a mature warrior's head, rested in their individual warming chambers, their numbers multiplied out to infinity by the reflective properties of the enclosure's rounded walls. Gog'resssh took quiet comfort from the humid, sultry air that wafted up around the footbridge out of the chamber below, where it nurtured the orderly, greenish-white ranks of the eggs. Those rows of enshelled younglings represented the future—a future that Gog'resssh was committed to safeguarding from any threat that might arise between now and the day those younglings acquired the ability to fend for themselves.

Gog'resssh reveled in the anticipatory stillness of the eggs, which he likened to sentries standing an unrelieved, almost one-suncircuit-long duty shift; he regarded their apparently endless vigil as a positive augury—a portent of the disciplined Gorn shock troops they would one day become. Their first tour of duty would begin a mere handful of diurnal cycles after the growing fetuses finished clawing through their protective membranes; they would embark upon the rigorous, lifelong regimen of training and combat that was their elite military-caste birthright almost immediately after their emergence into the world.

Today, however, nearly two local suncircuits into his current tour of crèche-guardian duty, Gog'resssh looked upon the vista arrayed across the sprawling incubation floor beneath him with a far more jaundiced eye than had been his wont on that memorable first diurnal cycle at Sazssgrerrn. What he had once found awe-inspiring now seemed almost quotidian, a font of impatience and ennui rather than a source of wonder and fulfillment.

Of course, Gog'resssh was careful not to articulate any such thought aloud, particularly so close to the workspaces of so many technological- and artisan-caste types, some of whom were no doubt inclined to send unfavorable reports about him to his military-caste superiors. Fortunately, the many adjacent environmental-regulation stations, offices, and laboratories were silent today, as though the staff had decided to take the morning off.

It was odd, if also incidentally something of a relief, to find the crèche's nerve center all but deserted on what should have been a typical workday. Although he was duty-bound to protect the tech-casters, Gog'resssh nevertheless found that their relatively large numbers, close proximity, and overall omnipresence grated on him.

Gog'resssh tensed as he suddenly became aware of a familiar, reedy voice just behind him. "I see that you remain troubled, First Myrmidon Gog'resssh. Were your higher-rankers unable to give you any reassurance?"

The warrior silently cursed himself for allowing the voice's owner to approach him so closely without being noticed. He turned quickly toward the speaker, an elderly member of the technological caste, and carefully avoided staring directly into his eyes for any longer than a moment or two. Although the scientist's two golden orbs stared out in typical Gorn fashion from beneath heavy crests on either side of his skull, they lacked the hundreds of facets that comprised a warrior's motion-oriented compound eye; instead each visual organ displayed a single, eerily mammalian-looking vertical pupil.

Keeping his voice as guttural and inflectionless as possible, Gog'resssh said, "Why do you believe me to be troubled, Doctor Rreszsesrr?"

"Because your back is bowed as though it bears the weight of worlds," the oldster said, speaking as though he were describing some matter of indisputable fact, such as the behavior of objects falling inside a gravitational field.

Straightening his spine, Gog'resssh treated Rreszsesrr to a contemptuous glower before he focused his gaze back upon the apparent infinitude of warrior eggs that spread out in all directions beneath the polysteel footbridge. "Nonsense, Doctor. My back is no more bowed now than it has ever been."

"Then the time you have spent living among us technologists has affected you more profoundly than you realize," Rreszsesrr said. "For instance, you appear to have acquired our alleged inability to tell convincing lies."

Gog'resssh felt the scales on his crest tighten slightly; he had to struggle consciously to prevent them from bristling forward into an obviously aggressive posture. His annoyance at the oldster for being right only increased the difficulty of the effort.

"I have lied to no one, Doctor," the warrior said. "I have broken no oath. And I will do my duty to the Hegemony, exactly as my superiors have ordered."

"But I sense you are doing so only under protest."

"What have I to protest, Doctor? Protecting the next generation is one of the worthiest of tasks. And it is a task that can be done properly only by members of the strongest of Gorn castes." Gog'resssh gestured with one five-clawed manus toward the multitude of gestating eggs below. "Or so the Hegemonic High Command tells me."

Rreszsesrr spread both of his complexly articulated forelimbs before him, the short claws on each of his three-fingered hands contrasting sharply with Gog'resssh's larger, blunter, and far deadlier-looking talons. "Your misgivings are understandable, First Myrmidon. Even by a member of the technological caste."

"I do the work of the Great Egg Bringer S'Yahazah on this crècheworld, Doctor. I harbor no misgivings whatsoever about serving here."

Rreszsesrr regarded him with what looked to the warrior like vague amusement. "Don't you? Your fellow warriors are fighting and bleeding as we speak, out beyond the Hegemony's furthest reaches. I know that they are attempting even now to repel an invasion fleet that has so far cut through friend and foe alike as easily as a Gorn landing trooper's killclaws can gut beached lakeprey."

"The machine-mammals and their cube vessels," Gog'resssh said, doing his best to keep his words free of bitterness. He could no longer deny the essential truth of the oldster's words. *I should be out there now in the Great Cyan Starcrèches with my warrior brethren and their new alien allies,* he thought. *To send those unnatural creatures back to whatever cursed mammalian underworld burrow spawned them.*

Rreszsesrr's head bobbed in affirmation atop his relatively narrow neck. "Yes. The B'orrg. The enemy that you and every other warrior now stationed on this world would rather face right now. It would be far better, would it not? Certainly far preferable to standing guard at what most of you regard as a mere backwater hatchery world."

Leave it alone, Doctor, Gog'resssh thought, carefully swallowing his emotions to avoid lending any credence to the scientist's thesis. He momentarily considered demanding an explanation for the oldster's intimate knowledge of confidential Gorn military matters, but held himself back;

Rreszsesrr was a highly accomplished member of the technological caste, so his ability to obtain classified information really shouldn't have been all that surprising.

"As I have said, I will do my duty to the Hegemony, without question," Gog'resssh said at length.

"Of that I have no doubt," Rreszsesrr said even as his forked tongue slithered quickly past his lips twice, a gesture of obvious skepticism. For one who had access to so many sensitive technological secrets, the old scientist had great difficulty concealing unspoken truths; Gog'resssh found him easy to read, even for a tech-caster. "But asking questions is no breach of discipline, Gog'resssh. Perhaps if more of your peers could find it in themselves to make the occasional harmless query, then perhaps the rest of your garrison would be less restive and angry."

Gog'resssh attempted to look pleasant. "What are you talking about, Doctor?"

"I mean that far too many of you crècheguardians do not appear to appreciate how critically important *this* hatchery world is to the continued survival and health of the entire Gorn Hegemony."

"Of *course* this world is important. *All* the hatchery worlds are important." Of course, Gog'resssh found it debatable that the importance of protecting this particular hatchery world was in any way comparable to the urgent need to mobilize every available Gorn warrior against the marauding machine-mammals. "But important or not, when the Hegemonic High Command sends me to protect any such place, I shall do as I am bid." *No matter how many Gorn worlds fall before the machine-mammal onslaught as a consequence.*

"I do not doubt the truth of that either, First Myrmidon. You warrior-casters are creatures of duty, and the political caste in particular is quite content to exploit this fact. I am simply wondering whether your superiors ever told you *why* this particular world is so uniquely important to us as a species."

Gog'resssh bared a good many of his meticulously sharpened teeth. "The Hegemonic High Command is not obliged to furnish its servants with rationales or explanations for its orders."

The oldster made a huffing exhalation, perhaps to demonstrate his impatience with the military worldview. Gog'resssh tried not to take offense, reminding himself that the scientist was a product of a nonmilitary caste, which made him infinitely less disciplined by definition.

"Indeed," Rreszsesrr said. "But explanations are my stock in trade, and the same may be said for most of my crèchebrethren. And an explanation is definitely in order here, no matter what your superiors may have decided to tell you—or, conversely, to withhold from you."

Gog'resssh allowed his nostrils to flare and bared several more of his very sharpest teeth. "You would dare to question the wisdom of the upper echelons of the warrior caste?"

"I do not answer to *any* echelon of the warrior caste, my good young fellow," Rreszsesrr said, taking no apparent notice of Gog'resssh's rising indignation. "And in my judgment, you need to understand why this world is so *especially* important—specifically to *your* caste, if only indirectly to mine. You see, this place requires warrior protection as no other Gorn hatchery planet does. For without this planet, the entire Hegemony would quickly find itself defenseless."

The oldster was speaking in increasingly eccentric circles. "What are you talking about?" Gog'resssh said, repeating his earlier question in more demanding tones.

"All of the non-warrior castes have established their respective reproduction crèches on multiple worlds all across the Hegemony," Rreszsesrr said. "But the eggs that nourish and protect you warriors as they grow from blastocyst to hatchling will grow properly only here, on Sazssgrerrn. Nowhere else."

The notion struck Gog'resssh as entirely preposterous. "Why would the High Command tolerate such a liability?"

"It isn't as though your superiors have any choice in the matter, First Myrmidon. The environmental requirements of your caste are extremely exacting, much more so than any other caste. Worlds appropriate to the warrior caste's unique nutritional requirements and gestational vulnerabilities have always been rarer than mammal-gizzards. Even the world upon which our people were believed to have evolved originally is no longer climatically fit to serve as a warrior-caste hatchery."

Although Gog'resssh found the old scientist's story incredible, he felt a chill settle deep inside his guts nonetheless. What if this addled ancient's ravings were true?

"Why would the High Command conceal such a terrible weakness from the rank and file of the warrior caste?"

"Who knows, First Myrmidon? Perhaps they reasoned that a weakness of which no warrior is aware is a weakness that cannot be revealed inadvertently to an enemy."

Gog'resssh thought that made a certain amount of sense, although it was hard for him to imagine a Gorn warrior worthy of the description revealing a military secret of any kind to an enemy, be it by accident or as a consequence of torture.

And Rreszsesrr's explanation left behind another vexing question as well.

"Why are *you* telling me this?" Gog'resssh asked, the scales on his head crests slowly standing up as if in expectation of imminent combat.

Frustratingly, Rreszsesrr still appeared utterly unintimidated. "Because, regardless of your superiors' decisions, I believe that you . . . need to know."

"All right," the warrior said. "But why do I need to know it *now*? Why did you fail to tell me this story—if indeed it is anything more than merely a story—two local suncircuits ago, when my tour of duty here began?"

Despite the scientist's pretense of openness, Gog'resssh knew that Rreszsesrr was holding back something else, something crucial. In his own way, the oldster was doling out information on a "need to know" basis himself, just as the Hegemonic High Command that he so clearly enjoyed criticizing had always done.

"Something is happening to Sazssgrerrn's primary," the scientist said after a brief pause.

Primary. It took Gog'resssh a moment to understand. "You speak of the sun that shines upon this world." Why couldn't technologists ever speak plainly?

"Yes. I have explained to you the long-term variable nature of this star, have I not?"

"You have. I did not understand much of your explanation. But I did gather that the star's radiation output can change greatly over periods of many millions of suncircuits."

"It can, First Myrmidon. And we now appear to be

very near the threshold of just such a change at the present moment."

Another interior chill assaulted Gog'resssh; this one began making a slow ascent along the length of his backbone. "I thought that such a thing was highly unlikely."

"It is. The odds always favor any particular Gorn generation coming and passing in the midst of one of Sazssgrerrn Prime's eons-long periods of stability. But my measurements are incontrovertible: you and I both have the misfortune of being here when one of the star's violent transitions is imminent. Our lives stand astride the boundary."

Gog'resssh slowly shook his great head. "It seems an intractable problem, Doctor. What do you propose I do about it? Do you expect the warrior caste to intimidate the local star into better behavior?"

"Of course not, First Myrmidon," the oldster said, finally beginning to sound nettled. It was gratifying to break his insufferable equanimity at last. "But I *do* expect you to inform the rest of your garrison. Very little time remains, and precautions must be taken. You and Second Myrmidon Zegrroz'rh must begin the process of relocating the eggs to the lower levels, where the solar shielding is strongest—"

Gog'resssh cut the oldster off with a wave of his claws. "Eggs are fragile things, even those of the warrior caste. You of all people should understand the risk involved in moving them from the incubation chamber, Doctor."

The oldster's weirdly mammalian-looking pupils narrowed even further, giving his eyes an even more disconcerting aspect than before. "I do not make this request lightly, First Myrmidon."

"Why have you waited until so little time remains to inform me of this? Why have none of your colleagues mentioned anything about this earlier? Why have *they* not already begun moving the eggs?" *Could it be,* he thought, *that none of them believes your measurements are quite so "incontrovertible" as you believe them to be?*

The footbridge beneath their feet shook for a moment. The eggs arrayed across the floor below took no notice.

"Please," Rreszsesrr said, a tone of pleading entering his voice. "I need your help now."

"I would think that you would turn first to *your* people, Doctor. Where are they?"

"My colleagues have all gone to the stellar observatories. They are studying the latest evidence that I have collected, and are busy comparing it to their actual observations."

"What evidence?" Gog'resssh growled.

"Evidence of a phenomenon that most of us have been denying for far too long."

"Do you believe they will find this . . . latest evidence convincing?"

"Certainly. But probably not in time to allow us to do what must be done."

Gog'resssh recalled an ancient tactical axiom that might have been as old as the Gorn Hegemony itself: *An incoming blade is all the proof that a Gorn warrior needs that an enemy wishes him ill. But if he waits for such proof to come to him, then he has waited too long.*

The footbridge shook again, this time considerably harder. It rattled loudly, as though an invisible hammer had struck it.

Gog'resssh placed a heavy claw upon the comm device

on his uniform collar and activated the emergency channel. "Second Myrmidon Zegrroz'rh," he said in his most guttural military tones. "Report to the central crèche immedia—"

A blinding flash of searing white light transformed the dome overhead into fire, immolating all sound, sight, and thought in a span of heartbeats.

"Where am I?" Gog'resssh said shortly after consciousness of a kind returned. His voice sounded alien in his own ears, distorted, processed. Though he knew he was awake, he nevertheless seemed to float in a lightless void; Gog'resssh felt more disoriented than he had as a hatchling during his first martial training sessions.

A voice spoke to him from the darkness. It, too, was slightly distorted, as though it had to pass through some viscous medium in order to reach him. But it was soothing nonetheless. Sibilant. Female.

"You are aboard the *S'alath,*" the voice said.

The *S'alath.* Despite Gog'resssh's disorientation, he had no difficulty recognizing that name. S'alath was the Gorn captain whose heroism had driven the vile human K'irrk and his Federrazsh'n from Inner Eliar, one of the Far Edgeworlds, more than a hundred Gornar suncircuits ago. True, the Gorn political caste had subsequently agreed to share the planet with the primates, who eventually brought distant Inner Eliar into their Federrazsh'n under the human name "Cestus III." But that unhappy result was no fault of S'alath's; it came about because the policy-casters lacked the strength of will to resist the diktat of the Met'rr'onz.

"The Gorn Hegemony warship *S'alath,*" Gog'resssh

said, relieved to learn he was in the claws of his caste-peers, at least nominally. "And who . . . who are you?"

"I am Z'shezhira."

"Technological caste?" Gog'resssh said.

"Yes. Communications specialist."

"Communications. You would seem to have strayed from your specialty."

"The fight against the machine-mammals has cost the *S'alath* dearly in terms of personnel. The threat has now passed, but the crew shortages remain acute. I have also had medical training, so my captain has posted me here."

Gog'resssh noted the apparent defeat of the machine-mammals without comment; he looked forward to reading the official reports from his caste's hierarchy. Not wishing to shine a light on his feelings of disappointment for having missed the opportunity to defend the Hegemony, he decided to steer well clear of the subject.

"You saved my life?" he said.

"I assisted, First Myrmidon," Z'shezhira said, the distortion in her voice doing nothing to filter out the self-deprecating tone. "The medical team nearly lost you."

Gog'resssh felt a surge of gratitude toward her for his survival. Then despair as black as space descended. "I cannot see. A blind warrior is a liability. You must euthanize me."

"No, First Myrmidon. Your head is bandaged. But we expect you will recover your vision soon."

That was fortunate, but was not in itself a justification for continuing to live as a weakling to be cared for by others. And that was precisely the fate he feared lay ahead. "Why do I not feel my body?"

"You are floating in a regeneration tank, First Myrmidon. The gel that surrounds you has dulled your nerve endings while your hide heals."

Gel tank. That explained the muffled quality of Z'shezhira's voice. He suddenly became aware of a strange, crowded sensation in his skull's maxillary region. A breathing tube, no doubt, probably attached to an amphibious microphone.

"From what am I healing?" he asked.

"Severe radiation burns, sustained during the mishap on Sazssgrerrn."

"Mishap?" Why couldn't he remember what had happened?

"I am told it was an extremely large solar-mass ejection, First Myrmidon. It occurs when the balance of forces within a star's photosphere becomes—"

"Such things are known to me, Z'shezhira." Gog'resssh had never had any patience for tech-caste lecturing. "What, precisely, was the outcome of this 'mishap'?"

Silence followed, irritating Gog'resssh further.

"I regret to inform you," Z'shezhira said at length, "that Warrior-Caste Hatchery Crèche P152 was destroyed."

"My soldiers?"

"We extracted nineteen warrior-caste survivors and twenty-two from the technological and artisan subcastes. All survivors immediately underwent treatment. Several have since died. The prognosis appears good for the rest, if guarded. Still, the neurological damage was ext—"

This was too much to get his mind around. "What of the eggs?" he said, interrupting.

"Gone."

"*All* of them?"

"I fear so. Sazssgrerrn itself is now uninhabitable."

My mission was to defend those eggs. And if Dr. Rreszsesrr—the ancient scientist who had probably been reduced to a clawful of ashes by the Sazssgrerrn "mishap"—was to be believed, those eggs had represented the entirety of his own caste's hopes for the future. Not to mention the future of the Gorn Hegemony itself. The black pit of despair into which Gog'resssh had narrowly avoided plummeting moments earlier suddenly returned with a vengeance.

This time he tumbled headlong into it.

Intermittent voices reached across the sedative-saturated void in which Gog'resssh floated. Tech-casters speaking in their uniquely opaque argot.

He heard something about severe radiation exposure. And burns. And "radiogenic damage" to someone's genes. Were they discussing his officers and troops? Or were they talking solely about Gog'resssh himself? He decided it probably didn't much matter.

Then he heard one of the male doctors say "study them all, then euthanize them all" before going on to explain to somebody—Z'shezhira, perhaps?—that genetically-damaged Gorn soldiers could never be permitted to pollute what remained of the warrior caste's gene pool.

"After all," the voice continued, "we cannot compromise the Gorn Hegemony's health and safety."

Consciousness returned more easily the next time, and the time after that. Gog'resssh was pleased to be out of the tank, though he could have done without the pain that the cessation of neutral buoyancy had brought him as he began getting used to Gorn-standard shipboard gravity. His recovery continued apace over the next several diurnal cycles, despite the awful knowledge that had settled upon him like a heavy shelf of granite sitting on his chest.

My caste's next generation has been burned to a cinder, along with any prospect of replacing it. And these tech-casters will probably put us all down without a thought once they've extracted whatever useful data our suffering may generate.

Though Gog'resssh studiously avoided giving voice to those thoughts—particularly when paying a supervised visit to Second Myrmidon Zegrroz'rh or any of the seventeen other officers and men who had survived the Sazssgrerrn "mishap"—he knew he could never be rid of his self-immolating misgivings.

Not until he found a way out of here, preferably for both himself and his troops, and began trying to secure a new crècheworld for his caste.

It wasn't until his sixth diurnal cycle aboard the *S'alath,* during one of Z'shezhira's infirmary visits, that Gog'resssh dared hope that his dream might be realized.

"You say the search for a new warrior hatchery planet is among this vessel's mission objectives?" he said after Z'shezhira had mentioned the topic in passing while moving a scanner over the steadily healing scales of his back and shoulders.

"It's one of several," she said, her vertical pupils riveted to the readout on her medical scanner. "But it has been a high priority for this vessel for many Gornar suncircuits. Since the events at Sazssgrerrn, the political, technological, and labor castes now regard it as a matter of the highest priority."

Of course they do, Gog'resssh thought bitterly. *Now that it is too late to save any part of the Sazssgrerrn Crèche. Now that it is too late to cleanse me of my shame, my failure.*

"Does this mean that you have identified some candidate replacements for Sazssgrerrn?" he asked.

Her scaled, heavy brow ridges crumpled into a thoughtful posture. "Perhaps. Perhaps not."

Gog'resssh bared his teeth to convey his impatience with that answer. "I do not understand."

"It is difficult to explain."

"You tech-casters appear to enjoy explaining things. Please, allow me to indulge you."

She answered with a good-natured snort. "Very well, First Myrmidon. First, do you understand the rarity of worlds capable of supporting large-scale warrior-caste reproduction?"

"I understand the fact, if not the reason." Such subjects had never been included in Gog'resssh's training. All he had ever known was the highly structured life of a combat soldier, the uncompromising discipline and relentless chaos of warfare, and the extensive, all but ceaseless preparation that such a martial existence required.

"Then we are equals in this matter, First Myrmidon. Despite the extensive study my caste has lavished on this matter we cannot yet satisfactorily explain why so far only Sazssgrerrn, out of all the worlds in Gorn space, has nurtured the eggs of our warrior caste."

"That is interesting, I suppose. But it doesn't answer my question: have you found any worlds as yet that might take Sazssgrerrn's place?"

"Perhaps. Perhaps not. We must conduct experiments first before we can answer that question definitively."

"What sort of experiments?"

Z'shezhira looked down uncomfortably at the metal grillwork of the deck beneath her bare footclaws. "Perhaps I have said too much."

"Nonsense. You were merely giving a recuperating patient a measure of hope. Please, tell me of these experiments."

Z'shezhira's head bobbed forward and back in a gesture of assent. "All right. Before the machine-mammal crisis diverted us, the *S'alath*'s crew had discovered a number of ancient technological artifacts. Items that may provide the key to a technological solution to the Sazssgrerrn dilemma."

"What sort of technological solution?"

"Worldsculpting. Ecoshaping. The wholesale changing of a planetary biosphere. The idea is to find the world that represents the closest analog to Sazssgrerrn, and then apply this technology to it."

"You sound as though you believe you have tamed the power of the Egg Bringer S'Yahazah herself," Gog'resssh said with an awed growl.

The scales from Z'shezhira's snout to the crests between her wide-set golden eyes reddened, as though the praise embarrassed her. "I would not go quite that far, First Myrmidon. But the technology does hold great promise. Hopes are high throughout the technological and political castes."

The political caste, Gog'resssh thought with distaste as she explained some of the technical particulars at too great a depth for his tastes. *Politics. The vice of the bloodless weaklings who saw fit to diversify the crècheworld holdings of every caste save the only one that is indispensable to the Hegemony's security. S'Yahazah's* cloaca, *even the lowly laborer caste has incubation facilities on at least a half-dozen worlds.*

The political caste obviously feared the warrior caste. That had been so ever since the warriors of the Black Crest had attempted—and failed—to seize the reins of power within the Hegemony almost eight Gornar suncircuits ago. Those would-be insurrectionists had failed, and now the political caste had finally exacted its patient vengeance by keeping the warrior caste vulnerable to a single calamitous extinction event. Gog'resssh's mind had hearkened back to the one and only time he'd met the legendary Captain S'alath, this vessel's namesake. S'alath had told him that while he stood vigil at one of the first Gorn-human territory negotiations that had followed his initial encounter with K'irrk, he had picked up a human aphorism: "Don't put all your eggs in a single basket."

The political caste had allowed all the warrior caste's eggs to remain in one basket. And catastrophe had been the result.

Banishing those thoughts lest he grow visibly angry enough to frighten Z'shezhira out of the infirmary, Gog'resssh tried instead to concentrate on what the female was telling him, in her caste's typical loquacious fashion. According to her, the warrior caste's future might not be so bleak as he had feared. Hope sparked within Gog'resssh's belly; it was his first experience with hope since he'd learned of his abysmal failure at Sazssgrerrn.

"Your captain must take this vessel to your best candidate world now," Gog'resssh said. "He must apply this new technology there immediately. He must use it to pull my caste back from the brink of oblivion."

Z'shezhira raised a restraining manus, its three delicate yet sharp claws extended in a gesture of warning. "Much testing remains to be done first. Worlds similar enough to Sazssgrerrn to be good ecoshaping candidates are too rare to risk ruining. We must run a great many simulations before we can deploy the technology safely."

The spark of hope quickly fanned itself into white-hot impatience. "How long a wait do you foresee?"

She made a noncommittal gesture with both sets of claws. "Adequate testing could require a good many Gornar suncircuits. Especially if we experience setbacks during the simulations."

"The Hegemony cannot continue to defend itself if the supply of new Gorn warriors remains interrupted for suncircuit after fallow suncircuit." *Not that you expect me or my warriors to be around long enough to observe that sad outcome.*

"I understand the drawbacks of caution as well as those of haste. But it really doesn't matter what I think. Such decisions are the province of the political caste."

Perhaps. But perhaps not.

Z'shezhira put the scanner on a tray with a number of other obscure-looking medical instruments. Apparently satisfied that he was mending satisfactorily, she bid him farewell.

He called out to her as she reached the threshold, stopping her. "May I speak to Second Myrmidon Zegrroz'rh?" he asked.

After pausing to look into the adjacent healing bay, she turned toward Gog'resssh and dipped her head in a gesture of assent. "He is conscious, though he still requires somewhat more healing than you do. Please do not tire him."

"I understand," he said.

After Z'shezhira departed, Gog'resssh rose from the steeply inclined resting board and walked across the infirmary toward the other healing bay. Since the other injured officers and enlisted troopers were recovering elsewhere, he and his lieutenant were all alone but for one another's company.

"First Myrmidon," Zegrroz'rh said as he tried to stand, his pain evident. Gog'resssh needed no special medical expertise to see that his Second had suffered more extensive burns than he had.

Gog'resssh gestured for Zegrroz'rh to stay down, and the injured Gorn sagged gratefully back onto the inclined resting board where he'd been recuperating. "The techcasters aboard this ship have made plans to kill us all," Gog'resssh said without preamble.

Zegrroz'rh's brow folded forward in a puzzled frown. "Why did they not do so when we were all more helpless than we are now? Why do they delay?"

Gog'resssh issued a low growl that signaled his displeasure at being questioned. "Why do they do *anything*, Second? They probably wish to make further observations of the radiation damage we have suffered before deciding they are finished with us."

"If you are right, we must stop them," Zegrroz'rh said, demonstrating his usual keen grasp on the obvious.

"Of course I am right. And we *shall* stop them. What's more, we are going to repair the damage that the politicals did to us at Sazssgrerrn. And we will find and safeguard a new crècheworld for our caste, without relying on any further 'help' from the politicals."

Zegrroz'rh appeared mystified. Or perhaps he was even more radiation-damaged than Gog'resssh had initially believed. "First Myrmidon?"

Gog'resssh leaned in close to the other warrior and hissed into the earhole just above his radiation-seared zygomatic bone. "Listen very carefully, Zegrroz'rh. We will begin by taking this ship. . . ."

1

U.S.S. TITAN, DEEP IN THE VELA OB2 ASSOCIATION, BETA QUADRANT

The aquamarine world that turned serenely on the main viewer had seemed hospitable enough when Captain William Riker had first looked upon it from orbit. It had seemed so when he had first set foot upon one of the small rocky continents that punctuated a planet-girdling, highly saline ocean. Other than the prevalence of strong winds, and the clouds of grit and dust they kicked up, the place had been very accommodating to *Titan*'s survey teams—it offered breathable air, middling-warm temperatures, and fair-to-tolerable humidity levels.

But the sometimes all-but-invisible fabric that nearly always accompanied such humanoid-compatible environments—an oft-taken-for-granted little thing more commonly known as *life*—was conspicuously absent from this place, from pole to pole and meridian to meridian.

William Riker leaned forward in his command chair, resting his chin on his fist as he regarded the dead world that even now *Titan*'s planetary-science specialists were still busy trying to understand.

"Deanna, what do you think about naming this place

'Doornail'?" he said, turning to his left just far enough to see an amused smile split his wife's face.

"'Doornail,'" repeated Commander Deanna Troi, *Titan*'s senior diplomatic officer, chief counselor, social-sciences department head—and beloved *Imzadi* of the captain. She pitched her voice low, as if to be audible only in Riker's immediate vicinity. "That's a curious choice, Will."

He repaid Deanna's grin with interest. After spending the past six hours down on that sterile, rocky world, he was grateful to be back aboard *Titan* and in the warmth of her presence. "'Doornail,'" he said, matching her sotto voce delivery. "As in 'dead as a.'"

She shrugged. "I understand the idiom, Will. My father came from Earth, after all."

"But you don't seem to be falling in love with it."

"No, it's a fine choice," she said, though a slight wrinkling of her nose belied her endorsement. "Besides, assigning names to new worlds is one of your prerogatives as captain."

Commander Christine Vale, who was seated in the chair to Riker's immediate right, chimed in quietly, "At least until the Federation Science Council settles on something a little more, um, dignified."

"Ouch, Commander," Riker said as he turned his command chair so that he faced Vale. "Way to show loyalty to your captain."

Vale answered with mock solemnity. "I wouldn't be much of a first officer if I didn't point out the captain's mistakes, sir."

"Touché. But as I recall, you were quite a bit more eager than I was to get away from that dustball."

"I was just more vocal about it, Captain. After all, a healthy set of lungs and a lack of hesitancy to use same are the main keys to success in this job."

"So . . . an exec's job amounts to either arguing with the captain, or just bellowing the captain's orders to the crew at the top of her lungs?"

Vale smirked as she pushed several strands of her shoulder-length auburn hair from her eyes. "I learned from the best, sir—aboard two ships called *Enterprise*. That reminds me of another nice thing about the planet: good acoustics."

Riker heard Deanna snicker behind him. "It sounds to me as if you like the planet a lot better now that you're safely back aboard *Titan*."

"Places like that always look better in retrospect," Vale said, gesturing toward the bluish orb that hung in the viewscreen's center. "Not to mention from nearly five hundred kilometers away. Besides, it could have been worse. At least there weren't any mosquitoes—"

With an almost Vulcan-like calm, Deanna said something that Riker belatedly recognized as "Incoming!" Simultaneously, Vale interrupted herself by letting out a yelp—accompanied by a brief chorus from Lieutenant Sariel Rager at ops and Lieutenant Aili Lavena at the conn—that startled the captain into turning toward the section of the bridge at which his exec's eyes had been directed: the main viewer.

An apparition had suddenly appeared directly between the screen and the forward helm and ops consoles, where it rapidly took on solidity—or at least the appearance of solidity. In the space of a few heartbeats, it had become recognizable as the high-fidelity holographic avatar of Lieutenant Commander Melora Pazlar, even as it continued to hover several centimeters above the deck directly in front of the wide central screen.

"I don't think I'm ever gonna get used to that," Vale said.

"Nor will I," said Lavena. The Pacifican flight controller shuddered as though something had gone wrong with her hydration suit's temperature controls. The suit made a barely audible sloshing sound in response to her brief startle reaction.

"Sorry, Commander," Pazlar said. "Lieutenant."

The senior science officer entered a command into the padd she carried; in response, *Titan*'s holographic telepresence system gingerly shifted her toward an open space on the bridge's port side. Pazlar's willowy form was outfitted in an ordinary duty uniform rather than in one of the slightly bulkier contragravity suits she wore when venturing outside the comfortable variable-*g* environment of her stellar cartography lab or her living quarters. Being an Elaysian born, bred, and raised in the microgravity environment of the planet known as Gemworld, Pazlar's body was structurally incompatible with a Federation starship's standard one-*g* environment.

Riker turned his chair toward Pazlar's floating image. "Commander, I assume you're here because the department heads have reached a consensus about the origins of this planet."

"Yes, Captain," Pazlar said. "At least insofar as our current knowledge can take us."

"Are most of you still convinced that this planet's M-class environment didn't come about naturally?" Deanna asked.

"As surprising as you might find this," Pazlar said, "the answer is 'yes.' "

Riker smiled. "Huh. Maybe 'Doornail' will stick after all." As dead as they were, even doornails did not spontaneously generate themselves.

Pazlar's V-ridged forehead wrinkled in puzzlement. "Sir?"

"Never mind. As I recall, you were part of the 'this planet's environment is a natural product of planetary evolution' camp."

"I was, Captain. At least at the beginning of our analysis."

"What changed your mind?" Riker wanted to know.

"Well, to give credit where credit is due, Captain, Eviku and Chamish were the first to notice the pattern—a pattern that appears to have played out in several other star systems scattered throughout the Vela OB2 Association, and perhaps even much further into deep Beta Quadrant space."

Commander Christine Vale, *Titan*'s executive officer, spoke up from the seat at Riker's right hand. "If anybody aboard *Titan* was going to find that sort of pattern, it would be our resident xenobiology and ecology experts."

"Apparently," Pazlar said with a nod. "Unfortunately, my expertise in those fields doesn't overlap all that much with that of the biospheric scientists. My specialties are cosmology and big-bore physics. Since we hadn't found a clear-cut footprint indicating intelligence the way we had with the Sentries, I still needed a little more convincing at the outset."

"Sounds like you got what you needed," Vale said.

The Elaysian nodded. "Torvig and White-Blue crunched

the numbers—twice, I might add—and the end results finally made a believer out of me."

SecondGen White-Blue was the designation of the eight-limbed artificial intelligence that Riker had allowed to remain aboard *Titan* a few months back, following the starship's harrowing encounter with White-Blue's kind, the ancient AI civilization whose members referred to themselves as "the Sentries." Although Riker couldn't deny that White-Blue had been invaluable in preventing *Titan*'s destruction, both at the hands of White-Blue's own kind and via the destructive energies of their extradimensional nemesis, the Null, he was also keenly aware of how much trouble the little AI had brought to his ship. The fact that White-Blue had violated the ship's security and privacy protocols on numerous occasions—to say nothing of its having briefly "uplifted" *Titan*'s main computer to full sentience—left the captain still wary of any judgments White-Blue might care to render. That White-Blue's conclusions were supported by calculations run by Ensign Torvig Bu-Kar-Nguv—a Choblik science specialist whose own sentience depended upon an extraordinary degree of integration between his natural biological form and his bionic components—made Riker feel only slightly better.

Riker's face felt flushed as he noticed Deanna regarding him curiously from her station at his immediate left. He stood, straightening his uniform tunic as he got to his feet.

"Give me the gist of it, Commander. Why are you convinced that this planet couldn't have produced its atmosphere on its own the way billions of other planets across the galaxy have?"

"The long and short of it is the balance of gases in this planet's atmosphere, Captain," Pazlar said. "You'll note that the sensors have corroborated Lieutenant Chamish's early contention that the eighty-twenty nitrogen-oxygen mix we observe here could only have been produced by nonbiotic processes."

"Are we certain of that?" Deanna asked. "Couldn't this planet's atmosphere have been produced by a thriving biosphere that was wiped out by some catastrophe in the relatively recent past?"

Pazlar shook her head, her fine white hair following a heartbeat behind owing to her protective cocoon of microgravity. "None of the scans we've done so far have turned up any evidence that there's *ever* been any life on this planet, let alone life that was catastrophically wiped out after producing a Class-M atmosphere."

Riker was no scientist, but he had enough scientific training to know that all Class-M planets' atmospheres were significantly out-of-equilibrium in comparison with those of lifeless worlds. Dead places tended to have atmospheres that were devoid of free molecular oxygen, a gas that tended to get bound up in planetary crusts as oxides, as had occurred billions of years ago on Mars. Lifeless worlds whose atmospheres were "in equilibrium" routinely became anaerobic carbon dioxide hells like Venus, deserts like Mars, or stillborn "primordial soups" like his ship's namesake, Saturn's moon Titan.

Facing Pazlar, Riker said, "Correct me if I'm wrong, but there are still only two known ways to create an M-class environment, broadly speaking. The action of organic photosynthesis or similar biospheric processes on a planet's surface over eons is one." He began ticking off his points on his fingers. "And terraforming technology is the other."

"That's the basic shape of it, Captain," said Pazlar's image. "We have the evidence presented by the composition of the atmosphere itself. Our survey scans have already determined to a high degree of certainty that no biosphere has ever existed on this world. Doctor Chamish, our senior ecologist, triple-checked the figures." Although Riker didn't know Chamish all that well, he understood that Chamish's people were generally gifted with the ability to communicate telepathically with lower animals, and that their homeworld, Kazar, was renowned for producing gifted ecologists.

"Wait a minute," Vale said. "I may have stumbled into this exploration business by way of law enforcement and security instead of through a lab, but even I can see a flaw in your methodology."

Pazlar nodded. "You mean that no matter how many numbers I might crunch, I still can't really prove to a fare-thee-well that there never really was any biota on the planet."

"Indeed," Commander Tuvok said from his position behind the tactical console. "I trust that I need not point out that proving a negative is a logical impossibility."

Turning her chair halfway toward Tuvok, the exec nodded in agreement. "Isn't absence of evidence sometimes just that? Absence of evidence?"

"As opposed to evidence of absence," said the stellar cartographer. "Point taken. But biospheres *always* leave a mark on the worlds that host them. Even small, tenuous biospheres will make their presence known if your instruments are good enough. And our instruments are *damned* good."

Riker considered the most tenuous native biosphere that existed in his own species' backyard—that of Mars. The Martian ecology, marginal though it was by the time humans had developed any capability of studying it to any significant extent, had made itself known only by dint of the traces of atmospheric methane it released and maintained at slightly-above-equilibrium levels. Absent the continued action of a relative handful of hardy subsurface extremophile native microbe colonies, that methane would have quickly been photodissociated into its component elements and then dispersed or absorbed. And before Mars had been scrutinized under a sufficiently sensitive lens, those molecular traces had been undetectable; Mars, with its whisper-thin, oxygen-free atmosphere, had appeared already to be in an equilibrium state consistent with an eternally dead, lifeless desert.

"But as good as our instruments are," Riker said, "couldn't there still be an ancient biological marker that nobody's been able to find yet—something so old it's literally buried at the very bottom of the rock pile?"

"There's a sharp limit to how old a fossil biosphere like that could be, Captain, given the atmosphere we've observed here. Class-M atmospheres are inherently out of equilibrium with the surrounding environment. Without biota to maintain them, they always deteriorate into something much less friendly—especially after a few tens of millions of years go by."

Deanna shrugged. "Suppose this atmosphere is being created right now by life so alien that our sensors simply couldn't recognize it *as* life?"

"According to Eviku, that's still just barely possible," said Pazlar. "But it isn't likely. Life processes, even extremely exotic ones, must involve some sort of metabolism that takes advantage of natural energy gradients—that is, materials moving from a high-energy state to a lower one. Predictable patterns of internal order being created in exchange for increased external entropy. But we simply haven't seen anything remotely resembling that here."

Riker nodded toward the blue world on the screen. "So nothing is maintaining this world's atmosphere. Or at least nothing we've detected so far."

"That's right," Pazlar said. "In fact, Chamish and Bralik have both confirmed that the oxygen in the atmosphere is slowly combining with the surface through natural weathering processes, even as it's being broken down by exospheric solar ultraviolet radiation. Since no detectable process is acting to maintain the atmosphere, it will succumb given enough time. Most of the free oxygen will end up in the rocks, and much of the rest will ultimately bleed off into space."

"In other words," Riker said, "what looks nominally like another Earth now will someday deteriorate into another Mars."

"Assuming that the atmosphere's rate of deterioration remains relatively consistent over time, it should be possible to estimate the approximate age of this . . . non-biogenic atmosphere," said Tuvok, who had raised an eyebrow. Though the phlegmatic Vulcan's current post was tactical officer, it seemed obvious to Riker that his scientific curiosity was now fully roused.

"My department thought the very same thing," said Pazlar. "Bralik locked the core probes onto the rock strata that corresponds to a time-depth of about five million standard years. And that's where we've found a marker of sorts—just not a marker made by life."

"What sort of marker?" Deanna asked.

"A very thin layer of klendthium that seems to cover the entire planet at that depth," Pazlar said.

Riker nodded. "The same way a subsurface layer of radioactive iridium marks the asteroid collision that wiped out the dinosaurs on Earth around sixty-five million years ago."

"Exactly," Pazlar said with a nod.

"Klendthium," Tuvok repeated. "That is an extremely rare mineral that I have only seen associated with Vulcan terraforming techniques, such as the ones historically employed at the Loonkerian outpost on Klendth."

Hence the name, I suppose, Riker thought.

Deanna turned to face the tactical station. "Other cultures have employed methods similar to the Vulcan universal atmospheric element compensator, Commander. Vulcan is only one of that technology's more recent users."

"Quite right," Pazlar said.

"It sounds as though you think we may have found another," Riker said.

"Wait a minute," Vale said, waving her hands before her as though she was dispersing a cloud of smoke. "Couldn't this 'marker' we're talking about here simply be evidence of something that could have wiped out a previously existing biosphere?"

Pazlar shook her head. "Something that seems to have left no trace anywhere on the planet of the billions of years of biological and chemical evolution that must have preceded it? That doesn't seem likely. Not without destroying the planet itself—or at least creating geologic stresses that would still be detectable today."

"What about comet collisions?" Deanna asked. "Couldn't the constituents of this planet's present-day atmosphere have rained down from the system's Kuiper belt?"

Pazlar folded her arms before her, her body language radiating skepticism. "It's a possibility. But this system doesn't appear to have much of a Kuiper belt. And those sorts of impacts would have left behind some geologic evidence *somewhere.* This planet looks to be almost in mint condition, so to speak. Not even a geologically active world like Earth can cover up every last one of its old scars."

"Add that to the implication of a global terraforming operation being conducted here millions of years ago," Deanna said, "and you've got a fairly tantalizing mystery."

"You might have even more than that, especially if you consider two additional factors," Pazlar said, her gray eyes beginning to flash with a rare enthusiasm.

"What are those?" Riker said.

"The telemetry from our probes and the results of our long-range scans. They show that several adjacent systems have bodies that fit the general profile of *this* planet—"

"Doornail," Riker said, glancing in Deanna's direction momentarily to underscore his determination to keep the name in place as long as possible.

"Doornail?" The look of perplexity Pazlar had displayed earlier abruptly returned to her face.

"It'll have to do until something better comes along, Commander," Deanna said around an incompletely suppressed smirk.

Pazlar blinked at the counselor. "All right." Focusing her telepresent gaze back upon Riker, she added, "Doornail it is, Captain. And it looks as though there could be a bunch more Doornails out there—nominally Class-M worlds that apparently got that way via unconventional means."

"A series of artificially terraformed planets spanning an entire sector or more?" Vale said. She didn't sound quite convinced.

Deanna, however, quickly took up the more optimistic side of the discussion. "Why not? We already have evidence that ancient starfaring species have transplanted entire humanoid societies from star system to star system. Some of those interventions may have even involved making deliberate, intensive genetic alterations to the relocated sapients."

"Exactly," Pazlar said. "It's not much of a stretch to imagine that some long-vanished alien civilization may have manipulated whole planetary environments in much the same way. We may be on track to settling the matter definitively. There are several other Doornails within easy reach of our current position. And if any or all of those worlds appear to be as artificially created as this one does, then we could gain some insight into precisely how it was done. If we're fortunate, we might even stumble across some technological relics."

Echoing Pazlar's mounting enthusiasm, Deanna said, "And if we're *really* lucky, we'll find some intact machinery, or maybe some still-readable computer data, that could give us a way to reverse engineer whatever technology these paleo-terraformers were using."

Riker stood in silence in front of Lavena's conn station

and studied the viewscreen's image of a dead-yet-life-friendly world whose stately, eternal rotation was rapidly carrying its nearer hemisphere into night. The allure of seizing long-forgotten knowledge that had once made a dead world—or perhaps even countless dead worlds—capable of supporting life was undeniable. The Federation was still in the process of recovering from the devastation the Borg had wrought during the previous year. Deneva had been laid waste, as had parts of Vulcan. Beyond the Federation, Qo'noS had suffered cruelly from the invasion. If a means of accelerating the recovery of those wounded worlds really existed out here, it deserved serious attention from *Titan*'s captain and crew.

But such a discovery also demanded a fair amount of caution. Riker was well acquainted with the dangers posed by Project Genesis, the code name of a Federation terraforming initiative. Not only had Genesis's initial deployment nearly a century ago proved it far more effective as a biosphere-destroying weapon than as a means of planet-scale creation, the powerful, molecular-level matter-reorganizing force known as the Genesis Wave had also threatened the Federation's very existence much more recently.

Once released from their bottles, genies were often notoriously difficult to coax back inside.

But maybe I can afford to let the ethical agonies wait a while longer, Riker decided, chiding himself gently for getting so far ahead of himself so quickly. *We don't even know whether or not this thing still exists—if it ever really did.*

Turning to face Lavena, he said, "Lieutenant, get the coordinates for the nearest candidate star system from Commander Pazlar and lay in a course, best speed.

"Let's find out how lucky we can be."

2

Despite his most disciplined efforts to clear his mind for meditation, Tuvok's thoughts took wing. He was sitting before an old-style Starfleet copilot's console, alternating between sending repeatedly unheeded hails and watching through a curved transparent aluminum window as a battered, airless moon drew inexorably closer. A half-shadowed jovian planet loomed in the space beyond, its ocher-and-ivory cloud tops striated by fierce cyclonic winds. Just visible near the partially obscured satellite's eastern limb, a motley, asymmetrical spacecraft orbited.

Tuvok turned to his immediate left and saw that his old friend and superior officer, the Halkan pilot Lojur, was handling the controls.

"It's too bad it wasn't the shuttlecraft Fujitsubo *and L. J. Akaar's team that managed to track these people down, Ensign," Lojur said, his bantering tone belying the sincere emotion he seemed to be struggling so hard to master. "Have I mentioned yet how much I hate this mission?"*

It came to Tuvok with no small degree of either surprise or fascination that he was back aboard the shuttlecraft Amagiri, *one of the auxiliary vessels the* U.S.S. Excelsior *had carried during the years he had served as one of that starship's science officers. The moon that the* Amagiri *was approaching circled the gas-giant world Eurymede VI, about a parsec from Klingon space. Captain Sulu had pursued this mission using* Excelsior's *entire complement of shuttlecraft because of the extensive battle damage that the starship had recently sustained at the hands of rogue Klingons; at the present moment,* Excelsior *needed every available hand to effect repairs and to tend to her scores of injuries and casualties.*

"I am certain that no one regards any assignment such as this one as a pleasant undertaking, Commander," Tuvok heard himself saying in response. "However, our duty is clear. We cannot permit these individuals to deploy the device. And we are empowered to use whatever means may be necessary to ensure that outcome."

Tuvok remembered that he had been but a lowly ensign at the time of the Eurymede mission. Matters of friendships aside, had he really spoken so pedantically to his superiors in those days?

"We're here to confiscate the device," Lojur said grimly. "As the Terrans say, 'We get in, we get out, and no one gets hurt.'"

Tuvok nodded. "That would be the ideal outcome. However, whether or not we will achieve that result is largely dependent upon the actions of the privateers who are holding the device—privateers who, I might add, are continuing to ignore my hails." Tuvok's gaze moved back and forth between his controls and the motley vessel, which was still growing considerably in apparent size moment by moment.

"Privateers? I thought they were refugees."

"So they have told us, Commander. The fact remains, they have come into possession of illegal technology that endangers not only this entire star system, but perhaps others as well."

"Give me a damage assessment on the other ship, Ensign," Lojur said.

Tuvok studied the slowly approaching ship through the for-

ward windows as he ran another sensor scan. Thanks to Lojur's delicate handling of the Amagiri*'s phasers, the other vessel's single torpedo bay was visibly scorched and melted.*

"Warp capability has failed, but there appears to be no immediate danger of a core breach. Minimal impulse power and life-support are available, so they cannot outrun us."

"Can they deploy the device?" Lojur wanted to know.

"The vessel has only one torpedo launcher, but it has sustained heavy damage," Tuvok said.

The comm console near Tuvok's right hand flashed, heralding an incoming signal. He tapped the console and a small viewscreen lit up, displaying the sad, careworn face of an elderly humanoid male.

"Please, Starfleet vessel. Withdraw. Leave us."

"This is Lieutenant Commander Lojur of the Federation Starship Excelsior,*" Lojur said. "I'm afraid I can't do that. You are in possession of a Genesis-wave generation device, in violation of the laws of the United Federation of Planets. It is an illegal weapon of mass destruction."*

"In the wrong hands, perhaps. But it is also an engine of creation. And I assure you, Commander, that we soon won't be in possession of any such device—not after we activate it, that is. Once the Genesis Effect runs its course, we'll have a new, living planet on which to settle."

"Negative," Tuvok said. "Your torpedo bay is nonoperational. You lack the means to deploy the device in a manner that will produce the result you seek. Besides, the Genesis Effect has never produced lasting, stable results."

"I don't believe you. This technology has performed miracles. Your own Starfleet has acknowledged that it has raised the dead."

Having met Ambassador Spock, Tuvok knew that he could not dispute that last point. But he decided that no good could come from acknowledging the fact aloud.

Lojur scowled at the image of the old man on the flight-control console's small viewer. "My science officer is correct. If you attempt to use the device, you will create an uncontrolled detonation that will kill everyone aboard both our vessels. Turn it over to us now, and the Federation magistrate may grant you some leniency. But if you detonate it, you'll—"

"The Federation seems to be nowhere near so assiduous in protecting border worlds from the Klingons as it is in guarding its military secrets. Starfleet did nothing to stop the Klingons from annexing our homeworld and making us refugees. It seems to me that your Federation owes us assistance, not harassment."

"Even if you were to succeed in using Genesis to create a new home on this moon," Lojur said, "how long do you think it will be before the Klingons discover what you've done and chase you away yet again?"

Stepping into the thoughtful silence that followed, Tuvok added, "The Klingons are certain to uproot you again once they discover that you have terraformed a world using Genesis—which I strongly suspect that you acquired from them in the first place." Of course, Tuvok could provide no hard proof for this assertion. But it was already common knowledge among Starfleet's officer corps that Klingon spies had somehow obtained a great deal of classified information about Project Genesis—information that easily could have passed from corrupt Klingon intelligence officers to private technology merchants willing to invest enough darseks *in bribes to the appropriate officials.*

"Please," *the old man said at length.* "We are only refugees. We pose no threat to you."

"Then prove it," Lojur said. "Let us take the device and dispose of it safely. You can petition the Federation for help. If you're willing to cooperate, I will personally vouch f—"

The old man interrupted. "If you attempt to board this vessel, I will activate the device, right here aboard my ship."

"That would be a foolish decision," Tuvok said. "Once you begin to generate a Genesis wave, the process will be unstoppable. An uncontrolled blast will annihilate the moon, the gas giant it orbits, and perhaps the rest of this system as well."

"Then back off."

"We can't do that," Lojur repeated.

Tuvok nodded. "Indeed. The planet this moon orbits harbors a complex ecosystem, and perhaps even intelligence." While it was true that higher-order sentience had never been conclusively found among the drifting herds of gigantic jellyfishlike creatures that filter-fed on the less complex life that teemed in the planet's cloud bands, it was nevertheless true that the creatures were alive, part and parcel of a flourishing alien ecosphere. It was also true that any number of natural phenomena, ranging from radioactive upwellings from the planetary core to local stellar mass ejections to the action of distant supernovae could easily summarily sterilize this world. Tuvok knew there was nothing that he or anyone else could do about such things.

He simply wasn't prepared to give the illegal actions of renegades as much leeway as nature demanded.

The slight distortion created by the subspace communications bands took none of the steel from the tone of the old man's reply. "I'll do it if you don't withdraw, I promise you that. Now. Don't test me. Please."

"Heave to and surrender the device," Lojur said, matching the old man's tone and timbre. He paused to take a deep breath. "You have one minute to comply, or we will open fire."

"You can't *do* that. There are twenty-two others aboard this ship, Commander. Women. Children."

"Get them to the escape pods, and we will rescue them," Tuvok said, tapping his console several times to fully activate the shuttlecraft's targeting systems. Next, he took the precaution of arming one of the Amagiri*'s small complement of photon torpedoes. Then he looked toward Lojur, who was making a slashing gesture across his throat. Tuvok responded by muting and blinding the cockpit's comm pickups.*

"He has us, Ensign," said the Halkan. "We're caught in a standoff."

Tuvok had served alongside Lojur for several years, and he thought he knew the commander quite well by now. He believed he had acquired a fairly thorough understanding of the man's culture, which was rooted in a deep pacifism. Lieutenant Akaar had once described Halka's peace-at-all-costs *philosophy as so profound that, to use Akaar's words, "it made Vulcan look like Romulus."*

"We need not be caught in a standoff, Commander. Not if we act before the privateers activate the device. Once the Genesis device begins powering up toward detonation, not even a valley of photon torpedoes will be able to stop it."

Lojur's dark eyes grew huge and desperate. "You scanned that ship, Ensign. You confirmed that there are twenty-three humanoid life signs aboard, just as he says."

"I did, Commander."

"I can't authorize firing on that ship."

"You did *make the threat already, Commander. The Gen-*

esis device has not yet been activated. And that minute you gave the privateers is almost up."

Despite the fact that Lojur had been cast out of Halkan society long ago for the crime of taking up arms against the Orion raiders who had attacked his village, his people's ingrained pacifism was clearly paralyzing him. Firing upon armed belligerents, apparently, was one thing; employing the same tactic against unarmed civilians was evidently quite another, even though the latter were arguably far more dangerous than the former.

"I remind you, Commander, that Starfleet Command and Captain Sulu have authorized the use of whatever force may be necessary to either reacquire or neutralize the Genesis device."

"I can't,*" Lojur repeated, his face a study in ashen agony.*

Tuvok nodded his acknowledgment of Lojur's decision. He placed the shuttlecraft's sensors on active scan and noted with relief that the distinctive wave-pattern of an impending Genesis detonation had not appeared on the console's small screen. At least not yet. But it almost certainly would sometime during the next several seconds.

Once that occurred, there would be no way to prevent the molecular-level immolation of the biosphere of Eurymede VI.

Tuvok glanced down at the console chronometer and noted that the minute Lojur had granted had just run out.

"I understand, Commander," Tuvok said. "I shall relieve you of the burden."

Steeling himself to do what they both knew had to be done, he tapped a control and consulted a readout, confirming his target lock. Then he touched another nearby switch and entered the "fire" command.

• • •

T'Pel opened the door to the officer quarters that she and her husband shared and entered to find the lights dimmed in the austerely-furnished main living area. The only light came from the stars beyond the wide window and the small meditation candle that burned atop the low table in the room's center. Her eyes adjusted quickly to the crepuscular illumination, which revealed that her husband, dressed in a brown-and-black robe, was sitting cross-legged on the floor of the common area. She turned back toward the door that led to the exterior corridor, not wishing to disturb his meditations.

She paused on the threshold when she heard his voice. "Please remain, my wife."

"You may continue your meditations undisturbed, my husband," she said. "There are child-care duties I can perform while you complete them."

"Your presence is no disturbance, T'Pel."

She stepped back into the room and allowed the door to hiss closed behind her. "You appear troubled. Perhaps some additional time in meditation—"

"No," he said as he rose to his feet in a single graceful, fluid motion. "I believe I have exhausted the utility of meditation for the time being." He extinguished the candle by squeezing its wick between his thumb and forefinger, then raised the lights to normal levels. The unblinking stars beyond the window remained as brilliant as ever.

She approached him and extended her parallel index and middle fingers toward him. "Speak to me, my husband."

Tuvok mirrored her gesture, and their fingers touched. Then he withdrew and began speaking. She listened in attentive silence as Tuvok explained the nature of *Titan*'s recent discovery while slowly pacing the living area.

"A world shaped by an ancient and powerful form of terraforming technology," she said after he had finished, allowing a slight overtone of awe to color her tone. "The discovery of extant machinery capable of making such transformations reliably would be highly significant."

He nodded, his jawline set, the muscles in his neck obviously tense. "Indeed it would."

"Yet you have misgivings about this matter," T'Pel said.

Tuvok turned and walked toward the starscape framed in the window, apparently gathering his thoughts. Turning again to face her, he said, "My initial service in Starfleet began at a time when the terraforming technology of Project Genesis posed a serious danger to Federation security."

She nodded. "Before we married."

"Yes."

"I assume you are referring to the possibility that other powers, such as the Klingons, might have gained access to the technology and employed it as a weapon."

Tuvok nodded. "Obviously a technology capable of almost instantaneously transforming dead worlds into living ones is also equally capable of effectively doing the reverse—were it to be unleashed on a planet that already harbors life."

"Of course. Ever since deep antiquity, technology has always been subject to misuse, all the way back to the discovery of combustion on the Fire Plains. It would be illogical to suppose that the technology that remade the planet *Titan* has just finished surveying would be any different."

"True. However, no technology of which I am specifically aware has ever posed such profound dangers as Genesis did."

"And you are uneasy because the possibility now exists of recovering an alien version of that same technology."

Tuvok's eyebrows pulled closer together slightly, noticeably accentuating the upward slope of their outer edges. "I am not 'uneasy.' I am merely highly cognizant of the dangers inherent in such a discovery."

T'Pel didn't believe for a moment that her husband was anything *but* uneasy, but she concealed her incredulity. She did, however, allow her curiosity to propel one of her own eyebrows aloft.

"Tuvok, you were a science officer when the Genesis technology first threatened to proliferate beyond the Federation, were you not?"

He nodded. "I was."

"Given the priorities of your job at that time, you must have found the technology fascinating, at least on a purely scientific level."

He paused. At length, he said, "I did. Nevertheless, Genesis became a hazard that claimed many lives before the technology was finally dismantled and suppressed."

Had an early encounter with Genesis precipitated Tuvok's decision to leave Starfleet's sciences track in favor of the tactical and security work he had pursued over the intervening decades? Though Tuvok had always been notably reticent about discussing that traumatic period in any degree of detail, it was clear that the skill set he had developed since his departure from *Excelsior* would be indispensable in dealing with the dangers posed by any technology as potent and unpredictable as Genesis.

"Did you know any of those who died as a consequence of Genesis?" T'Pel asked.

He grew silent, evidently carefully considering her question. Finally, he said, "No. At least, I knew no one who suffered any permanent direct effects."

"Then you can draw comfort from that," she said.

"No, my wife," he said, speaking almost in a whisper. His dark eyes had gone cold and distant. "I cannot."

3

GORN HEGEMONY RECONNAISSANCE VESSEL *SSEVARRH*

The stack of stellar cartographical data flimsies on the desk of General Technologist Third Class S'syrixx grew slowly higher, no matter how much effort he applied to the task before him.

S'syrixx's recognition of the fact that the job might well prove impossible wasn't helping matters any. *All we have to do is find at least one new crècheworld to support the warrior caste's entire reproductive enterprise,* he thought as he pulled another starchart flimsy out of the computer terminal's reader. Disgusted, he sent it fluttering to the moist deck with a distracted flick of his claws.

Also working against him were his omnipresent thoughts of Z'shezhira, who would have been his mate by now had she not disappeared along with the entire crew complement of the warship *S'alath* more than a full Gornar suncircuit ago. Now that the Hegemonic government had declared Z'shezhira and her shipmates officially dead, S'syrixx seemed to be the only one who held any hope of finding and recovering her.

Though his sense of hope for Z'shezhira's safe return

was higher at some times and lower at others, he was determined never to surrender that hope, however slender it might be, until her body was recovered.

The hatch behind S'syrixx irised open sibilantly and wafted a slight breeze through the dimly lit work chamber's warm, damp air. The draft carried the distinctive scent of S'syrixx's old friend R'rerrgran, the ship's physician.

"How are the environmental cross-comparisons proceeding, S'syrixx?" R'rerrgran asked.

S'syrixx swiveled his head almost all the way around and fixed the older tech-caster with a withering stare. "How well do you think? The developing warrior-cast fetus has extremely exacting biochemical requirements. On top of that, the planetary magnetic field can neither exceed nor lie below a critical threshold value. And the most frustrating thing is that there seems to be no shortage of 'almost right' worlds—but 'almost right' might as well be an airless void, or the surface of a star. So out of all the tens of thousands of worlds accessible to us, how many do you think are likely to provide an environment capable of nurturing our race's strongest caste?"

R'rerrgran's facial scales ruffled in response to S'syrixx's sarcasm. "I presume you speak ironically about strength to accentuate the warrior caste's present unseemly state of vulnerability."

"Do not worry about my words being overheard," S'syrixx said with a derisive snort. "War-casters' understanding of irony is on a rough par with their comprehension of even elementary mathematics." He knew he could have cited his present mission as an illustrative example of the Gorn soldiery's latter failing. *Why do these five-fingered, bug-eyed idiots believe the odds in favor of their quest to be any better than the chance that my beloved Z'shezhira might yet turn up alive and well, a castaway on some remote planet? They'll spare no expense pursuing the one goal while completely ignoring the other.*

"Whether they are irony-impaired or not, the warriors can smell disrespect. You don't want Captain Krassrr to overhear your comments, even if you don't believe him capable of understanding them. He may be tempted to gut you anyway."

"And diminish his own caste's already slim chances of survival by eliminating one of the relatively few Gorn capable of finding him a new nursery planet? The war-casters may be stupid, but they're not crazy. Or is that the other way around?"

R'rerrgran bared about half of his razor-sharp teeth and displayed a highly textured frown. "You may not be so indispensable as you seem to think, old friend."

S'syrixx didn't like the sound of that. "What are you talking about?"

"Can you access the command deck display system from here?" R'rerrgran said, pointing an index claw toward the terminal that glowed in the semigloom of S'syrixx's narrow workspace.

"Maybe," S'syrixx said. He began tapping at the controls of his terminal with all six claws. A security block appeared on the screen, and S'syrixx spoke a series of numbers and letters in Captain Krassrr's guttural voice. The pictographs for AUTHORIZATION ACCEPTED flashed on the screen.

"You should also take care never to let Captain Krassrr hear you do that," said R'rerrgran. "Though I must admit that it was nicely done, even for a member of the arts subcaste."

S'syrixx accepted the accolade with a simple head nod. Still, he was proud that his arts subcaste status mirrored his proficiency in the mainstream disciplines of the larger technological caste, such as computer science and the various maths. He also knew that he wasn't the first member of his family to demonstrate a theatrical-quality arts-caster's gift for mimicry; according to family lore, his great-granduncle Zsraszk—an arts-caster renowned for his talents using the Voice—had drawn upon intercepted Sst'rfleet communications to mimic the speech patterns of the commander of a mammalian outpost on Inner Eliar more than a century ago. Old Zsraszk's gift for copying speech—even notoriously difficult-to-manage non-Gorn speech—had enabled Captain S'alath's warriors to score the first blood in the wars against the expansionist Federrazsh'n. It was a pity that the subsequent untimely intervention of a meddling elder race, as well as that of the hated Federrazsh'n mammal K'irrk, had sullied S'alath's initial victory, along with Zsraszk's part in it.

The text on the terminal screen suddenly vanished, displaced by a spacescape whose deep blackness was relieved by the steady cold glow of countless distant stars. Near the bottom of the image was the limb of a partially daylit planet, a green world that looked like so many of the colonies the Gorn Hegemony had established on environmentally compatible worlds throughout nine adjacent and nonadjacent sectors of space.

A few heartbeats after the image appeared, S'syrixx noticed something else—the presence of an artificially constructed object orbiting high over the planet. In the top left corner of the screen one of the other recon vessels in the *Ssevarrh*'s six-vessel flotilla hove into view, apparently to make close observations of the object, which S'syrixx could now see consisted of a broad, micrometeoroid-scored metal platform out of which projected a tall, equally beat-up-looking towerlike projection. Although there was no way S'syrixx could accurately estimate its size, it gave him the impression of hugeness.

As well as almost unimaginable antiquity. From the look of it, the construct could well be older than the approximately half-million suncircuits that the Gorn civilization had endured.

"Could that be what I think it is?" S'syrixx said.

"Captain Krassrr will no doubt expect an answer to that question," said the physician. "However, if this is indeed a working version of one of the devices responsible for altering the climates of so many of the planets we've found throughout this sector of space—"

"Then Krassrr will expect to use it to create a new crècheworld for his caste should we fail to find one ready-made," S'syrixx said, interrupting. "This was not the way I had hoped to spend my career." Like most members of his particular subcaste, he had anticipated a long, quiet life creating and maintaining the Gorn Hegemony's intellectual demimonde—the eons-old pre-technological oral tradition of preserving and ritually reciting the most cherished documents of Gorn science, religion, literature, theater, and music.

"Don't worry," said his friend, who laid his claws companionably across the scales of S'syrixx's bare shoulder.

With his other manus, he pointed toward the ancient platform/obelisk that drifted far above the alien world on the screen. "Should the captain find the results of your inquiries into that ancient object unsatisfactory, he will probably take pains to make your new paleo-terraforming career a brief one."

S'syrixx nodded mutely as a feeling of intense foreboding tightened his *cloaca.*

GORN HEGEMONY WARSHIP *S'ALATH*

Z'shezhira feared that Gog'resssh might finally be about to pick a fight he couldn't win—a fight that would almost certainly result in the destruction of the *S'alath,* the deaths of Gog'resssh and his troopers, and the demise of the relative handful of surviving tech-caste hostages the radiation-addled war-casters had enslaved since they'd wrested control of the ship from its rightful crew—most of whom had long since been summarily ejected into hard vacuum.

Z'shezhira was surprised at the sanguineness with which she regarded the inevitability of her own death in such a scenario. *Perhaps,* she thought as she worked wearily at the multiple-application console to which Gog'resssh always exiled her during her interminable work shifts on the *S'alath*'s command deck, *I should welcome oblivion.*

Using the small viewer built into her console, Z'shezhira watched in silence as the image of oblivion approached almost closely enough for her to make out its shape.

She glanced toward Gog'resssh, whose gold-and-silver multifaceted eyes appeared to be riveted to the command deck's central viewer, which displayed a larger though equally indistinct version of the same distant, vague image that Z'shezhira had been studying on her console.

"Helm, has the approaching vessel detected us yet?" growled the *S'alath*'s renegade commander.

"Not so far as I can determine, First Myrmidon," replied the young trooper who was operating the flight control console. Z'shezhira recalled that his name was Sk'salissk.

"Good," Gog'resssh said in a voice that sounded like two tectonic plates grinding together.

Second Myrmidon Zegrroz'rh, Gog'resssh's second-in-command, lumbered from the clawholds that encircled the command deck toward the helm station near the center. Though his radiation burns had mostly receded—Z'shezhira had been forced to see to that personally—one of his multiple-lensed eyes was permanently clouded, damaged beyond repair. Z'shezhira had no doubt that both his ruined eye and his remaining good one concealed far deeper and more profound injuries, if only barely.

"Helm," Zegrroz'rh rumbled, "can you continue to keep us concealed from the approaching vessel?"

"I believe so, Second Myrmidon. Presently we are concealed from their sensors, but not necessarily from visual detection—that is, if the unknown ship approaches us closely."

Z'shezhira understood, of course, that the planet the *S'alath* now orbited—one of the outermost ice worlds of the system Gog'resssh had just sent some of his crew to explore in the furtherance of his quest for a new warrior nursery world—did much to obscure the *S'alath*'s presence; not only would the planet's frequent cryo-volcanic eruptions tend to scatter active sensor scans, but the very distance between the remote ice world and the more temperate bodies that orbited deeper in the local primary star's gravity would ensure the *S'alath*'s concealment.

Until, of course, Gog'resssh decided to make his presence known.

"The vessel crossed this world's orbit," the helmsman said, "on a heading for the inner worlds we just finished surveying."

"We should attack," Zegrroz'rh said, his unnerving white eye seeming to burrow into Z'shezhira even though she knew he was looking in Gog'resssh's direction.

"Not yet," Gog'resssh said.

Relief at the realization that her demise might not be imminent after all warred with disappointment as it occurred to Z'shezhira that her servitude to this aggressive creature and his henchman was to continue. *At least if I remain alive,* she thought, consoling herself, *then at least the possibility of someday seeing S'syrixx again remains.*

Zegrroz'rh released a deeply hostile growl as his brows crumpled in a manner that emphasized the unnervingly insectlike quality of his one good eye. "No doubt they are heading toward the world in this system that might one day support our caste's next hatchery, First Myrmidon."

Though he hadn't been addressed, the helmsman growled affirmatively. "They are on precisely that heading."

"Toward *our* world," Zegrroz'rh said, prompting the scales on Gog'resssh's broad neck and shoulders to rise defensively. Obviously, he perceived Zegrroz'rh's words and body language as a challenge to his authority.

As she always did during such tense moments, Z'shezhira

spared a moment to wish that the two senior war-casters would resolve their differences through combat—preferably the mutually lethal kind. Instead, her innate builder/nurturer's instinct intervened, moving her to try to keep Gog'resssh calm, despite the possibility that doing so might further prolong her current unacceptable circumstances.

Z'shezhira moved from her station to take up a position directly between the two warriors. "Before we take any rash action, should we not try to determine whether or not we have just witnessed the approach of another Gorn vessel? Perhaps it is another recon ship, part of the convoy that we saw coming through here as we prepared to survey this system."

It took a moment for her suggestion to penetrate, but that proved to be enough to break the tension. "See to it, Zegrroz'rh," Gog'resssh said. "But do nothing for now to compromise our concealment."

The second myrmidon backed away muttering and growling, then approached a nearby data console and began tapping into the long-range scan functions.

Moments later a grainy yet intelligible image of the other ship became visible on the command deck's central viewer. The resolution was poor—no doubt an artifact of the passive scanning techniques Zegrroz'rh had been obliged to use in order to avoid giving away the *S'alath*'s location—but the vessel was unquestionably not of Gorn origin.

"Disc-shaped forward section," Zegrroz'rh grunted, with no small amount of enthusiasm. "Two aft engine nacelles."

"Federrazsh'n," Gog'resssh said, displaying wicked

ranks of serrated teeth. Z'shezhira shuddered, not in response to the warrior's impressive dentition, but rather at the thought of the freakishly soft, hairy, mammalian life that doubtless infested the other ship.

"Which ship is it?" Gog'resssh asked.

Zegrroz'rh sniffed loudly. "I recognize the configuration. *Luna*-class."

"But *which ship*?"

Realizing that her ability to read the Federrazsh'n's standard written tongue was probably unique on the command deck, at least at the moment, Z'shezhira focused on the alien characters she saw emblazoned upon the Sst'rfleet vessel's egg-white hull.

"U.S.S. Titan," she said. "Registry number eight-zero-one-zero-two." She wondered if that last detail—the high registry number—would push Gog'resssh toward exhibiting caution when it came to an adversary possessed of such prolific shipbuilding capabilities. Or would it provoke him instead into testing his mettle in yet another unnecessary combat situation?

"We cannot allow the Federrazsh'n to annex any worlds in Gorn Hegemony space," Zegrroz'rh snarled.

Once again, Z'shezhira found that she was speaking almost without consciously willing it. "Officially, this system lies far outside Gorn space, First Myrmidon."

Gog'resssh released a small roar, which made Z'shezhira flinch. "*No* system is outside Gorn space, officially or otherwise, until *I* make that determination."

He really wants *to fight them,* Z'shezhira thought, astonished at the workings of the mind of a war-caster, albeit a damaged one. *Even though these Federrazsh'n mammals never seem to attack unless attacked first—even though they've forged mutually beneficial alliances with us in times past—he's going to let Zegrroz'rh goad him into doing this.*

Though she was tempted by the possibility that such a tack might finally put them all out of their misery once and for all, Z'shezhira decided to cast her lot with staying alive—at least for now.

But would Gog'resssh allow her to calm him down this time?

"First Myrmidon," she began, "need I remind you that these creatures come from the very same Federrazsh'n that somehow managed to end the threat of the galaxy's entire population of machine-mammals?" *Or that this very vessel,* she thought, *was one of the ships intimately involved in obtaining that victory?*

"Watch them, but continue to keep us out of their sight," Gog'resssh said at length, much to Zegrroz'rh's evident disappointment. "For now, we will follow where they go, like a shadow."

GORN HEGEMONY RECONNAISSANCE VESSEL *SSEVARRH*

S'syrixx knew he was concealing his impatience as the engineering team ran the final tests on the consoles that Captain Krassrr had set up along the perimeter of the observation deck. The panoramic crysmetal window revealed the ancient alien artifact, framing the flat, meteoroid-pitted platform that formed its base as well as the tall, needle-like structure that towered over it like the trunk of some colossal and impossibly straight tree. The platform was oriented to be parallel with the surface of the blue-green planet that was turning serenely below.

A planet that had evidently felt this artifact's touch on at least one previous occasion.

Setting up the experiment had required three full rotations of the planet, during which technical challenge had piled upon technical challenge. The science and engineering teams had, after all, been asked to do the all but impossible. But in the end, they had pulled off a successful, if low-powered, initial test; despite the apparently advanced state of decay of the alien equipment, the vacuum of space had entombed it well enough to make it relatively easy to render at least partially operational once again.

After an initial circuit failure had prompted Captain Krassrr to direct a withering, bug-eyed glance in S'syrixx's direction—which had, in turn, prompted R'rerrgran's quiet offer of a mild sedative to S'syrixx—the ancient platform awakened, summoning a primordial lightning that might have frightened even Egg Bringer S'Yahazah herself.

The energy beam appeared wide enough to have instantly cleaved through all six ships in the science convoy simultaneously. Although S'syrixx had to avert his eyes like everyone else on the *Ssevarrh*'s observation deck (except perhaps for Krassrr and his bug-eyed war-caste peers), he vividly imagined the beam lancing down to the planet's surface to near-instantaneous effect. Putting the almost agonizing brilliance out of his mind as best he could, S'syrixx tried to concentrate instead on his console's readouts, one of which consisted of a clock intended to prevent the ancient platform's hastily restored circuits from overheating and destroying themselves.

Not eager to displease or disappoint Krassrr, S'syrixx transmitted the cutoff command to the platform when the short, conservatively prescribed span of time had elapsed. He was gratified a moment later that he hadn't found himself tumbling into the airless vacuum beyond the windows, a victim of some unforeseen catastrophic failure of overstrained alien technology.

He felt even more gratified two dayturns later when the latest atmospheric and soil tests confirmed that the test-firing of the artifact had indeed increased the net life-supporting potential of the planet below, at least in the one small, sheltered valley that had been encompassed by the device's brief operation.

Later, R'rerrgran accompanied S'syrixx back to the wide observation deck, which now was thankfully free of scowling, impatient war-casters; those worthies were now busy providing muscle to the engineering teams, which even now were proceeding with the delicate task of attaching a complex lattice of tractor beams to the ages-old alien ecosculpting platform. S'syrixx watched through the great crysmetal windows as the faintly glowing beams lanced out at the venerable structure, grasping it with a surprisingly gentle touch.

"Imagine," R'rerrgran said in an awe-tinged, breathy growl. "That device is capable of rearranging matter on a submolecular level. Molding whole worlds to accommodate whatever biochemical demands we care to make."

"The war-casters may have a new crècheworld sooner than they had dreamed possible," S'syrixx said, watching as the flotilla prepared to tow the device away from what might well be the only world it had known since its construction perhaps half a million suncircuits ago. "Once the device is ready for use on a planetary scale, of course."

"Of course," R'rerrgran said. "I am certain that Captain Krassrr has every confidence that you will make that possible in due course."

S'syrixx experienced a surge of relief; R'rerrgran seemed to be implying that the war-casters needed time to decide upon the first and most appropriate world to transform from "almost right" to "just right" as the replacement for the late, lamented Sazssgrerrn crècheworld. Even given the recent successes of the science and engineering teams, powering up the ecosculpting platform enough to subject an entire planet to the device's full metamorphic effects would be no small achievement. Given enough time, S'syrixx knew that he and his colleagues could do a great deal to reduce, if not eliminate, the chance of some random malfunction bringing this entire endeavor to a premature and catastrophic end. If only the war-casters could be counted upon not to decide to rush matters. . . .

"Which planets are being considered for the next phase of this project?" S'syrixx said.

R'rerrgran's neck and brow scales rose inquisitively. "Planets? Plural?"

"Yes. The list of worlds on which we might do further testing."

"I think you may have misunderstood me, S'syrixx. There is no 'list' of which I am aware."

S'syrixx could feel his heavy eyeridges folding forward in irritation. "There has to be a list. And the next destination Captain Krassrr has selected for testing the device has to be on it."

"Oh, the device is definitely bound for a destination," R'rerrgran said, his flaring nostrils conveying a look of comprehension. "But I'm told that Krassrr expects to fully deploy the technology there."

"Where?" S'syrixx said, an inchoate anxiety stiffening his neck scales. He upbraided himself for being deluded enough to think that Krassrr might remain reasonable, especially when his now-endangered caste had so much at stake.

Although no one other than the two tech-casters was present on the observation deck, R'rerrgran leaned toward S'syrixx conspiratorially and spoke in a low growl. "It's a planet known as Hranrar."

Confusion caught up with S'syrixx's irritation and passed it. "Hranrar? I've never heard of it."

"Neither have I. Is that really surprising, S'syrixx? Stellar cartography is neither your primary discipline nor mine."

Hranrar. All S'syrixx knew about it was that the name had an unfamiliar, non-sibilant alien stink to it. Somehow, that name sounded insufficiently Gorn to be appropriate as a test bed for the Gorn Hegemony's newly acquired and still unreliable ecosculpting technology, let alone as a replacement for Sazssgrerrn.

Determined to discover why an alien place name he'd never heard before struck him in this manner, S'syrixx walked to an alcove near one of the bulkheads to consult a data terminal. He tapped into the stellar cartography files and swiftly located Hranrar, whose system lay in yet another remote hinterland of Gorn territory.

Claws of pure dread closed tightly about his heart when

the stellar cartographic find directed him to the sociological database for more information.

R'rerrgran's claws clattered on the duranium deck plating as he approached. "What's the matter, S'syrixx? Your scales look as white as the hide of an Outer Eliar salamander."

S'syrixx ignored his friend as he continued reading the surprisingly lengthy entry on Hranrar. "This can't be correct, R'rerrgran. According to this, there's already a thriving civilization on Hranrar."

"That is unfortunate," R'rerrgran said. He smelled of both sorrow and fatalism.

"'*Unfortunate*'? Do you understand what this means? If you're right, if Krassrr really is planning to do a full eco-sculpt on Hranrar, then an entire civilization will be wiped out, probably in less than a dayturn."

R'rerrgran's great scaled head drooped in a melancholic fashion. "Such, apparently, is the will of both the warrior and political castes, S'syrixx. And probably the leadership of our own, for that matter. After all, who else could have determined that Hranrar's environment is the one world in the entirety of Gorn space that is most likely to serve as the new Sazssgrerrn?"

Who else indeed, S'syrixx thought, *but a famously impatient warrior caste?*

Assuming his friend's question to be purely rhetorical, S'syrixx declined to answer it. Instead he turned his gaze back toward the broad windows and the spacescape beyond. The alien ecosculpting platform was already slowly moving out of orbit, pulled toward its date with destiny by the complicated webwork of coruscating tractor beams that each ship in the recon flotilla was generating in tandem operation.

The Gorn Hegemony's complex ecosystem of complementary castes and subcastes would soon be made whole again with the creation of a new warrior-caste crècheworld.

All it would cost was another civilization's very existence.

"Do not torment yourself, my friend," R'rerrgran said, speaking as though he had read S'syrixx's mind. "It is the way of the universe, as old as life itself. There are always winners and losers. Predators and prey. The eaters and the eaten."

S'syrixx looked sadly at his friend. "Survival is a zero-sum game?"

"In my experience that is usually so," R'rerrgran said.

S'syrixx nodded, fighting to keep his scales from bristling. There was no point in rousing suspicions, even among his closest confidants.

Perhaps not this time, my friend, he thought as he watched the ecosculpting platform disappear from his line of sight, to be replaced by some of the *Ssevarrh*'s sister ships as the flotilla arranged itself for warp travel. The stars smeared into streaks as the towing convoy coordinated its transition from sublight to superluminal speeds.

Perhaps not this time.

4

U.S.S. TITAN

Captain's Log, Stardate 59641.5

The second "Doornail" we've run across since our return to the Vela OB2 Association—this one located in the system officially designated Vela OB2-396—has proved to be every bit as dead as the first one, but perhaps a little more habitable. Our close-range scans and surveys turned up two other important differences as well: one is the presence of traces of sentient-manufactured alloys and artifacts in orbit around this dead-yet-likely-artificially-engineered world; and the other is evidence that someone else has visited this place recently. *Titan*'s sensors have picked up strong impulse signatures and vestigial warp trails, along with particle emissions consistent with the use of a powerful tractor beam. Unfortunately, factors such as the local system's intense solar wind and the powerful local planetary magnetic fields have effectively scattered most of these emissions, making it difficult, at best, to determine the heading of these visitors when they left the system.

So far, I have only questions. Has someone else found something significant here just before our arrival, such as the extremely powerful ancient terraforming artifact that our science team suspects may once have been used to create so many life-capable worlds throughout this sector of space?

And more importantly, has somebody recently dragged such an artifact away from this system?

Since the gamma shift encompassed the small hours of the ship's night, the lights on *Titan*'s sparsely crewed bridge were reduced almost to twilight levels. Riker sat back in his command chair and tried to let the diminished bridge illumination relax him, since nothing else he had tried this evening had succeeded in getting him anywhere near striking distance of sleep. On the main viewer, the second Doornail world continued its slow, oblivious rotation several hundred klicks below *Titan*.

Lieutenant Commander Tamen Gibruch, the scheduled gamma-shift watch officer, had expressed surprise at the captain's unexpected appearance at such a late hour. The Chandir officer's prominent facial brow wrinkled in apparent worry until Riker explained that he wasn't checking up on him.

"I've just decided to see if a little extra work will cure insomnia better than warm milk does," Riker told him, not straying terribly far from the plain truth. Ever since he'd become aware of the possibility that a supernally powerful planet-altering technology might be literally wandering through—or might have been deliberately taken from—this part of the galaxy, he'd found it extremely difficult to relax at all, let alone sleep. And since there was no use in letting his own futile tossing and turning jeopardize Deanna and the baby's sleep, here he was.

Ensign Dakal suddenly half rose from behind the main science console, his usually subdued voice now buoyant upon an uncommon enthusiasm. "Captain, I think we've established an outbound direction for one of the warp trails."

Riker heaved a sigh of relief as he checked out the redundant readouts on the right arm of his command chair. Sure enough, the young Cardassian's declaration looked promising; the navigation computer had drawn a bold yellow line that represented the best estimate of the most recent path taken by another warp-powered vessel out of the Vela OB2–396 system, *Titan*'s present location.

More than seven solid hours of continuous scanning and analysis may have finally paid off. "Ensign, you're a magician," Riker said, favoring the youthful sensor analyst with a small grin.

Dakal's gray skin turned ashen with evident embarrassment at the attention. "I'm afraid I can't take all the credit, sir. The trail is dilute enough to be virtually undetectable. If I hadn't had the benefit of Chaka's search-algorithm enhancements and overall number-crunching, I'd still be groping in the dark."

With a nod Riker acknowledged the invisible yet critical contribution of Crewman K'Chak'!'op, the Pak'shree information specialist whose native language—including her name—was simply beyond the capabilities of *Titan*'s human minority and humanoid plurality. As a compromise, and a bridge between the culture of the arachnidlike computer scientist and those of the various other members of *Titan*'s crew, most everyone aboard called her "Chaka" by way of approximating "K'Chak'!'op." The Pak'shree, by contrast, could speak Federation Standard by means of an electronic vocoder that transformed her movements and mouthpart stridulations into humanoid-intelligible speech. Sometimes the content of that speech proved exasperating, steeped as it often was in the matriarchal assumptions of the Pak'shree.

"I'll bet she told you that you're a credit to your gender for being able to keep up with her, Ensign," said Chief Axel Bolaji, who ran the flight-control console during the night watch.

Dakal looked offended, but Riker thought he might have been kidding. "That's *exactly* what she said. You have to take such things in the spirit in which they're intended."

I suppose you can take the spider out of the nest, but you can't always take the nest out of the spider, Riker thought. He was aware of how tough it was for Pak'shree females to take males of any species seriously, given the fact that for Pak'shree "maleness" was simply a transitory juvenile phase, to be sloughed off when the immature males metamorphosed into fully adult Pak'shree females.

"Where does the trail lead, Ensign?" Riker wanted to know.

Dakal paused for a moment to consult another display. "Projecting what we know of the departure trajectory, my best estimate is Vela OB2–404, which is less than two parsecs away. We'll need to run continuous long-range scans along the way, of course, to make certain we're still on the correct heading."

"Planets?"

"Yes, sir. According to Commander Pazlar's stellar cartographic data, the system contains a mix of gas giants and terrestrial planets, all laid out in stable, almost circular orbits. Vela OB2–404 strongly resembles the Sol system in that regard."

Riker wondered what would lay at the end of the trail. Another Doornail? The ultimate power of creation? Or something else entirely, something utterly unanticipated and unforeseeable?

Fortunately, he knew he didn't have to limit his options to merely wondering. Just as when he played the trombone in his holodeck recreation of the New Orleans jazz scene, he had the authority to call the tune.

"Let's take this one from the top, Mister Bolaji," Riker said. "And make our best speed that won't lose the trail."

"Aye, sir," Bolaji said as he worked his console.

"Take it away."

Although SecondGen White-Blue lacked his friend Torvig's discomfiture with microgravity environments, he acceded to the Choblik's request that he keep the gravity levels set at *Titan*'s standard one-g value during their current shift together in the stellar cartography lab. Since Commander Pazlar was presently in her quarters, presumably engaging in the regular pattern of nocturnal dormancy that appeared to characterize most humanoids, there was no reason to maintain the freefall conditions that Pazlar's delicate physiology required. In addition, the Choblik's comfort would probably make him far less distractible should the errant signal reappear—

—*there!*

"Interrogative," White-Blue said. "Question. Enquiry. Did you perceive that?"

The cybernetic organism with whom White-Blue shared the lab's catwalk waved his two primary cybernetic limbs as well as his metal tail, spreading the hands on the ends of each artificial extremity in a gesture of affect that presumably came from careful observation of the mannerisms of some of Torvig's humanoid shipmates.

"Perceive *what*?" said Torvig, his voice conveying a note of something that White-Blue could only interpret as an emotion. Could it be exasperation because this would be the third time he had diverted his friend's attention from the measurements he was taking?

"The signal I picked up a short time ago," White-Blue said. "I believe I have detected it again. Can you verify my observation?" Using his hard interface with the lab's main control console, White-Blue adjusted the section of the cosmos currently being displayed in the chamber's vast, full-surround holographic display. The effect looked uncannily like actual instantaneous travel across light-years of space. Perhaps that was the reason for Torvig's insistence on a strong artificial gravitational field: to help him remain cognizant that he was still aboard a starship rather than flying bodily through the cosmos.

"There seems to be something there, in the lower subspace bands," Torvig said, his voice registering a quality that White-Blue had learned to associate with surprise. "No, it's gone again. Whatever it was, it appeared to be badly attenuated."

"And therefore extremely difficult to distinguish from the cosmic background radiation," White-Blue said.

"Exactly," Torvig said.

"Interrogative. Should we report it to the bridge?"

The Choblik spread his cybernetic hands again as he waved his tail at the lab's representation of the vastness of this sector of the Beta Quadrant—a sector that now betrayed no trace of the intermittent subspace signal. "Report *what*?"

Deanna Troi awoke to find that Will's side of the bed was undisturbed; he'd more than likely pulled an all-night shift on the bridge. She didn't need her Betazoid gift of empathic awareness to understand the reason: the potential discovery of an ancient power equally capable of wholesale creation and destruction was weighing heavily on him, both because of the vast promise it held for a still-wounded Federation, and because of the existential threat it posed.

After scooping up little Natasha and giving the year-old child her morning feeding, Troi replicated a light breakfast of uttaberries and *swix* for herself and ate about half of it before sending the meal's remains back into the quantum limbo from which it had emerged. She then took a quick sonic shower, changed into a regular duty uniform, and dropped Natasha off with T'Pel at the day-care quarters that adjoined sickbay. After she kissed her daughter goodbye, and exchanged a dignified farewell with T'Pel as well as smiles with two-year-old Totyarguil Bolaji and eleven-year-old Noah Powell, she stepped out into the corridor.

It was only then that she began to observe that something wasn't completely right. Something was happening up on the bridge. She sensed Will's ebullience at the prospect of a new discovery, which sounded a psychic note that nearly (but not quite) masked his misgivings about whatever *Titan* might find in the next system. And suddenly she noticed something else: emotions that denoted high intelligence, but also primal, almost atavistic feelings. She sensed territoriality, anger, and aggression, but also a familiarity with music, literature, and art. Fear, but also passion. It was difficult to tell which, if either, was ascendant.

As she walked toward the nearest turbolift, Troi touched her combadge. "Commander Troi to the bridge. Have we reached the next system?"

An answer came immediately, courtesy of *Titan*'s first officer. *"We have, Commander."*

"I was just about to call you to the bridge," said Will. He sounded distracted by the developing crisis, whatever it was.

"Not necessary, Captain. I'm already on my way." *Thank you so much,* she thought into their telepathic link, *for almost letting me sleep through whatever's going on up there,* Imzadi.

I wanted you to be rested, he thought back to her. Although her extraordinarily difficult pregnancy had ended happily some twelve months earlier with the birth of little Natasha, Will still hadn't entirely shaken the annoying habit he'd developed of treating her like a fragile pane of Betazoid stained glass.

Rested, she thought as she recalled whose side of the bed had been left in close to mint condition last night. *I suppose that makes* one *of us.*

At first Troi resisted the urge to run the rest of the way to the turbolift. She gave in to the impulse a few seconds later, however, after the Red Alert klaxons began to sound. Perhaps half a minute later, she stepped breathlessly off the turbolift and onto *Titan*'s bridge, where she found Will and Christine already hard at work. The image of a spectacularly ringed, brilliantly sunlit sapphire planet turned slowly on the main viewer.

In the foreground lurked several sleek, multi-nacelled alien ships whose aspect she could describe only as predatory. The ships were in motion, and at the moment she could see four of them gathering around a collision-pitted orbital platform which hung over the alien world just inside the boundary of the planet's innermost golden ring. The platform's flat base and long, needle-like projection dwarfed the largest vessel that Troi could see. At first, she thought the alien ships were massing to attack the platform, until she began to sense proprietary, protective thoughts coming from the aliens. In the parlance of the old western novels her father had shared with her during her childhood, these vessels were "circling the wagons."

A growling, sepulchral voice suddenly began to issue from the bridge comm system. *"This is Captain Krassrr of the* Ssevarrh. *Earthers, you have no claim to this system. It has been annexed by the Gorn Hegemony. Withdraw now, or suffer the consequences."*

"The Gorn vessels' weapons remain charged," Lieutenant Rager reported from ops. "They are raising shields."

"Raise ours," said Vale. "Gorn. I really hate the way they sugarcoat everything."

Troi took her seat at the left side of the command chair

just as her husband rose from it. He looked tired, which was to be expected, but she also could feel how energized he was with determination and purpose. He noted her arrival with a nod and a small smile, then resumed giving the matter at hand his full attention.

"This is Captain William Riker of the Federation *Starship Titan,*" he said. "This system is at least a full parsec outside any of the previously recorded formal boundaries of the Gorn Hegemony. In fact, Vela OB2–404 lies outside *both* of our jurisdictions."

"Your star charts are evidently badly out of date, Captain. Withdraw. Now."

Will made a slashing gesture in the direction of the ops console, and Ensign Dakal immediately interrupted the comm system's audio pickup. Turning toward Commander Tuvok's tactical station, he said, "How many Gorn vessels are you picking up, Commander?"

"Six so far," the Vulcan said in his customary even tones. "Although they match the known configuration of Gorn scout vessels, they are all well armed and well armored. The odds in a direct confrontation would be very much against us. And they are certainly prepared to use deadly force to defend the orbital platform."

"Orbital platform?" Troi asked, turning toward Will. "Could that be the terraforming artifact you think might have remade some of the other planets in this sector?"

"We don't know yet, Deanna," he said. "But I'll be damned if I'm going to leave here before I find out."

"Why don't we have visual communications?" asked Vale, apparently speaking to no one in particular.

"Because the Gorn seem to prefer it that way," Troi

said. "At least when it comes to communicating with non-reptiloid species." Among the many intense, primitive emotions she'd been sensing was a strong feeling of cross-phylum revulsion, not dissimilar to the ingrained fear of reptiles or insects that many humanoids routinely experienced.

After ordering Rager to reactivate the comm pickup, Will began to respond to the Gorn commander's demand. "Under every agreement between the Federation and the Gorn Hegemony that I'm aware of, we have as much right to conduct research here as you do."

"Is that truly what you are doing here, Captain, in orbit of a world I have already explained to you belongs to the Hegemony? You claim to be conducting research?"

"Research. That's pretty much *all* we do, in fact. *Titan* is a ship of exploration."

"Titan *would also appear to be one of the Federrazsh'n war vessels responsible for stopping a mass-attack by the machine-mammals more than a suncircuit ago."*

Machine-mammals, Troi thought. "The Borg," she whispered.

"We did take part in that battle," Will said. "It was necessary to ensure the Federation's survival."

"You won decisively. But only after the machine-mammals devastated an entire Gorn fleet. How very convenient for you."

"We would have taken down the Borg sooner, Captain, if we'd had the means."

"I do not believe you, Earther. My original demand stands. Leave this system. Immediately."

"I'm prepared to accommodate you, Captain, as a

gesture of goodwill. But we'd like the answers to a few questions first."

Using the telepathic-empathic link she shared with Will, Troi spoke wordlessly to him. Imzadi, *shouldn't* I *be the one asking him questions? I* am Titan*'s senior diplomatic officer, after all.*

Not until you're up to speed on everything we've just learned about what's going on here, he thought back to her. *Now, if you don't mind . . .*

His request was certainly a reasonable one. Since she knew she was not yet in possession of all the relevant facts, she nodded her assent and allowed him to continue without distracting him any further. Still, she couldn't quite shake the impression that he was somehow . . . babying her again.

"Questions?" demanded the Gorn captain.

"About the device that's orbiting this planet. Your ships seem to be conducting an operation of some sort with it. In fact, our sensor readings indicate that your vessels towed it here from another star system nearby—"

"You are inquiring into matters that are none of your concern. If you do not leave now, my vessels will open fire. And they *will soon be joined by reinforcements. This will be your final warning."*

And with that, the comm channel abruptly closed.

Will stared forward, apparently rapt with the image of the meteoroid-scarred artifact that orbited the brilliant blue world.

"Mister Tuvok, Ensign Fell: Can either of you confirm that Gorn reinforcements are on their way?"

"Negative," Tuvok said after a brief pause to check his console.

"My scans are also negative, Captain," said Fell, who was running the science console. "Of course, that doesn't necessarily mean the Gorn captain is bluffing."

Tuvok nodded. "I concur. We might not yet be able to pick up the incoming hostiles, either because of stealth technology or because they're still too distant for our sensors to resolve them."

In answer to Will's questioning glance, Troi said, "Captain Krassrr isn't lying. He honestly believes that reinforcements are coming. So I'd assume he also wasn't bluffing when he said he'd attack us if we don't lea—"

Something on Fell's console suddenly drew the relief science officer's full attention. "Captain, the Gorn vessels are engaging their weapons locks!"

Imzadi, *now would be a prudent time to withdraw,* Troi thought, projecting in Will's direction. She considered the six Gorn ships out there, the escalating anger she sensed from them, and the vulnerable children belowdecks whom T'Pel was doubtless working very hard to keep calm right about now. *Don't you think?*

Troi felt the tension growing thicker all around the bridge. Just as it increased to a nearly unbearable level, Will said, "Lieutenant Lavena, get us out of here, maximum warp. Once we've passed the likely range of their long-range sensors, put us on a heading back for this system's Kuiper belt. We'll conceal the ship behind one of the belt's bigger cometary bodies and keep an eye on the Gorn from there."

Will announced that he would be in his ready room if anyone needed him. Without asking his permission, Troi followed him inside the small but tidy office.

"I don't understand the risk you're taking, Will," she

said after the door hissed closed behind her. "Why give an already bad-tempered Gorn captain a *good* reason to destroy us?"

His back was to her as he looked out the ready-room window, which displayed a weird panorama of the stars that *Titan*'s velocity had smeared into multicolored streaks. "I've just received some new intelligence from Starfleet. It seems that the Gorn lost a critical breeding planet to a natural disaster last year. Ever since then, they've been desperate to find a replacement—or, failing that, to make one."

He turned away from the speed-distorted starscape. "I have to find out whether that orbital platform the Gorn are defending really is that theoretical terraforming artifact we've been talking about ever since we started finding these Doornail planets out here."

She approached him. "And what if it is, Will?"

"Then the Gorn may just have gained a huge technological advantage over the Federation. Not to mention a new metaweapon that will almost certainly end up in the hands of the Romulans, the Tzenkethi, the Breen, the Kinshaya, the Tholians—every one of the Gorn Hegemony's allies in the Typhon Pact."

"But we don't know yet whether that . . . platform really has any such capabilities. Right?"

He shook his head. "No. But the Gorn obviously plan to deploy it on the second planet of Vela OB2–404. And they *did* go to all the trouble of dragging the thing all the way from system OB2–396. They must be reasonably confident in their chances of success."

"So the Gorn see Vela OB2–404 II as the best choice to replace their lost breeding world?"

"It will be," he said, nodding. "Once they finish adjusting the planet's climate, that is. Apparently they believe they have the means now. If it turns out they do, then we have a very big problem on our hands."

"I understand. The Gorn—the whole Typhon Pact—will have a metaweapon to deploy against us, unless we put a stop to it."

"That's a huge dilemma, Deanna. But I'm afraid it's not the most immediate one."

She took his hands, which she noticed were clammy with the terror he had been struggling so hard to conceal from his crew. "What is, then?"

"The planet the Gorn want to terraform," he said. "It's no Doornail, Deanna."

A bottomless pit of realization opened up deep in her belly. At last, she began to comprehend his terror. *No. Oh, no.*

He extricated his hands from her grasp and crossed back to the star-streaked window. "The long-range scans show there's already a civilization there with a hundred or so large cities. They have advanced telecommunications and a thriving culture.

"I can't sit by and let the Gorn destroy it."

5

GORN HEGEMONY RECONNAISSANCE VESSEL *SSEVARRH*

They're going to do it here, today, S'syrixx thought, the small monitor before him displaying the eerie yellowish glow of the ecosculptor as the great generation systems deep within its core gradually powered it up. *And there's no way I can persuade them to find another place or time to do this deed.* As much as the presence of fur-shedding, homeothermic mammals unnerved him, he almost wished the Sst'rfleeters that Captain Krassrr had chased away had chosen to challenge Krassrr's highly questionable plans. Unfortunately, that was not to be.

Soon, very soon, the surface of Hranrar would suffer devastation comparable to what a supernova might deliver. And then, assuming all the theoretical work and partial tests that had been carried out thus far proved reliable, that surface would be replaced by a new hatchery world specifically tailored for the Gorn warrior caste. The Hranrarii would instantly be reduced to a thing of memory, of interest only to academics and preservers of the past like S'syrixx.

But despite his mounting despair, S'syrixx knew that he was far from helpless to prevent the slaughter that Krassrr was about to unleash upon Hranrar. Alone in his quarters, he accessed his data terminal and began surreptitiously working his way into a "back door" he had quietly built into the software that the science team was using to feed instructions to the improvised interface between the Gorn flotilla's computers and the ancient hardware and software that drove the enormous energies contained in the ecosculptor artifact. The claws on his left manus trembled slightly as he began entering the string of commands he had already decided would prove most effective in feeding the escalating power emanations of the ecosculptor back into itself. In theory, the computer core that governed the artifact—a vastly powerful system that S'syrixx had to admit remained nearly as mysterious as the object itself—would suffer a flash overload that should leave it inoperable, at least for a time.

After he entered the penultimate command, S'syrixx hesitated. *What if I damage the ecosculptor beyond all possibility of repair?* he thought. He knew that he was taking a tremendous risk—that of relegating the Gorn warrior caste to the extinction that would inevitably await them in the event they never found a naturally generated hatchery world to take the place of dead Sazssgrerrn. He had little regard for the war-casters, whom he regarded individually as bullies and imbeciles for the most part. But he also bore them no special antipathy, since as a member of a technological caste he was well schooled in the necessity that every caste flourish for the Gorn Hegemony—and for the very Gorn race as a whole—to survive and prosper into the next generation and beyond. Although the relationship between his own caste and that of the warriors was distant and somewhat indirect, no one but the dimmest war-caster groundpounder or meanest labor-caste scat-shoveler could deny the interdependence of all Gorn castes and subcastes.

But if I do not act, and act now, a billion or more innocents will die—even if this damned thing merely clears the way for a new biosphere that it ultimately fails to deliver.

Grasping the necessity of his actions, at least for the moment, S'syrixx entered the final command, hopeful that he would not change his mind during the next few heartbeats. He entered ENABLE next, and felt a surprising calm descend upon him as he realized that he could no longer reverse what he had just done. All he could do now was hope that his act of compassion for the Hranrarii had not just written a premature end for both the Gorn warrior caste and the Hegemony that it defended.

And, of course, pray to the Egg Bringer S'Yahazah that Krassrr and his war-casters would fail to sniff out the source of the sabotage he had just committed.

U.S.S. TITAN

Anticipating a little time away from both his mother and *Titan*'s other child-care providers as only an eleven-year-old can, Noah Powell strode into the mess hall to have some lunch. He considered the available replicator options—being the son of *Titan*'s health-conscious head nurse Alyssa Ogawa, Noah hadn't been cleared to order absolutely *anything* he wanted—as he moved toward the four science specialists who were seated around what had come to be called the Blue Table.

Instead of passing the scientists on his way to the replicator, Noah stopped dead in his tracks, fascinated—not so much by the scientists, whom he had gotten used to seeing frequently since he and his mother had come to live aboard *Titan* nearly three years ago, but by whatever it was that seemed to so fascinate *them*.

What absorbed the attention of Ensign Zurin Dakal, Ensign Peya Fell, Lieutenant Savalek, and Dr. Se'al Cethente Qas—and now Noah Powell as well—was the strange, grainy holographic image that floated about half a meter above the table. For the most part it was a long cylinder, apparently made of an incredibly pockmarked, ancient-looking metal. The upper end terminated in a kind of spire, while the bottom was capped with a wide, blunt disk, itself a short, flattened cylinder.

"What is *that*?" Noah asked, enthralled.

Cethente, *Titan*'s senior astrophysicist, said, *"That is a very good question."* The sensory clusters on his hard, fluted exterior apparently focused on the hovering image, Cethente lapsed into a silence that Noah regarded as one of thoughtful study, though it was impossible to tell what the Syrath scientist was really thinking. Cethente wasn't remotely humanoid; in fact, he reminded Noah of a picture he'd seen of the Cardassian Galor emblem.

"We have very little information about this construct as yet," said Savalek, whom Noah knew was a botanist.

"Well, we probably know it isn't some new kind of flower," Noah said with a shrug, though he knew he probably wasn't being helpful.

Dakal chuckled. "It might not be a flower, but under the right circumstances it might enable quite a few new gardens to bloom."

"Once it clears all the weeds out of its way," said Peya Fell. As the relief science officer spoke she shook her head, which was hairless per Deltan tradition.

"Weeds?" Noah asked, confused.

"This object is in orbit around the second planet in this system," Cethente said in his electronically synthesized voice. *"The image here represents a mere first glimpse. But we are seriously considering the possibility that this . . . device may be an ancient, extremely powerful machine designed for the purpose of large-scale planetary engineering."*

"Planetary engineering," Noah said. "As in rebuilding planets?"

Ensign Fell said, "It's possible that at one time in the remote past, this artifact or something very much like it created whole biospheres. Many planets in this sector of space appear to have been altered in this manner—perhaps even some of the worlds in this very system."

A terrible understanding was beginning to dawn on Noah. He pointed at the floating hologram. "So the planets would get altered once this thing got done pulling the weeds."

"In a manner of speaking," Cethente said. *"It is at once an engine of creation and destruction."*

It was all starting to make sense. "Brahma and Shiva," Noah said. "Together."

"Excuse me?" Fell said, tipping her head in unconcealed curiosity.

Noah flushed, realizing that he'd usurped the artifact's status as the focus of attention. "I've been studying Earth religions in school. We just started exploring Hindu mythology. One of the Hindu gods—Brahma—was supposed to have created the universe. Another one, somebody called Shiva, is supposed to destroy it off in the far future."

"'Now I am become Death, the destroyer of worlds,'" Dakal said, still staring at the image.

"I've heard that somewhere before," Noah said, aware that the Cardassian officer had quoted a famous saying.

"It's from a poem written long ago by one of your people," Dakal said, resting his gaze on Noah. "One of the inventors of Earth's earliest atomic weapons quoted the line before I did. I think he may have been talking about the same destructive deity you just mentioned."

"Creation and destruction at the same time," Noah said, overwhelmed; he thought his eyes must have looked like pinwheels. "Shiva and Brahma head-butting each other."

"A crude but apt analogy," Savalek said.

Noah had an inspiration. "This thing needs a name."

"Like 'Bob' or 'Kevin'?" Fell said with an impish grin.

Noah frowned, wanting to be taken seriously. "Let's name the thing after both of the Hindu gods. You could call it Brahma-Shiva."

"Or Shiva-Brahma, depending on what mood it's in," Fell said, still grinning.

"I must point out," Savalek said, "that Vulcan mythology has its own gods of creation and destruction, life and death. Those deities could also provide our nomenclature."

"Except that nobody but Vulcans can pronounce their names," Fell said.

Cethente said nothing, and remained even less easy to

read than the unemotional Vulcan botanist. Fell seemed not to be taking the idea of naming the object seriously.

Dakal, however, was stroking his gray chin thoughtfully. "Brahma-Shiva," he said. "That just might catch on."

"Captain, the long-range sensors have detected a significant power spike in the inner system," Tuvok said, his dark gaze riveted to the tactical console before him.

Riker turned his chair toward the aft section of the bridge, and Tuvok's station; the forward viewer, now behind the captain, was split between two sets of images: a false-color display of several of the nearer icy bodies that made up the local Kuiper belt within which *Titan* had been concealed since her ostensible "departure" from the Vela OB2–404 system, and a long-range-sensor-generated shot of the ancient alien artifact that hung balefully above a distinctively ringed world.

"Can you pinpoint the source?" the captain said.

Tuvok nodded. "The readings originate from inside the artifact the Gorn have placed in orbit around the second planet."

"Which is an *inhabited* planet," said Vale, who was examining Tuvok's readouts on the small display that was built into the arm of her chair.

For the moment, Riker thought. The distinct possibility that this world's inhabitants might soon be summarily wiped out left him feeling more glum and helpless than he had at any time since the superpowerful Caeliar had made prisoners of Deanna and the yet-unborn Natasha.

Riker rose from his chair and straightened his uniform tunic. Facing Vale, he said, "Gather the senior staff in the main observation lounge. I want everyone to see what we might have to face."

Although Troi wasn't crazy about the short notice she'd received for the meeting Will had called—since it was near the end of the alpha watch, the time when she usually picked up Natasha from T'Pel's child-care facility, she'd had to impose upon T'Pel to watch her daughter for at least a little longer—she had to admit that receiving short notice about a meeting was a lot better than being left to sleep through it.

"Sorry I'm late," she said as she stepped into the wide observation lounge. She made her way to the large meeting table and took the seat—the only one not occupied—to Will's immediate left. Casting her gaze around the table, she exchanged smiles and murmured greetings and acknowledgments with everyone assembled; in addition to herself, Will, and Chris, Commanders Tuvok, Ranul Keru, Xin Ra-Havreii, Lieutenant Commander Melora Pazlar, Dr. Shenti Yisec Eres Ree, and Lieutenants Sariel Rager and Aili Lavena were present.

The room was infused with a kind of nervous energy, as though everyone shared a collective sense of purpose but lacked anything tangible upon which to focus it. Although it felt to Troi a great deal like impatience, empathically speaking, she also could sense very clearly that none of that impatience was directed toward her for her tardiness. It was instead directed toward the panoramic transparent aluminum window, through which the faintly reflecting surfaces of several shadow-engulfed comet fragments could be seen framing the distant ember of the star known as Vela OB2–404.

"I've called you all here because the situation with the second planet could come to a head at any moment," Will said without preamble. He nodded toward Vale, who touched a control on the padd she held.

The room's holographic projectors replaced the window's view with a high-resolution shot of Vela OB2–404 II, and the mysterious alien object that hung above its sky, like a knife poised to strike at the planet's vitals. Columns of figures were superimposed over the image, changing too quickly to interpret.

Troi didn't need any real expertise in the actual math to conclude that those numbers augured an outcome that was probably both imminent and terrible.

"Mister Tuvok," Vale said, setting aside her padd as she gave the tactical officer what appeared to be her full attention. "Have you noted any changes in the energy patterns since you first detected them?"

"Only that their rate of increase has continued to climb over the past several minutes," the Vulcan said. "The internal power level being generated already exceeds that of a standard *Intrepid*-class warp core. In approximately ten minutes, I expect it to exceed that of the original Genesis device."

Troi felt her jaw fall open; she managed to close it only with a firm act of will. Gesturing toward the alien object, she said, "Tuvok, are you saying that the Gorn have actually succeeded in *activating* the device?"

"Apparently so," Tuvok said.

"So it appears we're about to find out whether this thing really works the way the Gorn seem to think it does," said Melora Pazlar, whose appearance in a standard Starfleet duty uniform betrayed the fact that she was attending the meeting via *Titan*'s shipwide telepresence system.

"And if that thing really *does* work as advertised," said Keru, "then an entire civilization gets flash-fried—and there's not a damned thing we can do about it." Like all the other senior officers present, the huge unjoined Trill had already been brought up to speed on the latest intelligence concerning the recent destruction of a Gorn hatchery planet, a world critical to the survival of the Hegemony's warrior caste—as well as the great pains to which all the Gorn castes were presently going in their efforts to find (or create) a replacement for that ruined planet.

Dr. Ree nodded his great reptilian head in Keru's direction, his inhuman Pahkwa-thanh features looking somehow wistful despite the ostentatious visibility of a good half-dozen of his steak-knife-sized teeth. "We would appear to have very few available options, Commander."

But Keru clearly didn't want to hear that. Though usually possessed of a gentle demeanor, the security chief was now as angry and frustrated as Troi had ever seen him. "We could put a stop to this," Keru said, staring urgently at Will. "We could take *Titan* into the inner system at high warp, drop to sublight just long enough to treat that flying weapon to a brace of quantum torpedoes, and then throttle back up to warp nine or better before they even know what hit them."

"There's nothing about that maneuver that my helm can't handle," said Lieutenant Lavena. The words of the Pacifican conn officer were distorted slightly by her hydration suit's faceplate.

"Sounds good to me," Vale said, interlacing her fingers on the tabletop.

"I'm for imposing our will on the situation as well," said Ra-Havreii, *Titan*'s chief engineer. "Why should we sit idly by when lives—perhaps many *millions* of lives—are at stake?" Troi could feel the pain that lay beneath the Efrosian's words. During Ra-Havreii's earlier career as one of the chief designers of Starfleet's *Luna*-class starships, a horrendous accident had befallen his prototype engine room, an incident that had cost several *U.S.S. Luna* personnel their lives. The guilt Ra-Havreii still felt over the *Luna* affair followed him like a second shadow even now.

Vale nodded at the engineer and then cast a questioning look at Will. "Captain, just give the word, and—"

"By whose authority?" he said, cutting her off. He looked haggard and inadequately rested, conditions that all too often seemed to go with his job.

"Captain?" said Vale, sounding confused.

"This system is a long way from Federation space, Commander," Will said, his tone growing more stern and formal to cover the momentary lapse in his command persona. "The Gorn have never been gentle in handling incursions into territories they've claimed. Moving unilaterally against them will have consequences—especially since they decided to cast their lot with the Breen and the Tzenkethi and the rest of the Typhon Pact."

"If Starfleet Command would sign off on a plan of action, we wouldn't exactly be acting unilaterally," Keru said.

"That doesn't seem to be in the cards, unfortunately, at least for the moment," Will said. Turning his head toward Rager, he said, "Lieutenant?"

"About half an hour ago, a hitch developed in our

comm system," said the senior operations officer. "Something is jamming every attempt I make to raise Starfleet on any of the subspace bands." Though Rager was outwardly calm, to Troi's Betazoid senses she was almost refulgent with frustration. "I have to assume it's something the Gorn are doing, though there's still no evidence that they've located us here in the local Kuiper belt. And I also have to assume that Gorn subspace communications are still open."

"Which means that we must further assume that Gorn reinforcements are already en route to this system," Tuvok said. "Just as Captain Krassrr claimed."

"All right, so the odds against us stink, and we're on our own," said Keru.

"And don't forget that we're racing against a ticking clock," Ree said. "Even though we might not know exactly how much time is left on that clock until it's too late."

Keru's massive shoulders moved up and down in an elaborate shrug before he focused his gaze on the captain. "Ticking clock or no, our response to this . . . Gorn genocide is entirely up to you, Captain. Please don't tell us you expect us to just sit on our hands out here, sir."

Troi watched her husband as he sat in silence for an uncomfortable span of time. That he was in agony would have been obvious to the least empathic being in the galaxy.

At length, he said, "I'm afraid my hands may be tied. As far as we can tell, Vela OB2–404 II is subject to full Prime Directive protection."

"Which means, ironically, that we're forbidden to protect the natives from a bunch of genocidal lizard-men,"

Vale said. Turning to face Dr. Ree, she added, "No offense intended, Doctor."

The reptiloid chief medical officer seemed grimly amused by the exec's gaffe. "None taken, Commander. Besides, I'm more often likened to a Terran dinosaur than a lizard."

Will looked toward Vale, his frustration beginning to defeat his best efforts to contain it. "Damn it, Chris, I don't like this situation any better than *you* do! And I don't think I understand the constraints of the Prime Directive any better than you do, either. Or do you need a refresher course?"

Though clearly angered by the dressing-down she'd just received right in front of the rest of the senior staff, Vale presented an all but emotionless wall to *Titan*'s CO. "Of course not, Captain," she said after a brief, thought-gathering pause. "I suppose I'm just hoping for one of those proverbial rabbits you always seem to pull out of your hat—and always in the proverbial nick of time, no less."

Will's irritation softened at that, and he released a chuckle that seemed to soothe the rising anxieties of everyone else in the room, at least a little. "I think that hat may be fresh out of rabbits this time."

"Perhaps what really needs to come out of the hat this time," Troi said, "is a Starfleet JAG attorney with a specialty in Prime Directive law."

"Somehow, I doubt even that would do us any good," Will said. The small smile that had accompanied his mood-defusing laugh faded and vanished. "Unfortunately, the circumstances here are about as cut and dried as they come. None of our scans of Vela OB2–404 II have shown any evidence whatsoever that they've developed any spacefaring infrastructure of any kind. No ships. No orbiting ship-repair facilities. No outposts on any of the planet's five moons. Not even communications satellites or buoys. Nothing that gives them peer standing with the Federation. Therefore we can't simply intervene on their behalf, any more than we could with any pre-warp society."

"The Prime Directive requires us to avoid contaminating them through contact," Keru said. "But suppose we were to intervene *without* making contact? If we can destroy that terraforming platform without contributing anything more to the native culture than a mysterious fireworks display, then I think we ought to do it."

Will nodded as he quietly absorbed the Trill's suggestion and processed it. "Get in, get out, nobody gets hurt. Do I understand you correctly, Commander?"

"You do, sir."

"The idea looks pretty good, at least on paper. It might even pass muster on the Prime Directive front. But in practice, it might not be quite that simple. Even if we managed to blow that artifact to quarks, we'd still have to get away from a half-dozen very fast, very well-armed Gorn vessels, and with no prospect of any Starfleet support for *months*. Mister Tuvok, what are the odds of *Titan*'s survival given those circumstances?"

The Vulcan's grimmer-than-usual demeanor told Troi everything she needed to know. "There are a great many variables and unknowns in such a scenario, Captain, not the least of which is the possibility of the imminent arrival of Gorn reinforcements. However, I would estimate our long-term survival odds to be less than five percent. Should

Gorn reinforcements come into play, I would revise those odds downward precipitously."

Vale slapped her hands onto the tabletop in frustration. "So what do we do? Just sit up here, hiding in the weeds, *watching*?"

Will started to reply when Ensign Dakal's voice interrupted him from his combadge. *"Captain, our probes and long-range sensors have picked up something strange. The energy signature inside the terraforming platform is . . . fluctuating."*

Will nodded to Vale, who grabbed up her padd and began keying in the commands necessary to synchronize the holographic display with Dakal's new incoming data. "Good eye, Ensign," Will told Dakal. "We're watching it in here."

The holographic image being projected across the observation window rippled momentarily as the data being gathered remotely from Vela OB2–404's distant second planet began to refresh. Troi realized only then that she was holding her breath, expecting the next image she saw to be that of a lethal energy-beam of some sort tearing a swath of destruction across the planet's unprotected blue-green surface.

Instead the image settled down to reveal a bizarre mottled light-show encircling the alien artifact. The brilliance intensified, prompting Troi and others to raise their hands to protect their eyes even as the emergency illumination dampers cut in to ensure that no one was blinded. Spots swam before her eyes momentarily.

When they cleared, the alien artifact merely continued tumbling in its orbit, its pitted gray skin appearing as cold and dead as the surface of a multi-billion-year-old comet.

"What the hell just happened?" Will said, breaking the room's stunned silence.

"The device appears to have malfunctioned, Captain," Tuvok said, using a padd to consult his tactical station remotely.

Will stood, signaling that the meeting was at an end. "Has the planet been affected in any way?"

"Evidently not," said Tuvok, also getting to his feet, as was everyone else, with the exception of Pazlar, who hovered about half a meter above the carpet. "I suspect that the Gorn have just experienced an unanticipated technical failure of some kind."

Will nodded his acknowledgment. Addressing the room, he said, "I want a full analysis and report within the hour, people. Let's get to it." He remained standing at the head of the conference table, as did Troi, until the last of the other senior officers had finished filing out of the room.

"I believe I already have a preliminary report for you, Captain," Troi said, trying to lighten his confused, frazzled mood by speaking with mock-officiousness.

He favored her with a small smile. "Go ahead, Commander."

She stepped toward him so that the new imagery from Vela OB2–404 II framed them both. Since they were alone in the room, she took the liberty of taking both his hands in hers. "I think the universe may have just granted you another one of those proverbial nick-of-time rabbits."

6

GORN HEGEMONY RECONNAISSANCE VESSEL *SSEVARRH*

The "mysterious breakdown" of the ecosculptor threw tech-casters and war-casters into near identical flurries of panic throughout the *Ssevarrh,* and probably aboard the other ships in the flotilla as well. As S'syrixx had expected, his fellow technologists overcame the initial chaos first and began applying analytical thinking to the problem.

What he didn't expect was the voice that roared at him less than a mealtime later as he traversed the corridor that took him to the door to his quarters. Though he cowered instinctively, S'syrixx turned toward the sound even as his door slid open.

Out of his peripheral vision, S'syrixx could see through the irised-open hatchway that his personal work desk lay upended, his data terminal broken and smashed. Tools, clothing, padds, and data flimsies were strewn about the floor. Obviously, the captain had searched his quarters while he had been working elsewhere.

"Do you really believe members of the warrior caste to be stupid?" Captain Krassrr bellowed, flecks of cold spittle spraying from the scaly corners of his mouth. The countless facets of his metallic silver eyes appeared icier than Gornar's most frigid northern glacier. "Did you believe that your crime would not be traced back to you?"

"Crime, Captain?" S'syrixx said, his voice a weak croak as he vainly strove to keep his trembling under control.

Krassrr continued as though S'syrixx hadn't spoken. "I am told that yours was the only personal data terminal that was speaking with the ecosculptor at the time the tampering must have occurred. Your claws may as well be adrip with Gorn warrior blood." A quartet of highly intimidating armed enforcers suddenly seemed to appear out of nowhere, converging on S'syrixx from two directions.

S'Yahazah does indeed answer our prayers, S'syrixx thought as he stared down at his footclaws, his posture a motley mix of shame and defiance. *And sometimes her only answer is a resounding "no."*

"I was merely acting to *prevent* the shedding of blood," S'syrixx heard someone say before belatedly realizing that he had been the speaker. "And our shaming in the eternal eyes of the Egg Bringer S'Yahazah."

The war-caster's claws grabbed the body harness in which S'syrixx kept his various scientific tools and hoisted him clear off the deck. S'syrixx gasped as his footclaws sliced helplessly, out of contact with anything.

"You have committed an unconscionable act of sabotage!" Krassrr said in a voice like an avalanche. "You may have doomed my caste to extinction—and with us, the entire Hegemony!"

Despite his rising feelings of panic, S'syrixx found a split second to wonder why any of the non-warrior castes—the labor caste, say—couldn't adapt itself to the purpose of defending the Hegemony and take the war-casters' place. But there was nothing to be gained from giving voice to any such thought; nothing he could say was likely to calm Krassrr down.

"Extinguishing an entire civilization," S'syrixx said tremulously, "is a deed unworthy of your caste."

"The warrior caste does whatever is necessary," Krassrr said. "Starting with meting out the wages of treason." With that, he slammed S'syrixx to the deck hard enough to force the air from his lungs. The technologist gasped again and howled in pain as the deck plating scored the scales on his knees and elbows. He noted wryly that now blood really *was* on his claws, dripping from a laceration on his right forearm.

"Take him," said Krassrr, then turned away in disgust.

The armed troopers hustled S'syrixx back to a standing position and used the barrels of their pulse rifles to prod him forward down the corridor and into one of the radial passages that led toward the outer hull. The procession took on a bizarre sense of unreality, as if it were occurring in a dream.

They marched him to an inner airlock door, which obediently opened for one of the troopers.

No!

"Get in, traitor," said the nearest soldier, a nasty fellow whose distinguishing characteristic was the broad swatch of burn-scarred scales that ran diagonally across his blunt face.

S'syrixx spread both manus before him in what he hoped was a beneficent *let-us-reason-together* gesture. "Let's not do this thing in haste. I should be entitled to due process."

"You've *had* your 'due process,'" said the trooper that S'syrixx was coming to think of as Scarface. "Captain

Krassrr has found you guilty of treason. And treason is punishable by death." He raised his rifle and adjusted something on its stock so that it made a menacing *clack.* "Now get in the airlock, or I will shoot you dead."

Moving at the same dreamlike pace he had taken during the long march from his quarters, S'syrixx meekly did as he was bid. He stepped into the small, iris-hatched chamber, noting that the trooper who had his hand on the wall-mounted control pad was oozing drool onto the deck. *Bloodthirsty bastards,* he thought. *The warriors just* live *for this sort of thing. S'Yahazah help me, but the Hegemony would be better off without them.*

The door irised shut behind him, leaving another similar door—also closed for the moment—as his only protection from dying in the airless cold of space. Through the talk box on the inner airlock wall, he could hear the warriors laughing and growling in anticipation of their imminent entertainment.

But he also heard something else: a familiar voice. *"Stop this!"*

R'rerrgran! He's trying to rescue me!

"Don't interfere, physician," S'syrixx heard one of the warriors scoff. *"Unless, of course, you'd like to suck space with your friend."*

Through the inner airlock door's narrow crysmetal window, S'syrixx could see R'rerrgran making pleading gestures. Unfortunately, whatever any of them might be saying had evidently grown too indistinct for the comm to pick up. S'syrixx couldn't tell whether R'rerrgran was making any headway in pleading for his life, but he had to regard the still-closed outer airlock door as a good sign.

Good work, R'rerrgran, S'syrixx thought with no small amount of gratitude. R'rerrgran was the physician who had cleared him and Z'shezhira for reproductive bonding; R'rerrgran would never abandon him.

An eternity later, the inner door hissed open again. Scarface leaned into the chamber and roughly dragged S'syrixx back into the corridor.

"You've been granted a temporary reprieve," the warrior snarled. "Thanks to a point your doctor friend raised."

"Sorry to disappoint you and your friends," S'syrixx said as he wiped the blood from his lacerated foreclaw onto his tunic.

Scarface leaned toward S'syrixx, invading his space in the warrior caste's uniquely intimidating manner. "Don't worry. I'm sure we'll all be back here before the end of my shift—once we finish interrogating you for the identities of your secret confederates."

GORN HEGEMONY WARSHIP *S'ALATH*

On the command deck, Gog'resssh leaned once again across the sensor console with that almost-amorous warrior swagger that Z'shezhira found so distasteful. She remained seated at her station, sitting rigidly at attention and determined not to give offense through her body language. There was certainly nothing to be gained by going out of her way to antagonize the war-caster leader—just as there was nothing to be gained by revealing *everything* she had just discovered.

She could only hope that the ambient fear-chemicals that had proliferated among the conquered tech-caster crew ever since Gog'resssh had taken charge would work to keep her own interior emotional state obscure—along with her long-term plans to be rid of the mad warrior and his henchmen.

"What in the name of S'Yahazah's nether regions are they *doing*?" Gog'resssh wanted to know.

He was referring, of course, to the six Gorn recon vessels that had lately taken such an intense interest in the inhabited planet known in the astrometrics database by its native name of Hranrar. The small recon fleet's commander had evidently felt territorial enough about Hranrar to intimidate a Sst'rfleet vessel—allegedly an exploration ship with no military agenda—into fleeing the system.

Z'shezhira had been almost unable to contain the relief she felt after she'd persuaded Gog'resssh and Zegrroz'rh not to continue pursuing the retreating Federrazsh'n ship, at least for the moment, in favor of secretly monitoring the Gorn flotilla's activities over the system's second planet. Whether this was because they feared the vessel that had played such a pivotal role in the defeat of the machine-mammals, or because they were genuinely curious about what their conspecifics were doing on Hranrar, she neither knew nor cared; she was simply grateful to have been allowed such relatively close proximity to ordinary Gorn ships of the line, albeit only as a surreptitious presence watching them from the system's edge.

"I've already had several passive-scanner probes sent out to try to determine why the recon fleet has come here," she told Gog'resssh. That all but undetectable chain of small remote-sensing drones and outbound signal relays had told her a great deal about the flotilla of Gorn vessels, right down to the names painted on their hulls.

She'd felt a poignant mixture of joy and unrequited longing when she first saw the recon vessel *Ssevarrh* among those names.

Gog'resssh leaned unfortunately close to her, prompting her to notice that his breath stank of something that had been killed far too long before he had finally consumed it. "I hope you have kept your probes at a . . . discreet distance from those vessels. I would hate to misinterpret your commendable sense of scientific curiosity as an attempt to alert the recon fleet to our presence." As if to prove a point, he reached for one of the switches on her console—he probably hadn't bothered to make note of what it did—and snapped it into pieces.

Wonderful, she thought. She wondered how long it would be before the quartermaster and the engineers could no longer accommodate her requests for spare parts—component replacements that First Myrmidon Gog'resssh's ever-more-frequent demonstrations continued to make necessary on nearly a daily basis.

How delightful it would be indeed to be rescued from this increasingly unstable war-caster, not to mention his lieutenant, Second Myrmidon Zegrroz'rh, whom she noted was once again leering at her from an engineering station whose workings he almost certainly did not comprehend. But as much as she would relish any opportunity to get away, Z'shezhira was pragmatic enough to understand the odds against the prospect, particularly with the *S'alath* so well hidden at the moment among the boundless population of icy bodies that made up this system's periphery—and with Gog'resssh so obviously paranoid, so primed and prone to kill her at the first sign of treachery.

She breathed a silent prayer of thanks to Fertile S'Yahazah that no war-caster had ever been known to possess any telepathic abilities.

"We all saw those recon vessels towing that strange metal object in from outsystem, First Myrmidon," she said, "and settling it into orbit around this system's second planet. And they seem to have tried repeatedly to activate some sort of inner mechanism ever since. I'm not sure, but one of the power spikes the sensors picked up makes me think they may have nearly overloaded and detonated the entire thing a little earlier this very dayturn."

"So what do you believe it all adds up to?" Gog'resssh asked, his cavernous, scale-covered brow ridges folding in a rare approximation of real curiosity. Of course, his concerns were almost certainly strategic rather than scientific.

She debated for a moment how much she should tell him. What action on his part might her most tentative conclusions precipitate?

"Were I to speculate," Z'shezhira said at length, "I'd say that the recon fleet believes it has found one of the ancient technological artifacts that was responsible—eons ago—for altering so many of the planetary environments throughout this sector. They must be trying to use it to remold one of these worlds yet again."

"Why?" he said. His breath stank of rotting meat. Though she was thoroughly carnivorean herself, the odor was nearly enough to turn her into a dedicated leaf-eater—to say nothing of making her consider staying away from males entirely.

"I think they believe they've found a potent machine from out of the Hegemony's prehistory," she said. "A . . .

planet maker of sorts. Perhaps even a device that might enable them to re-create Sazssgrerrn, and restore generational security to your caste."

She was thankful when Gog'resssh, and his malodorous breath, took a long step back from her console. The fire that she saw burning behind his metallic, insectoid eyes, however, was anything but reassuring.

"It is a weapon," he said. "A weapon like no other."

"I suppose," Z'shezhira said, increasingly uncomfortable with the direction this conversation was taking. "But if this . . . artifact really can do what the fleet evidently thinks it can do, its best application would be to restore your caste's lost hatchery world. Would it not?"

He paused, as though weighing the possibilities. She dared to allow herself to hope that he might actually be listening to her.

Then Second Myrmidon Zegrroz'rh left the helm console and approached Z'shezhira's station. He showed an unnerving number of his knife-sharp teeth. Addressing Gog'resssh, he said, "That can wait until we have used the device to give the other castes a taste of the loss ours has suffered."

Whatever hope Z'shezhira had that reason might prevail abruptly evaporated. "Yesssss," said Gog'resssh.

Apparently relishing having captured his superior's imagination, Zegrroz'rh continued. "Long have the other castes envied us our strength. Our resolve."

Gog'resssh nodded. "Yesss."

"Now we will give them further cause to envy us. We will be the heralds of an entirely new, divinely-ordained incarnation of the warrior caste."

Gog'resssh seemed close to reaching the same fever

pitch that Zegrroz'rh had. "A warrior caste that will never shirk its duty in the eyes of fate, the universe, and Great S'Yahazah herself."

"A warrior caste that will rule all the *other* castes, rather than the other way around," Zegrroz'rh said.

Zegrroz'rh's one good eye shone with a light that Z'shezhira had seen before only in the orbs of those dying of severe radiation poisoning or some other wasting disease. Given the intense rad exposure these warriors had experienced during Sazssgrerrn's destruction, she wondered if that was the inevitable direction their mutual madness—a progressive insanity that neither warrior seemed to notice at all—would lead them.

"Do you really expect the other castes to just fall into line behind you?" Z'shezhira heard herself saying.

"Not immediately, no," Gog'resssh said. "And the political caste will be the most difficult of all to persuade, because of their arrogance. But they are every bit as jealous and fearful of us as is everyone else in the Hegemony. If the politicals will not assume an appropriately subservient role, we will destroy them."

"And remake their worlds for ourselves," Zegrroz'rh said. "As well as *yours*." Z'shezhira realized with a loosening of her guts that Gog'resssh's lieutenant was addressing her directly. Leaning menacingly forward in order to bring his phalanx of sharpened teeth to an uncomfortable proximity with her throat, he added, "When we were first brought on board the *S'alath,* you tech-casters tried to have us destroyed as genetically unfit. Do not believe for a moment that any of us have forgotten that."

"We will have to act decisively, Second Myrmidon,"

said Gog'resssh. "To ensure that none of the other castes ever gets to attempt such a travesty again."

At a gesture from the first myrmidon, the two warriors exited the command deck, the better to refine their grandiose new military plans in privacy. Z'shezhira hoped this meant that she could count on them not to act rashly or prematurely, despite their apparently accelerating descent into madness.

It suddenly struck her yet again how profoundly dangerous these paranoid troopers could be, despite their having been half-crippled by radiogenic illness. The fact that they had only a relative manusful of grunt troops at their disposal in no way appeared to diminish the threat they posed, so long as they could maintain control of the *S'alath*. *And if those two really do get their hands on that ecosculpting device—assuming that's really what it is—the damage they might inflict upon the Hegemony could be irreparable. Unless someone does something about it.*

Unless I *do something about it.*

She thought about the flotilla of Gorn vessels that even now was trying to wrangle that object in the skies over Hranrar.

And she wondered whether she really could get away with using the very same sensors she had used to monitor those vessels to send a covert warning to the *Ssevarrh*—the very ship to which her beloved mate-to-be S'syrixx had been assigned before the uncaring claws of fate had separated them.

7

U.S.S. *TITAN*

Riker slowly paced the length and breadth of his ready room, feeling like a caged tiger. Forcing himself into a semblance of calm, he came to a stop behind his desk and leaned with his hands against it, facing his two most trusted officers and confidantes. "If the Gorn can find a way to do it, they'll try to fire that device up again. And they won't waste any time doing it, given what seems to be at stake for them." According to the analysis of Starfleet Intelligence, the stakes might be nothing less than the entire defense capability of the Gorn Hegemony.

Vale offered a glum nod. Like Riker, she was standing, and she, too, seemed to radiate the nervous energy of a person trained to take action, yet prevented by circumstances from doing so. "In other words, we're right back where we started."

"Not entirely," Deanna said, leaning against the wall near the ready-room door. "At least Starfleet Command has been apprised of the situation."

At least there's that, Riker thought, though he wasn't sure how much good that would do anybody aboard *Titan*. True, the shuttlecraft *Handy* was on its way back from its voyage past Vela OB2–404's distant heliopause, the vast spherical boundary that marked the distance at which the incoming winds from other, more distant suns overwhelmed the local star's outbound particle flux. The purpose of the *Handy*'s flight had been to deploy a series of subspace radio relay buoys between the heliopause and the relatively more confined space of Vela OB2–404's Kuiper belt and points sunward.

Thanks to the efforts of two accomplished shuttle pilots, Ensign Olivia Bolaji and Ensign Waen—and Ensigns Crandall and Kuu'iut, specialists, respectively, in engineering and tactical—*Titan* now had an open subspace channel to Starfleet Command, at least as long as the series of subspace relays remained capable of piercing the local interference. Admiral Alita de la Fuega, the commander of *Titan*'s base of operations at Starbase 185, had listened to Riker's verbal report with rapt attention and was now up to date on the Vela OB2–404 situation. She had enthusiastically endorsed Riker's every decision up to this point.

But when Riker asked for permission to use force to neutralize the Gorn terraforming operation—and requested that Starfleet send slipstream drive-equipped reinforcements to counter the phalanx of Gorn vessels Captain Krassrr said he was expecting—de la Fuega's enthusiasm appeared to have reached its limit.

On the terraforming matter, the admiral had said she'd need time to consult with Starfleet Command before any decision could be made. And regarding Riker's request for reinforcements, she reiterated how terribly overstretched Starfleet was at the moment because of the destruction the damned Borg had wrought. "We'll try to shake a few ships loose," she'd said just before signing off.

Riker, who was already more than familiar with Starfleet's post-Borg circumstances, had immediately parsed the true meaning of the admiral's parting words: *I'll do what I can, but I don't expect that to amount to much.*

Or, more plainly: *You're on your own.*

Shaking the captain from his reverie, Deanna said, "I suppose we ought to be thankful that the Gorn's little technical snafu bought us at least *some* additional time."

"Which could run out at any moment," Vale said, folding her arms across her chest. "Suppose the accident that aborted the Gorn's first attempt to use that device didn't do any appreciable damage? They could have it up and running again in next to no time. And fate might not intervene again to save the inhabitants of Vela OB2–404 II."

Whatever ultimately happens to those people could be up to us, Riker thought. Correction: *Up to* me.

Riker watched his wife take one of the padded seats that faced the desk, evidently attempting to defuse the tension in the room. He welcomed the gesture, though he doubted it would do him any good.

"Point taken," Deanna said. "I recommend that we use the meantime, however long that might last, to find a way to save the planet's native civilization that both the Gorn and Starfleet Command can live with."

"Is that all, Counselor?" Vale answered with ironic blandness. "I thought we might have to accomplish something *really* difficult today."

Riker cast a warning frown at his exec. "It seems to me that's one of the better options we have at the moment: trying to convince the Gorn to spare this planet and do their terraforming someplace else."

"They didn't seem all that keen on talking the last time we tried to reason with them, Captain," Vale said, matching Riker's frown.

He cast his gaze at Deanna. "Maybe that's because I let the wrong person try to reason with them then."

"I'm game to try," she said without any hesitation, just as he knew she would.

Vale held up both hands in a *stop* gesture directed at both at Riker and Troi. "Now wait a minute. Commander, I understand that trying to reason with the unreasonable is right in your wheelhouse as *Titan*'s senior diplomatic officer. But given the low probability of success—and you've got to admit that the Gorn have never been easy to deal with—we need to consider *all* our options before we put *Titan* in harm's way again."

"You're talking about Commander Keru's idea," Deanna said, not asking a question.

Vale's frustration seemed to be close to coming to a head. "Why the hell *not*? If we take them by surprise and blow up that terraforming dingus, those Gorn ships will no longer have the means to wipe out an entire civilization."

"But if we were to do what you're suggesting," Deanna said, countering Vale's heat with her own cool calm, "the Gorn might see it as a justification for going to war against the Federation. And with the Gorn Hegemony now formally aligned with the Typhon Pact, we could easily end up with the Tholians, the Breen, the Tzenkethi, the Kinshaya, and even the Romulans at our throats as well."

"And then there's the little matter of *Titan*'s chances

of surviving the immediate aftermath of a raid like that," Riker said, recalling his tactical officer's vehemence—for a Vulcan—in supporting his own bleak analysis of the problem. He was determined to avoid the *blow-it-out-of-the-sky* option—a course of action that would deny the alien terraforming technology not only to the Gorn, but also to the Federation—while any other alternative remained.

Vale waved a hand before her as though erasing an invisible chalkboard filled with flawed equations. "Well then let's just tuck our tails between our legs and go home? Damn."

Riker considered that. True, he could order *Titan* entirely out of the system. But had he taken every opportunity to dissuade the Gorn from their present course of action?

Focusing his attention on Deanna, Riker came to a decision. "Commander Troi, I want you to put your diplomacy hat on. We're going back to the second planet. Once we're there, you're going to appeal to the Gorn's better nature."

"That's assuming," Vale said sourly, "that they have one."

Bathed in the blue-green brilliance of the main viewer's rendition of the reflected light of OB2–404 II, Troi found Captain Krassrr's reaction to her overtures to be entirely predictable.

She felt a keen sense of disappointment just the same.

"Earther, did your translation devices suffer damage sometime prior to our last communication?" Krassrr's guttural, annoyance-tinged voice rumbled from the bridge's audio speakers. *"I thought I ordered your commander to withdraw your vessel from this system."*

As before, the commander of the *Ssevarrh* was reticent about using visual communications with his adversaries—or at least with this *particular* adversary. And although thousands of kilometers still separated *Titan* from the *Ssevarrh* and her sister vessels, Troi once again sensed a powerful emotional undercurrent of revulsion coming from Krassrr. It reminded her of own reaction the first time her father had taken her to see—and touch!—the Jalaran river eels at the Rixx Aquarium.

But for Troi's conversation with the Gorn captain, the bridge was utterly silent. Will and Chris sat at their respective stations, listening attentively. The rest of the bridge crew, from Lavena at the flight-control console to Rager at ops to Dakal at sciences to Tuvok at tactical, were equally quiet and motionless. But they were all poised like coiled springs, ready to take whatever split-second action circumstances might require their captain to order.

"I acknowledge that you are uncomfortable with our presence here, Captain Krassrr," Troi said, raising her voice to its most sincere diplomatic pitch; she could only hope that the Gorn version of the universal translator was doing justice to her efforts. "Please let me assure you that we have come in peace. We merely wish to talk with you."

"'Talk,' mammal? The way you and your Met'rr'onz allies 'talked' your way into domination over Inner Eliar?"

It took Troi a few moments to process the unfamiliar place name into something more generally recognizable: Cestus III, the initial flashpoint of every Federation-Gorn conflict over the last century. "We have no designs on any of the planets in this sector, Captain Krassrr. Our interest is purely scientific and humanitarian."

During the lengthy pause that followed, Troi wondered whether the word "humanitarian" was giving Krassrr even more trouble than the Gorn name for Cestus III had briefly given her. The question briefly reminded her of a joke that she'd overheard *Titan*'s reptiloid chief surgeon, Dr. Ree, telling Commander Tuvok nearly a week ago during lunch in the officers' mess: "Commander, if vegetarians eat only vegetables," the carnivorous Pahkwa-thanh physician had asked the sedate, *plomeek*-soup-sipping Vulcan tactical officer, "then what do you suppose 'humanitarians' eat?"

"Permit me to make my meaning as clear as crysmetal, mammal," the Gorn captain said. *"You are not welcome here."*

Beyond Krassrr's obvious annoyance at *Titan*'s return and his profound but unsurprising sense of revulsion at having to speak (again) to a humanoid, Troi sensed something else coming from the Gorn vessels as well: anger, though not all of it was aimed toward *Titan*. She also picked up impatience, directed both internally and externally. There was fear as well, as though death was imminent, which Troi herself knew might very well be the case. And mixed in with all those intricately braided emotions, like the sound of a single voice that was nearly being drowned out by a chorus of others, was something that felt vaguely like unease.

Or possibly even regret.

On the main viewer, some twelve thousand klicks below *Titan*, the planet designated in Starfleet's stellar cartographic database as OB2–404 II serenely continued its eternal rotation. Near the planet's eastern limb floated the alien artifact—some of the crew had lately taken to calling it Brahma-Shiva—which pointed straight down like a cold, dead finger at a world that would soon be shorn of all the life that currently dwelled upon it should the Gorn move their plan forward unopposed.

Could that fact have been the source of the emotion that so smacked of regret?

Did someone among one of the Gorn crews, either on the *Ssevarrh* or one of the other vessels, feel strongly that what they were attempting to do here was wrong?

And just how much influence, if any, might such a person exert over Captain Krassrr?

"Do we understand one another?" Krassrr continued.

"Perfectly, Captain," Troi said. "Just as you must surely understand that *Titan* poses no threat to the operation you are presently conducting. You are expecting reinforcements to arrive soon, after all, and I assume you could always summon more at any time."

Troi felt an odd emotional response coming from the Gorn captain; it felt almost as though he disagreed with what she had just said, or at least some portion of it. Doing her best to put this ambiguous information to one side, she continued: "Since you are in a position of such obvious strength, you have nothing to lose by negotiating with us."

"Negotiating, mammal? Negotiating what*?"*

"The possibility of your choosing a different planet on which to conduct your . . . tests."

The Gorn commander made a derisive snort that the universal translator passed along unchanged. *"What could you know of our . . . tests?"*

"Probably a good deal more than you realize. Certainly enough to know that they threaten the existence of a civilization native to this planet."

"That is unfortunate. But it cannot be avoided."

"That isn't true, Captain. The Federation can help you locate an uninhabited world that will suit your purposes as well as this one."

Krassrr snorted again, but this time the noise sounded vaguely like laughter. *"We are already receiving more than enough help from our Typhon Pact partners."*

"Are you, Captain?" Will said. "The only Typhon Pact-aligned ships I see here so far belong to the Gorn Hegemony."

"That will soon change, mammal. You would do well to be elsewhere when that occurs."

"Thank you for the friendly warning, but I'd like to talk with you a little more first. Our offer of assistance is sincere."

"It is also useless. Your Federrazsh'n would conveniently delay even beginning any such search until after my caste had already suffered so much attrition that the Gorn Hegemony could never again raise its claws against your never-ending expansions and incursions. The stakes are far too high for us to take your offer seriously, Captain."

"Are the stakes so high that they would turn the Gorn Hegemony into a genocidal nation?" Tori asked.

"I regret the necessity of destroying Hranrar," Krassrr said, and Troi sensed a kernel of sincerity buried beneath innumerable thin layers of studied hostility. *"But that is the Hranrarii's problem, not ours."*

Troi suddenly heard a series of incoherent growls coming through the bridge speakers, as though somebody had interrupted Krassrr to present him with some urgent news—none of which, unfortunately, was being translated for her, either because it was too indistinct or too guttural for the translation systems on either end of the connection to handle.

The subspace link closed down in a burst of static. On whatever *emotional* channel she had managed to open with Krassrr, Troi registered only confusion and distraction. There was no sign, however, that an attack on *Titan* was imminent.

"What are they planning to do, Commander?" Vale wanted to know.

Troi turned toward the exec and shrugged. "I honestly don't know."

"Then for now at least, we watch," Will said. "And we wait."

8

GORN HEGEMONY WARSHIP *S'ALATH*

During the latter half of the more than one Gornar sun-circuit that had passed since her capture, Z'shezhira had begun to notice a change in Gog'resssh—beyond the obvious fact of his steadily escalating paranoia. He seemed to have come to trust her on some level, despite the huge gulf of caste-difference that separated them. It struck her as almost paradoxical, especially given the thickening cloud of suspicion that surrounded Gog'resssh and the twenty-odd other remnants of the former Sazssgrerrn garrison as he and his second myrmidon drew their plans against the Federrazsh'n vessel and those of their fellow Gorn.

But it was also highly fortunate, since it enabled her to hide certain information from the first myrmidon—information such as the sensor returns that revealed that the Federrazsh'n vessel had surreptitiously returned to the Hranrar system, where it had hidden its presence among the system's remote zone of icy rubble, just as the *S'alath* had done elsewhere in that selfsame immensity. And then there were the readings that, upon careful study, would have revealed that the Sst'rfleet ship had sent one of its auxiliary craft far out-system, and then back. Z'shezhira felt it was necessary to do whatever she could to "manage" what Gog'resssh learned about what was happening elsewhere in the Hranrar system, the better to keep his mind focused on whatever the Gorn recon flotilla was doing on Hranrar proper.

For keeping his attention focused there was the only way she could think of to maintain any hope of being reunited with her beloved S'syrixx, who had been serving on one of those recon ships at the time of the Sazssgrerrn catastrophe. But when the mammals' ship left the concealment of the ice belt and suddenly headed sunward, any chance of hiding the fact from Gog'resssh evaporated like the tail of a comet at perihelion.

"How could the Earthers have penetrated so far into this system without anyone having noticed their approach earlier?" Gog'resssh bellowed at her without preamble as he came storming onto the command deck, presumably upon having received word of *Titan*'s presence from Second Myrmidon Zegrroz'rh.

She assayed her sincerest expression, keeping her facial scales as flat as possible, and hoped for the best. "I am at a loss, First Myrmidon. It's as though the Federrazsh'n vessel just came out of nowhere."

Gog'resssh bared his unattractive ranks of teeth. "It is a gift from Blessed S'Yahazah herself. We are in need of supplies. We shall take whatever we require from the mammals."

Z'shezhira watched with rising trepidation as Gog'resssh lumbered toward the helm station, where Sk'salissk patiently awaited his commander's orders.

"Helm, plot an intercept course," Gog'resssh rumbled.

GORN HEGEMONY RECONNAISSANCE VESSEL *SSEVARRH*

"The legal subcaste tribunal has completed its deliberations," said Dr. R'rerrgran as he stepped across the threshold to S'syrixx's now computerless quarters. Through the briefly opened door, a vigilant pair of hulking war-caster guards, as hard and stolid as boulders, were visible.

S'syrixx, who had been confined to said quarters since his actions had first earned him Captain Krassrr's unwanted scrutiny, could tell from his old friend's scent as much from his ruffled facial scales and the convoluted topography of abject misery that twisted his dual sagittal crests, that the news he was about to impart was not good.

"I did everything I could, my friend, to intervene on your behalf," R'rerrgran said. "In fact, I have done little else since I stopped your initial summary execution. But the law is the law. Once the tribunal has delivered an official sentence, it must be carried out immediately."

"I am aware of that," S'syrixx said.

"Had I done any more . . ." The physician trailed off.

"I understand." S'syrixx felt far more calm than he had expected. He supposed he'd experience his emotional meltdown when his execution became more imminent than it was presently; perhaps he still needed time to process what was about to happen to him. "Had you done anything more, then we would probably have to share an airlock together."

R'rerrgran tipped his head forward in miserable assent. Then he reached into a pocket on his eggshell-hued medical tunic and withdrew a small hypo injector.

S'syrixx felt a sharp jolt of fear. "Is *this* how it is to be done, R'rerrgran? An injection?"

R'rerrgran's vertical pupils looked strangely opaque. "No. A short time ago I was granted permission to administer an analgesic to you. When death comes, her embrace will at least be a gentle one."

S'syrixx held out his still-lacerated foreclaw, and R'rerrgran dutifully administered the injection.

"Would you like me to repair that?" R'rerrgran said, indicating S'syrixx's foreclaw wound.

The idea sounded so absurd that S'syrixx found he couldn't restrain himself from an intense emotional release. He suspected his meltdown had finally begun. Out in the corridor, as the guards prodded him toward the outer hull—toward, presumably, the nearest airlock—he began issuing peels of deep, chuffing laughter. He willed the unwelcome yet cathartic sensation to stop, but it wouldn't, even as the unamused troopers marched him past the scowling bulk of Captain Krassrr and the three spindly legal-casters who had no doubt unanimously condemned him. His mad chortles continued even after he once again found himself inside a cramped airlock, where he stood hunched between the two heavy pressure doors.

The sense of risible absurdity persisted, even after the outer airlock door irised open and allowed a powerful blast of escaping air to deliver him into the vacuum's cold embrace.

It continued even after his lungs ceased functioning and a darkness that he recognized as death's cloak swaddled him, pushing aside all thought save a final regret that his separation from beautiful, lost Z'shezhira had now been made permanent. . . .

GORN HEGEMONY WARSHIP *S'ALATH*

"I mean no disrespect, First Myrmidon," Z'shezhira said. "But are you certain this is the wisest course of action?"

Gog'resssh's neck scales separated from one another until they stood almost perpendicular from the radiation-scarred flesh his sleeveless military tunic revealed. "You forget your place, female," the war-caster growled, baring his innumerable teeth. "Who are you to question my wisdom?"

Z'shezhira felt her heart race as though it were a warp core. All too aware that she had to defuse her captor's easily roused anger as quickly and deftly as possible, she allowed her head to loll to the side, exposing her neck to a potentially fatal bite in an ages-old Gorn gesture of submission.

"I did not mean to question your wisdom, First Myrmidon," she said. "My intent was to direct your attention to an easier and more desirable target than the mammal vessel."

Gog'resssh's frown deepened until his face resembled a seam of old, weathered copper jutting out of a mountainside. "*Which* target?"

She turned toward the command deck's central visual display, which showed a tactical diagram of the Hranrar system on which the relative positions of the *S'alath,* the Sst'rfleet vessel, and the Gorn recon flotilla were both clearly limned in amber. Z'shezhira also noticed that Sk'salissk's claws were frozen over his helm controls as he awaited either confirmation or rescission of Gog'resssh's most recent order. And on the other side of the helm console, Second Myrmidon Zegrroz'rh was regarding her in a cool, appraising silence, his one good compound eye seeming able to bore a hole through her scales.

"Well?" Gog'resssh roared.

"I'm speaking of the Gorn vessels in orbit of Hranrar, First Myrmidon," Z'shezhira said at length.

"But there are six Gorn ships to our one," Gog'resssh said. "The Federrazsh'n ship is but a single vessel."

"But it's hardly worth raiding, at least for the purpose of restocking our provisions. I've studied the habits of the Federrazsh'n mammals, First Myrmidon. They keep no live food aboard their vessels."

Gog'resssh's jaws slackened with evident horror. "No live food? Nauseating."

"Nauseating indeed," she said. "Nearly as nauseating as the horrible dander being produced by all those mammals. The vessel's corridors are literally acrawl with such creatures."

The first myrmidon stood in contemplative silence, apparently shuddering slightly in response to his own imagination.

"The human ship would be a far easier target to take down," said Zegrroz'rh, to whom Z'shezhira had never attributed a surfeit of imagination.

She struggled to exhibit the same poise and confidence she would have brought to a technical briefing. "Do not be deceived, Second Myrmidon—their ships have surprisingly effective weaponry and evasion capabilities. And even if we were to 'take down' the Federrazsh'n ship, there would still be next to nothing aboard that we could eat."

"I should think that the crew of that vessel would qualify as 'live food,'" Zegrroz'rh said. Snorts and huffing chuckles passed quietly among the half-dozen or so other war-casters now present on the command deck.

Gog'resssh, however, wasn't laughing. "So, Z'shezhira, you suggest instead that we take supplies from six Gorn recon vessels—in fact, from six apparently very *well-armed* Gorn recon vessels."

"Yes, First Myrmidon," she said.

Gog'resssh's teeth reappeared. "The *S'alath* is critically short of personnel in departments throughout this ship."

That's what you get for being so quick to order summary executions, you crècheless bastard, she thought as she struggled to prevent her neck scales from rising into agitated postures. Aloud, she merely said, "True. But the *S'alath* also boasts more than twenty of your strongest fighters, First Myrmidon." Or at least twenty of those who had proven themselves the least easy to kill.

But Gog'resssh appeared to be in no mood to accept flattery. "Even so, we would still be significantly outgunned. The *S'alath* would have to engage up to six well-armed adversaries simultaneously."

"Six well-armed adversaries who would have no reason to expect hostilities from us," Z'shezhira said. "They have called for reinforcements to encourage the Federrazsh'n ship to leave the Hranrar system. Were they to see us, they would believe us to be one of the reinforcement vessels they are awaiting."

A glimmer of understanding appeared to be dawning in Gog'resssh's dull, silvery insectile eyes. "And we can raid their stores of live food and other supplies while their guard is down."

"You are indeed wise, First Myrmidon," Z'shezhira said

with as much humility as she could muster—which wasn't nearly enough to cover the intense loathing she felt for this vile creature.

This creature who was enforcing her separation from her betrothed.

"It is decided, then," Gog'resssh said, snapping Z'shezhira out of her reverie. "Helm, enter a new course. We will approach Hranrar, and our fellow Gorn."

Though she couldn't be certain she wasn't merely indulging her own wishful imagination, Z'shezhira thought she could sense relief in the manner of both Zegrroz'rh and Sk'salissk—relief that they were no longer contemplating an imminent encounter with the hideously alien Federrazsh'n mammalians.

"As friends?" Zegrroz'rh asked. He appeared confused. "Do you really think they might accept the *S'alath* as a reinforcement vessel?"

"Not unless they are unforgivably stupid," Gog'resssh said. "Even if we were to try to obscure this ship's identity with a falsified transponder, they'd no doubt check its authenticity."

"With respect, First Myrmidon, I think you give the tinkering subcastes too much credit."

Gog'resssh's nostrils flared, but he restrained himself from any deeper display of anger. "Never underestimate the tech-casters."

"Perhaps we could alter the markings on our hull," Zegrroz'rh said.

"It won't fool them long enough to do us any good," Gog'resssh said, this time with a hoarse growl obviously intended as a warning that he would brook no further discussion of the matter. "They will recognize the *S'alath,* and then they'll want an explanation for her sudden return to ship-of-the-line status after such a lengthy absence. We might not be able to fight our way out of that eventuality—at least not against six vessels. So we will approach by stealth instead."

Zegrroz'rh and Sk'salissk both acknowledged their superior's order with nods and grunts. Z'shezhira had to suppress a cunning, tooth-baring grin of her own when Second Myrmidon Zegrroz'rh approached, his one good eye flaying her with his obvious suspicion. Ever since her initial encounter with Zegrroz'rh, she'd imagined that he'd always hated and feared the technology caste and his other cultural betters.

"You will continue to monitor the recon fleet's communications," Zegrroz'rh said with a brusque growl. "And never forget, tech-caster: I will be keeping my eye on you, to be certain you hold nothing back. Do we understand each other?"

She nodded mutely. *I understand that you trust* me *about as far as I trust* you. Which was to say, hardly at all.

After the uncomfortable silence between them ran its course, Z'shezhira returned her attention to the console before her and began executing passive scans of the recon flotilla, as well as of the subspace frequencies the other ships most commonly used.

When she slipped the personal receiver unit into her ear canal, she found herself immediately immersed in a flurry of intership comm traffic. The gabble of overlapping voices startled her at first, until her sensitive ear began to separate them, enabling her to hear their reptilian character. She could hear the distinctive plodding cadence of Gorn warriors as well as the quicker, more nimble locutions of comm specialists. Not only members of her own species, but her fellow caste-mates as well, all of them stationed on the various ships of the recon flotilla.

Despite having the lone watchful eye of the hateful Zegrroz'rh trained upon her back, she thought there had to be a surreptitious way she could get a message to one of those comm specialists. A way to let her beloved S'syrixx know that she was still alive. Then she heard S'syrixx's name uttered in the gabble, and her hopes rose.

But only until she heard and sorted out a few more words from the surprisingly chatter-filled ship-to-ship channels. *S'syrixx. Tribunal. Treason. Execution.*

Airlock.

Z'shezhira redirected one of the remote superluminal subspace scanners and began looking for biosigns in the immediate vicinity of the *Ssevarrh,* the vessel upon which S'syrixx had served. In defiance of her will, the scan revealed the presence of a Gorn body adrift beyond the vessel's hull. She divined from the weakness of the bio-readings that this body had exited the ship both unwillingly and without protection. She could also see that the tumbling, distant shape was rapidly cooling toward the ambient temperature of space. Her spine experienced a chill that very nearly matched it.

S'Yahazah's blood, she thought, sagging heavily into the comm console's too-broad chair. *They've just murdered S'syrixx.*

U.S.S. TITAN

"What the hell happened to Captain Krassrr?" Vale demanded, apparently speaking to no one in particular.

Standing in front of his command chair, Will nodded. He was staring at the image of Vela OB2–404 II, the world that Krassrr had called "Hranrar." The ancient, micrometeoroid-pitted orbital platform hung above it like an ill omen, and several Gorn vessels were visible in its vicinity.

"One minute Krassrr is about to run us out of town by force," Will said. "And the next minute he just disappears. Doesn't seem like typical Gorn behavior."

Troi was beginning to think she might have an explanation. "Krassrr's behavior doesn't appear to be typical of the Gorn *warrior* caste."

Will regarded her with a wry smile. "Krassrr certainly seems as warrior-like as any Gorn soldier I've ever encountered."

"And I have no doubt that that's exactly what he is," Troi said. "He probably wouldn't be in command if he belonged to one of the other castes. But the relationship—the *balance*—between the various Gorn castes aboard those ships may be severely out of equilibrium at the moment, in view of the eco-crisis they've been forced to deal with."

"Meaning that the demands of the other castes may be forcing Krassrr to change his methods."

"This is a hell of a change. Damned sloppy, if you ask me."

Troi shook her head. "I'm picking up a great deal of vigilance from each of those Gorn ships, Will. The warriors among those Gorn crews are keeping a very close watch on everything we do. It's just not their place to speak for their captain when he's . . . preoccupied."

"So what do you suppose he's preoccupied *with*?" Vale asked.

Troi shrugged. "Underneath all that vigilance, I'm picking up a strong undercurrent of confusion. Agitation."

"As though there's some sort of power struggle going on between the castes?" Will asked.

Before she could answer the question, another sudden jolt of emotion struck her like a fist to the abdomen, forcing her to wince involuntarily. It was still more imminent death, but it was a far stronger sensation than anything she'd yet experienced with the Gorn.

"Counselor?" said Will, moving toward her seat on the bridge. She realized she was clinging to the chair's arms as though she feared falling.

"Someone's dying, Will," she said, breathless, gazing up at him through a shroud of tears. She gestured toward the main viewer. "Out there."

"Captain, one of the Gorn vessels has just ejected something into space," Ensign Dakal said.

"Red Alert!" Vale shouted.

"Belay that," Will said as he moved toward Dakal's station. "Exactly *what* did that ship eject?"

"A body, sir. A Gorn male."

"Part of a stealth boarding party?" Vale asked.

Dakal shook his head. "Not unless they're sending their troops out without environment suits. This one appears to be all alone, and lacks any apparent life-support apparatus."

Will moved back to Troi's side. "Maybe this explains the undercurrent of emotion you're picking up, Deanna," he said quietly. "This might be a burial in space."

But every instinct Troi possessed argued against that. "No, Will. He's alive."

"Only for the moment, however," said Tuvok, whose hands were moving quickly over the tactical console as he ran scans of his own.

"Mister Dakal," Will said. "Can you get a transporter lock on that individual?"

"I think so, Captain."

Vale cut in: "But can you do it without being noticed by all those vigilant Gorn eyes that must be studying our every move?"

Although the Cardassian ensign at ops looked distinctly uncomfortable, he wasted no time activating the remote transporter system's targeting scanner. "No pressure," Troi heard him mutter. "Lock established."

"Don't energize just yet," Will said. "We're going to need to find a way to cover our tracks first."

"I have just the thing," Vale said, rising from her chair. Troi glanced toward the exec in time to see a grin spread across her face as she moved toward Dakal's station.

GORN HEGEMONY RECONNAISSANCE VESSEL *SSEVARRH*

Krassrr silently cursed the laws that only members of the sedentary castes—who threatened to overwhelmingly outnumber Krassrr's own caste should his present mission fail—would think to invoke. The *Ssevarrh*'s ill-hatched law-caster contingent, no doubt annoyed by the summary execution that had been only narrowly thwarted by the *Ssevarrh*'s chief medical officer, were now insisting upon the strictest possible interpretation of the law and the warrior caste's duty to it. So the tribunal had demanded that the traitor's death sentence be carried out immediately upon the announcement of its final and irrevocable Decision of Condemnation. Unlike the informal execution that Dr. R'rerrgran had stopped, a formal, tribunal-ordered killing such as this one legally required the captain's presence, regardless of how this might conflict with his many other duties.

The fact that a Federrazsh'n vessel had remained in the vicinity of Hranrar despite repeated warnings had mattered not at all to the blinkered law-clawers, whom Krassrr was imagining sending out to keep the traitor company.

Krassrr was in such a foul humor by the time he made it back to the command deck that he didn't bother growling to encourage the two maintenance technicians who stood in his path to make way. Instead he simply swatted them aside with the backs of his leather-scaled manus and stomped between them the rest of the way to the tactical consoles, where a trio of junior officers had been assisting his Second in maintaining watch over the Federrazsh'n vessel during his brief absence.

"Report."

"They've done nothing yet, Captain," said Grezzsz, Krassrr's Second. Grezzsz was also his most experienced tactician. "Other than hail us repeatedly."

"Have you returned their hails?"

"No, Captain. Nor have we usurped your place by speaking with them during your absence. Per your orders."

"Very good." Krassrr turned his bulky upper body toward the communications console, which was attended by a much older but alert-looking warrior-caste female. "Open a channel."

"Captain Krassrr!" Grezzsz roared. Krassrr turned back toward him in time to see the junior officer's keen, sparkling silver eyes focus intently upon the incoming data being displayed on his personal console. "The mammalship has just launched several objects. They are moving at high sublight speed."

"Alert status!" Krassrr rumbled, pitching his deep, cavernous voice at its loudest volume. Klaxons shrieked. The command-deck crew responded instantly, like a complex but well-maintained projectile launcher. "Lock weapons onto the Federrazsh'n vessel! Fire on my command!"

Grezzsz huffed his assent, then returned his full attention to his console.

A moment later, a wrinkle of surprise crossed the tactician's twin sagittal crests. "Captain Krassrr, whatever the mammalship just launched is not heading directly toward us."

It was Krassrr's turn to feel surprise. A salvo of antimatter-tipped Federrazsh'n torpedoes he could understand. But this . . .

"They're only probes, Captain," said Trr'reriss, the techcaster responsible for the command deck's most technical scientific and engineering-related functions. "The Earthers didn't launch any weapons."

The scales across Krassrr's jaw pulled involuntarily taut, resulting in what he knew was a formidable display of teeth. "No. They merely wish to spy on us. Grezzsz, track down each and every last one of those Federrazsh'n probes and destroy them. Trr'reriss, open a channel to that ship."

U.S.S. TITAN

"The last of the probes is away, Captain," Dakal said.

Riker nodded. "Very good, Ensign."

"Wait for it. . . ." Vale said quietly.

As she continued watching the silent Gorn vessel displayed on the main viewer, Troi assessed the intensified hostility and fear that had just begun radiating from the other vessel's bridge. Though these emotions remained as highly unpleasant as the first time she'd felt them, the distilled, almost refined quality of their psychic fingerprint made them easy to recognize.

"Captain Krassrr is about to work us back into his busy schedule," Troi said. "One way or another."

Her weapons ports and impulse engines aglow with barely restrained power, the Gorn ship suddenly began to move.

"Damn," Will said. "I hope our little gambit didn't just backfire on us."

"Wait for it. . . ." Vale repeated, frowning at the viewer.

Troi felt an almost palpable tension enfold the bridge. Everyone present knew that *Titan* now stood only seconds, or perhaps fractions of seconds, away from becoming embroiled in a potentially lethal combat situation.

"The Gorn vessel is moving away from *Titan,*" Tuvok said in crisp, military tones. "She is firing her forward particle weapons—but only at the probes we just launched."

Relief began permeating the tension. Suddenly aware that she hadn't been breathing, Troi allowed air to resume coursing in and out of her lungs.

Vale turned to her and grinned. "I *told* you this was going to work, Counselor."

Thanks to the universal translator's high-fidelity positronic mimicry, the comm system's speakers suddenly reverberated with deep, guttural tones. *"Federrazsh'n vessel, this is Captain Krassrr of the* Ssevarrh. *We are presently destroying the spying devices you have deployed. If we find that you have chosen to remain here after that task is complete, then your vessel shall be our next target—and you will have to contend with every ship at my disposal at once. You will be warned no more."*

Troi felt Will's gaze upon her, and she turned to look into his deep blue eyes. "There's no sign yet that the Gorn have noticed any transporter activity aboard *Titan,*" she said in answer to his unspoken question.

"So far so good, then," he said and rose from the captain's chair. After he directed Lieutenant Rager to open a channel to the *Ssevarrh,* he said, "Captain Krassrr, this is Captain Riker. We have no intention of . . . further provoking you. We'll withdraw immediately. *Titan* out."

Lieutenant Rager and Lieutenant Lavena wasted no time laying in an outbound course. Moments later, Vela OB2–404 II—Hranrar—had disappeared from the screen as *Titan* began to retreat once again to the system's periphery.

"The Gorn have just destroyed the last of the probes, Captain," Tuvok said as his hands moved quickly across the face of his tactical station. "However, the probes yielded several gigaquads of scans of the artifact prior to their termination."

"Good, Mister Tuvok," Will said. "Get it straight

to Commander Pazlar and the other science department heads. I want to know everything I can about that thing as soon as possible."

"Aye, Captain."

"Captain," Dakal said. "I'm picking up traces of alloys that strongly resemble the outer hull of that artifact."

"Where?" Vale said.

"All around us," the young Cardassian said. "Tiny fragments, ranging from dust grains to some the size of a ripe *yamok*. It's as though another one of those artifacts, or at least something made of the same stuff, was destroyed out here. Probably eons ago."

"Why didn't we pick this up earlier?" Will asked, frowning. Troi felt his frustration—it was obviously inconvenient to make this kind of discovery while simultaneously trying to tiptoe away from an adversary as touchy as the Gorn.

"We approached the inner system on a very different trajectory sir," Dakal said. "And our last departure heading was also very different from our current one."

"We need to analyze this stuff as well, Captain," said Ensign Crandall, who was running the main engineering console.

"Should I bring us to a stop, sir?" Lavena asked.

Titan was still close enough to the Gorn fleet to enable Troi to feel the hostility radiating from it. "I wouldn't recommend it," she said.

Will nodded. "Continue to withdraw, Lieutenant. But keep us at high impulse. Mister Tuvok, can you lock onto some of that material and beam it aboard?"

"I believe so, Captain," Tuvok said. Troi thought she felt an uncharacteristic uneasiness beneath the Vulcan's outwardly serene manner. Then it was gone, vanished beneath Tuvok's hard, disciplined exterior.

"Then do it," Will said.

Vale rose from her chair and turned in Tuvok's direction. "But try not to wake the dragon in the process, Commander."

Will tapped his combadge as Tuvok busied himself at his console. "Riker to sickbay. Doctor Ree, how's your new patient doing?"

"Unconscious, Captain. Other than that, he's in surprisingly good condition, considering the ordeal he's just endured."

Once again, Troi felt a familiar emotional jolt. Confusion. Fear. Terror.

Only this time, it was coming from *inside Titan*. From sickbay, in fact.

She rose quickly from her chair. "Captain, I think we'd better get down there." Her heart pounding in sympathy with the being Dakal had just snatched from the jaws of death, she made haste for the turbolift without even bothering to check if Will was behind her.

9

S'syrixx became aware of a pinpoint of light.

One of the cold, indifferent stars, perhaps. One of the last vestiges of reality his eyes had been able to resolve before consciousness had fled from him forever. Even accounting for his thick hide, S'syrixx imagined that his lungs must have burst just a little later, after his optic nerves had registered that terminal vision. He wondered if the subsequent effects of exposure to vacuum would have caused his eyes to burst from their sockets, or merely to freeze solid in their orbits as his cryo-stiffened corpse tumbled endlessly about the ill-fated planet Hranrar. . . .

The pinpoint of light steadily grew until it no longer reminded S'syrixx of the stars. Then it occurred to him that he shouldn't be able to see *anything,* be it a distant star or the nearby light fixture that had slowly resolved into sharpness as his pupils adjusted to the somewhat too-bright chamber in which he now found himself.

A chamber filled with air—somewhat oxygen-poor, judging from his present somewhat lightheaded condition, but air nevertheless—that his tormented lungs were now hungrily taking in. And the place wasn't merely filled with air and excessive illumination—it was also fairly crammed with technology: narrow beds that hardly looked sturdy enough to hold anyone, along with banks of improbably delicate-looking computers and visual displays. With considerable discomfort, he craned his neck straight up. Although he still lay supine on a flat surface—one of the narrow beds, he surmised—he could see part of a computer display mounted on the wall almost directly overhead. He supposed it was a display of his vital signs, though he wasn't certain how to interpret the alien graphics beyond the obvious measurements of his cardio-pulmonary rhythms.

Where in the name of the S'Yahazah's sacred ovipositor am I? he wondered as fragile hope warred with a rising sense of foreboding. *It's obviously an infirmary of some sort. But where?* Surely not any of the other ships in Krassrr's flotilla. None of their officers or troops—let alone their tech-caste specialists—would dare put themselves in the way of Krassrr's wrath.

Moving with the utmost caution, he used his elbows very slowly to push himself up into a semi-recumbent position on the table upon which he lay. He froze in place when he heard the sound of something shifting elsewhere in the chamber, followed by an approaching shadow, evidently cast by whoever had made the noise. S'syrixx's heart pounded in his chest like a war-caster's blunt fist pummeling a heavy swampwood door. He braced himself for the worst.

"Hello," said the reptiloid shape that followed the shadow into S'syrixx's line of sight. "You shouldn't try to move so much. At least not yet."

S'syrixx experienced a rush of relief that he hadn't been confronted by some Federrazsh'n mammalian-type. But even though it was not nearly so repulsively alien as those monsters that still lurked within his imagination, there was still a terrible strangeness about this creature, which resembled no Gorn he had ever encountered. S'syrixx could intuit from the long, gracefully short-clawed fingers at the ends of its upper limbs that it would have been a fellow member of one of the technological subcastes—were it a Gorn. But he'd never seen such highly articulated digits anywhere in the Hegemony, not even on the manus of highly skilled surgical specialists.

"Which . . . what is your caste alignment?" S'syrixx said, his tongue feeling too large and heavy to function properly. Had it frozen after he had been blown out the *Ssevarrh*'s airlock?

"My name is Shenti Yisec Eres Ree," said the creature, which S'syrixx intuited to be a male from the sound of its voice. There was a slight mismatch between the motions of the being's toothy jaws and the arrival of the sound of its voice, a barely perceptible echo effect as though he were speaking through a translation system in some language other than the Common Tongue. S'syrixx also noted that his—captor? host?—had come to a stop just beyond arm's reach.

So you don't trust me any more than I do you, S'syrixx thought. Paradoxically, this realization calmed him, possibly because it was a recognition of common ground. Perhaps an acknowledgment of mutual distrust could lead to an alliance of sorts.

"Shen'tree Yiz," S'syrixx said aloud, aware that he was mangling the creature's decidedly non-Gorn name.

"You may simply call me Doctor Ree if you prefer."

"Doctor . . . Ree," S'syrixx croaked. His throat felt drier

than Gornar's equatorial belt during High Summer; he supposed that his exposure to hard vacuum accounted for that.

"Doctor Ree, that's correct," said the strange not-quite-Gorn creature. "I hold the rank of lieutenant commander."

Was this creature—this Dr. Ree—now trying to tell him he belonged to the military caste? That struck S'syrixx as highly unlikely, given his obviously technological-caste physiological adaptations. "Rank? Rank in what?"

"Why, in Starfleet, of course. I am this vessel's chief medical officer."

S'syrixx's jaw fell open. "Sst'rfleet. You serve . . . aboard a Federrazsh'n vessel?" Doubtless the very vessel, S'syrixx suddenly realized, that Captain Krassrr had so obviously feared would prevent the ecosculptor from being used to remake Hranrar into a new warrior hatchery.

S'syrixx had been surprised at Krassrr's obviously high opinion of the Federrazsh'n's capabilities, no doubt because of the fluke that had enabled them to rout the recent machine-mammal invasion. Since it was common knowledge that the Federrazsh'n was largely run by humanoids and other mammalian types, S'syrixx had always viewed their technological prowess with a more jaundiced, skeptical eye.

But if they were placing their minority *reptiloid* species into key positions now, S'syrixx supposed he might have to rethink his earlier uncharitable appraisals of Federrazsh'n achievements. Perhaps this ship was entirely crewed and commanded by one or more species kindred to that of Dr. Ree. And why not? Who better for the Federrazsh'n to send into territory claimed by the Gorn? He had read several reliable reports on the existence of single-species Sst'rfleet vessels. Unless such a crew turned out to be as blinkered and hidebound as the Gorn warrior caste, they might not only be reasoned with, but might also offer a solution to the hatchery problem that didn't require the casual destruction of an entire civilization at the order of brutes like Captain Krassrr.

The thought buoyed up S'syrixx's flagging sense of hope.

"You're aboard the Federation *Starship Titan,*" Dr. Ree said. "The captain just told me he's coming down from the bridge to speak with you. Our senior diplomatic officer will accompany him."

"*Tie-tan,*" S'syrixx said, doing his best to pronounce the strange syllables as he heard them. Soon he would meet this vessel's commander. Although he knew that much would depend upon that individual's mettle, the hope within S'syrixx's chest flared ever brighter. Perhaps Hranrar's chances of survival weren't so dire as he had feared.

Keeping Dr. Ree's warning about excessive movement in mind, S'syrixx carefully pushed himself the rest of the way up into a sitting position and allowed his bare, scale-covered feet to swing over the side of the surprisingly sturdy little infirmary bed. He was determined to make a good first impression with this vessel's captain, as well as to demonstrate his gratitude to the person who was ultimately responsible for his rescue.

"My name," he said, "is S'syrixx."

Ree displayed an impressive assemblage of long, sharp teeth. "Welcome aboard, S'syrixx."

S'syrixx heard a brief pneumatic hiss, which drew his

attention to an open doorway that hadn't been in his line of sight before.

A pair of uniformed humanoids entered the chamber and slowly approached the bed. S'syrixx suddenly felt unsteady. Had something gone wrong with the ship's environmental systems, or its artificial gravity generators? His claws tore into the bed's edges as he hung on, suddenly desperate to steady himself.

The room spun, and he felt long, scale-covered fingers and forelimbs pushing him gently back onto the bed.

"Mammals," he muttered as darkness made another bid for him. "Why did it have to be mammals?"

GORN HEGEMONY WARSHIP *S'ALATH*

Z'shezhira had found precious little time to mourn her beloved. She had been far too preoccupied by the imperative of not joining him in death.

"The braking thrusters are firing too hot!" she said, shouting to be heard above the overstrained sublight propulsion system that seemed about to rattle the ship apart.

"Imbecile!" Gog'resssh roared as he swept the back of his thick, armor-scaled manus across Sk'salissk's stupefied face. The young helm officer went sprawling over the top of the console and met the deck with a bone-jarring crash.

Another young war-caster wasted no time taking Sk'salissk's place, stepping over his predecessor's still and supine body on the way.

After a seeming eternity, the harrowing deceleration maneuver was complete. The thick Hranrarii atmosphere had somehow managed to trade much of the *S'alath*'s excess velocity for heat without immolating everyone on board in the process. The warship's badly strained braking thrusters had done the rest.

Z'shezhira experienced no small amount of relief as she studied the readout confirming that the ship was presently keeping station over the planet's northern polar zone, from which Hranrar's intricate system of rings were visible just above the horizon only as a long series of distended, nested loops. Though she had finally released the death grip she had maintained on her console ever since the braking sequence had begun, she didn't resume her normal breathing pattern until after the inertial damping system had restored some stability to her relationship with gravity and inertia—with an emphasis on the basic directions of "up" and "down," between which the contents of her anterior stomach-chamber had lately developed some trouble distinguishing.

Across the entirety of the dim, cramped command deck's forward viewer, the vast nightside bulk of Hranrar loomed, rendered by the main computer in high-contrast, false-color imagery. The planet and its delicate adornment of rings looked nearly close enough to reach out and touch. Per Gog'resssh's plan, the *S'alath* had approached Hranrar at high impulse. The vessel's lack of a perceptible warp signature, combined with its arriving on a heading that used Hranrar itself for concealment, had given the hijacked warship better-than-even odds of reaching the planet undetected—assuming that nothing untoward occurred during the brief-but-tense inbound voyage. Once the *S'alath* reached Hranrar's northern polar region—the auroral zone where the planet's potent magnetic field was perpetually challenged by the nearly equally powerful particle flux from the Hranrarii sun—the vessel would have all the camouflage necessary to keep its presence obscured.

"Was our approach observed?" bellowed Second Myrmidon Zegrroz'rh, his single multifaceted eye seeming to bore right through her hide and into her soul.

Does he know? Z'shezhira thought, struggling to maintain the outward appearance of complete and utter smooth-scaled equanimity. *Can he tell that some of Gog'resssh's hostages are finally prepared to move against him when the time is right?*

Once a good portion of the first myrmidon's troopers were off the ship, raiding the recon vessels for their supplies, the time would indeed be right.

"Well?" Zegrroz'rh demanded.

Z'shezhira focused her attention back to the console readouts for the passive-action sensors. So far, none of the vessels in the Gorn flotilla had altered their standard orbital paths, and the Federrazsh'n ship appeared to be on an outbound trajectory, as it had been during the *S'alath*'s stealthy approach to Hranrar.

"I can see no sign that we've been detected, Second Myrmidon," she said. "So far as I can tell, no one else knows we are here, except perhaps for some of the natives."

"I can believe we have caught our own vessels unawares," Gog'resssh said. "But I want to maintain a special degree of vigilance against the Federrazsh'n mammals."

"They seem to be leaving the system, First Myrmidon," Z'shezhira said.

Gog'resssh shook his huge, burn-scarred head. "They appeared to have done that once already. But then they returned unexpectedly, after hiding at the edges of the great swamp, like the egg-thieving parasites they are."

Z'shezhira shuddered involuntarily. Gog'resssh had used imagery straight from the sleepchamber tales she'd heard as a hatchling. Youngling-devouring predators with parasite-infested hair and salamander skin. Autotrophs who feed their own young with glands that they replenished with Gorn blood and ovifluids.

Had Gog'resssh become so unhinged from the injuries he had sustained at Sazssgrerrn that he could no longer distinguish between mythological demons and real creatures that were merely the product of an alien biology?

Z'shezhira feared she already knew the answer to that question.

"The Federrazsh'n mammals covet those things that might bring them power," Gog'resssh said. "Things such as the ecosculpting artifact."

"It is the artifact that worries me most of all, First Myrmidon," Zegrroz'rh said. "We are deep inside Hranrar's atmosphere. If the artifact should become active unexpectedly and begin transforming this world, we would be defenseless."

Gog'resssh made a dismissive, air-clawing gesture. "The *S'alath* has more than enough speed to save us. Provided we remain vigilant."

The commander's claw came down on Z'shezhira's shoulder with an impact that made her wince. "Now direct some of that vigilance toward the mammals. See that they do not seek to fool us again by doubling back here a second time."

"Yes, First Myrmidon," she said as she directed the passive scanners outward, along the Federrazsh'n vessel's last known trajectory. Obviously lacking the patience to continue observing her, Gog'resssh stomped away, leaving the command deck alongside Zegrroz'rh, no doubt in order to plan the fine details of the raid they were about to conduct against the ecosculpting fleet.

The ship she sought was easy enough to locate, since it remained relatively close, at least in interplanetary terms. Although it was unquestionably still on an outbound course, she found it odd that it had not yet gone to warp.

And why is it raising and lowering sections of its energy-shielding?

It was only then that she detected the telltale signature of a matter-transmission beam, being operated in intermittent bursts. It was difficult to determine whether the Federrazsh'n ship was taking something aboard or leaving something behind. But the gaps in the vessel's shielding, necessarily synchronized with the operation of the beams, gave her one brief opportunity after another to peek inside the vessel in search of clues.

Because of her grounding in the life sciences, she dedicated her scans—still in passive mode to prevent an accidental giveaway of the *S'alath*'s location for which Gog'resssh would surely blame her—to biosigns.

The glimpses those intermittent scans gave her were nothing short of astounding. Of the over three hundred biosigns she detected, perhaps a third were nonmammalian. The crew appeared to be drawn from a vast galactic bestiary of sentient races. It bespoke a civilization that either placed a high value on diversity, or else was fond of displaying its conquests to its adversaries.

The mammals-as-conquerors idea immediately struck her as specious. Why would the oppressive, egg-stealing predators that populated Gog'resssh's nightmares allow the sullen, angry ranks of the conquered to make up such a large proportion of their starship crews?

By the fifth scan, Z'shezhira confirmed that some of the biosigns were, in fact, as far from mammalian as it was possible to be. A few of these biosigns were, like those of all Gorn castes, endothermic or poikilothermic—dependent upon external factors for the regulation of body temperature.

The seventh scan revealed that at least one of these biosigns belonged to a member of the last species she would have expected to find aboard a Federrazsh'n vessel.

The reading was unmistakably Gorn. And just as unmistakably alive.

Z'shezhira could feel the delicate claws of hope reaching toward her, but she quietly evaded them. After having spent more than a Gornar suncircuit as the slave to a cadre of rogue war-casters, she had learned to keep hope at a safe distance.

But if this biosign does not belong to S'syrixx, then whose could it be?

And how much longer could he hope to survive in the clawless, deceptively soft manus of the Federrazsh'n?

GORN HEGEMONY RECONNAISSANCE VESSEL *SSEVARRH*

As he made a quick, scrolling survey of the latest batch of infuriating excuses and equivocations from the tech-casters who were charged with repairing the damage that S'syrixx had dealt to the ecosculptor, Captain Krassrr caught a tentative movement out of the most peripheral of his right eye's compound lenses.

"What do you want?" he bellowed at the cowering young sensor technician who had approached his seat at the command deck's center.

"I have observed something . . . unusual, Captain," the tech said haltingly.

"What is it?" Krassrr rumbled, in no mood to have more of his time wasted with trivia.

"Evidence of unusual atmospheric ionization, near the polar region at the terminator."

Krassrr pushed his document reader back into its slot in the broad arm of his chair. "What of it?"

The tech answered with a slightly quavering voice. "It might be evidence of an enemy ship approaching the planet by stealth. Perhaps you should consider sending one of our ships to investigate it up close."

"It could just as easily be evidence of a meteor burning up in the atmosphere. Do you have any definitive proof that you've seen anything more worrisome than that?"

"I suppose not, Captain," the tech said, his shoulders slumping, the scales on his crests drooping slightly.

Krassrr displayed his entire armory of razor-edged teeth. "Then don't expect me to deploy any vessels for the purpose of chasing phantoms—especially not when I need every manus bent to the task of getting that ecosculptor up and running."

"Yes, Captain."

"Continue scanning," Krassrr said, cuffing the technician hard across his earpit to signal his dismissal. "But don't bother me with the results unless you actually *find* something."

U.S.S. TITAN

Carried aloft on his integrated directional antigravs, SecondGen White-Blue extended one of his cybernetic servomechanical limbs to the keypad that allowed him to open the materials science lab's doors. He resisted the urge to rush across the threshold the instant the aperture opened; he already knew, thanks to a number of near-collisions, that unexpected eye-level encounters with free-floating artificial life-forms had an unfortunate tendency to unnerve most humanoids.

After a slow count to three, White-Blue floated deliberately into a brightly lit space in which several crewmembers stood around a large rectangular table, using their tricorders to scan what appeared at first glance to be several dozen random pieces of metallic and rocky debris, the largest piece being approximately twice the size of a humanoid fist. White-Blue noted that Ensign Torvig Bu-Kar-Nguv was present—each of his segmented bionic appendages wielding a scanning device—as were relief science officer Peya Fell, the Ferengi geologist Bralik, the Selenean cryptolinguist Y'lira Modan and the human engineers Mordecai Crandall and Tasanee Panyarachun. Everyone present wore regular Starfleet duty uniforms, with the exception of White-Blue and Torvig, the latter being adorned with markings denoting affiliation with and rank in the organization.

"Persuading the captain to beam this stuff aboard while

the Gorn were distracted by our sensor drones was a stroke of genius," Ensign Crandall said.

"If you do say so yourself," retorted Ensign Panyarachun.

Crandall paused in his tricorder scans to make an incongruously long appraisal of his neatly trimmed fingernails. "I do indeed."

"I hope there's no emergency EVA drill in your immediate future, Mordecai," Ensign Modan said. "I'm not sure you could squeeze that big head of yours through the neck-ring, much less pull a helmet over it."

Crandall muttered something whose meaning eluded White-Blue's flexible linguistic systems, as well as every translation matrix he knew.

"Maybe we ought to save the real praise for Torvig," Panyarachun said to Modan. "Mordecai wouldn't have any reason to boast if our Choblik friend hadn't discovered a belt of interplanetary debris so rich in this stuff in the first place. Besides, if we find anything among these relics that resembles language, that's when we'll all get to see *real* genius at work."

The golden tones of Modan's epidermis modulated in apparent response to Panyarachun's praise, taking on a vaguely coppery hue.

Bralik, who stood a short distance from Modan, directed what White-Blue could only interpret as a sour expression at the objects of everyone else's apparent fascination. "Looks to me like a pile of rocks and metal on a table. A truly stunning achievement." Crandall regarded her in silence, his eyes narrowing to slits, though Bralik appeared not to have noticed.

"That's a pretty strange reaction coming from a geologist, Bralik," Modan said. "I thought that rocks and metal were your stock in trade. Especially exotic ones like these."

Adjusting the sash of her colorfully printed work coverall, Bralik said, "You're right, Goldie. These particular rocks and metals don't match anything in any of the existing mineralogical and metallurgical databases. They even appear to have some curious energy-absorption and -storage capabilities. Who knows, they might even end up giving some clever Starfleet engineer the key to perpetual motion someday."

"I find that highly doubtful," Modan said. "But I find it even more curious now that you'd be so dismissive of this discovery while still acknowledging its unrealized potential."

"That's easy enough to explain," the Ferengi said, scratching one of her earlobes. Although those lobes were the biggest in the room, White-Blue recalled having read that the ears of male Ferengi were considerably larger. "I think the Thirteenth Rule says it best: 'Anything worth doing is worth doing for money.' "

Modan shrugged. "I'm not sure I understand."

"All right, I'll pretend for a moment that you're just another garden-variety, economics-challenged Starfleet *hew-mon* and explain this in simple terms."

"I'd be grateful if you wouldn't use a lot of big words or math," Modan said in oddly flat tones that White-Blue suspected might have been deliberately calculated for ironic effect. Despite all the time he'd spent aboard *Titan* studying its personnel and their complex interpersonal interactions, it still found such things extraordinarily difficult to read.

"All right," Bralik said. "It's just that I find exotic rocks and metal a lot more interesting if I can extract 'em in bulk and then use 'em in the ancient Ferengi art of alchemy."

Crandall sniffed. "Alchemy is a pseudoscience, Miz Bralik. Superstitious nonsense. Surely you know that."

"Here's what I know, kid," the Ferengi woman said, baring her teeth in what White-Blue thought might be either a grin or a leer. "Even if I can't change lead into gold without access to a replicator or the heart of a supernova, I suspect it wouldn't be too difficult to convert a ton of this stuff into an extremely respectable stack of gold-pressed latinum bricks."

"Ah," Modan said. "You're talking about *economic* alchemy."

"Of course. It's the only kind that works," Bralik said a moment before her grin-that-might-have-been-a-leer fell in on itself and morphed into an expression that White-Blue recognized immediately as sadness. Gesturing toward the samples on the table, she added, "But even if we could find this stuff out here in that kind of quantity, the Gorn aren't likely to let us extract it."

Ensign Peya Fell chose that moment to step away from the table, presumably to give her colleagues additional room in which to carry out their studies and analyses. Fell then approached White-Blue, acknowledging his presence with an unsmiling nod. Although White-Blue still found many nuances of humanoid emotion and expression elusive, he had no difficulty divining that the Deltan woman felt uncomfortable around him.

"Aren't you supposed to be in stellar cartography, helping Commander Pazlar keep an eye on what the Gorn are up to, Mister, ah, Blue?" said the smooth-scalped female.

"I have accepted a number of stellar cartographical duties, to be carried out under Commander Pazlar's authority and supervision," White-Blue said, hovering in place two meters from Fell. "But the commander and I need not always be physically co-located for me to perform those functions."

"Oh. Right. So . . . what brings you to the materials lab?"

White-Blue pondered that question for a moment as he processed Fell's somewhat imprecise idiom. He finally decided it was safe to assume that she wasn't inquiring into the technical specs that governed his multidirectional antigrav units or his pneumatic thrusters.

"Ensign Torvig informed me of the science team's initial findings," White-Blue said as he waved two of his cybernetic arms toward the objects that so engrossed everyone else in the room. At that moment, the lab doors hissed open again, and White-Blue used his aft sensory cluster to observe Commander Tuvok entering the chamber, his hands clasped behind his back.

"What exactly did Mister Torvig tell you?" the junior science officer asked White-Blue after pausing to greet Commander Tuvok.

"He wrote an initial report indicating that we have collected some debris near Vela OB2–404 II," White-Blue said. "Debris that bears the same chemical, radiolytic, and quantum signatures as the large alien artifact that the Gorn have appropriated."

"Huh," Fell said. "I suppose I'd better remind him to run those preliminary reports past me first in the future." She turned to cast what could only have been a reproachful glance at the little Choblik engineer, who appeared far too preoccupied at the moment to show any sign of having noticed.

"I have seen the report in question," Tuvok said from the lab's doorway. "It raised the distinct possibility that we have found the pulverized remains of another device like the one the Gorn have captured."

"I'm impressed, sir," Fell said. "Materials science isn't exactly a required area of knowledge for a tactical officer."

"Before developing my expertise in tactics and strategy, Ensign, I served as a Starfleet science officer," Tuvok said evenly. Though White-Blue wasn't certain, he suspected *Titan*'s chief tactitian and second officer was working to conceal an emotional undercurrent of irritation. "I am as well acquainted with the scientific underpinnings of exotic materials as I am with their tactical applications."

Fell's pigmentation abruptly lightened by a noticeable gradation. "Of course, sir. I never meant to imply that—"

"Have any of the recovered fragments been positively linked with the alien artifact that now orbits Vela OB2–404 II?" Tuvok asked, interrupting. "And do any of the pieces your team beamed aboard contain traces of anything you recognize as high technology?"

While the Vulcan was speaking, Panyarachun turned away from the table and toward Tuvok, apparently listening attentively. Raising her tricorder, presumably to make the device's readouts more visible, she approached Tuvok.

"I'd have to answer 'yes' to your first question, Commander," Panyarachun said. "The specimens are definitely made of the same stuff as the orbiting artifact. As for your second question, that's beginning to look like another affirmative as well, if only tentatively. We still have a lot more scans to run, but I'm already seeing what appear to be traces of microcircuit patterns. They're all highly degraded, of course, since they're at least hundreds of thousands of years old. But I don't think these are the result of scanning aberrations. They look real."

Tuvok raised an eyebrow in response, a mannerism that White-Blue had come to understand was as close as Vulcans generally ever came to making highly emotional interjections. However, the overall level of physiological agitation that White-Blue detected in this particular Vulcan made him question whether the vaunted emotional control of Commander Tuvok's species really lived up to its reputation.

"So it's possible that this debris might hold at least some of the secrets to the terraforming technology the Gorn have been attempting to wield," Tuvok said. "If we are forced either to attempt to board the terraforming device or disable it from a distance, we will need to know as much about its underlying technology and composition as possible. Your scans might conceivably yield, for example, maps of circuit patterns related to the device. Or perhaps even some partially intact data-storage media."

"I suppose that's all at least theoretically possible, Commander," Panyarachun said.

"But I wouldn't bet the rent on it," Bralik said.

According to White-Blue's sensors, Commander Tuvok's cardial organ had increased its rate of operation slightly but measurably. Clearly the ancient alien artifact was a source of great anxiety for the tactical officer.

At that moment, White-Blue experienced another flash

near the ragged edge of its perceptual powers. Was he receiving an artificially generated EM signal? The sensation was not dissimilar to the three incidents he had already experienced in the stellar cartography lab—events he had since attributed either to scanning errors or to random spikes in the noisy background blanket of EM and subspace radiation—but it was also quite different this time, at least in terms of its "color," or wavelength. With local impediments like Vela OB2–404 II's powerful magnetic field distorting such weak signals almost past the threshold of detection, White-Blue could determine little else.

How satisfying it would be, he thought, *to find the means of tracing these errant, intermittent signals all the way back to their sources?*

But like the first three incidents, this latest pulsation had disappeared almost as quickly as it had attracted White-Blue's attention, making him wonder yet again whether the signal had ever really been there in the first place. Was it simply what Commander Pazlar referred to as a "glitch?" Although he knew it was probably a futile gesture, White-Blue dedicated the bulk of the portion of his consciousness that had remained linked with *Titan*'s stellar cartography systems to finding any repetition of the most recent "blip."

Panyarachun and Tuvok continued to discuss the scientific and tactical ramifications of the technological fossils the specialists were still busy analyzing. White-Blue continued to listen attentively, both to the humanoids and to the vast universe that lay beyond the confines of *Titan*'s hull.

Although White-Blue found Tuvok's evident distress at the science team's discovery puzzling, he was unsurprised by the sustained "white-noise" silence he heard as he listened for a repetition of the latest transitory signal.

Unsurprised, but also unsatisfied.

"May I, too, assist your team, Ensign Fell?" White-Blue asked, eager to focus more of his attention and resources onto a new scientific puzzle—and away from the disquieting new internal sensation he was coming to think of as "frustration."

10

"What the hell just happened, Doctor?" Riker said.

"Unless I'm very much mistaken, Captain, my patient just fainted," Ree deadpanned as Lieutenant Alyssa Ogawa, *Titan*'s head nurse, checked his new patient's vital signs.

"I'm not certain it was such a good idea to keep me out of sight after he started to regain consciousness," Ogawa said after she'd finished confirming that the creature on the biobed was in no immediate danger of expiring.

"I am inclined to agree with you, Alyssa," said the doctor, hissing out the sibilant phoneme in his head nurse's name.

Deanna, who stood at Riker's elbow, was regarding the unconscious Gorn with remarkable poise. "But I can certainly understand why you might take that precaution. He must have found the sight of a reptiloid face reassuring."

Ree nodded, his long forked tongue darting out and disappearing again. "Unfortunately, his seeing only me at first might have led him to believe he had come aboard a ship populated entirely by reptiloids."

Riker looked down at the insensate Gorn and felt a peculiar mixture of wonder and revulsion. Like many humans, he wasn't overly fond of terrestrial reptiles. Why so much of

H. sapiens shared this general predilection was something that had always intrigued him. Since the notion of the "evil snake" figured so prominently into so much of his world's mythology, he'd always assumed it to be a deeply ingrained attitude—perhaps too deeply ingrained ever to be excised entirely, whatever level of enlightenment humanity might attain. He'd been forced to confront that ancient prejudice directly almost immediately after taking command of *Titan,* when Dr. Ree had come aboard to assume his duties as chief medical officer. Riker had talked very proudly then about the unusually high degree of diversity—even by Starfleet standards—that characterized *Titan*'s crew.

But it wasn't until he'd found himself standing toe-to-claw with his new CMO, a creature whose brilliance and expertise was housed in a form that strongly resembled a two-and-a-half-meter-long velociraptor, that he came to understand just how shallow his understanding of "diversity" really had been. After that initial encounter, Riker began to wonder whether Ree had to work just as hard to overcome an equally visceral anti-mammalian bias.

"Then Commander Troi and I sauntered into sickbay," Riker said, "and scared the hell out of him."

"Your analysis is essentially correct, Captain," said Ree. "The Gorn are well known for being xenophobic and territorial, of course. Their Linnaean-class-specific prejudices may be less well documented than are their more general hostilities, but they are every bit as real. It's a strange thing, too, since humans bear no genetic relationship to any mammal-analog species native to the Gorn homeworld of Tau Lacertae IX, nor are any such species kindred to any other humanoid race known to the Federation."

"Go figure," Riker said with a shrug. "Appearance and perception sometimes matter a lot more than the actual facts. That's probably why fear has always been such a handy way to manipulate the masses throughout my planet's history."

"This creature is a lot different from any Gorn I've ever seen," Deanna said.

Riker nodded in agreement, recalling the failed political coup that he and the rest of the *Enterprise*-E crew had helped to stop on the Gorn homeworld about eight years ago, and the Gorn treaty negotiations Captain Picard had undertaken near the end of his tenure aboard the *Enterprise*-D.

"His body is . . . slighter," he said. "And take a look at his hands."

"Almost the claws of a surgeon," said Ree, lifting one of his patient's slender-yet-deadly-looking manus with his own claw-tipped hands.

"And right before he collapsed, he locked eyes with mine," Deanna said. "Just for an instant."

Although those eyes had since retreated behind a pair of leather-scaled lids, Riker had seen them as well, if only for a split second. "He doesn't have the same multifaceted silver bug eyes that I've seen on other Gorn," he said. In fact, the newcomer's eyes were different from those of any Gorn he'd ever encountered before, and during the Gorn coup attempt he'd seen more than enough Gorn to last him a lifetime. The golden orbs not only appeared to carry only one lens each, they were split vertically by dark pupils that reminded Riker of a Terran lynx, or a Capellan power-cat.

"Are you certain this creature is actually a Gorn,

Doctor?" Deanna asked. "It's almost as though he belongs to a different species."

"I noticed many of the same differences when he was beamed aboard," Ree said. "Once Alyssa and I had stabilized him, I ran several quick genetic scans. Although it's still possible that he belongs to a species separate from that of other Gorn the Federation has encountered so far, his DNA overlaps with known Gorn DNA almost completely. While he obviously differs from other Gorn we know of in terms of phenotype, his genetics are clearly linked to theirs, and bear no resemblance either to my own or to the other reptiloids who serve aboard *Titan*. The creature's relationship to the other Gorn could be analogous to that of the various sentient Xindi races, each of which sprang from a common biology despite some of them being on evolutionary pathways as far removed from each other as humans are from orcas, or reptiles from insects."

As fascinating as all of this was, Riker wasn't eager just yet to get lost in the weeds of scientific detail that were already springing up so swiftly around this strange creature. "We already have intelligence indicating that the Gorn civilization is split up into many more castes than we knew about previously," he said. "So far, we've only had direct encounters with their military and political castes. Maybe he"—Riker paused as he gestured toward the being on the biobed—"is a member of one of those newly discovered castes."

"That sounds reasonable," Ree hissed. "After all, they can't all be warriors and prime ministers."

"Whatever his caste affiliation might be," Deanna said, "we still don't know why he was . . . thrown overboard."

"Maybe his shipmates thought he was dead," Riker said, spitballing, though without much conviction. The Gorn had always struck him as methodical to a fault, and thus extremely unlikely to make any mistake of that sort. "It's possible we interrupted a burial at sea, so to speak."

Ree shook his great scaly head. "With respect, Captain, I find that doubtful. Judging from his rather impressive dentition," the doctor said, pausing to make a brief display of his own oral cutlery, "not to mention the size of his brain's olfactory region, this creature is the product of a long line of hunting carnivores, just like his warrior cousins. Such species are unlikely to confuse 'alive' for 'dead,' or vice versa."

"So the Gorn were evidently executing one of their own," Deanna said.

"Given his abrupt ejection into hard vacuum," Ree said, "and his ostentatious lack of protective gear, I *would* tend to concur."

"You *would*," Riker said. "But you don't."

"I'm not yet certain."

"Why?" Deanna said.

Ree moved sinuously to a monitor on a nearby wall. In response to a few quick taps of his razor-sharp claws, the darkened screen lit up and displayed what was obviously a highly magnified view of a complex molecular form, its toroid surface studded with innumerable side chains; it reminded Riker of one of the perceptually deceptive drawings of M. C. Escher.

"Because of *this*," Ree said. "I found this substance in the creature's blood. It's a drug, apparently designed to slow down certain Gorn metabolic functions. I can't think of any reason for the Gorn to have administered this drug, unless their intention was to prolong their . . . victim's survival time in hard vacuum."

Riker turned his gaze away from Ree and back to his slumbering patient. "So you're saying that in spite of appearances, he might really be a spy. That his apparent execution may have just been a cover. Maybe Captain Krassrr *wanted* us to 'rescue' our friend here."

Ree spread his claws in a reptilian shrug. "I'll admit that's a possibility. However, there's something wrong with that hypothesis as well: the drug seems to have been administered too recently to have taken full effect in time to have offered our guest any significant protection from being 'spaced.' It's almost as though he received this drug as an afterthought. I know none of this makes much sense, Captain. But there it is." His long tail snaked toward the biobed and its occupant in much the same way a humanoid might have made a hand gesture.

"I don't believe this Gorn has come aboard to spy on us, Will," Deanna said.

Riker turned to face his wife. "Why not?"

"Because of the intense hostility I picked up from the Gorn fleet."

"Gorn hostility is to be expected, Deanna. It's a well-established fact that they don't like us very much."

"No, Will. I'm talking about the hostility I felt being directed *inwardly*—toward *him* when he was still aboard Krassrr's ship." She pointed at the patient on the biobed. "Hostility that's largely evaporated now that everyone in the Gorn fleet believes he's been executed."

But Riker wasn't convinced, at least not yet. "You may be detecting a lot less emotional intensity from the Gorn because the distance between them and *Titan* is increasing at a pretty fast clip."

She folded her arms across her chest, a clear sign that she was prepared to dig in and defend her assertion. "I'll admit that the emotional 'volume level' is dropping off quickly. But it's like the singing of a distant choir. It might be faint, but I can still hear every note, every chord."

"All right." Turning back to face Ree, Riker said, "I suppose there's only one way to get at our . . . guest's real intentions. Can you wake him up, Doctor?"

"If I work quickly to neutralize the drug in his system," Ree said. "Otherwise he may soon slip into a coma. Should that happen, I have no way to determine precisely how long it may be before he again becomes conscious and lucid enough to interview."

With a nod, Riker said, "Do whatever you have to do."

"In the meantime, I'd like to gather an assemblage of bedside faces he might find friendlier than either of ours," Deanna said. "Or even Alyssa's."

Riker could guess where she was going with this. There was no good reason, after all, not to do whatever was possible to put their guest at ease once he regained consciousness.

"Since you're this ship's chief diplomatic officer, first-contact specialist, and senior counselor, I'll defer to your judgment," he said. "At least until our unexpected passenger does anything that might endanger *Titan*."

The light returned yet again, dazzling S'syrixx's eyes.

And with the renewed brilliance the room—no, the *infirmary*—also sprang back into being. Though S'syrixx couldn't yet see anything with absolute clarity, he was immediately quite certain that this was the same room in which he remembered having awoken once already. He tried to rise.

Claws reached for him. He tried to bat them aside with his own, but found he couldn't muster the strength to do so effectively.

"Eassssy," said a soothing, sibilant voice as those other claws eased him back down.

Three shapes resolved themselves around his bed, as did their faces. Reptiloid faces, to be sure, yet all three were still something other than Gorn. But at least there were no mammals in sight this time. Was this place really infested with such creatures, or had he merely had a nightmare?

"Doctor, he's regaining consciousness," shouted one of the three strange-yet-almost-familiar beings who stood surrounding S'syrixx's bed.

A fourth shape suddenly hove into view, one that he had seen before. The physician.

"Ree," S'syrixx croaked.

"Very good," the doctor said. "I'm delighted to see you again, Mister S'syrixx. Once again, welcome aboard the Federation *Starship Titan.*"

S'syrixx wondered how the doctor knew his name, but supposed he may have mentioned it to him before his most recent lapse into unconsciousness. "Federrazsh'n. *Tie-tan,*" he repeated, still unused to the slight echo-like lag between speech and hearing that this vessel's translation system was apparently causing.

Titan.

"How am I . . . alive?" S'syrixx asked.

"You mean after being jettisoned from your vessel," Ree said. "Do you remember what happened to you before you came aboard *Titan*?"

"Of *course* I remember, Doctor," S'syrixx said acidly. "Being blown out into space is not an experience one soon forgets."

"So you were ejected deliberately?"

"Quite so," S'syrixx said, then paused to cough. He marveled that he wasn't experiencing more pain, that his lungs were in such relatively good condition after the ordeal he had just endured.

"Why?" Ree asked. "Why did your shipmates . . . *space* you?"

"Captain Krassrr grew . . . annoyed with me."

Ree fixed him with a penetrating stare, making it clear that he wasn't entirely satisfied with S'syrixx's answer. S'syrixx decided to say no more on the subject for the moment, at least until he'd figured out the reason for his unlikely survival. Had the pain-suppressant that R'rerrgran gave him just before his enforced departure from the *Ssevarrh* had anything to do with it?

Apparently realizing he wasn't going to learn much more any time soon, Ree took a step back and said, "While you're a guest aboard *Titan,* Mister S'syrixx, I'd like you to get to know a few members of our crew."

"I am Ensign Ot Rynaph," one of the other three reptiloids said. The creature's eyes, the nearest of which was fixed upon S'syrixx, were set on opposite sides of its heavily ridged, pink-scaled skull. This feature, along with its wide mouth, reminded S'syrixx of the images of the Hranrarii he'd found in the Gorn fleet's planetary database shortly before Krassrr had . . . dismissed him. "I work in the ship's airponics lab."

"I am Chief Garem Urkral," said the reptiloid who stood nearest to Ree. "I serve aboard *Titan* as an engineer." This creature, whose femaleness S'syrixx intuited because of her slight frame and high-pitched voice, had the gray-green skin of a jaundiced Gorn hatchling. She also possessed front-facing yellow eyes that were startling for their sheer size; they seemed nearly twice as large as the eyes of any Gorn he had ever met.

"And what of *you*?" S'syrixx said after turning his head toward the only reptiloid who had yet to speak, a mottled-gray-skinned, stooped-postured creature who almost could have passed for a member of the Gorn labor caste but for its long tail, its startling, ruby-hued eyes, and the single scaly horn that rose to a sharp point near the top of its serpentine head.

"I am Lieutenant Qur Qontallium," said the indeterminately gendered being as it extended both manus toward him, palms and claws downward in what S'syrixx surmised was a gesture of greeting. "I am a security officer."

S'syrixx allowed his gaze to drift down to the security officer's hip, upon which a small, unobtrusive device was clearly visible. It was no doubt a deadly weapon, and probably a fitting complement to the creature's formidable-looking claws.

It occurred to S'syrixx then that none of the reptiloids with whom he was speaking were wearing uniforms as such. Each of them sported various items of uncoordinated apparel, but none showed any indication, at least from their highly individualized modes of dress, that they were crewmates on a ship, or members of a quasimilitary organization. S'syrixx suddenly realized that this lack of uniformity had to be part of a deliberate effort to put him at ease.

And that thought put him distinctly *ill* at ease.

"You . . . you aren't Gorn," he said, addressing the group as one. Though he still felt weak, he nevertheless managed to push himself up until he had almost reached a sitting position on the narrow bunk. "*None* of you are Gorn."

"Please," Ree said, trying to push S'syrixx back down into a supine position. Though the physician's grip was as strong as it was gentle, S'syrixx managed to shake it off and raise himself until he was sitting completely upright. This time he experienced no sensation of lightheadedness.

"None of you are Gorn," S'syrixx repeated to the pink reptiloid. "Which worlds do you come from?"

"I come from Kashet," the creature called Rynaph said.

"I don't know that world," S'syrixx said, feeling belatedly dizzy. Perhaps Ree had been correct in directing him to lie still. "Where in the Hegemony is it located?"

"Kashet is not affiliated with the Gorn Hegemony," the alien said. "It has been a member of the United Federation of Planets for more than a century."

"As has my homeworld of Sauria," said Urkral, the engineer.

Qontallium, the security officer, said, "Gnala, the homeworld of my Gnalish Fejimaera people, is a longtime Federation member as well."

"My homeworld is Pahkwa," Ree said. "My species, the Pahkwa-thanh, joined the Federation only about two decades ago."

Federrazsh'n, S'syrixx thought. *Perhaps the Federrazsh'n is not quite so mammal-infested as the political caste would have us all believe.*

The comfortingly reptilian hiss of a portal opening across the chamber startled him out of his reverie. When he looked up to see who had entered, he was startled even further. Mammals! A pair of them strode toward him, perhaps the very same two that had surprised him earlier (he wasn't certain because it was inherently difficult to distinguish between individual members of the softpink races). The four other reptiloids noticed the mammals' entrance immediately, and made deferential noises, which included addressing the fur-faced male as "Captain."

The other reptiloids spread out to allow the mammals to pass—all except Dr. Ree, who interposed himself protectively between the captain and his patient. The inaudible conversation that passed between the physician and the two mammalians no doubt also served the purpose of bringing the captain up to speed on everything S'syrixx had revealed about himself so far, deliberately or otherwise.

He felt his *cloaca* muscles involuntarily tighten as he noticed the mammals watching him with their small, clever eyes. Then Ree abruptly withdrew, leaving S'syrixx defenseless as the mammals approached to within nearly a fully extended arm's length. S'syrixx snorted in response to an unpleasant aroma, which might have arisen from either the creatures' hair or epidermis.

"I'm Captain William Riker," said the facially hirsute mammal. Gesturing with one fleshy, clawless manus toward his shorter, more cranially hairy companion, he added, "And this is my senior diplomatic officer, Commander Deanna Troi. You seem to be recovering nicely, Mister S'syrixx. I'm glad to see it."

Why? S'syrixx thought. *So you can fatten me up and add me to your crew's list of dining options?* He wondered if this Rry'kurr would have his remains fashioned into apparel and other adornments once the feasting was done—and whether they would kill him before or after Krassrr finally succeeded in bringing the ecosculptor back on line and wiping out the Hranrarii with it.

Aloud, he said only, "Thank you, Captain. It was my good fortune that you and your vessel were in a position to pick me up when you did."

"Apparently that wasn't your only bit of good luck today," said the mammal captain. "Doctor Ree found a paralytic compound in your system that might have had something to do with your surviving long enough for us to reach you."

R'rerrgran, you old rogue, S'syrixx thought. He hoped his longtime friend's kind but ill-advised action wouldn't rebound badly on him later. If Captain Krassrr were ever to discover that the execution over which he had presided today had been thwarted . . .

"It would seem there's plenty of good fortune to go around," the female mammal said.

S'syrixx tipped his head to the side, confused. "I do not understand."

The one Rry'kurr had called Troi took a seat on a nearby platform that resembled the one that supported S'syrixx. She folded her slender forelimbs across her chest, momentarily sparing S'syrixx the sight of her ostentatiously mammalian contours. "Well, you're obviously a member of one of the Gorn technological castes. We believe that you've come to the planet Vela OB2–404 II in order to—"

"Hranrar," S'syrixx corrected, his broad snout wrinkling in response to the mammals' sterile designation for such a vibrant, living world. It reminded him of the bloodless machine-mammals the Hegemony had spent so much of its precious blood and treasure fighting off during the previous suncircuit.

"Hranrar," the Troi-mammal said with a nod that made her long, dark hair move about as though it were an independent life-form that might pounce on him of its own accord. "We believe you've come to Hranrar as part of a team that's deploying a powerful terraforming technology."

"Terraforming?" S'syrixx asked. He supposed the mammals' translator was unable to cope with certain technological terms, especially when it came to rendering them in intelligible Gorn Standard.

"Terraforming is the science of rebuilding planetary environments," said Rry'kurr. "It's a means of remaking dead worlds into places where life can flourish."

Terraforming, S'syrixx thought, though he believed "Gornarforming" might be a more appropriate, albeit still not perfectly precise, term. Aloud, he said, "Do you speak of ecosculpting, Captain?"

"Ecosculpting," Rry'kurr said, apparently pleased by the way the new term sat upon tongue and teeth.

The Troi-mammal nodded again, though S'syrixx found the movement of her hair somewhat less alarming this time. "Ecosculpting, yes," she said. "We know that your fleet plans to use this technology on Hranrar."

"We think it has something to do with an ecological

disaster that occurred sometime last year," Rry'kurr said. "An event that left your warrior caste without a hatchery planet."

"Your government apparently thinks Hranrar is the best candidate to become a replacement for that hatchery planet," said the Troi-mammal.

S'syrixx's throat went suddenly dry. How could the mammals have learned so much about the ecosculptor? Perhaps they were merely speculating, waiting for him to fill the gaps in their knowledge.

It came to him then that his "rescue" might not redound to *anyone's* good fortune. Despite the presence of kindred-appearing reptiloids here and there within this Federrazsh'n and its Sst'rfleet, surely the mammals who dominated both would do everything in their power to thwart the Gorn Hegemony's efforts to replace the dead, sunscorched warcaster crècheworld of Sazssgrerrn. No, they would try to seize the fires of creation for themselves—perhaps after first allowing the Gorn ecosculpting team to finish testing and fine-tuning the ecosculptor for them. The consequences, whether for the innocent natives of Hranrar, the warrior caste, or the defense of the entire Gorn Hegemony itself, would be immaterial to the furry parasites of the Federrazsh'n.

Great S'Yahazah, I have been delivered straight into their grasping, fleshy little paws, S'syrixx thought, a deep sense of desolation sweeping across his soul like an equatorial sandstorm on Gornar. *Captain Krassrr will have much to answer for.*

But in the end, it wouldn't matter who was ultimately to blame for what was to come. The warrior caste would die off through attrition, all for want of a suitable crècheworld. The mammals would merely have to play a waiting game.

And when the time was finally ripe they would overrun all the Hegemony's crècheworlds and colonies, sparing none of them—not even ancient Gornar itself. Then the Hegemony would die, and the mammalians would gnaw at its bones with their tiny yet wickedly sharp teeth. And the mammalian infestation would rule the entire cosmos, as it now ruled distant Inner Eliar. . . .

S'syrixx suddenly became aware that Rry'kurr was speaking sharply to him. "Are you still listening to us, Mister S'syrixx? We *know* that you're knowledgeable about that artifact—what you might call an 'ecosculptor.' And we think you know something about why the Gorn haven't yet been able to get the thing through its preliminary trials."

S'syrixx bared his teeth and hoped the sight made the mammals uncomfortable. "I don't know what you're talking about, Captain. I'm only a lowly kitchen worker. You're interrogating the wrong person."

Rry'kurr paused to exchange a quick but apparently significant glance with the Troi-mammal; she responded with a silent shake of her head.

The mammal captain stepped closer, coming almost nose to snout with S'syrixx. Surprised, S'syrixx inadvertently received a partial lungful of the stink of Rry'kurr's cranial fur; he barely restrained himself from gagging.

"Please don't try to deceive us," Rry'kurr said.

"Why would you think I'd do that?" S'syrixx said, knowing he sounded pathetic. He struggled not to display any fear before the fur-bearing creatures. He knew they could smell such emotions, that they reveled in them.

"Mister S'syrixx, you're simply not an accomplished enough liar to fool my half-Betazoid diplomatic officer," the captain said, his face flushing redder as his voice boomed in very evident anger. "The planet your people are using as a petri dish supports an indigenous civilization. If they activate this . . . ecosculptor there, millions of innocent people will die. I'm not going to just sit here and let that happen."

S'syrixx couldn't have been more surprised if the mammal had just offered a proposal of marriage. Was it even barely possible that he had misjudged these beings, or that his caste superiors had done so? Or was it likelier that this was some devious interrogation trick, employed without remorse by clever but conscienceless mammals?

"Why should you care about what happens to a few million Hranrarii?" he said. "You're Federrazsh'n, aren't you?"

Rry'kurr seemed about to hurl an angry retort, only to be interrupted by the Troi-mammal, who suddenly jumped up from the bed upon which she sat.

"Mister S'syrixx, I think a better question would be why *you* seem to care so much about what happens to a few million Hranrarii."

Rry'kurr displayed a look of surprise that S'syrixx thought must have mirrored his own. How had she known that? Could she detect chemical-pheromonic cues, as he could? Or was she some sort of telepath? What other potent secrets had these creatures managed to keep concealed from the Gorn Hegemony's fund of general knowledge?

S'syrixx felt the abrupt return of the intense lightheadedness that had taken him down mere moments after his initial return to consciousness aboard *Tie-tan*. The room suddenly spun crazily about him, and he belatedly realized that someone was grabbing him, pushing him gently backward onto the bed.

Someone with comfortingly scale-covered and claw-tipped limbs. He chose not to fight the ministrations of those limbs.

"Captain, my patient needs a break from this . . . interrogation," S'syrixx heard Ree say, a perilous anger evident in his voice. Although he was clearly subordinate to his mammalian captain, the physician was just as clearly unafraid to advocate on behalf of those in his care.

"We're not done here yet, Doctor," Rry'kurr said.

"Yes, you *are,* Captain," Ree said. From his supine position on the bed, S'syrixx watched as the doctor interposed himself between his commander and the narrow bed on which S'syrixx lay.

"Doctor," said the captain, "the Gorn have seized a machine that will kill millions if they manage to get the damned thing started. That could happen any minute now. To prevent that, I need to know whatever your *patient* knows about that machine."

"My patient was near death less than an hour ago, Captain," Ree said, his words carried along on a dangerous growl that might have given the doughtiest Gorn war-caster pause. "I will not have him badgered in this manner. Not in *my* sickbay. I will have you removed first. Please, Captain. Do not make me warn you again." The physician punctuated his last request by displaying his double ranks of long, sharp carnivore's teeth.

S'syrixx noticed only then that the other three reptiloids were uncomfortably milling about the room's periphery, as though unsure whose side to take. Was phylum-loyalty colliding with command discipline, right before his eyes?

"Ree's right, Will," the Troi-mammal said, laying one of

her pink paws on Rry'kurr's arm in a manner that appeared strangely intimate. "S'syrixx needs to rest."

The mammal captain appeared to hesitate. Patting the Troi-mammal's hand, he turned back to face Ree and said, "Fine, Doctor. Just make sure your patient understands that I don't intend to play games with him. Not when the stakes are this high. If he won't share his expertise with us—help us deal with the terraforming artifact over Hranrar—then I'll repatriate him to the Gorn fleet at the earliest opportunity."

"Repatriate?" S'syrixx asked, once again unsure of the translator output he was receiving.

The Troi-mammal drew uncomfortably close to him. "It means that the captain wants to send you back to the Gorn fleet."

"Once Doctor Ree certifies you fit and ready to travel, of course," Rry'kurr said.

S'syrixx experienced a jolt of panic; he considered trying to sit up again, but swiftly abandoned the idea. "You can't do that," he said.

"Why not?" Rry'kurr said. "Because you'd find it inconvenient to be handed over to the same fine folks who made you walk the plank in the first place?"

S'syrixx strongly suspected the translator was again having trouble rendering certain of Rry'kurr's terms or idioms in Gorn Standard. Even so, there could be no mistaking the captain's meaning.

"Please . . ." S'syrixx said. If the mammal captain was sincere in his threat to hand him over to Captain Krassrr, his life would be finished in very short order. Krassrr would leave nothing to chance in his second attempt to carry out the tribunal's final and irrevocable Decision of Condemnation. In addition, S'syrixx knew that his having survived the initial execution would implicate his old friend R'rerrgran, earning him an execution of his own.

Then there would be no one left to speak for the Hranrarii. No one save these savage warmbloods, whom every fiber of his being told him couldn't be trusted not to pervert his knowledge of the ecosculptor. What, save S'syrixx's own silence, was to stop them from turning it into a superweapon to be wielded remorselessly against every caste in the Gorn Hegemony?

"Think about that while you're . . . convalescing," Rry'kurr said as he turned on his heel and stalked toward the exit, the Troi-mammal following close behind him.

S'syrixx came to a decision then. For better or worse, it might be better to find a way to survive among the unclean endotherms than to die at the cold claws of his own people. Summoning what little strength remained to him, he pushed himself back up onto his elbows despite Ree's best efforts to make him recline.

"Wait, mammal!" he cried.

S'syrixx saw the two mammals pause on the threshold of the open doorway.

Rry'kurr and the Troi-mammal turned back to face him. "I'm listening, Mister S'syrixx," Rry'kurr said.

"If you are truly as concerned about the survival of others as you would have me believe, then you will not return me to those who would execute me," S'syrixx said. "Whether I cooperate fully with you or not."

"Why do you say that?" Rry'kurr asked.

"Because, Captain Rry'kurr," S'syrixx said as he felt his body lowering itself back into a recumbent pose, "I now formally request your protection from Captain Krassrr and the Gorn military."

Will obviously wanted to continue the conversation with S'syrixx, but Troi could see immediately that this wasn't to be—at least not at the moment. First, Ree's exhausted Gorn patient appeared to have once again lapsed into unconsciousness. And second, an angry Dr. Ree was insisting, in guttural, growling tones that brooked no argument, that everyone except essential, care-providing personnel had better exit his sickbay *now.*

Out in the corridor beyond the main sickbay entrance, Troi reached out to touch her husband's arm, bringing him to a stop. Though he showed only the most subtle of outward signs, it was clear to her that he was in a state of emotional upheaval.

"Will, what's wrong?" she asked quietly, so as not to be overheard by any of the various *Titan* personnel who were walking past them in either direction along the curved corridor.

"Besides the obvious?" he said. "Besides the fact that we now know for sure just how dangerous that ancient artifact is?"

"At least we don't have to speculate about the device's purpose anymore."

"At least there's that," Will said, leading the way to the nearest turbolift as Ensign Rynaph and Chief Urkral hastened past, both radiating waves of discomfiture that even Will must have felt. Troi had rarely seen the Saurian engineer's large webbed feet carry her across so much distance so quickly.

It was obvious that neither Rynaph nor Urkral were eager to speak with Troi or the captain at the moment, no doubt because of the tense near-confrontation they had both just witnessed in sickbay. Troi turned her head in time to see Lieutenant Qontallium from security walking away from sickbay in the opposite direction, thereby avoiding her and Will entirely; the retreating Gnalish radiated a sense of relief that the captain hadn't pushed Ree far enough to force him to choose between Ree's authority under the Starfleet medical regs and Will's authority as *Titan*'s CO.

She made a mental note to speak with all three of the reptiloid crewmembers at her earliest opportunity; after all, they had done everything possible to make S'syrixx feel comfortable, in the hope of making him more cooperative than he might have been away from any remotely kindred faces. Troi knew she might need to call upon them to do so again soon—particularly if Will treated S'syrixx's formal request with all the seriousness it would seem to merit.

Mentally filing all of that away for later, Troi turned toward Will and said, "So we're back to the obvious—the obvious being the fact that an entire civilization could be reduced to atoms without so much as a moment's notice."

They came to a stop in front of the turbolift, whose doors slid obediently open to admit them. A moment later, they were alone together as the lift began to carry them toward the bridge.

"I'm glad *that* much is obvious," Will said. "It's too bad that the solution to the problem isn't equally obvious."

Using her most soothing counselor tones, Troi said, "S'syrixx might hold the key to that solution, Will."

"Unless he's actually a Gorn saboteur. A tactical weapon fired at us by Captain Krassrr."

"He's requested asylum, Will. You can't just ignore that."

During the silence that followed, she could feel the tension that was tearing at him, an almost tangible emotional torque. On the one hand, he had to protect his ship and crew in a perilous region of deep Beta Quadrant space that was certain to grow even more perilous the longer *Titan* remained in it; the prize for staying could be a miracle technology that might heal a Borg-ravaged Federation almost overnight. On the other hand, an entire civilization—a Prime Directive "hands-off" civilization at that—was in imminent danger of receiving a summary death sentence.

And the solution to one problem might bring a catastrophic resolution to the other.

"What are you going to do, Will?" Troi said as the turbolift doors opened onto *Titan*'s bustling bridge.

He paused briefly on the threshold and smiled at her. "I won't ignore S'syrixx's request, Deanna. I know which side of caution I have to err on."

She nodded and returned his smile as they made their way to the center of the bridge, though she experienced no relief upon hearing his decision. After all, she had never believed he would willingly send a refugee back into the hands—or the claws—of his would-be killers; she had never doubted his core humanity.

Christine Vale vacated the center seat, exchanging it for the one to her immediate right as Will assumed his place in the very heart of *Titan*'s bridge. Troi took her customary seat to Will's left as he brought Vale up to speed about S'syrixx's urgent request.

"Captain, has anybody told our Gorn guest yet about your decision to grant him asylum?" Vale asked.

Will shook his head. "I thought I'd send Deanna down to do that in a few minutes. Or else have Ree handle it."

"Can I make a recommendation?" Vale said.

"Shoot," Will said with a nod.

"There's no regulation that says you have to tell him right away, is there?"

Will shrugged and looked to Troi for help. She returned the shrug. "None that I'm aware of," she said. "Why do you ask?"

"Because being kept waiting on tenterhooks overnight might make him a little more cooperative," said Vale. "You know, wondering whether he's going to get to stay aboard this nice comfy starship, or whether he'll be zipped out of one of Captain Krassrr's airlocks again."

Will seemed to mull that thought over for a few seconds before he consented with an unhappy nod. He turned toward Troi. "Let him know first thing in the morning," he said.

Troi nodded. "You're still uneasy about having S'syrixx aboard," she said.

"Or maybe I'm just uneasy about my own . . . parochial reaction to him," he said.

"What do you mean, Captain?" Vale asked.

With a weary sigh, he leaned his bearded chin on his fist. "It's just that it's hard to shake the feeling that I'm about to let a poisonous serpent loose in *Titan*'s garden."

11

Vale had always made a point of being the first to arrive at morning staff meetings whenever the relentless exigencies of her executive-officer duties didn't make it impossible. As she walked briskly through the doors to the observation lounge, she noticed that it was already oh-six-five-five hours, a fact that made her feel almost tardy. The doors parted to admit her and she was mildly surprised to find Captain Riker and Commander Troi already in their customary seats at the broad, round table that was framed by the observation windows' view of *Titan*'s bow and the star-bejeweled darkness beyond.

"I just received a very interesting upload from sickbay, Chris," Riker said as he tapped the controls of a small padd he had laid on the table. She was relieved to see that he seemed better rested this morning than he had at the previous senior staff meeting. Perhaps the unexpected arrival of *Titan*'s Gorn "guest" had been a game-changer for him. She could only hope that whatever action the altered circumstances might lead him to take against the Gorn wouldn't trap the ship and crew in a deadly no-win scenario.

"Something from our visitor?" Vale asked as she sat at the table. As on the bridge, she took the seat to Riker's immediate right.

"Mister S'syrixx appears to have been burning the midnight oil to give us information about the Hranrarii," Troi said. "Not to mention some beautiful artwork. It certainly looks like an act of good faith to me."

"Can't argue with that," Riker said as he continued scrolling through the contents of the padd. "It might even turn out to be useful."

"We'll see," Vale said noncommittally as he slid the padd toward her. She wasted no time picking it up and examining the surprisingly detailed table of contents of the document in question.

"I've just finished uploading everything on that padd into the senior staff's general database," the captain said while Vale continued skimming the data. "Deanna and I will walk everybody through what we know about the particulars during the briefing."

Though she was scrolling through the material quickly, Vale couldn't help but be impressed. What S'syrixx had composed was nothing short of a comprehensive monograph about Vela OB2–404 II and the biology and civilization of the planet's inhabitants. Despite its stilted language—doubtless an artifact of having been drafted in the Gorn tongue and subsequently machine-translated into Federation Standard—the document looked to be quite the achievement, especially considering the fact that its author had had only a few scant hours to assemble it.

"Looks like your instincts were spot-on, Chris," Riker said. "Keeping our guest waiting seems to have motivated him quite a bit."

Vale grinned. "You can blame my cop background. I

simply harnessed the positive power of uncertainty and worry."

Instead of returning her good humor, Riker regarded her with a vaguely pained expression—which she also saw mirrored, if only involuntarily, on Troi's usually placid features.

Ouch, Vale thought, recalling just how much extreme "uncertainty and worry" that she, Troi, and the entire crew of the *Enterprise*-E had experienced after Riker's capture by Kinchawn, the mad prime minister of the planet Tezwa. Vale knew that Kinchawn's tender mercies had taken Riker to the absolute limits of human endurance, if not farther. The torments the Tezwan dictator had inflicted on Riker had demonstrated graphically that whatever might create uncertainty and worry could easily glide down a slippery slope that ends at terror, torture, or even murder.

On the other hand, Vale's law-enforcement experience had taught her long ago that Samuel Johnson had made an excellent point with his observation that nothing focused the mind quite like an impending hanging. And the punctiliously cooperative Gorn down in sickbay still had no assurance that he wasn't about to end up at the end of Johnson's metaphorical rope.

Vale was grateful when the observation-deck doors suddenly distracted her from this train of thought. The brief pneumatic hissing heralded the arrival of Commanders Tuvok, Ra-Havreii, and Keru, who were followed moments later by Dr. Ree and Commander Pazlar.

Vale was pleased to see that Pazlar had walked into the meeting room with the assistance of a contra-gravity suit instead of simply manifesting in the room as a remotely generated apparition via *Titan*'s omnipresent holoemitter network. *Good for you, Melora,* she thought. *For a while there you were on your way to becoming a stellar-cartography-lab shut-in.* She wondered whether Pazlar's ambiguous romantic relationship with Chief Engineer Ra-Havreii was in any way involved in the science officer's new found positivity.

"We appear to owe our guest, Mister S'syrixx, a debt of thanks," Riker said, addressing the room once everyone had finished settling into their seats. "Thanks to him, we now know a hell of a lot more about Vela OB2–404 II—or Hranrar—than we did before. Including the likely fate of the planet and its people if something isn't done on their behalf, and soon."

"That is assuming, of course, that Mister S'syrixx is being forthright with us," Tuvok said, his fingers steepled before him.

"I've seen no indication so far that he's told us anything but the truth," said Troi.

At least the truth as he *understands it,* Vale thought, though she kept her doubts to herself for the moment to forestall a potentially time-wasting debate. The last thing she wanted was for anyone, even Troi, to try to intellectualize away her legitimate doubts.

Vale watched Troi turn toward Dr. Ree. "Doctor, what is Mister S'syrixx's condition this morning?"

"I'm pleased to report that my patient is much improved, Counselor," said the physician. "Save, of course, for his rather acute anxieties, which are perfectly understandable under the present circumstances."

"I've heard a little bit about Mister S'syrixx's 'anxieties,'" said Ra-Havreii, his mild amusement not at all obscured by his drooping white mustachios. "Is it true that he's upset mainly because he's cooped up on a starship full of biologically objectionable life-forms?"

"My patient has exhibited a certain . . . reticence around placental mammals," Ree said as he nodded his great velociraptor head. "However, I believe his decision to seek asylum among those selfsame mammals may be a sign that he is learning to overcome some of his ingrained fears."

Vale shrugged. "It could also be a sign that he now thinks that living among beings that his culture has labeled as bogeymen is his best choice out of a very bad set of options. After all, his own people gave him the heave-ho straight out of one of their airlocks. Almost any alternative to going back to them must look pretty attractive to him."

For an absurd moment, she wondered whether anyone had considered sending Crewman Chaka down to speak with the Gorn, just to see if he also had a thing about spiders.

"I sincerely hope that the option of staying aboard *Titan* remains open for him," Ree said, his tone deferential though his yellow eyes became less so as his gaze fell upon Riker's.

The captain nodded. "I've decided to honor his asylum request, Doctor."

"He'll be very relieved to hear that, sir," Ree said. "I've been dreading the possibility of having to send him back to Captain Krassrr."

"At least we finally have a good idea of *why* Krassrr dumped Mister S'syrixx into space," Troi said. "Namely, his affinity for the Hranrarii."

"I obviously haven't had time to really read any of this

stuff yet, Counselor," Vale said. "But I won't complain if you decide to spoil some of the good parts right now."

Troi activated a small keypad on the table before her, and a heartbeat later a half-meter-long holographic representation of the terraforming platform that orbited Hranrar appeared like a genie from a lamp and hovered at approximately eye level over the center of the meeting table. Vale supposed this was another one of the Gorn's renderings, only displayed in three dimensions.

"S'syrixx was condemned for sabotaging Krassrr's terraforming efforts on Hranrar," she said.

"So he says," Vale said, folding her arms across her chest.

"I'll grant that I can't independently verify a lot of what's in S'syrixx's report," said Riker. "But at least this part of his story is consistent with his getting chucked out an airlock."

"As well as with the fact that the Gorn flotilla hasn't yet been able to fully power up Brahma-Shiva," Troi said. "Much less use it to alter Hranrar's biosphere."

Vale nodded as she recalled the most recent Gorn attempt to power up the device—an effort that ended in a hasty shutdown that could have been accompanied by untold amounts of damage to Brahma-Shiva's ancient internal systems.

Riker stroked his beard thoughtfully. "While I'd prefer to interpret the respite the Gorn have given the Hranrarii as evidence that our senior diplomat has shown his people the error of their ways, I can't ignore reality. Not only haven't the Gorn withdrawn from the system, they're still busy trying to do *something* with that artifact. So the reason they haven't turned the terraforming tech loose on Hranrar yet isn't because they've decided *not* to do it, but because they've discovered that they *can't*. At least for the moment."

But Vale was still having trouble buying some of this. "All of which makes our gallant Mister S'syrixx look like quite the hero."

"Indeed," Tuvok said. "He clearly has a strong motivation to furnish you with information designed to lead you to certain self-serving conclusions."

Keru nodded. "Hear, hear."

A slight frown creased Troi's forehead as her gaze drifted first to Tuvok, then to Keru, and finally settled upon Vale.

"Ever since we first encountered Krassrr's fleet," Troi said, "I've been detecting discord among the Gorn crews, presumably related to the Hegemony's plan to wipe out and annex Hranrar. It's obvious that they're not completely unanimous in their opinions about the Hranrarii. Why is it so hard for you to believe that a Gorn—particularly a non-warrior—might have some compassion for the plight of an alien race?"

Vale wasn't entirely sure how to answer that question; she found it difficult to apply words to the subject, since her objection was admittedly more gut-level than cerebral, more a product of inchoate feeling than of conscious thought. All she knew for certain was that the idea of trusting the Gorn made the tiny hairs on the back of her neck stand at attention, like a parade ground full of Izarian police cadets.

"Perhaps it is a biological issue," Ree ventured into the silence that had followed Troi's question.

Vale found that surprising, especially coming from Ree. "Doctor, you're not saying you think that all Gorn are biologically predisposed toward being violent blockheads?"

The doctor snorted, as though amused. "Not at all, Commander. I'm merely saying that it is well understood—at least by most of the Federation's nonhumanoid sentients—that Starfleet's much-publicized prohibition against xenophobia is a work in progress, at best. It is quite common for Federation humans and humanoids to assume that certain of the 'softer emotions' are distinctly mammalian traits."

"Pardon me, Doctor," Keru said, the Trill spots that ringed his face flushing with emotion as he straightened in his chair and glared at the Pahkwa-thanh surgeon. "But that's the biggest load of *mreker* droppings I've ever heard."

"Belay that, Commander!" Vale snapped at Keru, even though she largely agreed with his assessment.

Ree raised one of his delicate yet deadly looking manus. "I am not offended in the least. I far prefer honest discourse to—what is the term?—'sugarcoating' such weighty matters."

Vale shrugged and looked toward Riker. The captain nodded back, then nodded at Keru, though he didn't look pleased by the senior security officer's turn of phrase.

"My apologies, everybody," Keru said. "But this sort of broad-brushing really gets under my skin. I've always believed that the Federation's relations with new species—whether they're adversaries or prospective new members—were based on practical experience. After all, isn't that what the whole protracted Federation member-admission process is supposed to be all about? We trust you and your Pahkwa-thanh countrymen, Doctor, because you have *proved* yourselves to be trustworthy. The same can be said of the natives of any Federation member world."

Vale reflected momentarily on the irony built into Keru's observation. Though the security chief was not joined to a Trill symbiont, his people had kept the dual nature of a prominent elite minority of their race a secret until well after Trillius Prime's entry into the Federation. And until very recently, they had kept the truth about their symbiont population's kinship to a conquest-driven race of alien parasites even more deeply buried.

She hoped nobody present would have the poor taste to bring any of that up.

"I agree," said Tuvok. "To date, the Gorn have given us little reason to trust them."

"Good point," Vale said.

"You're forgetting about the help they provided during last year's Borg attacks, Mister Tuvok," Riker said. "They suffered some very significant losses in that fight."

Tuvok nodded in acknowledgment. "I have not forgotten that, Captain. Nor have I overlooked their subsequent decision to abandon all détente with the Federation in favor of entering the Typhon Pact. Therefore I see no logic in imputing any motivation other than enlightened self-interest to their brief participation in the Borg conflict."

Though Vale wasn't any more inclined to trust the Gorn than Tuvok was, she also wasn't certain that the Vulcan's "enlightened self-interest" hypothesis panned out either. Most of the territory controlled by the Gorn Hegemony lay deep enough in Beta Quadrant space to have been well out of harm's way during the Borg invasion. And the Borg's beef, as it were, had been with Earth, not with Gornar.

But Vale knew what Tuvok and T'Pel had lost to the Borg: one of their adult children, as well as a daughter-in-law, both of whom had perished while helping others escape from their adopted homeworld of Deneva. *Maybe Tuvok blames the Gorn for that,* she thought. *Maybe he thinks the Borg might not have had time to wipe out Deneva if only the Gorn fleet had put up more of a fight.*

"Not being a Federation member," Pazlar said, "the Gorn Hegemony wasn't obligated to assist us at *all.*"

"No," said Ra-Havreii. "But it also wasn't obligated to join up with a Federation-hostile power the minute it got a bloody nose for making common cause with us."

Shaking her head, Troi said, "Until now, we've only had dealings with the Gorn Hegemony's warriors and political leaders. But those account for only two of the Gorn civilization's social castes, and there appear to be a lot more of those than we'd ever suspected before. S'syrixx says he belongs to one of their technological castes, and the fact that he differs biologically from members of the castes we are more familiar with tends to bear that out. He's also part of an *arts* subcaste, according to his report, so he may have an entirely different perspective than any Gorn we've ever encountered before. He could give us unprecedented insights into Gorn psychology and politics."

Arts subcaste, Vale thought as she glanced down at the padd and its copious diagrams and illustrations. *I suppose that explains all the pretty pictures he's uploaded onto this thing.*

"Or he might merely be a hostile spy with an elaborate cover," Tuvok said. "Furthermore, if we take Mister S'syrixx's own report at face value, then we must necessarily believe that his own people regard him as a saboteur—and therefore as an untrustworthy liability."

Riker held up both hands and spread them in the universal imploring gesture of the peacemaker. "I'm well aware that there may be as much reason to distrust Mister S'syrixx as to trust him. Once I inform him of my decision regarding his asylum request, I'll expect you to keep him under discreet but constant surveillance, Mister Keru."

"I won't let him out of my sight, Captain," said the big Trill. "My people are already watching him like Arbazan vultures."

"Then let's table the political discussion for the moment," Vale said, delighted at the opportunity to move on to more urgent matters. "While there's a lot we still don't understand about the Gorn, we do know that they're no slouches when it comes to engineering. Between their technical people and those of the other Typhon Pact powers"—she paused to gesture toward the floating holographic rendering of the orbiting terraforming platform—"they're bound to get that damned thing running again sooner or later."

"And I'd wager much more heavily on 'sooner' than on 'later,'" Ra-Havreii said.

Vale nodded. "And that naturally raises the question, 'So what are we gonna *do* about it?'"

"That's why we're having this briefing," Riker said. "To fully examine our options, and all the likely outcomes."

"I know we've discussed this before, but why don't we start with the direct approach?" Vale asked. "Storming the castle, as it were."

Pazlar reached toward a keypad before her on the table and tapped its control face twice. At once, the holographic platform that hovered above the table vanished, to be replaced instantly by a detailed wire-frame diagram depicting the very same object. As the wire-frame of Brahma-Shiva began slowly rotating along all three of its axes of motion, Vale could see rough indications of large hollow interior spaces, juxtaposed with vaguely opaque portions that might have denoted interior walls or support beams or even banks of indistinct machinery. The totality of the image resembled a half-done schematic drawing executed by a bright but inexpert child architect.

"What you're seeing is the latest set of computer-enhanced images generated from the sensor returns we received from the probes the Gorn destroyed."

"Our decoys," Vale said.

"Fortunately, those sensor drones turned out to be a good deal more than mere decoys," Pazlar said. "Before the Gorn ships finished zapping them all, they gave us the best glimpse we've had so far into Brahma-Shiva's internal workings."

"Fascinating," Tuvok said. "I thought that the alloy that comprises the object's outer hull was largely resistant to our sensor scans."

Pazlar nodded. "It is. But Hranrar's natural magnetic field is far more powerful than our most sensitive active scanning equipment. Evidently, it's capable of penetrating the hull enough to act like an old-style radiological scanner."

"What they used to call an 'X-ray machine' on Earth a few centuries ago," Riker said. "Or a fluoroscope."

"That's the general idea," Pazlar said. "By taking advantage of this 'fluoroscope effect,' we managed to pick up a surprisingly large volume of interior data via the passive sensors on the probes."

"Maybe we'll luck out," Vale said, "and discover that millennia of constant exposure to this 'fluoroscope effect' has baked Brahma-Shiva's interior so completely that it just plain won't work when the Gorn finally do get it powered up and switched on again."

"I might be straying a little bit out of my field here," Keru said, "but I'd have to say that that's a distinct possibility."

"It is, no question," Pazlar said as Vale's gaze followed the three-dimensional diagram's almost hypnotically slow omnidirectional spin. "But we can't afford to make an assumption like that. It isn't safe for us, or for the Hranrarii."

"Regardless, the data appears to be somewhat incomplete," Tuvok said. "Any plan for an assault on this structure using this data will necessarily be highly problematic."

"Probably," Riker said. "Unless Mister S'syrixx can fill in some of the blanks for us. He says he knows how to monkeywrench the thing. Maybe he could also help us get a tactical team inside it. Help us figure out how to take control of the artifact directly."

"Perhaps he could even help us take Brahma-Shiva away from here entirely," Troi said. "Or at least help us refine our scans to the point where the Federation could reverse engineer the underlying technology later."

Tuvok's mostly impassive face immediately drew Vale's attention, only because his left eyebrow seemed to be trying to climb entirely off the Vulcan's forehead. Obviously, the prospect of using this technology to restore the worlds the Borg had ravaged was an attractive one.

But just as obviously, to ask Tuvok to trust S'syrixx enough to make such a thing possible was asking a hell of a lot of him, the teachings of Surak notwithstanding.

"As I said, I want to consider *all* our options," Riker said. "Particularly those that might give us the best chance of keeping this ship in one piece, and saving the Hranrarii as well."

The Hranrarii. Vale suddenly found herself all but consumed with curiosity about this mysterious race. It occurred to her that the crew of *Titan* had risked quite a lot—and was preparing, potentially, to risk even more—on behalf of a species she had never before laid eyes on.

"About the Hranrarii," she said. "Who are they? What do they look like?"

Troi tapped another command into her keypad. The schematic of Brahma-Shiva vanished, to be replaced at once by a depiction of a being that could be described as human-like only in the broadest of terms. The unclothed yellow-green form stood on two powerfully muscled legs, each of which came equipped with a pair of knees that bent in opposing directions, giving the creature an almost cricket-like aspect at first glance. The upper body sported two long arms, and all the extremities possessed long digits draped in thin folds of skin that appeared to be adaptations to an aquatic environment. The neck was striated with grooves that had to be gills, though the chest cavity looked robust enough to have supported a decent lung capacity as well. The noseless and thick-lipped head evoked Vale's childhood memories of catching transplanted Terran frogs and native fanfish on Izar, and the enormous, forward-facing eyes brought to mind images of Izarian barn owls. The image began slowly revolving as it hovered, allowing everyone present to see the creature from every angle.

"Like the primary Gorn homeworld of Tau Lacertae IX, Hranrar lacks large bodies of water," Troi said. "Hranrar differs, however, in that its temperate zones support a large number of water-rich marsh ecologies. There is little seasonal weather variation because of Hranrar's minimal axial tilt, and the gravitational of interactions between the planet and its five small natural satellites appear to have kept the rotational axis stable for eons. These conditions appear not to have changed significantly for many millions of years, during which time the Hranrarii wetlands have given rise to sapient life."

But sapient life, Vale thought, *that looks a lot more Gornish than humanish.* She couldn't help but wonder whether Mr. S'syrixx would have been so determined to save these people if they'd come equipped with hair and lactation glands instead of gills and webbed digits. She suddenly felt her neck and face flushing with shame. Ree had been right: Humanity's commitment to excising its worst prejudices was indeed an incomplete exercise, perhaps even a beginner's art. *Would I be more gung-ho about taking down that world-wrecker out there if the people in harm's way looked more like my family than S'syrixx's?*

"The planet's only evident sentient species—the Hranrarii—are very well adapted to this kind of climate," Troi continued. "Like the amphibians and amphibian-analogs of many worlds, the Hranrarii are extremely sensitive to even small changes in temperature and atmospheric composition. Fortunately for them, variables of that sort have never posed a serious threat to them, especially during their present era of high technology. Of course, Hranrar's relatively gentle conditions have had a lot to do with the emergence of the Hranrarii's highly advanced civilization."

"As highly advanced as this society may be," Ra-Havreii said, "its accomplishments don't yet appear to include a capacity for spaceflight of any kind."

"True enough," Troi said. "Perhaps they have been so successful in living in harmony with their environment—and maybe with each other as well, since S'syrixx made no mention of warfare between Hranrarii tribes or nations—that they never developed any serious impetus to find other worlds to colonize, or even to take the strategic 'high ground' of low orbit."

As she continued to study the holographic Hranrarii, Vale noticed that the creature's eyes periodically closed, then opened again, blinking in an irregular, slow-motion rhythm. The eyelids, when they became visible, revealed a complex pattern of markings that Vale interpreted as alien writing or pictographs, their lines, loops, and swirls rendered in luminescent oranges, blues, and purples. She figured them for tribal tattoos of some kind.

"So we know that Hranrar has been kind to the Hranrarii until now," said the captain. "But that could all go right out the airlock once Captain Krassrr's terraforming team finishes undoing whatever damage S'syrixx did to Brahma-Shiva."

"Then we'd better be ready to do something before that happens," Vale said. "Assuming, of course, that our good friend Mister S'syrixx has been leveling with us about all of this."

Riker nodded. "That's my assumption, for the sake of

the Hranrarii. And against the chance that we might grab that terraforming tech for the Federation. It could hold the key to restoring entire ecosystems virtually overnight."

"To say nothing of its value to us simply in terms of the balance of power between the Federation and the Typhon Pact," Vale said. "Having the tech would help us defend against its being used against us as an offensive weapon—in addition to giving us the use of that very same offensive weapon. A triple threat, so to speak."

"An apt description," Tuvok said drily. "And perhaps an equally apt reason to choose the option of destroying this technology rather than allowing it to proliferate."

"Nonsense," Ra-Havreii scoffed. "Suppose that 'proliferation' could put right the damage the Borg did to us in a small fraction of the time nature would take to do the same job?"

A frown like a thunderhead wrinkled the Vulcan's brow. "Some damage can never be undone, Commander. There are limits to what even the Federation's best and brightest can do."

Ra-Havreii folded his arms across his chest, standing his rhetorical ground. "The only limits are those that we impose upon ourselves."

A sad, almost stricken look crossed Troi's face. "Tuvok may be right."

"Oh, please, Counselor," Ra-Havreii said disgustedly. "Not you, too. If your Terran ancestors had exhibited this kind of diffidence in the face of the new and the different, their revered Zefram Cochrane wouldn't have gone anywhere, boldly or otherwise."

"I'm not talking about technology," Troi said, holding

up a hand almost in a "warding-off" gesture. "I'm talking about law, and Starfleet regulations. Realistically speaking, what *can* we do here? We're still just as constrained by the Prime Directive as we were when we first arrived."

Vale didn't much like thinking about it, but she knew that Troi was correct. Under a strict interpretation of the Prime Directive, *Titan*'s officers and crew would be forbidden even to warn the Hranrarii about their impending doom. The Hranrarii, after all, had yet even to put one of their own into low Hranrar orbit; the discovery of warp-drive technology, the traditional benchmark of Federation first-contact scenarios, was doubtless several generations away.

And the Hranrarii generations alive today could well represent the last the species would ever produce, thanks to the Gorn.

"Maybe our hands aren't tied completely," Pazlar said. "While the Gorn are still busy trying to repair Brahma-Shiva, can't we at least send an away team down there to do a little covert studying of the natives and their civilization? It wouldn't save the planet, but at least we could learn a little more about this society before . . ." She trailed off into a significant silence.

"The Gorn are likely to be vigilant against any further incursions on our part," Tuvok said.

Ra-Havreii shrugged. "My engineering team won't necessarily find that an insuperable problem."

"Approaching the Gorn flotilla too closely may be unwise," Tuvok said. "Simply leaving this system and reporting our findings thus far to Starfleet may be the best option we have."

"That would leave the Hranrarii on the chopping block," Riker said. "We're talking about millions of lives. I'd take a suicide run at Brahma-Shiva before I let the Gorn get away with genocide."

"So would I," Ra-Havreii said, his grim tone leaving no doubt about his sincerity—or about the ghosts that still haunted him, from the engine room of the *U.S.S Luna* to the much more recent death of *Titan*'s AI avatar, whose brief and now terminated existence as a sentient being the chief engineer had been unable to restore. He obviously had no intention of allowing anybody else to die because of his actions, or because of his failure to act.

A pall of thoughtful quiet had settled over the room. Obviously, nobody wanted to be stuck with the terrible final option Riker had just proposed, and that Ra-Havreii had just seconded—just as nobody seemed to be flinching from it, should the chips fall that way between now and this deadly game's last hand.

Troi was the first to break the contemplative silence. "We have to accept the possibility that the Gorn may succeed in denying us the 'suicide-run' option."

"Which is the same as saying that the Hranrarii are going to die no matter what we try to do about it," Keru said.

"As I said, we have to accept that outcome as a possibility," Troi said. "And that obliges us to use every bit of Prime Directive 'wiggle room' we have."

"What kind of 'wiggle room' are we talking about here, Counselor?" Vale asked.

"The kind that allows us to at least study the Hranrarii up close, but from behind concealment."

"You're talking about a duck blind," Riker said.

"It may be the only answer, Will," Troi said, her earlier sadness seemingly replaced by a gathering wave of enthusiasm.

"An away team would be at continuous risk of discovery by both the natives and the Gorn," Tuvok said. "To say nothing of the possibility that the Gorn may succeed in activating Brahma-Shiva while our away team is still on Hranrar's surface. The entire endeavor may be unwise."

"Maybe," Riker said. "But it might also be mandatory."

Tuvok's eyebrow again vaulted toward the ceiling. "Sir?"

Riker leaned forward and rested his elbows on the table. "I've been giving this a lot of thought since the first time we discussed our options vis-à-vis the Hranrarii. If they really *are* facing imminent extinction, then *Titan* has a legal, moral, and ethical duty to try to preserve their culture and language—at least to whatever extent that may be possible."

"As long as we do it without breaking the Prime Directive's first-contact protocols," said Troi. "As strange as that may sound in connection with a society that might soon be extinct."

"I believe I should caution you, Captain," Ree said. "You seem to be exhibiting a reflex that I have found to be all too common in Starfleet."

"What reflex is that?"

"The ingrained, knee-jerk belief that you can save everyone in the universe," the reptiloid said in surprisingly mild tones. "And therefore the delusion that you *must.* But as Commander Troi has already pointed out, you may be pursuing a cause that is already lost."

The captain flashed one of his more dazzling smiles. "As a great man once said, 'Lost causes are the only ones worth fighting for.' "

Vale couldn't quite place the quote; Zefram Cochrane maybe, or President Archer. She decided it didn't matter, since optimistic literary aphorisms never really stood much of a chance against the meat-hook realities of life.

Vale took a moment to break the captain and Troi's plan down into bite-sized practicalities. Though Riker's argument in favor of saving some part of an otherwise doomed race was compelling, the results didn't look promising, at least in pragmatic terms.

"So all the away team has to do," Vale said, "is tiptoe past an already pissed-off Gorn commodore and his six heavily armed ships, land a discreet distance away from the Hranrarii equivalent of Paris, then tell the natives, 'Hello, we're travelers from a far land. We're here to sample your cuisine, language, art, and politics. Sorry, we don't have time to stay for the apocalypse that we're not allowed to tell you about.' And then we tiptoe back to *Titan* and retrace our original steps right past Captain Krassrr. Did I leave anything out?"

Riker shook his head soberly. "All you forgot was the native disguises. But the rest of it had the makings of an outstanding away-mission profile." He grinned. "Which is why I'm putting you in charge of getting that option ready, just in case we come up short trying to stop this wholesale planetary engineering in its tracks. I want you put together a tactical plan for getting an away team on and off of Hranrar quietly while Commander Tuvok and Chief Ra-Havreii work out a means of either neutralizing Brahma-Shiva—or of taking it outright."

"Understood, Captain," Vale said, before looking first to Tuvok, who appeared slightly skeptical, and next to Ra-Havreii, who looked as determined as she had ever seen him. *Frog suits,* she thought. *Wonderful.* She hoped Ra-Havreii could spare the away team that last indignity through the magic of holotechnology.

"Of course, that's an option we might not have to pursue if we can shut down the Gorn's terraforming plans sooner rather than later," Riker said, addressing the room.

Vale was keenly aware that the resolution to this crisis would boil down to one person's decision. Her heart went out to her friend and CO for having to ride the hot seat, even as she felt relief that the choice was not hers to make.

Speaking directly to Riker, she said, "We're cut off from Starfleet, thanks to all the local subspace interference. Whatever we do next—whether we turn tail and run, attack Brahma-Shiva, or stay here and sit *shiva* for the Hranrarii—will be up to you. If this were a democracy, I'd cast my vote for option 'A.' But whatever you decide, sir, I want you to know that you will have my complete support."

"Hear, hear," Troi said.

Murmurs of assent went around the table, then faded away into renewed silence as the senior staff collectively awaited the captain's decision.

"Thank you," he said. "All of you. At the moment, we're not exactly ready to do anything. So we'll keep our powder dry for now. We'll continue monitoring Gorn activity over Hranrar from the local Kuiper belt, via sensors and drones. We'll watch, and we'll plan. Let's assemble again tomorrow, same time, to review those plans." Riker rose from his chair, a signal that the morning briefing was at an end. "In the meantime, I want everyone to become as familiar as possible with the data we've gathered about Brahma-Shiva, as well as everything we've received so far from our new friend S'syr—"

"Will!" Troi said, interrupting. "Something's wrong down in sick—"

The purring yet sibilant voice that exploded from Keru's combadge interrupted the counselor in mid-syllable. *"Ensign Hriss to Commander Keru."*

"Keru here, Ensign," said the big Trill, who was still seated while others were starting to rise around him. "Talk to me."

"We have a security situation in sickbay, sir. It's the Gorn."

Keru vaulted from his chair with surprising grace and ran for the door without waiting for a formal dismissal. "On my way."

"Right behind you," said Ree, whose long torso was nearly parallel with the deck as he hastened after Keru.

Vale wasted no time falling right into step behind them both.

12

S'syrixx willed his claws to stop shaking, but with only marginal success. *I made my move too early,* he thought, berating himself. His vocal cords had healed considerably since they'd been exposed to hard vacuum, but evidently not quite enough to pull off a completely seamless voice-imposture; he considered himself foolish ever to have thought that he might equal his great-granduncle Zsraszk's storied facility with the Voice. *I should have waited longer before making the attempt, at the very least.*

On the other manus, how much longer could he *afford* to wait? At any moment, he was bound to receive word of what seemed ever more inevitable with each passing heartbeat: Rry'kurr's formal decision to deny his request for sanctuary aboard *Tie-tan,* in favor of returning him to his would-be executioners.

Captain Krassrr wasn't infallible, as S'syrixx's survival of the first execution attempt attested. But neither was Krassrr known for repeating his mistakes. *Next time he will make certain of his work, either with a disruptor pistol or cold, sharpened polysteel.*

The gold-skinned creature around whose disconcertingly soft neck S'syrixx had hooked his left arm screamed at an alarming volume. He belatedly realized that the claws of his right manus, which he had brandished primarily as a threat gesture, had nicked the creature's unprotected flesh, producing an unintended trickle of translucent yellow fluid.

S'syrixx growled a guttural warning into the right ear of the father-crowned creature—it called itself Dr. Onnta—who quivered in his iron grasp. "Be. Quiet."

"Let him go," commanded one of the other *Tie-tan* crewmembers who had rushed into the room once he had decided he could no longer afford to await the captain's decision regarding his disposition. No fewer than eight of them had crowded into the vessel's infirmary. Five of these were armed with small, handheld weapons that S'syrixx had to assume were capable of delivering lethal particle-beam charges or disruptor blasts. He recognized one as one of the reptiloids who had greeted him after his second awakening here. The others were either mammals or belonged to species even more exotic, with epidermal colorations ranging from something roughly comparable to that of Rry'kurr all the way to cerulean blue and even Gorn war-caster green. One of these mammalian nightmares was even covered from crest to claw with a thick coat of fur!

"Let him go," the Sst'rfleeter repeated. This time S'syrixx was able to identify the speaker as the blue-skinned one. This creature, whom S'syrixx decided was a female, possessed twin cranial antennae that seemed capable of independent motion; they probed restlessly in S'syrixx's direction, making his *cloaca* muscles clench involuntarily.

S'syrixx tightened his grip slightly around Onnta's throat, while taking care not to injure the delicate creature again. "You know I can't afford to do that. You'll just shoot me where I stand."

"Not if you release him now," the hulking green mammal said. This one S'syrixx decided was a male.

"There's nowhere aboard *Titan* you can run, Mister S'syrixx," said the reptiloid.

Baring his teeth, S'syrixx said, "I know. That's why I need this chamber sealed until I can negotiate my way off this ship. Let no one else in or out of here until that is accomplished." S'syrixx paused to get his trembling manus under control again. Onnta yelped in pain. "Do this now, or your Doctor Onnta dies."

A brief tumult went up among the eight other beings who crowded the room. A small, unarmed, blue-furred creature that stood approximately knee-high relative to most of the others present was suddenly fighting its way through the quintet of armed—and suddenly very surprised-looking—personnel who stood in its way. The remaining two individuals who carried no visible weapons—one was the female medic Oh-Gow-uh, while the other was a portly, hirsute creature that bore an unseemly resemblance to a domesticated nonsapient mammal that every Gorn caste raised to serve as live food—tried and failed to stop the furry little being's advance.

The creature bounded to a stop right in between S'syrixx and the weapon-carrying crewmen. "Negotiate?" the fur-covered one said. "You say you wish to negotiate?"

S'syrixx stared at the being, both fascinated and horrified. Aside from one of the armed mammals, he had never seen so much fur adorning any one creature. The creature's eyes were enormous, and it sported a respectable array of teeth and claws, though nothing that any Gorn should have any reason to fear.

His manus shook anyway as he wondered what other weird surprises this ship might spring upon him at any moment.

"My name is Huilan Sen'kara," said the little blue being, whose gender S'syrixx couldn't immediately identify, though by now such distinctions were beginning to seem trivial, or at least academic. "I am a junior counselor."

"Counselor?" S'syrixx asked.

The furry blue head nodded. "I advise members of the crew regarding their . . . personal problems. At this moment you appear to be in desperate need of my help, Mister S'syrixx."

"You want to help me?" S'syrixx said. "Then help me get off this ship."

The fur above the little counselor's eyes knotted into a distinctly mammalian-looking frown. "Yesterday you petitioned the captain for asylum. Have you withdrawn that request?"

"You and I both know that any request I might make of your captain is entirely irrelevant. The outcome is a foregone conclusion."

The blue-furred head tipped slightly to the side. "Why do you say that?"

"Because your Federrazsh'n distrusts my people."

"That isn't necessarily so, Mister S'syrixx. Though I must admit that the Federation government wasn't very pleased by *your* government's decision to cut its diplomatic ties with us and become part of the Typhon Pact."

"I am not part of the political caste. Such things do not concern me. All I know is that your Captain Rry'kurr has yet to answer my request, even after I provided him with exhaustive information about Hranrar and my people's activities there. His intentions are therefore clear to me."

"Captain Riker is a very busy man, Mister S'syrixx—and since he received your information, he's no doubt become a great deal busier."

"I'm sure he's not too busy to save the life of a member of his crew," S'syrixx said, giving Onnta's neck another quick, yelp-generating squeeze for emphasis. "Rry'kurr plans to send me back to Captain Krassrr, who would execute me."

"If you were to leave this ship, Mister S'syrixx, where could you possibly go where Krassrr couldn't find you?"

How little they understand a properly authoritarian power structure, S'syrixx thought, amazed at the unsophisticated nature of the mammalian thought process. Aloud, he said, "That's not my plan, small one. I would go straight *to* Krassrr. But I would not come to him with an empty manus. This ship must have a number of auxiliary vessels. Get me to one of those, and secure me safe passage with it back to Krassrr's fleet."

"Release Doctor Onnta. Please. Afterward, I will argue on your behalf before the captain regarding your asylum request."

S'syrixx experienced a moment of vertigo as he questioned the wisdom of his actions. Would Ry'kurr really consider his case, even now? Could any mammal really be that naïve?

Snorting a derisive laugh, S'syrixx lifted Onnta entirely off the deck for a moment, shaking him as though he were a bag of feed intended for consumption by meatbeasts. "You have heard my terms. I give your captain ten of your minutes to meet them—without any attempt at trickery of any kind—or I will bite this creature's throat out."

S'syrixx's stomach heaved at the thought.

The effort of keeping up with Ree's powerful sprinting strides had left Vale mildly winded by the time she reached the closed doors to sickbay.

Somehow, Keru had beaten both Vale and Ree there. The big Trill stood before the doors with Crewman Ellec Krotine, one of Keru's junior security people. Both officers had drawn their phasers, and the AI Blue-White hovered at eye level about a meter away from both of them.

"It's no good, Commander," Krotine said to Keru; the female Boslic had pulled her shoulder-length violet hair back into a ponytail that swung slightly when she shook her head. "The doors are locked from the inside."

"Then I will smash them down," Ree growled, sounding like a predator who was both ready and eager to defend his territory. He pulled his powerfully muscled tail back, as though cocking a spring-loaded battering ram or siege engine.

"Stand down, Doctor," Vale said, getting her breathing back under control as she stepped between the CMO and the sealed doors. "I need a sit rep first."

Ree relaxed his aggressive posture with obvious reluctance.

Answering a nod from Keru, Krotine turned to face Vale. "Our . . . guest has taken Doctor Onnta hostage and sealed the sickbay doors. He's threatening to kill Onnta in ten minutes unless we give him safe passage off of *Titan* aboard one of our shuttlecraft."

"Oh, is *that* all he wants?" Vale said drily. In her peripheral vision, she noticed someone approaching.

"This seems completely out of the blue," Troi said as she came to a stop in a deliberate and decidedly un-winded manner.

"That's what I'm thinking, too," Vale said.

"Interrogative," SecondGen White-Blue said as he bobbed gently on his antigravs. "Question. Inquiry. 'Out of the blue'?"

"It's an old human idiom," Troi said. "We use it to refer to circumstances that completely surprise us."

"Understood," said the AI. "Perhaps it is an inapt metaphor in this particular instance."

"Why do you say that?" Vale asked.

The levitating robotic life-form seemed to be enjoying the attention it was receiving. "I noticed that Lieutenant Qontallium had taken the precaution of bringing a security team to sickbay approximately seven-point-five of your minutes ago."

"Why?" Keru wanted to know.

"Because someone tried to gain unauthorized remote access to one of the shuttlecraft in hangar bay one, using a sickbay computer terminal," Krotine said. "The suspected perp very nearly succeeded, too, from what I can tell."

"'Suspected perp,' Mister Krotine?" Vale said. "We're talking about S'syrixx."

Glaring at Krotine, Keru reddened. "Why wasn't I informed about this?"

"Evidently events overtook Lieutenant Qontallium's full attention before he had an opportunity to make a formal report on the shuttlecraft incident," White-Blue said.

Krotine nodded, though she looked embarrassed and chastened. "I just reviewed the security log about this, Commander Keru. Mister S'syrixx claimed to be Captain Riker when he tried to grab the shuttle."

The pieces of the puzzle were coming together in Vale's mind. "He must have planned to beam himself and his hostage out of sickbay using the shuttlecraft's transporter. Then he'd get clear of *Titan* and be under way before we could stop him."

"Probably figured we wouldn't pursue him," Krotine said.

"Or at least that we wouldn't get too grabby with our tractor beam," Troi said. "So as not to endanger Onnta."

"Those gambles sound like good ones, at least from a Gorn perspective," Vale said. "Chasing or tractoring S'syrixx would probably let Captain Krassrr know that we're still hiding in the weeds." It wasn't hard to imagine S'syrixx playing chicken with *Titan*'s tractor beam, stubbornly overdriving a stolen shuttlecraft's engines until he was either set free or ostentatiously destroyed.

Either way, it probably wouldn't be long before the ever-irritable Krassrr's fleet once again moved *Titan* into a fight-or-flight posture.

"Damn," Keru spat. "My people seriously misjudged how desperate our Mister S'syrixx is."

"Let's not burn any calories right now on blame," Vale said. "At the moment we have a problem to solve."

Keru nodded in agreement, though he still looked miserable. He clearly blamed himself for the events that were now unfolding—and just as clearly dreaded what might yet happen. "Of course, Commander."

"Our Gorn 'friend' must have made a quick study of our computer's remote command overrides," Ree said. "Getting as far as he did by putting manual commands into a sickbay computer interface is quite an achievement."

Krotine shook her head, once again making her ponytail swing like a pendulum. "But that's not what he did, Doctor. He used the standard voice interface. Even made a print match with the captain's voice. Damn near fooled the shuttlebay watch officer, from what I can tell so far."

A sly smile appeared on Keru's face. "Fortunately for us, he couldn't fake his way out of not knowing the captain's authorization code."

Vale scowled. "S'syrixx faked the captain's voice, right down to the voiceprint metrics? Isn't that supposed to be impossible?"

"Evidently not for the Gorn," Troi said.

Vale hated it—*hated* it—when an adversary surprised her like this. "Sounds like I need to bone up on Gorn tactical studies."

"That's what I started doing last night," Troi said. "I started by reviewing the Federation's first encounter with the Gorn."

"The Cestus III Massacre," Keru said. "But what does that have to do with voiceprint matches?"

"Actually, more than you might think," Troi said. "In the immediate aftermath of the Massacre, Gorn forces impersonated a Starfleet officer they'd just killed—specifically one Commodore Grant Travers. Someone posing as Travers lured Captain James Kirk and a landing party to Cestus III with a dinner invitation that turned out to be bait for a Gorn ambush."

"It's hard to imagine that monster who fought Kirk doing a convincing impression of a Starfleet officer," Vale said. For a fleeting instant, she had an absurd mental image of a toothy Gorn performing at a child's birthday party, carefully twisting balloons into alien animal-shapes while doing dead-on impersonations of household-name celebrities and politicians.

"You're talking about Captain S'alath," Troi said. "Don't forget, he was a member of the Gorn warrior caste. Each caste's talents seem to be determined biologically at least as much as culturally. So now we know it's highly probable that S'syrixx belongs to the same caste as whoever mimicked Commodore Travers at Cestus III."

"And we also know that S'syrixx has an agenda other than political asylum," Vale said. "It's strange that you didn't pick up on it earlier, Counselor."

"I'm not yet convinced that S'syrixx really *does* have a hidden agenda," Troi said. "Otherwise I believe I would have discovered it long before now."

Vale could appreciate optimism, but not after it turned the corner into full-blown delusion. "Come on, Counselor. It should be pretty obvious by now that S'syrixx was never sincere about wanting asylum. He's a spy who got caught red-handed—er, red-clawed—trying to steal some of our technology."

Troi folded her arms across her chest. "What's obvious to me is that S'syrixx is terrified of being put off this ship. He's assuming that that's what's going to happen to him, his asylum request notwithstanding."

"Because the captain hasn't answered his petition yet," Vale said, beginning to understand.

And just where the hell is *the captain, anyway?* the exec thought as she glanced quickly down the corridor in either direction, seeing no sign of Riker.

Vale turned back toward Troi in time to see the counselor's affirmative nod. "S'syrixx appears to have concluded," Troi said, "that his best and only option is to get off this ship on his own terms, rather than on ours."

Vale decided not to waste any more precious time debating the Gorn's motivations; Dr. Onnta's life was still in grave danger, and the clock was ticking. "We need to get somebody in there, ASAP. A negotiator."

"Counselor Huilan was in sickbay before the doors were sealed," Troi said. "He's already working with me on a plan."

"A plan," Vale said, grateful for anything that might turn the tables before the clock ticked down to zero. "Plans are good. Feel like sharing?"

Troi began spelling out the plan. A grin spread slowly across Vale's face. The grin halted and receded, however, after she began to consider the consequences of failure. If S'syrixx were to catch wind of what the captain was *really* up to, then Dr. Onnta was already as good as dead.

Glancing again at the chronometer on the wall, S'syrixx could see that the ten minutes he had allowed was very nearly up.

Does Rry'kurr have gizzard enough to test my resolve? he thought. *Or maybe these warmbloods simply don't have the same regard for the lives of their underlings as we Gorn do.*

S'syrixx heard a quick exchange of murmurs coming from the part of the room where the armed *Tie-tan* personnel continued to stand vigil. The murmurs ceased and the reptiloid crewmember took a single confident step toward the corner of the infirmary chamber where S'syrixx stood with the furry blue dwarf-thing.

The reptiloid came to a halt after S'syrixx raised his hostage in a warding-off gesture. The Onnta creature had gone limp in his grasp; S'syrixx judged his hostage to have fallen into a faint, since he felt none of the terminal muscle-loosening and smelled none of the stench that usually accompanied sudden death.

"What do you want?" S'syrixx snapped. He found it difficult to speak civilly to this reptiloid. The sight of a kindred species in Sst'rfleet livery now seemed like an affront.

"Captain Riker is out in the corridor," the reptiloid said. "He wants to come inside sickbay to speak with you."

Though S'syrixx was relieved to hear that, he tried to keep his affect as flat as possible. "Good. You must be aware that your Doctor Onnta's time is very nearly up."

"May I send the captain in?" the reptiloid asked.

"Only if he comes in alone and unarmed," S'syrixx said. "And only if you and the rest of your security force leaves."

"That would leave the captain as a second hostage," said the reptiloid.

"Those are my terms. Consult with your captain if you must, but know that I will kill this hostage if my instructions are not followed without delay."

The reptiloid withdrew with a curt nod and exchanged more murmurs with the communications device attached to its uniform tunic.

Moments later, everyone began filing out of the chamber. Another form entered—a lone mammal, bearing no obvious weapons.

"Captain Rry'kurr," S'syrixx said, the manus he had wrapped around Onnta's neck beginning to tremble once again.

"Let him go," the mammal said, spreading its two soft, pink manus before it in a gesture of supplication. "Take me as your hostage instead."

S'syrixx was taken aback momentarily by the captain's apparent courage and selflessness. He sniffed the air deeply, just as he would have done among his Gorn conspecifics, hoping to assess the mammal's true interior emotional state via the room's ambient chemistry. Unfortunately, the residual stench of Dr. Onnta's fear, liberally mixed with his own, made an accurate read impossible.

He carried Onnta to a chair in the corner and allowed the doctor's insensate form to slump into it. Then he turned back to face Rry'kurr, who did not resist when he wrapped his manus around the captain's throat.

"Order your people to clear a path between this chamber and shuttlebay one," S'syrixx said, using his meager talents in the Voice to copy the pitch, timbre, and meter of Rry'kurr's speech, almost without realizing he was doing it.

Astonishingly, the Earther still appeared unfazed by his dire circumstances. Exposing his alarmingly small and ineffectual-looking teeth, he said, "Not bad. No wonder you nearly managed to talk your way aboard the shuttlecraft *Armstrong*. I think I'm a bit more of a baritone, though—"

This was maddening. "Enough!" S'syrixx growled, his default Gorn gutturality returning to the fore as he choked Rry'kurr's taunting words off at their source. "Give the appropriate orders. *Now.*" S'syrixx released his hold, then gave the human a hard shove toward the door.

"Riker to Commander Keru," the mammal said as his breath returned. "I've agreed to let Mister S'syrixx take me down to shuttlebay one. Make sure the *Armstrong* is prepped and ready for launch. And send Ree back inside sickbay as soon as we're out. Doctor Onnta needs medical assistance."

"Understood, Captain," replied a deep voice from the communications device that adhered to Rry'kurr's tunic.

Within moments, the captain had led S'syrixx out into an empty corridor. Although he allowed Rry'kurr to lead the way during the tense march from corridor to turbolift to the hangar bay's heavy duranium bulkheads, S'syrixx never once removed his manus from the soft pink creature's throat—despite his disgust at the bristling of Rry'kurr's beard-fur against his scales.

A seeming eternity after their departure from sickbay, S'syrixx and Rry'kurr approached a shuttlecraft whose hatch yawned open, like a Gorn warrior preparing to swallow a small meatbeast whole.

Rry'kurr hesitated on the threshold, which probably represented the human's last opportunity to mount a survivable escape attempt. S'syrixx clutched the creature's throat more tightly and brandished the claws of his free manus before Rry'kurr's incongruously placid blue eyes.

"No deceptions, mammal," he said as he preceded the human through the hatch, then dragged him inside.

Servos whirred as the hatch sealed itself and Rry'kurr strapped himself into the pilot's seat. The human claimed to need to go through an elaborate preflight checklist, but

S'syrixx suspected this was a mere ploy to buy time and demanded an immediate launch. With a sigh, the human captain complied.

S'syrixx had to crouch on the floor to get a decent view through the forward windows. In front of the shuttlecraft, massive pressure doors parted slowly, revealing the glow of a permeable forcefield that framed a wide view of the limitless dark that lay beyond. In response to Rry'kurr's ministrations at his pilot's console, the little vessel vibrated slightly. The open aperture leading to space suddenly rushed toward the vessel's nose, and an instant later the craft was flying free and clear in the void.

I actually did it, S'syrixx thought. *I've beaten the humans!*

Rry'kurr turned in his pilot's seat and looked up at his passenger. "Where were you planning on heading, Mister S'syrixx?"

That seemed like a stupid question. "Back to the eco-sculpting fleet. Where else would I go?"

"Just about anywhere, I'd imagine. Or have you forgotten that Krassrr tried to kill you the last time you saw him?"

"The last time I saw Krassrr, I didn't have any gifts to present him with," S'syrixx said, baring his teeth in triumph. "But I have two very valuable ones now: this spacecraft, and you."

"I see," Rry'kurr said as he turned his seat back toward his console, into which he immediately began entering commands. S'syrixx instantly felt the heading of the shuttlecraft beginning to change, as well as a split-second surge of forward motion that revealed a large increase in speed before the little ship's inertial damping system discreetly concealed it.

The mammal's casual manner piqued S'syrixx's suspicion—as did his continued utter lack of the stink of fear. In fact, the mammal didn't seem to have any odor whatsoever now that he was away from *Tie-tan*'s internal atmosphere, with its highly heterogeneous mix of emoto-chemicals.

"Aren't you concerned about what Captain Krassrr will do with you?" S'syrixx asked.

The human's shoulders bobbed up and then down again in a gesture of ambivalence that S'syrixx recognized as a shrug. "Not particularly."

Astonishing. "Why?"

"Because this shuttlecraft is now filling up with anesthezine gas," Rry'kurr said, once again baring his underdeveloped dentition. "Probably enough to knock out half a dozen Gorns."

S'syrixx *was* feeling a little lightheaded, but he attributed the effect to his surprise at the human's baseless assertion. "Ridiculous. You would be affected as well, Rry'kurr. Perhaps even killed."

"That certainly *would* be true," Rry'kurr said. His face and his body seemed to be turning transparent before S'syrixx's eyes.

"*Would* be?" S'syrixx echoed. He tried to rise from his crouch, but ended up sprawling onto his side across the deck instead. When he craned his neck to take another look at Rry'kurr, he saw that the Federrazsh'n commander had faded away into translucency. Only his useless teeth looked tangible.

Was the crew of *Tie-tan* using one of their transporters? Or had Rry'kurr managed to engage the transporter system aboard the shuttlecraft? Neither theory seemed to hold up, since neither vessel's transporters should have been within beaming range of any destinations at this stage in the shuttle's flight.

Unless Tie-tan *is secretly pursuing us,* S'syrixx thought as he laboriously got his feet back beneath him. With a growl of rage, he swung his right manus directly at Rry'kurr's throat.

His claws passed through the grinning mammal just as they would have done through empty air.

"It *would* be true," the all but invisible Rry'kurr repeated, "if I were actually in the shuttlecraft with you."

No wonder he has no scent.

The shuttlecraft's horizon abruptly changed to vertical. The hard duranium deck grating rushed up to greet S'syrixx. Once again he felt a heavy cloak of darkness enfolding him, and then he felt no more.

Riker watched the Gorn who slumbered on the king-size bed across the room. Rather than following his instincts and assigning *Titan*'s troublesome passenger to the far more Spartan accommodations of the brig, he had reluctantly acceded to Deanna's request that S'syrixx awaken instead in less threatening surroundings. She'd suggested using a VIP guest suite, which Riker had thought excessive; why, after all, should a kidnapper and pirate be treated like a visiting dignitary?

Riker decided to split the difference between prisoner and VIP when one of the crew offered to lend his quarters to S'syrixx, for reasons that Deanna had been quick to endorse, if not to discuss in detail.

Congenial though these quarters might be, Riker had

ordered Keru to keep them under constant surveillance and heavy guard.

Riker heard the main door whisk open. A moment later Lieutenant Qontallium—the generous donor of these quarters—escorted Deanna Troi into the bedroom. A moment later, the reptiloid Gnalish security guard silently retreated back into the corridor.

"How's our guest?" Deanna asked.

"Sleeping like a baby. How's Doctor Onnta?"

"Ree says he won't be singing any Balosneean madrigals for a week or two, but he's expecting him to make a complete recovery."

Riker was relieved to hear that. Not only had nobody died because of S'syrixx's emotional meltdown, no one had been permanently injured. "Do you know what's ironic about all of this, Deanna?" he said at length.

"I'm not sure I'd classify this as an ironic situation, Will," she said quietly, as though afraid she might wake the Gorn.

"Really? Let's see. For starters, we have a sentient lizard who appears to be terrified of mammals."

"Don't be parochial, Will. You know as well as I do that every species has its own biologically and culturally determined predilections. Those of the Gorn are no weirder than ours."

"All right. If that fun fact didn't tickle your irony bump, then maybe this one will—until Mister S'syrixx went berserk, I was going to say 'yes' to his asylum request."

She looked at him expectantly. "And now?"

"Now?" He paused, sighing. "He ought to count himself lucky that I haven't given him the same old heave-ho that Krassrr did."

"You don't really mean that, Will."

"Of course not. But he's *dangerous,* Deanna. Dangerous and unpredictable."

"Especially when he suspects he's being used."

Though her tone was neutral, the implied accusation was plain. "Are you saying that S'syrixx's rampage happened because I decided to let him sweat a little?" he asked. "That it was *my* fault?"

"I'm not saying any such thing, Will. But I *am* suggesting that you might not understand S'syrixx quite so well as you *think* you do."

"I don't like endangering my ship or my crew."

"Of course you don't," she said. "But you also understand that you need to keep S'syrixx close at hand if we're to have any hope of helping the Hranrarii. You need more than his cooperation under duress. You need his goodwill."

Riker nodded wearily. There was no getting around that unpleasant reality.

"By the way, that was a very clever application of Commander Ra-Havreii's holographic telepresence system you came up with," she said. "That, and your decision to run the *Armstrong* in training simulator mode."

"Alien contact scenarios are a lot like jazz solos, Deanna. Sometimes you have to just watch the changes, try like hell to keep up, and improvise."

"I'm curious," she said. "Why didn't you just run the entire deception on one of the holodecks, instead of letting S'syrixx actually come aboard the *Armstrong*?"

"More than anything else, I needed to keep him calm. I wasn't sure how much knowledge he'd acquired about the ship's internal layout. If I'd tried to lead him onto a holodeck, he might have known he was being tricked. Besides, there would have been too much chance that he'd have noticed he was in a simulation—too much chance I'd completely lose control of the situation."

"Too much chance we'd end up having to kill him."

Riker gave her a solemn nod. "Confronting him with a single holographic element—a simulation of myself—was risky enough. Especially when he had his claws at Onnta's throat."

Right before Riker's eyes, Deanna's face abruptly went paler by nearly two full shades. "Deanna?"

The combadge on Riker's chest suddenly began to speak. *"Bridge to Captain,"* Vale said.

Riker tapped the badge. "Riker here, Chris. Go ahead."

"It appears we're going to have visitors, sir. And not the kind you'd want to invite over for dinner."

When it rains, it pours, he thought. "On my way."

13

"We haven't determined exactly how many of them are coming our way yet, Captain," Vale said as she relinquished the command chair to Riker and took the seat to its immediate right. "But we've detected at least two dozen warp signatures so far. They're all still at extreme range, but they're all definitely on a general heading for Vela OB2–404."

Wonderful, Riker thought, taking his seat. "How soon can we expect them?"

In answer to Vale's questioning glance, Tuvok quickly consulted his console and said, "ETA is approximately one standard day."

Riker allowed himself to frown. "Whose ships are they? More Gorn?"

"It's a mixed bag, sir," Vale said. "We're definitely reading Gorn warp signatures among them. But there are also Breen, Kinshaya, Tholian, Tzenkethi, and even Romulan readings in there as well."

"The entire Typhon Pact," Deanna said, standing beside her seat at Riker's left side. "Showing their colors."

Vale leaned toward Riker. "You don't suppose Starfleet just might come through for us with about that many reinforcements in, say, the next day or so?" she deadpanned.

"No," Riker said with a gallows chuckle. "Do you?"

"Of course not. Just making sure we're both on the same grim, fatalistic page as always. It's my way of fully embracing reality."

"Sometimes," Deanna said archly, "I'd prefer that reality and I just remain close platonic friends."

"One thing's for sure," Vale said, her tone suddenly sounding as serious as a heart attack. "If we're going to sneak an away team to Hranrar and back, the time to do it is *now.*"

The clock was ticking. The time for waiting had passed. Riker knew that if he were to abandon Hranrar in order to save *Titan* and her crew, no one would fault him for his decision. After all, all his other options involved more or less intolerable degrees of risk, particularly with an incoming Typhon Pact fleet only a day away.

So he made the obvious choice.

True to his word at the last senior staff meeting, Xin Ra-Havreii and his engineering team had devised an ingenious way to reach the surface of Hranrar with only the most minimal risk of detection by Captain Krassrr's terraforming flotilla.

Of course, Christine Vale would have felt a good deal more confidence in *Ra-Havreii*'s confidence were he beside her now, harnessed as she was into one of the seats aboard the shuddering, bucking shuttlecraft *Beiderbecke* as it made its ballistic descent to the nearest of the five small moons that orbited Hranrar, just beyond the planet's complex ring system.

A voice shouted out from the *Beiderbecke*'s forward section, barely audible over the rumbling of the shuttle as it aerobraked in the moon's surprisingly dense atmosphere. "Away team!" cried Ensign Olivia Bolaji, the shuttle pilot. "Are all of you still with me?"

To prevent straining her neck muscles by turning to look at her teammates during the jouncing deceleration, Vale contented herself with closing her eyes and listening to their responses.

Deanna Troi groaned, prompting Vale to imagine that she might soon need a change of uniform.

"This is fun," quipped Lieutenant Gian Sortollo from security. "I wanna go again."

Ensign Modan, the cryptolinguist, intoned a crisp, "Present!"

Ensigns Dakal and Evesh, sensor analyst and sensor technician respectively, seemed only able to make moist coughing sounds. It was probably getting a bit messy back there.

"Don't feel bad, kids," Vale said as she barely restrained her own stomach from performing an inconvenient triple lindy of its own. "You're in noble company. Some of Earth's first lunar explorers chundered all the way to the Moon and back." *It could be worse,* she told herself. *They could be yarking in microgravity.* The thought of blobs of vomit tumbling everywhichway in freefall almost made her join the chorus.

At that moment the *Beiderbecke* slammed hard into a particularly treacherous pocket of turbulence, which slammed Vale's teeth together painfully. *Why did I pick a shuttlecraft named after a self-destructive cornet player?* she thought, hoping that the choice wasn't subtle evidence that she was carrying a death wish. Her conscious intention had been to press the *Beiderbecke* back into the kind of service the little craft had performed the first time she'd been summoned out of *Titan*'s shuttlebay two: the mass rescue of aliens threatened with imminent destruction. She made a mental note to discuss the matter later with Deanna.

Assuming that either of them still had a later coming.

U.S.S. TITAN

When S'syrixx's senses returned to him, his first sensation was a feeling of intense astonishment even to be alive. He found himself in a semidarkened chamber, apparently alone. Despite the scant illumination, he could see well enough to judge it a living space, austerely decorated yet obviously inhabited by someone—living quarters no doubt designed for the comfort of *Tie-tan*'s mixed mammalian-reptiloid-alien crew. Realizing that he was lying supine on a large, surprisingly sturdy bed, he stood up and faced the nearest wall. His swift, sinuous movements placed him before a broad, rounded oblong window that displayed the star-strewn darkness into which he'd expected again to be cast.

Why hadn't the mammals taken the rational expedient of simply spacing him after what he had done? S'syrixx realized that his understanding of the mammal Rry'kurr was incomplete at best. Perhaps there was more to this creature than mere manipulation and deception, despite S'syrixx's most base-level expectations—and despite Rry'kurr's evident cleverness.

Was it possible that Rry'kurr's expression of concern for the imperiled Hranrarii had been sincere?

A flicker of movement at the base of the window caught his attention, and the scales on his dual cranial crests stood erect in response to his startle instinct. He felt foolish mere heartbeats later when he realized that the motion had come from a framed holographic image that someone—doubtless the room's usual occupant—had left perched on the narrow ledge at the window's bottom.

S'syrixx reached down and carefully lifted the frame to get a clearer look at the image within. He saw a pair of horn-headed reptiloid creatures, both of whom strongly resembled one of the non-mammals he had encountered in *Tie-tan*'s sickbay. The two beings faced each other in combat crouches, each clutching edged metal weapons. Every few heartbeats, the image would shift, depicting the duo engaging in what appeared to be a series of carefully choreographed combat exercises. Despite the obvious martial nature of the motions, S'syrixx saw none of the combat-fury that a Gorn war-caster might display during such activities.

A voice sounded behind him, startling S'syrixx yet again. "Her name was Sar Antillea." S'syrixx allowed the framed image to tumble to the carpeted floor as he turned to face the unexpected speaker. A barefoot yet Sst'rfleet uniform-clad reptiloid creature stood facing him from an entrance on the opposite side of the chamber, its short-clawed manus both spread before it in an *I'm-no-threat-to-you* gesture. S'syrixx inhaled deeply, but sensed no deception in the air, just as he saw no weapon on the creature's hip. Though he'd been exposed to the being's scent only once before, S'syrixx recognized it at once, along with its faint echoes, which he now noticed were part of the room's olfactory backdrop.

"Qontallium," S'syrixx said.

"Yes," the security officer said. "But you may feel free to address me by my first name. After all, we're kindred souls, at least in a manner of speaking. So you may call me 'Qur.' Welcome to my quarters. They will be yours for the duration of your stay aboard *Titan*."

S'syrixx nodded. "Thank you, Qurr," he said, maintaining his natural Gorn gutturality along with its tendency to transform many phonemes into protracted growls. He had always found it difficult to render non-Gorn names accurately without employing his caste-specific Voice talents to copy another speaker's pitch, emphasis, timbre, and rhythmic qualities. After his spectacular failure to get himself away from *Tie-tan* by replicating Rry'kurr's voice, he wasn't eager to call undue attention to his Voice abilities.

"I'm glad to see that you're none the worse for wear," Qontallium said, approaching S'syrixx slowly.

"I hope that is so," S'syrixx said drily. He lowered his guard somewhat, but not entirely. "Your captain dosed me with some sort of toxic gas. I am not certain exactly what it did to me."

"Doctor Ree has pronounced you fit. And speaking of the captain, he has authorized me to inform you of his decision regarding your formal request for asylum aboard *Titan*."

S'syrixx tensed. *Perhaps Rry'kurr allowed me to regain consciousness with such a spectacular view of trackless space,* he thought, *merely to tell me I'd have been better off had he simply allowed me to die out there in the first place.*

Bracing himself for the inevitable bad news, he said, "And what has Rry'kurr decided?"

"He has granted your request," Qontallium said in a tone

that suggested pride. "You will now receive the official diplomatic protection of the officers and crew of the *U.S.S. Titan,* Starfleet, and the United Federation of Planets. Provided that you—how did the captain put it? 'Mind your manners, behave yourself, and refrain from giving me any more goddamned grief' for the duration of this emergency."

S'syrixx tried not to display any surprise, allowing his ruffled crest-scales to settle down as he struggled to process the stunning news. Could any mammal—even one of such obviously exceptional cleverness as Rry'kurr—really possess such a surfeit of altruism? Or was this merely evidence of a hidden agenda? Though he was loath to say anything that might jeopardize his hosts' goodwill, S'syrixx couldn't resist probing the latter possibility, at least a little.

"Why did Rry'kurr send you to inform me of his decision?" he asked quietly, damping down the tone of challenge that his words suggested.

Qontallium's huge, ruby eyes blinked slowly in surprise. "Captain Riker is a very busy man."

"Of course," S'syrixx said. "I merely meant to ask why he sent you in particular, instead of, say, his . . . diplomatic officer." He had very nearly said "mate" instead of "diplomatic officer," since the pheromone emissions of both mammals had made the nature of their personal relationship abundantly clear; he'd decided to apply the latter term both out of simple prudence and because he didn't enjoy thinking about the rutting habits of mammals.

"I don't know," Qontallium said with a birdlike bob of the shoulders. "I didn't think to ask. Is it important?"

"It might be. But I believe I already know the answer. Rry'kurr placed me in your quarters—and therefore in your care—because he hopes I will form an interspecies bond with you that would be impossible for me to forge with him or with his m—"—S'syrixx paused to correct his near slipup—"his diplomatic officer."

Qontallium's shoulders bobbed again. "Sounds like a reasonable way to do the math. I'd probably do something similar if I were the captain."

S'syrixx chuckled. "Even in this grand Federrazsh'n of yours, what chance does a reptiloid like you really stand of gaining command of a vessel like this one?"

The ruby eyes narrowed in evident annoyance. "That's an excellent question, Mister S'syrixx. Maybe I'll ask Captain Sigrengar of the *Starship Galatea.* I'll be sure to bring it up the next time *Titan* rendezvouses with her ship, or when we're having shore leave at the same time—on our mutual homeworld of Gnala."

Whatever S'syrixx had planned to say next died forgotten before it got from his brain to his throat.

"Remember, Mister S'syrixx," Qontallium said, the horn atop the creature's head now standing taller and straighter than it had mere moments earlier. "The captain's decision to grant you a safe haven aboard *Titan* is not unconditional. He might be inclined to reevaluate your present immigration status should you create any more difficulties for him—such as that unfortunate incident in shuttlebay one. Likewise, you'd be wise not to regard a positive recommendation from me as a foregone conclusion simply because of our superficial biological similarities. I offered to loan you my quarters—not to become your default best friend. Do we understand each other, Mister S'syrixx?"

S'syrixx nodded, chastened. "I understand."

Could these Sst'rfleeters really be what they claimed to be? Were they truly concerned with the welfare of innocents like the Hranrarii? Were they actually as capable of delivering mercy and compassion to an adversary—one whose presence must have unnerved the mammals as much as the presence of so many mammals unnerved S'syrixx—as they were of dealing violence and cruelty? His own people's notable deficiencies made it difficult to believe in such notions, even as remote possibilities.

But even so . . .

Lowering his claws, S'syrixx took a tentative step toward Qontallium, but stopped when he realized he was about to tread directly on the framed holoimage he had dropped.

"What is the status of the Hranrarii?" he asked as he crouched and retrieved the framed image. "I hope that Krassrr still has yet to repair the damage I did to the ecosculptor."

"The Hranrarii civilization remains intact," Qontallium said. "But Captain Krassrr's crews are continuing to work around the clock on the terraforming artifact—what your people call the 'ecosculptor.' Hranrar remains in grave danger. An incoming Typhon Pact military fleet is only a day away. Once they arrive at Hranrar, there won't be much we can do to help the Hranrarii."

"I see," S'syrixx said. He digested the grim news, thankful at least that Krassrr had yet to extinguish the Hranrarii. Pensive, he stared at the holoimage he held in his manus, paying particular attention to the sword-wielding reptiloid who appeared to be fighting Qontallium. A question came to mind, though he suspected he already knew the answer.

"Who is Sar Antillea?"

The horn on Qontallium's head seemed almost to droop. The creature's ruby eyes quickly elided from pellucid anger to cloudy melancholy. "She is . . . she *was* . . . my mate."

S'syrixx grunted his understanding. Unbidden, an image of his beloved, lost Z'shezhira sprang to mind.

Qontallium approached S'syrixx closely and slowly took the holoframe from the Gorn's fingers. Moving with an almost ceremonial reverence, the security officer returned the object to its place of honor beneath the window.

"She was buried in space," the security officer said, only now tipping S'syrixx off that he was probably a male of his species. "It was what she'd always said she wanted, in the event she were to lose her life in the line of duty. Tradition, you see, would demand a riparian burial back home on Gnala. But she had always said she'd prefer to spend eternity amid infinity. That's probably why I like to keep her image here, right next to my own personal interface with that very same infinity."

"She served here? Aboard *Tie-tan*?"

"Yes. In my own department, security. She was a senior chief petty officer. To avoid any potential conflicts of interest, we made sure that she didn't have to answer directly to me. So she became part of Commander Keru's handpicked elite combat squad."

"She died defending *Tie-tan*?"

"During the Borg attack. Sar wasn't the only member of *Titan*'s crew that the Borg killed. Security was probably hit the hardest. We also lost Rriarr. Doron. Tane. Hutchinson. Seven others." The ruby eyes gazed past S'syrixx to the window, apparently fixed upon some extremely distant object.

S'syrixx felt a surge of sympathetic grief for Qontallium. He also experienced a flash of envy of Qontallium's definitive knowledge of his mate's demise; despite the grimness and finality of the fact, the security officer had at least obtained the kind of closure that S'syrixx was all but certain would forever elude him.

"The machine-mammals," he said. "I grieve with you."

Qontallium bowed his great horned head. "I thank you."

Something occurred to S'syrixx then: Whether these Federrazsh'n citizens were being sincere or cynical in their idealism, he *wanted* to believe as they apparently did. If his asylum petition was ever to be anything other than a last-ditch act of desperation, he *had* to believe—he had to back his request up with a statement of faith.

He sat heavily on the edge of the bed. "Would you convey a message to Rry'kurr for me?"

GORN HEGEMONY RECONNAISSANCE VESSEL *SSEVARRH*

As Krassrr emerged from his planning chamber, he nearly collided with a small, slight form. He growled and cocked a rigidly muscular arm, preparing to bat the quivering youngling out of his way. But he stayed his manus when he noticed that the obstacle was the same young techcaster who had approached him a short time ago with an overblown concern about some Hranrarii atmospheric phenomenon or other.

"What?" Krassrr roared, giving the youngling the benefit of the doubt.

"The ionization pattern I saw before has repeated itself, Captain," the tech-caster said.

"So what?"

"By itself, that may not be significant. This time, however, a subspace pulse accompanied the phenomenon. Or to be more precise, the pulse appeared moments after the ionization trail dissipated."

Now he calls it a trail, Krassrr thought. *And a trail implies a willful entity capable of leaving it—and with the capacity to transmit subspace signals.* His neck and crest scales rose into aggressive postures as he considered the possibility that the Federrazsh'n commander, Rry'kurr, may have yet again fooled him into believing he had withdrawn from the Hranrar system—only to sneak up on his flank like the furtive, scavenging mammalian vermin that he was.

But something about that scenario didn't quite sit right with Krassrr. "Why would the Sst'rfleet crew be so careless as to allow a subspace signal to be intercepted?"

"Perhaps they were insufficiently aware of the reflective properties of Hranrar's natural satellites."

Krassrr grunted. It was a stroke of luck he could hardly credit. Still, he wasn't about to look such unwonted good fortune in the maw. "Open a channel to the *Zzrorss,*" he said to the tech-caster. "Tell the comm officer there I have a new errand for his commander."

• • •

As he paced around his ready-room desk, Riker kept a weather eye on the chronometer on his computer terminal.

The door chime sounded.

"Come."

The door hissed open and admitted Commanders Tuvok and Ra-Havreii. In response to the captain's silent nod, the latter took a seat at one of the chairs in front of the desk, while the former remained standing at attention.

Something about the stiff manner of both men warned Riker that whatever his senior officers had to say was likely to be a mixed bag. "Report, gentlemen," he said as he took a seat behind his desk.

"Why don't you give him the good news first, Mister Tuvok?" the Efrosian chief engineer said wryly.

Riker flashed a hopeful smile at his tactical officer. "Don't tell me—the Typhon Pact fleet has suddenly changed its heading."

"To expect that would be excessively optimistic, Captain," Tuvok said. "However, we just received a subspace burst transmission from the away team, per the mission profile. The signal was more attenuated than I expected, but with the help of the main computer I was able to reconstruct its message quickly."

"And what did the message say?"

"Just that the away team has completed its passage to Hranrar without apparent incident. They seem to have eluded the detection of both the Gorn and the Hranrarii."

At least so far, Riker thought with no small amount of anxiety. Sending Deanna into danger had never sat well with him, but he had always known that his command responsibilities sometimes demanded it. She was *Titan*'s chief diplomat, after all; even if the mission involved only a covert form of alien contact, it nevertheless fell within her purview.

"Meaning that Captain Krassrr's terraforming fleet is still going about its business trying to repair the damage our resident Gorn did to Brahma-Shiva," Ra-Havreii added. "As my simulations predicted, they've shown no sign of having noticed our people's arrival on the opposite side of the planet."

"Therefore it may also be safe to assume that Krassrr's people failed to intercept the away team's subspace burst," Tuvok said.

Riker nodded. He hated being forced to rely so heavily on such brief "squirts" of information, but the interference that continued to foul so much of the subspace comm-spectrum throughout this system—not to mention simple prudence—gave him little alternative.

"Let's hope the away team's luck continues," he said. "Now what's the bad news?"

Tuvok's silently raised eyebrow was clearly a missile aimed in Ra-Havreii's direction.

"Besides the fact that the away team now has substantially less than a standard day to preserve whatever they can of a society that is all but marked for annihilation?" Ra-Havreii said.

Riker drummed his fingers on the desktop. "Go ahead, Commander. I can take it."

Ra-Havreii pulled a padd from the front pocket of his uniform tunic and slid it across the uncluttered desktop toward Riker. "Here's our preliminary tactical plan for boarding and neutralizing Brahma-Shiva."

"'Preliminary?'" Riker said as he picked up the padd and began scrolling through its contents. "I know that you and Commander Tuvok haven't had much time to work on this, but I was hoping we'd be a bit past 'preliminary' at this point."

Ra-Havreii shrugged, apparently unfazed by his CO's underwhelmed reaction. "I had the same hope, Captain. But we have to look at this realistically. Despite the luck we've had with passive, short-range drone scans, the metal in Brahma-Shiva's hull is extremely scan-resistant at a distance. And we can't do any further scans without alerting Krassrr that *Titan* is still hiding in the weeds, watching him. That platform has the potential to completely destroy the Hranrarii civilization—or at least it will once the Gorn get done fixing it. Whether or not they succeed in that effort any time soon isn't terribly relevant to us—assuming they don't manage to fire the thing up while our away team is still on Hranrar—because we're going to have to stay hidden or clear out of the system entirely when the Typhon Pact fleet arrives."

Riker scowled. "It sounds like you've given up," he said, addressing both men. He pushed the padd back toward the engineer.

"Not at all, Captain," Tuvok said, his countenance unyielding, his posture becoming even more ramrod straight than it had been a moment earlier. "We have merely acknowledged reality. To do less would be entirely illogical."

Ra-Havreii nodded as he recovered his padd. "Without the insight of somebody who really knows Brahma-Shiva inside and out, we're still only guessing at this thing's vulnerable spots. Even with the benefit of Mister S'syrixx's diagram, we're still not completely sure which parts of the beast's belly are safe to use as beam-in sites for Mister Keru's tac team."

Riker's combadge chirped, prompting him to tap it. "Riker here. Go ahead."

"It's Lieutenant Qontallium from security, sir," came the reply. *"Commander Troi asked me to inform you the moment Mister S'syrixx made any sort of friendly overture."*

"I take it he'd like to show his rescuers a little more gratitude?"

"I believe so, sir. Specifically, he's just offered to do whatever he can to help save the Hranrarii."

After signing off, Riker allowed himself to experience a brief surge of hope that the Hranrarii cause might not be lost after all. Despite the impressive package of information S'syrixx had produced before he went off the deep end and tried to return to Krassrr, Riker had felt from the beginning that his Gorn guest had been holding a great deal back. And why shouldn't he? He was, after all, a stranger in a strange land. Trust wouldn't come easily for the Gorn, and Riker knew he'd have to use every tool at his disposal to cultivate it—including guile.

When he considered how his decision to exploit S'syrixx's anxieties had led to a nearly disastrous encounter, he felt more than a little guilty about continuing to employ guile, however the exigencies of the moment might justify it. But Alyssa Ogawa and Dr. Ree had reported hearing S'syrixx talking in his sleep about a lost love, and Deanna had devised a plan to foster the Gorn's cooperation by keeping him in close proximity to Lieutenant Qontallium, who had suffered a similar loss during last year's Borg assault. Riker had felt uneasy about using such a manipulative technique on someone under his protection—even on an adversary, such as a Gorn national—until Qontallium himself had volunteered to do the job, despite being reminded that the task would force him to revisit his intense, still-healing grief over losing Senior CPO Sar Antillea during a Borg attack.

Riker rose to his feet. Addressing both Tuvok and Ra-Havreii, he said, "Have Lieutenant Qontallium set up a meeting with our guest, ASAP. I have a feeling he'll get your Brahma-Shiva assault plan past the 'preliminary' stage fairly quickly."

14

Vale felt a tingle of awe as she crested the hill and saw the forest of towers, minarets, tubular bridges, and glistening, raised waterways that lay beyond it. Spread like a prized collection of jewels beneath cloud-streaked, cerulean skies, the Hranrarii city rose from the endless marsh that surrounded it, extending to the limits of her vision toward the eastern horizon, and probably a good deal farther. A mighty river bisected the city, whose waterways sported a profusion of vehicles that gleamed in the golden afternoon brilliance of Vela OB2–404, which was making its inexorable march toward the western hills, at the away team's back.

The Hranrarii city, from its sky-piercing vertical scale to its vast network of natural and constructed subterranean water-channels that served as personal and vehicular transit connections to its nearest neighbors, was easily the equal of anything that any Federation world might have produced. But when Vale considered the likely future of this city—the probable fate of *all* Hranrarii constructs, everywhere on the planet—the awe the vista inspired quickly plummeted into a downward spiral of grief. *All of this could be reduced to quarks at any moment,* she thought. *Just to give the Gorn warrior caste a new place to lay its eggs.*

Ensign Modan, the cryptolinguist, was the first to

break the silence that had reigned ever since the city first came into view. "Soon it'll be as if none of this ever existed," she said. Like everyone else on the team, she now could pass—unless scrutinized very closely—for one of the green, gilled, moist-skinned, sentient amphibians who built and maintained the city.

"Whatever might become of the Hranrarii," said Troi, gesturing broadly toward the city with her webbed, lime-hued hands, "we have to make sure that all of this—everything they've achieved as a civilization—is never forgotten."

"And we have to cram that task into the span of a few hours," said Ensign Evesh, her brusque Tellarite manner setting her apart from the rest of the team despite the fact that everyone present looked almost indistinguishable from one another, thanks to Commander Ra-Havreii's specially modified isolation suits. Unlike an earlier generation of such suits, which used holographic technology to create a kind of functional invisibility—a sort of personal cloaking device—the chief engineer's variant model used that same technology to create a three-dimensional holographic disguise for its wearer.

"Let's stop here and check our holosystems for glitches before we go on," Troi said. "This could be our last chance before we get close enough to any of the natives to really put these suits to the test."

"Good idea, Deanna," Vale said. Hoping to lighten the team's dour mood, she approached the counselor, turning her ungainly amphibianoid body in a quick circle as she moved. "What do you think? Does this hologram make my butt look big?"

"Let's hope your butt is precisely as big as it needs to be so as not to attract the wrong kind of attention while we're down here," Troi said, speaking sotto voce as the junior officers began checking one another's suits. "Remember, Chris, it could always be worse."

Vale snickered quietly as she looked Troi's frog-and-grasshopper-chimera form up and down. "When have you ever looked worse than this?"

"About twelve years ago, aboard the *Enterprise*-D. I was probably a little more recognizable than I am now, but I certainly *felt* a lot worse."

"I take it you're not describing a typical bad hair day."

"It was more like the worst hair day imaginable," Troi said. "A mutant virus turned me into an ancient Betazoid amphibian. But maybe we ought to put the coiffure conversation aside. We're supposed to be passing ourselves off as natives, remember?"

"It's a little hard to forget," Vale said. She held one of her own holographically webbed hands before her eyes, which she knew looked just as oversized and yellow as Troi's now appeared to be. She tried to avoid catching sight of her hologram-enhanced lower body, which seemed to sport the grasshopperlike Hranrarii feature of redundant forward-and-backward knee joints; while this characteristic looked every bit as genuine as the rest of Vale's amphibious persona, she knew that it couldn't withstand a thorough inspection, such as a body search. And then there was the (potential) problem of the team's (perhaps) conspicuous lack of the tribal tattoos that S'syrixx had added to his visual depiction of the Hranrarii form, a decision Vale had made in an effort to sidestep the possibility of inadvertently offending any natives who might be aligned with a differently-tattooed social group. . . .

For those reasons, Vale had ordered the team to avoid close contact with the natives as much as possible. Her own law-enforcement experience told her that it would be particularly wise to avoid the local constabulary.

"I still don't understand why Olivia couldn't have beamed us down closer to the city," Evesh grumbled through her thick, fishlike lips once each and every one of the away team's isolation suits, along with their main and reserve power cells, had passed muster.

"I thought we already went through all that," Ensign Dakal said as he unhooked a tricorder from the belt that bisected his simulated native clothing, which consisted of little more than a complicated harness that seemed to have been designed for the express purpose of carrying things. With a deftness and grace that belied his large, webbed, and apparently three-fingered hands, the Cardassian activated the scanning device, pointing it toward the city.

"You don't have to be patronizing," Evesh said querulously. "I know that these holo-disguises won't stand up to close scrutiny, any more than a standard invisibility-equipped isolation suit would. And I'm more than passingly familiar with the Prime Directive, thank you very much. I understand that we're not supposed to frighten the pre-warp-drive natives by seeming to appear out of nowhere right before their eyes."

"So what's the problem?" Modan asked.

The Tellarite sighed. "Well, suppose a few natives *did* happen to see us materialize? How much damage could that really do here? What's the harm, really, when we're all operating under the assumption that this entire civilization probably won't be here by this time next week? Isn't following the letter of the Prime Directive in this situation a little like fretting about the sodium content of a condemned prisoner's last meal?"

Vale had to admit to herself that Evesh had made a good point. But in the interests of proper order and discipline, she wasn't about to agree with her out loud. "The Prime Directive doesn't give us that kind of leeway, Ensign. We don't have the discretion to say, 'these people will all be dead soon, so to hell with the rules.'"

"Besides, whatever might happen to this civilization tomorrow, they're here *today,*" Troi said. "And until the Gorn actually *do* wipe them out, there's always the hope that they'll survive this crisis somehow. The Prime Directive has to err on the side of optimism."

"Exactly," Vale said. *And sometimes even* foolish *optimism.*

Dakal apparently finished a sequence of scans and was reviewing the results on his tricorder's display. "Besides, Evesh," he said, "the best way to use our time is to tap directly into one of the city's data nodes. This city keeps its major data trunks near the outskirts, just like all the other cities we scanned from orbit. Which means we're better off approaching from the outside."

Evesh folded her froglike arms across her chest, her finned feet splayed in an aggressive stance. "The orbital scans weren't that clear-cut, Zurin, and you know it. There are more than a hundred cities like this one all across this planet, and each of those has hundreds of multiply cross-linked data hubs. You interpreted the readings to indicate that all the data hubs are located at the edges of the cities. But those energy readings coming from deep in the city cores created a lot of interference. The intensity of the planetary magnetic field could have distorted the readings as well."

"Enough to throw off Ensign Dakal's estimate about the location of the nearest data hub?" Vale wanted to know. This could be a problem.

Evesh drew her own tricorder and activated it. "I'm still picking up those interference readings. They're registering a lot more strongly here on the surface than they did when we scanned from orbit, and they're still muddying things quite a bit."

Dakal shrugged. "Which I suppose stands as proof that the nearest data hub is either precisely where I said it was," he said, "or somewhere else."

Vale sighed. Pointing toward the still-distant towers, she said, "There's only one way to find out who's right."

The energy readings Dakal had associated with a critical Hranrarii data hub turned out to lie about two hundred meters from the precise spot his tricorder had selected, as well as some thirty meters off the ground; the young Cardassian attributed the slight gap between theory and the real world to the combined effects of Hranrar's magnetic field and the interference-generating energy pulsations Evesh had detected coming from the deep core of the city. Dakal didn't let the slight discrepancy between his estimate and empirical reality discourage him. Factoring in Evesh's interference and local magnetism, the readings on Dakal's tricorder represented a highly fine-tuned estimate at best.

Dakal took the point climbing the narrow, apparently deserted tower that led to the node itself, with Evesh and Modan following close behind while the away team's non-technical personnel—Vale, Troi, and Sortollo—remained at the bottom of the tower to serve as lookouts, just in case a curious native should happen by.

Getting inside the small chamber that housed the node—the confined space was barely big enough to admit the entire trio at once—had been surprisingly simple, a mere matter of forcing a metal hasp open with brute strength. Dakal supposed the Hranrarii were an extremely honest people, materially speaking, since they seemed to have little use for complex locking mechanisms.

Once the team had crawled inside, Dakal wasted no time exposing the interior mechanism of the Hranrarii information node, which resembled a two-meter-long Cardassian cavegrub covered in a centimeter-thick layer of slimy, mucouslike material.

"It looks like organic technology," Evesh said. "Not unlike the bioneural gel packs that Starfleet uses to enhance computer performance. You were right, Ensign."

"Too bad I'm not a betting man," Dakal said as he opened his toolkit and began extracting a high-performance ODN cable that was already hooked into a series of high-capacity data modules, collectively capable of storing several hundred teraquads of information. "I could have collected a tidy sum."

"Don't count your *lek*s just yet," Evesh said, still running tricorder scans. "You still can't explain the interference coming from the city's interior any better than I can. And you don't know yet whether or not anything in your toolkit is compatible with the Hranrarii's information technology."

"I'll have a look at the interference issue later," Dakal said, preferring his own investigative approach to the Tellarite's more scattergun methodology. "As for the compatibility question, I can think of only one way to settle it." He raised the end of the ODN cable and brought it toward the slimy mass of the Hranrarii data hub's core, his eyes closed so he wouldn't have to watch himself touch the odious-looking thing.

Dakal felt a hand grasp his arm firmly, restraining him. He opened his eyes to see Modan holding him back. "What?"

"Wait just a moment," said the cryptolinguist. "All we know for certain about this . . . thing is that it's pulsing with energy. What we *don't* know is whether it's actually carrying any information."

Dakal scowled. "It certainly looks like an information hub to me. And to my tricorder. Not to mention the scanners aboard the *Beiderbecke.*"

"But those readings and the conclusions you've drawn from them could just be an artifact of the interference coming from inside the city," Evesh said.

Dakal thought he appreciated reasonable caution as much as the next person, but this was beginning to border on the absurd. "Oh, please."

Though the Selenean language expert was usually quiet, she was making it clear now that she had no intention of backing down. "Dakal, you might be about to tap into the main power-coupling for the entire city."

Dakal allowed himself to sit, splaying his webbed feet out as far as the chamber's limited space would permit. "All right. Just don't think I'm going to let you stick an arm or any other body part in there just to see if it's safe to do it."

"Don't worry about that," Modan said as she drew closer to the sluglike mass, while stopping short of actually touching it. She waved her tricorder just centimeters over the thing's slime-covered surface.

"What kind of scan are you running?" Evesh asked, saving Dakal the trouble. "And how can you tell whether or not you're dealing with a stream of data without actually tapping into it?"

"I've never seen a data conduit that was completely efficient," Modan said as she studied the device she clutched in her awkward-looking, froggish hands. "There's always at least a little bit of leakage. The bigger the data stream, the more leakage there is. And I only need a tiny amount of leakage to construct a quick Zipf plot."

Dakal frowned. He knew that Zipf plots dealt with a particular probability distribution, one in which the frequency of any point in a data set was inversely proportional to its rank in a frequency table.

"And what does a Zipf plot have to do with Gral's uppermost right teat?" Evesh said, saving Dakal the trouble.

Modan blinked several times in holographic-amphibian puzzlement as she continued her scan. "I suppose one might have to have a cryptolinguist's perspective to see the utility of what I'm doing. Zipf's Law underpins the basic operation of the universal translator, at least in part."

"I thought the UT worked by cross-comparing the

vocabularies and grammars of various languages," Dakal said.

"It does," Modan said. "But that isn't quite the whole story. The UT also looks for raw statistical relationships to which a simple Zipf plot might be applicable. Even before the translator understands a word of a new language, it calculates the relative frequency of word occurrences. The UT's basic Sato algorithms assume that all natural sentient languages have essentially the same Zipf distribution with regard to the words, phonemes, or pictograms that make them up."

"But that rule doesn't always hold true," Evesh said.

Modan assayed a salamanderlike shrug. "Of course not. But it holds up often enough to make a pretty good general rule of thumb. For languages, it works more or less this way: 'The' is the most frequently occurring word in Federation Standard and accounts for about seven percent of all word occurrences in that language, so we can place that word in the first rank. 'Of' comes in at the second rank, or second most frequent in occurrence, with a percentage frequency of three-and-one-half percent—roughly half the frequency of the first-rank word. And so on and so on, down the list of frequency rankings. Most humanoid languages fall into this pattern, more or less."

Dakal thought he was beginning to understand. "It's a way of determining that an actual language—whether understood or not—is being spoken."

"Yes," Modan said. "As opposed to a bunch of subsentient vocalizations."

"So by applying the same formula to whatever is pulsing through this conduit," Dakal said, gesturing toward the slime-covered bioneural apparatus, "you can distinguish a uniform stream of electrical energy from ordered, information-rich content—without necessarily having to understand that content."

"Fortunately, we'll be able to translate any such content later, once we're far away from here, provided we can copy it from the source," Modan said. "But if this conduit is carrying, say, raw electro-plasma system power, it won't show any such pattern, and therefore will yield nothing but a potentially lethal shock. In that case, the Zipf plot I am compiling will settle in at a value close to zero."

"So, an active EPS feed would plot out as information-null," Dakal said. "But if this conduit carried, say, the collected works of Ulan Corac, it would have a Zipf value of one."

"More or less," Modan said, waggling one webbed hand.

"Faugh," Evesh said. "Corac is an author that only a universal translator algorithm would find readable."

Dakal ignored the jibe, concentrating instead on watching over the Selenean's shoulders as her tricorder gradually gathered and processed whatever data points it could glean short of Modan risking any physical contact with the hub's slick surface.

Modan turned toward Dakal, her thick green holographic lips parting in a broad, blunt-toothed smile. "It appears you were right, Zurin," she said. "Go ahead and plug in—but do it carefully."

The Selenean backed away, giving Dakal full access to the glistening data node. Moving gingerly, he pushed the end of his cable into the pulsating mass; the cable's end sank into the spongy node with a vaguely nauseating wet sucking sound. Once the cable seemed firmly attached, he activated the storage modules, which immediately began soaking up data at the ragged edge of their maximum rate.

"Let's hope I don't burn anything out," Dakal said, focusing on the swiftly blinking lights that showed the ferocious speed with which Hranrar's planetary information stream was filling his data modules. Although the modules were capable of capturing prodigious amounts of data, Dakal noted with melancholy that he could capture at best only a tiny fraction of the planet's informational output. He knew that what he was gathering was of critical importance, to be sure. It was, after all, part of a unique sapienogenic digital noösphere that might very soon represent the last trace and cultural epitaph of the entire Hranrarii civilization.

But it was only a very small part. Dakal tried to imagine the fruits of his own civilization being subjected to such a terrible cultural bottleneck, with only the short stories of Ulan Corac surviving in complete form. Galactic scholars might be confined to sheer speculation regarding the significance of Corac's long-form repetitive epics; *The Never-Ending Sacrifice,* widely hailed as the finest novel in the history of Cardassian literature, might exist only in fragmentary form, or as a woefully inadequate description in some half-corrupted library index or literary abstract. Even the horrendous destruction wrought by the Dominion had failed to bring Cardassia to such a pass.

Dakal's tricorder emitted a shrill tone that hauled him out of his unpleasant reverie and back into the here and now. Seeing that the data modules were already nearly full, he began the process of shutting them down and disconnecting them. Then he noticed that something else was happening as well.

The sluglike data hub had begun . . . *writhing.*

"I'm no information systems expert," Modan said. "But I'm fairly certain it's not supposed to do that."

The writhing abruptly stopped. The ambient lighting inside the hub chamber, which had been present ever since the team's entry as a soft glow with no obvious source, abruptly faded into near-darkness.

"Oh, shit," Dakal said as he grabbed up his data modules and disengaged the cable. He heaved a sigh of relief when he saw that the storage devices had indeed grabbed a large chunk of Hranrarii data, on the order of two hundred teraquads' worth. Who knew what cultural treasures, literature, music, treatises on politics and science, might emerge from this mass of digital chaos once Modan and *Titan*'s other cryptolinguists had their way with it?

After stowing the data modules and the cable in his toolkit, Dakal saw that Modan was passing her tricorder over the apparently lifeless data hub. "It reads like a dead or burned-out bioneural gel pack. The datatap must have tripped some sort of failsafe, shutting this hub down. The network appears to have compensated by bypassing this node entirely. It's only one of thousands, after all."

Dakal experienced a frisson of disgust as he realized that his efforts may have just killed a living thing—perhaps even a sentient being, judging from the sophistication of the hub's function as an organic router of prodigious amounts of data.

"Zurin!" Evesh said, preempting Dakal's ruminations

with all the subtlety of a crashing shuttlecraft. Though Evesh had his full attention, she was too busy studying her tricorder's display to make eye contact with him. "You know those readings I got from orbit, and the ones I took from just outside the city?"

"I got the same readings," Dakal said. "But I had to screen them out in order to track down a usable data hub, remember?"

"Of *course* I remember," Evesh huffed. "But I've been *studying* the interference patterns, rather than simply screening them out. They were starting to look familiar to me before, but now that I can compensate for both the planetary magnetic field and the local effects of the data hub, the patterns look *really* familiar. Tell me what you think of this." She handed her tricorder to Dakal, who promptly began blinking at the display in disbelief.

Now that the mysterious emanations from the city's deep interior were no longer being obscured by the output of the now-defunct data hub, a pattern had emerged, one that anyone with some basic engineering experience would recognize instantly.

The sudden dryness in Dakal's throat belied his moist, amphibious appearance. "We have to get this to Commander Vale," he said. *"Right now."*

15

GORN HEGEMONY WARSHIP *S'ALATH*

A sinking feeling was developing in the pits of Z'shezhira's stomachs as she watched the tactical display, which showed one of Captain Krassrr's six vessels separating itself from the others. Not wishing to rouse First Myrmidon Gog'resssh's ever-more-easily-roused suspicions, she dutifully reported the development the moment she noticed it.

"I have confirmed it, First Myrmidon," Second Myrmidon Zegrroz'rh said moments later, his ruined compound eye seeming to stare into Z'shezhira's soul though she knew this to be an utter impossibility. "One of Krassrr's ships is breaking formation, moving away from the ecosculptor. It's the *Zser'resz,* Krassrr's best-armed vessel."

"Heading?" Gog'resssh demanded from the middle of the command deck.

"It's coming toward this hemisphere," Sk'salissk said from the helm console.

Gog'resssh pounded the arm of his chair, splitting it as though it were a cord of dunewood. "Have they detected us?"

"Negative," Z'shezhira said, focusing on her scanner's readouts. The *Zser'resz*'s trajectory suggested that the vessel might be seeking the source of the two subspace pulses she had detected earlier in the ship's day; Z'shezhira wasn't certain, but she thought they might have originated on one of Hranrar's five small moons, or else had been bounced off one of the satellites on its way elsewhere.

She hoped that Gog'resssh wouldn't act rashly—or at least not so rashly that he got everyone aboard the *S'alath* killed. But she knew how badly shipboard supplies had dwindled of late. The Gorn war-caster requirement for live food greatly constrained the size of each supply raid the *S'alath*'s de facto crew could conduct in its endless search for sustenance; therefore such raids had to be undertaken fairly frequently.

If Gog'resssh and his cronies wait much longer, she thought with an inward shiver, *then they will scarcely be able to restrain themselves from consuming me and the other technical personnel they have seized along with this vessel.*

Z'shezhira looked up from the tactical display and stepped into the harsh glare of Gog'resssh's insect-eyed gaze. "Call the auxiliary-craft team," he said as he rose from his partially wrecked command chair. "Tell them we must move immediately to take what we require from Krassrr's main supply vessel. We may never have a better opportunity."

Z'shezhira nodded, grimly aware that she, too, would soon have an unprecedented chance to do what had to be done. . . .

SHUTTLECRAFT *BEIDERBECKE*

"Welcome back to your own phylum," Ensign Olivia Bolaji shouted from the cockpit once the transporter's shimmer had finished dissipating.

"Ribit," Commander Vale said, reaching for the hidden control stud that caused her holographic Hranrarii disguise to vanish; her plain red isolation suit was once again in neutral mode. The rest of the away team immediately did likewise and began stripping off their isosuits while Vale made her way forward to the copilot's seat.

"I take it the mission was a success, Commander?" Bolaji said, turning her pilot's seat away from the aquamarine planet that dominated the forward windows in order to face the exec.

"I suppose that depends how you define success, Ensign," Vale said without looking up from the console into which she was already entering commands at a furious rate. A glance at Vale's console displays told Bolaji that Vale was preparing to send another subspace burst to *Titan,* probably consisting mostly of a preliminary after-action report. "The Hranrarii are still on the chopping block, even if they don't realize it. And the ax is getting closer to their collective necks hour by hour."

"But I'm guessing you succeeded in penetrating one of their data networks," Bolaji said, determined to remain hopeful in spite of the dire threat she knew would probably wipe this world from existence. As far as she was concerned, hope was its own justification, no matter how bad any given situation might look.

"We took as much Hranrarii data as Ensign Dakal could carry," Vale said as she connected her tricorder to the console and continued working the controls.

"Of course, we don't have any idea as yet what's in that huge pile of data," said Commander Troi, who had just advanced from the amidships crew compartment, her isosuit replaced with a standard duty uniform. "For all we know, Ensign Dakal's data modules could be filled with things that would embarrass a Hranrarii college student if his parents were to catch him looking at them."

Bolaji suppressed a snicker. She was no information systems expert, but from what she recalled of the history of computational technologies, the initial iteration of Earth's global infonets was all but dominated by prurient, if not outright pornographic, imagery and text.

"We can only hope," Vale deadpanned as she entered the "transmit" command. "I've just given *Titan* a little taste of what we found on Hranrar." She turned to face Bolaji, drawing her gaze. "Now we just have to get back to the ship so I can fill the captain in on all the fine details."

"You've got it, Commander," Bolaji said, and began laying in a course that would retrace the *Beiderbecke*'s inbound steps, tracing a route back to *Titan*'s Kuiper-belt hiding place while remaining discreetly out of the Gorn terraforming flotilla's line of sight.

Bolaji was half finished entering the necessary commands when an automated klaxon sounded. She responded by making a quick check of the passive scanners.

"Uh-oh," she said.

Then the first incoming salvo rang the *Beiderbecke*'s hull as though it were a colossal bell, nearly drowning out the shriek of the alarm.

U.S.S. TITAN

Riker leaned against the railings of the catwalk that bisected the stellar cartography lab. Beside him stood his chief engineer. Both men looked up at a synthetic vista of the Vela OB2–404 system, in whose glowing, dust-and-debris-peppered midst *Titan*'s senior science officer floated like some mythological sky goddess.

"Sorry about the delay, Captain," said Melora Pazlar. "But I wanted to triple-check Commander Vale's latest message the moment I saw Ensign Evesh's diagram attachment. Looks like my first impression was right. There's no longer any doubt about it."

"There never *was* any doubt about it," groused Ra-Havreii. "We both had the very same first impression, Melora. This *is* my field of expertise, after all."

Riker tried to suppress a sour frown, but failed. Were these two merely engaging in a robust argument as scientific colleagues, or were they having some sort of lover's spat?

"There's no longer any doubt about *what*?" the captain said.

"About the fact that this one diagram changes *everything,*" Pazlar said. With a wave of her hand, a dynamic, oscillating line drawing suddenly appeared, cutting a jagged swath across the majesty of the lab's holographically-rendered cosmos.

At first glance, it looked like a painting of a zodiacal constellation executed by a lunatic. But Riker quickly understood that this was only because it was cast against a backdrop of black space and its abundant embroideries of multicolored stars. The realization made him see the lines as an energy pattern not unlike those he had seen produced by medical diagnostic equipment, or seismographs, or even warp-field monitoring devices.

"In what way?" Riker said. Why did science officers find it so difficult to come straight to the point?

"You may recognize this as the signature of a warp drive," Pazlar said. "It appears to be produced by a warp core of considerably less power than those typically found aboard Federation starships. I'd say its maximum velocity output probably tops out at warp six."

"Closer to warp five, or possibly five-point-one," Ra-Havreii said. "It reminds me of the Henry Archer designs I studied back in grad school."

"This pattern was attached to Commander Vale's last subspace burst?" Riker said. Though he already knew from the last burst that Christine, Deanna, and the rest of the team were already on their way back to *Titan* from Hranrar, he was nevertheless beside himself with questions about their apparently successful mission.

"Yes, Captain," Pazlar said. "And Xin and I were as surprised as you are by the warp signature Ensign Evesh picked up on Hranrar."

"As far as anybody knows, the Hranrarii have never ventured into space, with or without warp drive," Riker said. "So this warp signature must belong to somebody else. Could the Gorn have been idling one of their ships on or near the planet's surface without us knowing about it?"

Ra-Havreii pointed up at the solar-system-spanning diagram with a shake of his head that made his long white mustachios sway like slender tree-limbs in a gale. "No, Captain, this appears to be a home-grown Hranrarii phenomenon."

This made no sense. "Explain."

"First, the Gorn aren't in the habit of using Archer-style

antique engines," Ra-Havreii said. "And second, Ensign Evesh reported that this pattern came from deep in the interior of one of the Hranrarii cities."

"And that's why it changes everything," Pazlar said as she descended toward the catwalk in a gentle glide.

Understanding struck Riker with the finality of a guillotine blade. "The Hranrarii must use controlled, force-field-mediated matter-antimatter annihilation in the central power plants for their cities. Too bad Mister S'syrixx didn't remember to include this little detail in his initial report."

Pazlar shrugged. "I wouldn't necessarily read anything sinister into that, Captain. Perhaps he didn't know about it, or didn't consider it worth mentioning."

"Warp power is certainly the best explanation I can find for the apparent material wealth of the Hranrarii," Ra-Havreii said. "At least judging from the images the away team attached to their last subspace burst. What I don't understand is why they never saw fit to apply this technology to its most obvious use—powering superluminal starships."

"Maybe that application isn't as universally obvious as we'd like to think it is," Pazlar said.

Riker looked up at the warp-field diagram through narrowed eyes. "You'd think we would have detected a warp signature like that from a long way off. Why didn't we notice this before an away team stumbled across it?"

"You'd think that the Hranrarii's warp emissions would be detectable from orbit, or even from across the system," Pazlar said with a nod. "But Ensigns Evesh and Dakal seem to have accounted for that as well. They've hypothesized that the planetary information network works in tandem with Hranrar's magnetic field to create an interference pattern that conceals subterranean warp signatures almost completely."

Ra-Havreii nodded. "And that can't be an accident. For this society to remain as peaceful as it appears to be, it must have taken measures not to attract undue attention. Otherwise it would have been preyed upon by warp-capable species who don't possess the Hranrarii's reticence about building starships."

"Unfortunately, merely keeping a low profile isn't always enough to keep people out of harm's way," Pazlar said with a melancholic expression.

Riker looked away from the hovering diagram, fixing his gaze instead on his senior science officers. "As fascinating as all of this is, I'm not sure why you keep saying it changes everything."

Looking mildly incredulous, Pazlar exchanged a quick glance with Ra-Havreii before replying. "Don't you see, Captain? The fact that the Hranrarii possess warp technology completely changes *Titan*'s duty toward this civilization vis-à-vis the Prime Directive."

"How? The Hranrarii still don't have any interstellar spaceflight capability. Hell, as far as anyone can tell they haven't even put an artificial satellite into orbit yet."

"Correct me if I'm wrong, Captain," Ra-Havreii said. "But doesn't the Prime Directive set *warp capability* as its main criterion for first contact?"

Riker nodded. "It does. But I think it also assumes that that development always coincides with warp-driven space travel."

"Well, whether the drafters of the Prime Directive assumed that or not," Ra-Havreii said, "the Hranrarii civilization stands as empirical proof that the assumption is wrong—or, at the very least, needs to be reexamined."

"I don't think I have the authority to do that," Riker said. "Starfleet Command takes a dim view of officers who legislate from the captain's chair."

"May I speak freely, Captain?" Ra-Havreii asked.

"Go ahead. And that applies to both of you."

The Efrosian stroked his pale chin as he gathered his thoughts. At length, he said, "Whether anybody serving aboard *Titan* understands it or not, there's one central principle this vessel stands for: honest confrontation with our deepest, least-examined prejudices and biases."

Riker nodded during the engineer's pause. He couldn't quarrel with anything Ra-Havreii had said so far, having already encountered—and, he hoped, subsequently removed—the ugly stain of prejudice on his own soul. That stain had not been evident to him until his first meeting with Dr. Ree, whose predatory, dinosaurlike appearance the captain had found intensely disturbing—at least at the beginning of his working relationship with *Titan*'s Pahkwa-thanh CMO, nearly three years ago.

"I'm no legal expert, sir," Ra-Havreii continued. "I'm just a lowly, hairy engineer. But I feel very strongly that the actual building and flying of starships shouldn't be the main consideration here. It *can't* be."

Pazlar was nodding vigorously. "I agree. Demonstrating warp-drive *capacity*—which really amounts to little more than sustaining and harnessing the mutually annihilative reaction of matter and antimatter, as the Hranrarii have done—is what determines whether a culture has attained warp *capability*."

"And the presence of warp capability cancels out a society's Prime Directive protection," Ra-Havreii said. "Because it signals that the world in question has reached the first contact threshold. Insisting that the threshold can only be crossed via a space vessel—well, that's just another human . . ." The engineer trailed off, his already pale complexion becoming even paler, as though he feared he may have said too much.

"Xin, I *did* give you permission to speak freely," Riker said with a gentle smile. "Go ahead and spit it out."

Ra-Havreii nodded. "I was going to say that the default expectation that the development of warp technology always follows a faster-than-light trajectory is just another unexamined prejudice. It may be a prejudice that the Prime Directive's drafters weren't even aware they had, but it's a prejudice nonetheless. A bias that every Federation member has shared without question, more or less, since the signing of the Federation Charter."

"Whether we think of it as a prejudice or a bias or an erroneous assumption," Pazlar said, "I think we can all agree that it's one of those things that *Titan* is all about challenging."

My God, Riker thought as he tried the notion on for size. He now wished more than anything that he hadn't made Deanna part of the away team; he could really use her counsel at the moment.

"Do you two have any idea what you're *actually* suggesting?" he said. "What it really means for *Titan*? For *all* of us?"

"I think so, sir," said Pazlar, looking glum. "It may be that you are no longer enjoined from intervening on behalf of the Hranrarii."

Ra-Havreii nodded in agreement, his mien as solemn as Riker had ever seen it. "I'm inclined to agree, Captain. But there's an even graver implication."

Riker nodded, his brow crumpling under the weight of his new knowledge and responsibility. "This might not be just a matter of my no longer being forbidden to act. I may be *required* to take action of some kind to stop the Gorn from wiping out the Hranrarii."

"I don't see how Starfleet could hold you to that," Pazlar said, a look of deep concern creasing her porcelain features. "I hope nobody needs to remind you that *Titan* is hiding out from a Gorn fleet at the moment. To say nothing of the incoming Typhon Pact armada that'll be breathing down our Bussard collectors by tomorrow."

"And add to that the fact that we can't count on any Starfleet reinforcements to come to our rescue," Ra-Havreii said.

"There's only so much Starfleet can expect of *Titan,*" Pazlar said. "Or her captain."

"She's right, sir. *Titan* is just one ship up against a multitude of others. You're just one captain. We're just one crew."

One ship, Riker thought. *One crew.*

Even though he was responsible for the safety of both, he couldn't restrain himself from imagining that one ship plowing straight into Brahma-Shiva on a high-warp suicide trajectory. How many millions of Prime Directive-emancipated Hranrarii lives might he save in a single stroke by taking this single precipitous—and final—action?

If no better means of saving the Hranrarii presented itself between now and the moment the Gorn activated the planet-altering device, could he live with himself afterward if he ultimately decided to do anything less? Could he really settle for the option of lodging ineffectual after-the-fact complaints with the Gorn Hegemony over its act of genocide against the Hranrarii?

Starfleet Command might very well commend his decision to save *Titan* and her crew—not to mention Riker's own family!—under the assumption that the Hranrarii simply couldn't be saved, given the present circumstances.

Gripping the railing before him as though he were in danger of tumbling upward from the catwalk's surface and into the lab's sprawling holographic cosmos, Riker felt far from certain that he could grant himself that same consideration.

A voice from his combadge startled him out of his musings. *"Captain, I just picked up a fragmentary signal from the* Beiderbecke," said Lieutenant Lavena. *"Their communications are being jammed at the source, but it's pretty clear that they're under attack."*

He tapped the combadge, then vaulted over the catwalk's railing as he spoke, trusting the lab's variable-gravity field to bring him to a soft landing. "Red Alert! And make best speed to the *Beiderbecke.*"

SHUTTLECRAFT *BEIDERBECKE*

"Get us out of here, Ensign!" Vale shouted, trusting Bolaji to do what was necessary while she concentrated on the comm system's controls. She disabled the insanely loud alarm klaxon, then fired up the comm.

"*Beiderbecke* to *Titan*! The Gorn have found us." She heard only a burst of static in reply.

The goddamned lizards are jamming us, Vale thought, watching as the once-placid planetscape swung crazily across her forward field of view, disappearing and reappearing in response to Bolaji's frenzied maneuverings along all three of the shuttlecraft's axes of motion. A greenish, angular, multi-nacelled vessel whose hull plating vaguely resembled reptilian scales appeared intermittently in Vale's field of view, its forward tubes exuding a baleful red glow that became visible in between the harsh white flashes from the Gorn ship's disruptors.

The *Beiderbecke* rocked and shimmied; Vale's stomach lurched in sympathy a split-second between the impact and the intervention of the shuttlecraft's inertial dampers, which Bojali's constant pitching, yawing, and spinning were already straining past their limits.

"Shields are down to twenty percent," Bolaji said as yet another energy barrage struck the shuttle with the force of a giant fist. "I'm afraid that first salvo really caught me with my pants down."

"Returning fire," Vale said, deciding she had no energy to spare on recriminations. She put aside her efforts with the comm system, switching instead to the tactical displays. "Deanna! Keep trying to raise *Titan.*"

"Are you sure that's wise, Chris?" Troi said from the aft cockpit console she had just occupied. "We'd be giving away *Titan*'s presence here."

"That train left the station the moment the Gorn found

us," Vale said as she engaged the *Beiderbecke*'s phaser-lock, which made contact long enough to score a brief but well-placed hit on the Gorn vessel's forward ventral area. "They already know that a short-range vessel like this one couldn't get this far from Federation space without a mothership hiding somewhere nearby. And the *Beiderbecke*'s markings ought to make it clear enough to Captain Krassrr which mothership that is."

Vale fired the phasers again, to little effect. The gauges and telltales on the tactical console were presenting ominous portents. "Damn. We're losing power."

As if in answer to Vale's words, the cockpit lights suddenly dimmed to a fraction of their usual brightness.

"I've just lost warp drive," Bolaji said. "Impulse engines and maneuvering thrusters are also failing."

Undeterred, Vale initiated a bypass to reroute emergency battery power to the tactical systems. The phasers remained dead, but the shuttlecraft's sole photon torpedo launcher showed as operational. She wasted no time arming it and loading the tube with the first of the *Beiderbecke*'s compliment of two photon torpedoes. The target lock was apparently fried, so she aimed by pure dead reckoning. When she was ready, she slammed her fist onto the icon marked "fire."

Vale felt the *Beiderbecke* shudder slightly from the recoil. "Torpedo one, away," she said. Without pausing to check the departing missile's trajectory, she loaded the second, then repeated the firing procedure.

This time the torpedo's gentle recoil was replaced by a violent, if momentary, shaking.

"Another disruptor hit," Bolaji said, her tone steely and

businesslike despite the dire circumstances. "Shields are down. Main power and secondaries are both out."

Every internally illuminated cockpit instrument winked out for a split second, along with the overhead lights. Vale checked her hiccupping tactical console, which would have been as black as space had the internal batteries not just kicked in.

"Oh, shit." The second torpedo hadn't made it out of the tube, which was evidently no longer in operational condition.

And the torpedo, along with its armed and ready antimatter payload, was lodged in the damaged launch mechanism.

"Olivia, I'm taking over at the stick," Vale told the pilot as she reconfigured her console for the task. "Help Deanna get everybody to the transporter. Sortollo, wrangle the emergency evac kits. Dakal, grab those data modules.

"We have to abandon ship, and *fast.*"

GORN HEGEMONY WARSHIP *S'ALATH* AUXILIARY VESSEL *DEWCLAW*

As far as Gog'resssh was concerned, the sudden and unexpected departure of one of the ecosculpting fleet's best-armed vessels—on a heading that would take it far from the *S'alath*'s hiding place in the planet's northern magnetic shadow—could have been a sign from divine S'Yahazah herself.

Gog'resssh allowed his second, the half blind Zegrroz'rh, to pilot the *Dewclaw* out of the *S'alath*'s ventral landing bay and into the far southeastward extremity of Hranrar's intense magnetic field.

"Hold position here," Gog'resssh said from his position in the cramped cockpit, crouched directly behind Zegrroz'rh as the second worked the pilot's console with plodding deliberation. Five warriors fidgeted behind them, spoiling for action. "Any closer and we may become all too visible, even to distracted eyes."

"Holding position, First Myrmidon," the pilot said, angling the thrusters to null out the *Dewclaw*'s forward acceleration. "Our unwitting resupply ship awaits our pleasure."

Determined to remain as serious in his focus as possible, Gog'resssh ignored his underling's guttural chuckles. He turned and took several loping steps until he reached the console near the auxiliary craft's small transporter stage. *We have drawn close enough to our target to be in danger of discovery,* he thought. *But are we still too far away to achieve our objective?*

Seeking a definitive answer to that question, he began synchronizing the transporter's targeting scanners to the standard deflector-shield frequency of a Gorn military recon vessel. . . .

GORN HEGEMONY WARSHIP *S'ALATH*

Although more than a suncircuit's worth of careful, clandestine planning was about to come to fruition—and though all the necessary components were in place to assure a successful outcome—an intense sensation of foreboding assailed Z'shezhira's innards.

As she sat watching her station on the command deck, she felt cold, unable to believe that the prospect of her long-dreamt-of reunion with S'syrixx might finally have drawn near enough to be within claw's reach.

But it was true. Mad Gog'resssh was now off the ship, for however briefly, along with his hideous second-in-command, Zegrroz'rh, and several others. Moreover, three of Gog'resssh's strongest war-caster subordinates had accompanied him on his little "shopping expedition" among the ecosculpting fleet. Never before had First Myrmidon Gog'resssh permitted the ranks of those who held the figurative shackles of the *S'alath*'s surviving complement of tech-casters to grow so thin. Gog'resssh had trusted her to help maintain order during his absence, and that error was to be his downfall.

Assuming that I do not lose heart before our captors return, Z'shezhira thought, struggling to keep her escalating fear invisible to the lone war-caster who was present with her on the command deck. Did Sk'salissk, Gog'resssh's helm officer, have any inkling of the turmoil she was barely managing to contain?

All I have to do is wait for the signal, she thought. The silent, mostly dimmed console before her would display a prearranged pictogram, sent surreptitiously by Vrezsarr, the engineer. *Then I have to do what must be done.*

The signal would come, and she would rise quietly and approach the helm officer, but she would take care not to do so stealthily. There was no point, after all, in alerting Sk'salissk of what was to come by acting as though she were doing something untoward and trying to conceal that fact.

She had seen the way Sk'salissk had been looking at her lately, despite the ingrained taboo against mating across caste boundaries. Fortunately, the helmrunner was a junior officer, and had interpreted her frequent proximity to Gog'resssh as an imperative to maintain an appropriate distance. But with the *S'alath*'s commander off the ship, she might catch Sk'salissk off guard by casually brushing against him as she passed his station. Thus distracted, the young war-caster wouldn't see the end coming before it was too late. And since they were the only individuals present on the command deck at the moment, neither would anyone else.

His death would come, S'Yahazah willing, courtesy of the small chemical injection-ampule she was even now concealing in her loosely closed left manus. Zzerrhezz, a fellow infirmary medic, had been able to synthesize only a very limited quantity of the substance in the ampule, so she knew she would have only one opportunity to use it.

Provided, of course, that Vrezsarr the engineer sent her the appropriate "go" signal, thus alerting her that he had just similarly dispatched his own specified war-caster target, further diminishing Gog'resssh's skeleton crew.

After that, everything would depend on whether she could summon the nerve to rise and cover the few short steps that separated her post from Sk'salissk's without giving him sufficient advance warning to enable him to evade or resist her attack.

She willed her left manus to stop shaking, but the effort met with only partial success.

Just when she was beginning to wonder whether something had gone terribly wrong down in the engine room, Vrezsarr's icon appeared on her panel like a silent apparition. Her fellow tech-caster had taken an irrevocable action, one that would surely get him killed—and might even get *her* killed as well—should she fail now to do her part before Gog'resssh and his raiding party returned to the *S'alath.*

Steeling herself and her flagging courage one last time, Z'shezhira rose from her seat and moved toward her target.

SHUTTLECRAFT *BEIDERBECKE*

With a quick glance over her shoulder, Vale confirmed that the small transporter stage was clear. She breathed a silent prayer that the rest of the away team had materialized on the planet's surface without incident—and that the emergency batteries that had powered the team's beam-out would continue to function for the few precious additional moments she needed.

Vale had one last task to complete before she'd get the chance to find out. Bringing the shuttlecraft abruptly about, she locked the helm on a collision course with the Gorn vessel, which arced high above Hranrar's dayside surface. Each of the aggressor ship's glowing forward disruptor tubes gaped like the maw of a leviathan as the gap between the two ships closed rapidly.

Almost simultaneously, Vale entered two final commands: the timed detonation of the photon torpedo that remained lodged in the *Beiderbecke*'s launcher, and the transporter's Mayday ENERGIZE command.

Half a heartbeat later, a shimmering curtain of light appeared, immediately followed by a flash of optic-nerve-searing brilliance.

U.S.S. TITAN

"Mister Tuvok!" Riker shouted as he leaned forward in his command chair. "How long until we're within weapons range?"

"Twenty-two seconds, Captain," came the Vulcan's crisp response.

"We're within visual of the *Beiderbecke,* sir," Lieutenant Rager said from ops.

"On screen."

The coin-sized but rapidly growing disc of Hranrar on the forward viewer abruptly vanished, replaced by a high-resolution image of a Starfleet shuttlecraft trading salvoes of weapons fire with an aggressively-postured warship that had a long, narrow primary hull and at least four clearly identifiable engine nacelles.

"Ten seconds until weapons range," said Tuvok.

"Ready phasers, Commander," Riker said.

The shuttlecraft abruptly switched from evasion to a pursuit trajectory that appeared to bring the two vessels into dangerous proximity. Though he knew Olivia Bolaji was arguably the most experienced combat pilot serving aboard *Titan,* he seized the arms of his chair in dual death grips.

Then he saw the flash of light and the ensuing fireball.

HRANRAR

Troi experienced a rush of gratitude when the transporter beam released her into the relative safety of the open air of a planetary surface. She turned to her right and saw the spires and minarets of a Hranrarii city. Looking in the opposite direction, she was further relieved to see several other members of the away team—Lieutenant Sortollo, and Ensigns Modan, Dakal, Evesh, and Bolaji—none of whom looked any more the worse for wear than she felt. At their feet she saw the customary emergency gear associated with a hasty bailout: A bulky but at least somewhat portable subspace transceiver; a duffel filled with field rations; another duffel crammed with thermal clothing; and a small carrying case that contained various tools, Dakal's data modules, the hand phasers, and the spare power packs.

Suddenly an alarming thought occurred to her. She turned in a full circle, praying she was wrong.

"Where the hell is Commander Vale?" Sortollo said just before Troi could articulate the same question.

"Look!" Evesh said, pointing with one chubby, hirsute hand toward the beautiful yet baleful fireball that had just pierced Hranrar's nearly clear blue skies.

"Oh, no," Troi said with a gasp as a wave of reptilian surprise and fear washed over her, threatening to knock her from her feet. Although the emotional onslaught stopped as quickly as it had begun, doubtless scattered by the deadly red-orange blossom overhead, its fading echoes pounded at her psyche like seismic aftershocks.

GORN HEGEMONY WARSHIP *S'ALATH* AUXILIARY VESSEL *DEWCLAW*

"The cargo hold grows overcrowded," Zegrroz'rh warned, raising his voice to be heard above the mewling bleats of the food animals. "Perhaps we should depart now before we are discovered."

Gog'resssh paused in his labors at the console long enough to give the cargo manifest assembled by his troopers in the hold a cursory glance. Reluctantly, he was forced to agree with his half-blind second. Though the need for live meatbeasts and medicine was urgent, only so much could be crammed into a single auxiliary vessel's hold.

"Very well. Take us back the way we came. *Discreetly.*"

GORN HEGEMONY WARSHIP *S'ALATH*

Sk'salissk's steel-muscled hand shot out and grabbed Z'shezhira almost before she realized what was happening.

"What are you holding in your claws?" the helmrunner demanded.

The injection-ampule fell from her suddenly nerveless manus and clattered impotently to the deck.

"An injection mechanism," Sk'salissk growled, his tones colored by both dismissiveness and disgust. "You sought to poison me?"

Sk'salissk released her while she searched for the words she needed to reply. But before she could complete the process, his other manus lashed out, striking her between the temple and her right cranial crest before she even saw the blow coming. Z'shezhira crumpled to the deck, her facial scales making sudden, painful contact with the command deck's unyielding duranium grillwork.

Even after she came to rest, facedown, the universe continued to spin around Z'shezhira, whose mind was suddenly bereft of all thoughts save one:

I will never see S'syrixx again.

Then the alarm sounded, startling her.

GORN HEGEMONY RECONNAISSANCE VESSEL *SSEVARRH*

"Captain Krassrr!" cried a junior member of the command-deck staff.

"Speak," Krassrr growled. "Have you received word from the *Zzrorss*?"

"Not since First Myrmidon Rraarsk reported having crippled the mammal vessel, Captain."

Krassrr didn't much like Rraarsk's silence, though he knew it could have been a simple matter of momentary interference radiating from the substantial explosion that the sensors detected all the way from the other side of the planet; the detonation had been the natural accompaniment to the delivery of Rraarsk's death blow.

Krassrr liked even less the idea of diverting more of his forces away from the task of protecting the precious eco-sculptor.

"What is it, then?" he rumbled, strongly implying that whatever tidings the junior officer bore had better not be trivial.

"Sensors have picked up a faint impulse wake, Captain. It forms a trail from one of our support vessels to the planet's northern polar region, where it is obscured by the local magnetic field. And one of the property officers has just reported significant losses in the fleet's supply stores."

"Thieving mammals," Krassrr hissed, his teeth flashing like daggers across his wide mouth. "*Tie-tan* must be nearby. Find it!"

GORN HEGEMONY WARSHIP *S'ALATH*

The next blow Z'shezhira had anticipated never landed. Very cautiously, she turned her head and tried to look up.

Sk'salissk had moved away from her, his rage forgotten, at least for the moment. He faced the main viewer, which displayed an image of an expanding fireball low on the horizon, as seen through the extreme northern reaches of the Hranrarii atmosphere, the *S'alath*'s current hiding place of choice.

Though she couldn't be certain, Z'shezhira thought that the fireball looked very much like an exploding space vessel; having been forced to serve the whims of First Myrmidon Gog'resssh for as long as she had, she had seen more than a few such sights.

As she began trying to get to her feet, one of her manus fell upon the injection ampule, which Sk'salissk appeared to have forgotten. She grabbed it as she rose and readied it for use.

Sk'salissk moved to a nearby console, at which he appeared to be studying the results of sensor scans on the still-expanding explosion. But he remained oblivious, showing her his armored back.

With a dreamlike sense of unreality, she set aside all doubt and hesitation in order to grasp at a second chance to be reunited with her beloved S'syrixx.

Leaping upon Sk'salissk's back, she jammed the business end of the injection ampule into the relatively delicate flesh at the junction between his jaw and neck.

Another alarm sounded, startling her. A harsh rasp of a voice followed it. Though distorted by the ship's communications system, its firm, obedience-generating quality was undiminished.

"Dewclaw *to* S'alath. *This is First Myrmidon Gog'resssh. Open the auxiliary vehicle bay immediately."*

For several protracted moments, Z'shezhira stood stock-still. As long as all the tech-casters aboard stuck to their plan and kept the auxiliary vehicle bay shuttered, Gog'resssh and what remained of his crew would be neutralized, either trapped belowdecks or locked out of the ship entirely. Then, once Vrezsarr the engineer put some distance between the *S'alath* and Gog'resssh's small vessel, the larger ship's weapons systems would swiftly put down Gog'resssh and his boarding party while the transporters could be used strategically to get rid of the remaining warcasters.

It was a good plan. All she had to do was stick to it.

"If the auxiliary vehicle bay is not opened immediately," Gog'resssh thundered, *"then I will ram it at this vessel's top speed. Everyone aboard the* S'alath *and the* Dewclaw *will die."*

Z'shezhira shuddered. She did not enjoy his anger. But neither could she bring herself to take the simple expedient of shutting down the comm channel.

We have a good plan, she reminded herself. *We merely have to follow it.*

But Vrezsarr might not be able to defeat Gog'resssh's patchwork of ersatz command codes in time to prevent the first myrmidon from making good on his threat. And

Z'shezhira felt certain that Gog'resssh was mad enough to actually go through with it.

Should that happen, she truly would never see S'syrixx again.

"Whoever takes immediate action to bring me back aboard will be rewarded," said the commanding voice.

Against her own better judgment, and in defiance of the internal warning klaxons that coursed up and down her spinal column, her manus began moving, as though propelled by a will of its own, across the late, unlamented Sk'salissk's control panel. . . .

U.S.S. TITAN

"You do beautiful work, Mister S'syrixx," Ranul Keru said. He had watched the deceptively thick-thewed hands of the Gorn as they moved the slender brushes across the canvas with a liberal mixture of speed and deliberation.

"You say you've never painted before?" Lieutenant Qontallium asked, sounding sincerely impressed.

"Not with materials such as these," S'syrixx said, working at the easel without pausing. "But I have created many similar renderings using electronic media, such as your own padds."

Keru knew that S'syrixx wasn't boasting. The creature that he and Qontallium were interviewing/guarding was a member of a Gorn arts subcaste, which in turn was part of the larger technological caste. And Keru had seen the many renderings and diagrams that S'syrixx had generated during the first night after his arrival aboard *Titan.*

But this, the end result of S'syrixx's present labors, possessed a sensitivity that bore no more relation to his previous effort than a hastily hand-rendered star map did to the immersive three-dimensional work of Trillius Prime's ancient holomasters.

The canvas carried an intensely photorealistic likeness of the head and shoulders of a Gorn. Despite the creature's obvious alienness, its golden, almost feline eyes carried none of the cold-blooded fury that Keru usually associated with the Gorn people in general. The being in the depiction almost looked . . . *kind.*

"Who is she?" Qontallium said, anticipating the question Keru had been about to ask.

"Her name is . . . was . . . Z'shezhira," S'syrixx said. "She is lost to me now."

Keru nodded silently. Having only recently come to terms with the death of his life partner, Sean Hawk, during a Gorn assault some nine years ago, he felt no need to pry any further into S'syrixx's grief. Keru saw that Qontallium, whose own loss to the Borg was far more recent and raw, was doing the same, his large eyes appearing to moisten with unshed tears.

GORN HEGEMONY WARSHIP *S'ALATH*

When Gog'resssh confronted Z'shezhira at her station on the command deck, he sounded preternaturally calm. For some unaccountable reason, she found that his current demeanor frightened her far more deeply than had even the most capricious and violent of his earlier paranoid tantrums.

"I could not help but notice," the first myrmidon said,

"that it was your authorization code that opened the auxiliary vessel bay for me."

Z'shezhira focused her gaze upon the deck grillwork beneath her bare, clawed feet. While she was ostensibly putting on a show of deference before a cross-caste superior, she was actually averting her eyes in shame over her weakness—and to avoid making contact with the soul-piercing lone good eye of the ever-suspicious Second Myrmidon Zegrroz'rh, who kept staring at her from the post of the late and unlamented helmrunner, Sk'salissk.

"I do not forget my friends," Gog'resssh said as he paced the deck near Z'shezhira with heavy but deliberate steps. "I do not hesitate to reward those who show loyalty toward me and my cause. That is why I have allowed you to remain at your post."

"Thank you, First Myrmidon," she said, the words an exercise in the purest form of survival-mandated rote behavior. In the tiny, private space in her head that she reserved for believing herself to be unconstrained and unbent by the bullying war-caster's duranium will, she wondered precisely what Gog'resssh's cause really amounted to other than a private Hegemony—a new autocracy at the summit of whose power structure would sit Gog'resssh and his fellow radiation-addled survivors of the Sazssgrerrn catastrophe.

"It may not be wise to count this one among your friends, First Myrmidon," said Zegrroz'rh. "This tech-caster killed Sk'salissk during our brief absence, here on this very command deck. She is as guilty as the other mutineers."

"I already explained that," Z'shezhira said, putting as

much confidence and defiance as she could muster behind the lie. "Sk'salissk attempted to take liberties with me. I merely did my duty to my caste."

"So you say," Zegrroz'rh growled. "Unfortunately, the only other witness to the . . . incident can neither corroborate nor dispute your story."

"Were I truly guilty of anything, would I have let you back aboard the *S'alath* after the mutineers had seized it?" she asked, hoping to score some points for sheer brazenness, a trait that the war-casters seemed to admire in other contexts.

"It does not matter," Gog'resssh told Zegrroz'rh, dismissing his lieutenant's concerns with a wave of one sharp-clawed manus. He approached Z'shezhira, his face drawing close enough to hers to force her to suppress a wince at the foulness of his breath. She noted a new scar on the scales of his neck, probably a disruptor burn received during the brief firefight that had just concluded.

"I wish you to understand the rare privilege I have granted you," he said, his deep rumbling voice reduced to a sibilant whisper as freighted with deadly promise as the hiss of a leaky airlock seal. "I trust that Zegrroz'rh has informed you that I authorized him to put four of your tech-caster colleagues off of this ship, once we regained control of it."

"He did," Z'shezhira said quietly. The second myrmidon had seemed to revel not only in carrying out Gog'resssh's death order with alacrity, but he had also made no effort to conceal the pleasure he had taken in her muted but noticeable reaction to the dispiriting news.

Zegrroz'rh flashed a grin that resembled a large collection of crookedly sharpened bone daggers. "Do not be concerned for your friends, noble Z'shezhira. I am certain that their suffering lasted no longer than it took for their lungs to explode into the void."

Four of my colleagues dead, she thought, miserable. *All because of my failure of nerve.*

"Before your medic friend Zzerrhezz tumbled out the airlock, he implicated you as a co-conspirator," Zegrroz'rh said. "The engineer Vrezsarr said much the same thing when his turn came to die."

Considering how badly she felt now, she would almost have been relieved were she to learn that she would soon share Zzerrhezz and Vrezsarr's fate. Even if her recent deeds somehow brought her and S'syrixx together again, she could scarcely face her beloved after what she had allowed to happen to members of their own caste.

Regardless, something within her forced her to seek whatever words might serve to soothe Gog'resssh and Zegrroz'rh's still potentially lethal anger; it remained imperative to her to keep her future with S'syrixx at least within the realm of the possible.

"Allowing Vrezsarr and Zzerrhezz to believe I would help them retake the *S'alath* seemed to be my safest course of action," she said, though she was too overwrought emotionally at the moment to tell whether or not the wordless languages of her posture, her scales, or her aromatic secretions had betrayed her as a poor liar.

Z'shezhira watched as Gog'resssh's face drew even closer. She closed her eyes in almost grateful anticipation of the war-caster's death blow, the terminal bite that would either mortally sever the largest artery in her relatively slender neck, or behead her outright.

Instead of the lancing sensation of knifelike fangs, she felt a powerful pulse of hot, foul breath against her neck scales. Something cool and viscous oozed down the side of her head.

Great S'Yahazah, she thought, blinking at the war-caster in disbelief. *He has initiated the mating ritual!* This was never done across caste boundaries. *Never.*

Except, perhaps, by the irredeemably mad.

"Remain loyal," Gog'resssh hissed quietly, dangerously. "Remain strong. And continue monitoring your communications post until I tell you otherwise."

"First Myrmidon, I must object to this!" Zegrroz'rh said as he bounded from the helm to the side of his superior officer. He looked and smelled as appalled as Z'shezhira felt about the taboo mating display he had just witnessed. Z'shezhira nearly succumbed to an ironic urge to smile at the notion that she might find herself in agreement with the second myrmidon about *anything.*

Moving faster than Z'shezhira could see, Gog'resssh took a long step backward, his manus lashing out in full force to catch his second-in-command squarely between the eyes. The second myrmidon went down hard, momentarily insensate.

Gog'resssh stepped toward his cowed subordinate. "I trust you recall the four tech-casters you just escorted into the Great Empty?"

"On your order," Zegrroz'rh said, his words sounding slurred by the blow to the head.

A great, dangerous growl grew deep inside Gog'resssh's chest. "Regardless of the source of the order, the loss of so many tech-casters, along with Sk'salissk and four more of our warrior brethren, has created a serious shortage in expertise aboard this vessel. Therefore Z'shezhira will remain at her post. This shall be so both because it is *necessary* and because *I wish it.* Do I make myself clear?"

Zegrroz'rh answered with a grunt and a sullen nod, whereupon Gog'resssh exited the command deck, doubtless to deal with some newly exigent consequence of the labor shortage that his orders and Z'shezhira's inaction had jointly caused.

Zegrroz'rh rose and carefully reassembled the tattered shreds of his dignity. He approached Z'shezhira, but did not draw nearly so close as Gog'resssh had, much to Z'shezhira's relief.

"The first myrmidon may trust you," he said. "But I am not as optimistic as he is. Nor am I as forgiving. I shall continue watching you—very closely."

An alert klaxon sounded on the helm console, prompting Zegrroz'rh to lumber back to his station.

"What is it?" Z'shezhira said after noting that the main viewscreen showed nothing but a display of Hranrar's tenuous but aurora-pinked upper atmosphere, the region of the planet whose northern electromagnetic hot spot served as the *S'alath*'s hiding place. Near the horizon she could see a still-expanding debris cloud, the last remnant of the fiery explosion that had recently consumed both the Gorn ecosculpting vessel and the Federrazsh'n auxiliary ship.

"It's another approaching vessel," Zegrroz'rh said.

Z'shezhira returned to her station and began listening for comm signals. Though her instruments had yet to yield any visual contact—the *S'alath*'s EM-swaddled hiding place was a two-edged sword against all but the nearest of vessels—she was able to detect the vessel's trajectory, as well as the presence of a Gorn transponder aboard it.

"It's another ship from the ecosculpting fleet," Z'shezhira reported with no small amount of relief. "The vessel is not heading directly for us. It's merely crossing the north polar region on its way to the more southerly latitudes. I don't think they've seen us."

"Confirmed," Zegrroz'rh said. "Once again, they seem to be preparing to confront an incoming Sşt'rfleet ship."

"Which ship?" Z'shezhira said, her innards growing deathly cold.

"Tie-tan," the second myrmidon said, forcing Z'shezhira to face the unpleasant but distinct likelihood that whatever she did to ensure her eventual reunion with S'syrixx might prove to be sadly inadequate.

HRANRAR

Her head filled with still-green empathic impressions of the Gorn crew's final moments, Troi stared skyward at the spreading bloom of fire and debris for what felt like an eternity.

Then she heard the hum of the transporter directly behind her.

She turned and saw Vale standing before the awe-inspiring Hranrarii cityscape. Apart from a slight unsteadiness, the exec seemed to have made it through the *Beiderbecke*'s death throes relatively unscathed.

"I *hate* it when people do that," Troi said.

Vale blinked in confusion. "Do what?"

"Beam off an exploding ship *after* the explosion."

"Sorry about that, Counselor." Vale grinned. "But if you want to get technical, I beamed off *before* the detonation. The rematerialization part always comes a couple of seconds later."

Troi approached Vale and gave her a quick hug. "Just don't make a habit of it."

"I'll try to be more careful, Counselor," Vale said. "At least as long as we're here." The exec paused to look toward the majestic Hranrarii city before turning back to face Troi. "By the way, where exactly *are* we?"

U.S.S. TITAN

Riker reflected bitterly on the irony of having rushed to get *Titan* within weapons range of a target, only to find that no targets were left once the starship had arrived on the scene. Only a spreading, fiery debris cloud high above the planet remained.

"Sensors confirm that both the Gorn ship and the shuttlecraft *Beiderbecke* were destroyed in the conflagration, Captain," Tuvok reported.

Riker swore under his breath. "Commander Vale must not have had a lot of better options."

Though he knew that the away team had been on its way back from the planet when they'd been forced into a ship-to-ship combat situation, Riker wasn't ready to assume the worst—at least not yet. *If Deanna were dead I would feel it,* he thought, having learned long ago to trust the psychic bond he shared with his wife.

Aloud, he said, "The *Beiderbecke* and the Gorn ship

were both within transporter distance of the planet when the collision happened. Maybe they had time to bail out at the last moment. Mister Tuvok, scan for survivors on the surface."

"I have already begun such a search, Captain. The results so far are inconclusive, owing to the overlapping effects of a number of atmospheric phenomena with which we are already familiar."

Riker nodded. On the viewer before him, the planet Hranrar turned slowly several hundred klicks below *Titan,* oblivious to his hopes and fears.

"Try raising the away team."

"Aye, sir." Rager manipulated her console with the grace and alacrity of a concert pianist. A full minute passed. "I'm sorry, Captain," she said with a frustrated shake of her head. "But there's a lot of interference on the standard combadge frequency. I'm not sure if—"

Riker's mind felt a familiar touch, tentative at first, then stronger. *Imzadi?*

"*—way team to* Titan,*"* sounded a garbled voice that was barely discernible against the oceanic background hash of static. "*—ade it down to—planet in one piec—*"

They're alive! Riker thought, belatedly recognizing the voice of Christine Vale, despite the distortion. He relaxed backward slightly into his command chair. But even though the relief he felt was almost palpable, he didn't want to surrender to it just yet, right here on the bridge. He'd postpone that moment until sometime after recovering the away team, and reuniting with Deanna. Sometime after he'd discharged his responsibilities to the Hranrarii.

Assuming, of course, that those responsibilities didn't

leave him, his ship, and his crew in a condition that strongly resembled that of the shuttlecraft *Beiderbecke.*

"*Titan* here, Chris," he said, speaking loudly and resonantly in the hopes of drowning out the static. "It's good to hear your voice again."

"I'm trying to establish a signal lock, Captain," Rager said.

"Good," Riker said. "Get the shields back up the moment the away team's on board."

"Aye, sir."

"Commander Vale, give me a sit rep," Riker said.

"*—raid I had to ram—Gorn ship,*" Vale said.

"I can see that. The Gorn vessel was destroyed, along with the *Beiderbecke,*" Riker said, speaking loudly again for his exec's benefit. He knew that Captain Krassrr wasn't going to be thrilled about that, but there was nothing he could do about that now, other than to get *Titan* hidden again before Krassrr could retaliate. "Right now we're trying to lock on and beam you up."

"*—utstanding plan, Capt—I second the—otion.*"

Riker chuckled. "In the meantime, I suggest you keep an eye peeled for any uninvited guests. If you had time to execute a last-second bailout, then maybe a few of the Gorn troopers on that ship did as well."

"Transporter lock established, sir," Rager said. "But I'm not sure how long it'll hold."

Lieutenant Lavena turned so quickly from her helm station that Riker could hear her hydration suit sloshing. "Captain, I'm picking up an incoming bogey."

"Confirmed," said Tuvok as he worked the tactical station with his customary calm but relentless efficiency. "It's the *Ssevarrh* again, Captain. And she's closing fast."

"She's charging weapons," Rager said.

"Do you have the away team aboard yet?" Riker asked the ops officer.

"Negative, sir. And I've lost Commander Vale's comm signal. Probably more Gorn jamming."

"What about the transporter lock?" Riker asked.

"I need just a little more time, given all the atmospheric effects down there."

Damn!

"Keep trying. Hail Krassrr, and tell him we're just trying to recover our away tea—"

"Incoming fire," Tuvok said.

"Raise shields!" Riker cried, springing out of his chair.

As the lights dimmed and the deck went nearly perpendicular, Riker realized that it was already too late for that.

16

HRANRAR, MINUTES EARLIER

"We beamed back to the very same Hranrarii city we were surveying during our first visit to the planet's surface," Troi said, answering Vale's earlier question. The counselor strove to recover at least a small degree of her customary professional demeanor now that she had obtained the much-needed catharsis of hugging someone she had feared dead only moments earlier.

"We still had a good line of sight to this location when we had to bail out," Olivia Bolaji said. The pilot was kneeling on the moist, mossy earth, inventorying the cache of emergency supplies that had accompanied the away team during their hair's-breadth exit from the doomed shuttlecraft *Beiderbecke*. "I'm afraid we didn't have time to be any choosier than that with the preprogrammed transporter coordinates. At least we're pretty well stocked with supplies."

"Let's hope it's enough to protect and feed ourselves until help arrives," Lieutenant Sortollo said. "*If* help arrives, that is."

"Captain Riker isn't going to leave anybody behind," Vale said, a stern edge in her voice.

"I hope you're right, Commander," Sortollo said. "But if *Titan* really *is* coming for us, then that had better happen before the Typhon Pact fleet arrives. Performing a rescue with the Gorn terraforming fleet here is almost too much already."

"Maybe it's not," Troi said, pointing up at the dissipating fireball that was still visible overhead through a scudding of low clouds. "Commander Vale appears to have thinned the Gorn ranks a little." The empathic memory of their passing made her shudder slightly.

"We don't know that for sure," Sortollo said.

"Unfortunately, staying aboard the *Beiderbecke* until I was absolutely sure the Gorn ship was destroyed wasn't one of my better options," Vale deadpanned.

Troi nodded sadly. "They're dead. I can tell." She knew she didn't need to offer any further explanation. Trying not to sound as though she were making an accusation, she added, "But I wish there had been another way."

"I do, too, Deanna," Vale said as she moved toward the mobile subspace transceiver, which Ensigns Evesh and Dakal were already in the process of setting up. "But if I hadn't set the *Beiderbecke* on her suicide run, the crew of that ship could have detected our beam-down site in real time, while we were using the shuttle's transporter. If I hadn't blown up their ship, we'd already be up to our asses in Gorn troopers right now."

"I have to agree," Sortollo said as he busied himself checking the charges on the phasers.

Now that she had an opportunity to think the matter through, Troi could see that both the exec and the security officer were almost certainly correct. But the necessity argument didn't make her feel any better about killing on such a scale.

"Much as I hate to recommend this," Evesh said, "perhaps it would be prudent to get back into our isosuits. If we are disguised as Hranrarii, any Gorn who come calling might not recognize us."

"Good plan," Sortollo said as he finished checking his sidearm and moved along to begin examining the contents of the field-ration case. "But it doesn't take into account the fact that we no longer *have* the isosuits."

"Come again, Lieutenant?" Vale said.

Sortollo paused in his labors and looked apologetically at the exec. "When we bailed out, we only had time to include the prepackaged supplies in our beam-out. Our isosuits had just come off a few minutes earlier; they hadn't been stowed yet when the Gorn ship attacked us."

Troi could sense that Vale had only barely overcome the temptation to bark something unkind at the security man. "Great," the exec said at length. "Does anybody else have some good news they'd like to share?"

"Well, there's still the undiscussed possibility that the Gorn crew actually *did* succeed in pinpointing this spot before they were vaporized," Dakal said. He spoke without making eye contact, kneeling on the ground as he methodically reconnected subspace comm components that had been disassembled to accommodate the limited storage space aboard the *Beiderbecke*. "They could have transmitted our present coordinates to the rest of Krassrr's fleet on the other side of the planet just before the explosion."

"Good point," Vale said.

"On the plus side of the ledger," said Evesh, "unless they really did follow our transporter beams down here from orbit in real time, the rest of the Gorn fleet should have considerable difficulty finding us just by searching randomly."

Dakal nodded. "We have the planet's magnetic field and atmospheric energy emanations to thank for that."

"Still," Vale said, "let's keep the comms quiet for the moment, just to avoid attracting any more unwanted attention. Mister Dakal, Mister Evesh, I want you to drag the comm unit out of sight." The exec pointed toward a nearby copse of gnarled, vine-draped, treelike vegetation. "That'll be our base of operations, at least for the moment. Once the comm gear is set up and running in there, I want you to monitor all Starfleet frequencies. But don't transmit anything unless it's to answer a call from *Titan*."

"And if you receive a call from *Titan*," Troi said, addressing both technicians, "give me a chance to verify it before you send any response. We can't afford to forget Mister S'syrixx's gift for mimicry. Captain Krassrr might have kept a few more like him in reserve."

Within a matter of minutes, the team had finished carrying its assorted matériel into the copse, which formed a crude arboreal fence that reached a height of some three-and-one-half meters. The concentration of vines, moss, and leaf-litter toward the bottom of the natural barrier provided a not inconsiderable amount of concealment.

A moment after Sortollo went out to start setting up the small proximity alarms that would alert the team of anything that might try to approach, Vale turned to Troi. "This reminds me of the treehouse I built on Izar when I was eleven."

Despite the smile on Vale's face, Troi could sense that her friend's memories of that time and place weren't entirely fond ones. "I suppose the present circumstances are somewhat less enjoyable."

Vale shrugged. "We'll see. At least this time I had the good sense to build my fort on solid ground instead of three meters up. Let's see if I can avoid falling and breaking my arm this time."

Troi's grinning reply was interrupted by a stereo wash of static, both from her own combadge and from Vale's. Buried in the white noise was a familiar sound.

"Sounds like a standard digital hail," Vale said. "From *Titan.*"

In response to Vale's questioning look, Troi closed her eyes and concentrated. *Imzadi?*

Troi opened her eyes. "It's genuine, Chris."

Tapping her combadge, Vale said, "Away team to *Titan.* We made it down to the planet in one piece."

Both combadges emitted more static. Whatever reply *Titan* might be trying to make was being drowned out utterly. Vale strode to the quarter of the perhaps five-meter-wide enclosure where Dakal and Evesh still labored to finish setting up the transceiver.

"I need that comm up and running, ASAP!" she said.

"Almost there, Commander," Dakal said, pausing momentarily in his labors. Evesh continued working as she muttered something that sounded profane. Vale showed no sign of having heard it.

Vale tapped her combadge hard, her frustration evident. She smiled in pleased surprise when the next burst of static carried with it a recognizable and moderately intelligible human voice. "Titan *here, Chris—good to hear y—r voice ag—"*

Another voice sounded, this one coming from the much larger speakers of the subspace transceiver. Troi recognized the voice as belonging to Lieutenant Rager; it was faint, in the bridge comm system's background. *"I'm try—g to—stablish a signal lock, Cap—"*

"Good," Will said, his voice equally faint against the backdrop of static. *"—shields back up the mom—th—way team's on board."*

"Ay—" Rager said.

Considering the end that the away team had just narrowly avoided, Troi sincerely hoped that Will wouldn't have to leave *Titan*'s shields down a moment more than was absolutely necessary.

"—ander Vale," Will said. *"—ive me a sit rep."*

"I'm afraid I had to ram the Gorn ship, Captain," said Vale.

*"I can see that. The Gorn ves—was destroyed, along wi—*erbecke. *Right now—e're tryin—lock on an—eam you up."*

With a relieved grin, Vale said, "An outstanding plan, Captain. I second the motion."

Troi could feel her husband's good humor and relief mix together and come close to overflowing into his words. *"—meantime, I suggest you keep an eye peeled—or any uninvit—guests. If you—d time to execute a last-second bailout—aybe—few of the Gorn troop—on that ship did as well."*

"Transporter lock established, sir," Rager said from the progressively less intelligible background. The static underlying every word being spoken aboard *Titan*'s bridge was

growing in intensity, like a wave front building slowly to tsunami strength.

"Captain—icking up—ncoming bogey." This was another background voice; though it was highly distorted, Troi recognized it as belonging to Lieutenant Lavena.

"Confirm—the Ssevarrh *again, Capt—."* This time the speaker was Tuvok. *"And—closing fas—"*

"Transceiver is online, Commander," Dakal said. "It's locked on the combadge frequency. Should be able to clean up some of the static."

Elbowing the two technicians aside, Vale knelt in front of the squat portable comm unit and began adjusting the controls with methodical yet quick motions.

Troi heard Rager's voice surface once again through the froth of whistling, popping interference. *"—lost Commander Vale's comm signal. Probably more Gorn jamming."*

Will's voice reappeared: *"What about the transporter lock?"*

Rager again: *"I need just a little more time, given all the atmospheric effects down there."*

"Keep trying," Will said. *"Hail Krassrr—tell him we—ust trying to recov—"*

"Incoming fire," Tuvok said.

The connection broke up.

"Away team to *Titan*!" Vale said. "*Titan,* come in." She repeated the hail three more times before stalking away from the comm unit in frustration. Troi could sense that it had taken every particle of will the exec possessed to resist the impulse to deal the transceiver a spinning *Jeet-Kune-Do* kick.

Wearing a grave expression, Vale approached Troi. "I

sure as hell hope Will got those shields back up before the fireworks started."

Troi felt her body tensing involuntarily as a jolt of unpleasant surprise shot up and down her spine. Something was very, very wrong. "I think we may have a more immediate problem, Chris."

Vale's combadge spoke up once again, this time without the static that had plagued it before. *"Sortollo to Vale."*

"Vale here, Lieutenant. How's the perimeter sweep going?"

"Something's following me, Commander," the big security officer said, sounding out of breath. *"I think it may be a Gorn landing party. I've made my way into a pretty vegetation-intensive area of the hillside for cover, so I haven't got a clear look at 'em yet. But I recommend that you and the rest of the team break out the phasers. Hunker down and stay out of sight until—"*

The channel suddenly went dead.

"Lieutenant?" Vale said. "Lieutenant?"

After ordering Ensign Dakal to start distributing the phasers, the exec flashed a silent, inquisitive look at Troi, whose only response was a small shrug and a shake of the head. While Troi was certain that Lieutenant Sortollo was no longer transmitting, she could not yet say precisely why.

A sudden wave of unfamiliar fear and anger, paired with the frantic rustling she could hear in the vines behind her, told her that this was about to change rather abruptly.

U.S.S. TITAN

Riker sat in his command chair, silently studying the long, angular vessel that hung in apparent motionlessness near the center of the bridge's forward viewer. It was definitely Krassrr's flagship.

"Our shields are holding," reported Tuvok. "However, numerous EPS relays throughout the primary hull overloaded during the Gorn vessel's initial salvo."

An initial salvo that had turned out to be the other ship's *only* salvo—at least so far.

"We've switched to backups," Rager said. "Commander Ra-Havreii reports repair teams dispatched."

"Phasers, photon torpedoes, and quantum torpedoes are ready for return fire," Tuvok said.

"Thank you, Mister Tuvok. Stand by. And keep those shields up." The away team on the planet's surface was simply going to have to fend for itself, at least for the time being. "Lieutenant Rager, hail Captain Krassrr one more time. Tell him I want to talk to him."

Once again, the Gorn vessel made no acknowledgment of the hail. But it also made no further aggressive moves. Riker found it immensely puzzling. The Gorn warriors he had encountered during the political crisis on their homeworld had been both ruthless and relentless. They weren't prone to indecision and didn't tend to spend all that much time engaging in what Riker considered minimally prudent tactical planning. When they received an order to attack, they would do so with a single-minded ferocity that he'd seen matched only by the Dominion's Jem'Hadar soldiers. They never considered casualties, or personal survival, and would fight to the last trooper without any hesitation. When they went into battle, considerations such as whether or not the odds favored them never seemed to enter their minds. They displayed no fear toward their enemies, no aversion, no emotion of any kind other than implacable hostility.

Riker heard the turbolift doors hiss open, and he turned his head in time to see S'syrixx step onto the bridge, flanked by Commander Keru and Lieutenant Qontallium.

"Thank you for agreeing to come to the bridge," Riker said.

Despite S'syrixx's evident discomfiture at the close proximity of so many non-reptiloids, Riker was impressed by the Gorn's new-found composure. "I am pleased to help you in any way I can, Captain Rry'kurr."

"After its initial attack, Krassrr's ship is just . . . *sitting* there," Riker said. "That doesn't match any Gorn M.O. I'm familiar with. I'd like an appraisal."

"We might interpret Captain Krassrr's lack of action presently as a sign of his extreme confidence in the outcome of any protracted battle between his vessel and *Titan,*" Tuvok said.

Keru nodded, stroking his chin with one large hand. "I suppose the fact that he has five other vessels to watch his back may make him feel fairly sure of himself."

"Four vessels," S'syrixx corrected.

Keru nodded. "All right, then, four vessels. That still represents enough firepower to outgun *Titan* by a considerable margin. And that fact begs the obvious question: why aren't those four other ships *here* right now, ganging up on us?"

"Captain Krassrr may believe that the reason for *Tietan*'s presence," S'syrixx said, "is to draw his ships away from their primary mission of protecting, repairing, and activating the ecosculptor. He may be biding his time, waiting for *Tie-tan* to make a tactical error, or to reveal the location of other hidden Federrazsh'n ships."

"I'm detecting sensor beams radiating from the forward section of the Gorn vessel, Captain," Lieutenant Lavena said. "Some are making contact with *Titan*. Others appear to be directed toward the remnants of the debris cloud."

"Confirmed," said Rager.

"So he must know by now that one of his ships got blown to Kingdom Come, half a world away from his precious terraforming artifact," Riker said, resting his bearded chin on one fist as he continued to study the image of the Gorn ship. "Maybe he's actually taking the time to find out just how mad he ought to be at us."

"Captain Krassrr is hailing *us* now," Rager said. "And I'm getting a visual signal this time."

Another surprise—so far Krassrr had studiously avoided visual communications, as though the sight of humans repulsed him. He doubted that Krassrr found mammalian life-forms any less repellent now than he ever did, and wondered if his willingness to do so now was a display of military theatrics, perhaps a move designed to strike fear into his adversary and to impress his own subordinates with a display of personal courage.

It was becoming crystal clear to Riker that he had badly underestimated the sophistication of the Gorn military mind by generalizing from the lockstep, robotic characteristics of the typical Gorn foot soldier.

"If Krassrr has scanned this ship," S'syrixx said as he stepped into the command well at the bridge's center, "then he knows that I am aboard."

"Maybe that's why he wants visual communications

this time," Riker said, looking up at the slender yet still fearsome-looking reptile that towered over the right side of his command chair. "He wants to look you in the eye before he tries to kill you again. Maybe you ought to get out of sight until aft—"

"No," S'syrixx said. "I will no longer allow war-caster bullies to rule my life." Though the Gorn technician was clearly afraid, Riker could see that he was determined to stand his ground anyway.

"All right. Mister Tuvok, prepare to initiate Tactical Plan Archer One, on my signal. I've already sent the heading data to your console and the helm. Make sure Commander Ra-Havreii is ready to do his part."

"Aye, Captain," Tuvok said. Despite his Vulcan equanimity, he looked almost impressed as his hands hastened to enter the relevant commands.

"Interesting," Lavena said over her shoulder a moment after she displayed the same data on her flight control console. "It might even work."

Grinning at his pilot, Riker said. "Sometimes there's just no substitute for the classics." He gestured toward the screen. "Lieutenant Rager, Captain Krassrr is a busy man. Let's not waste any more of his time."

The image of Krassrr's ship rippled for a fraction of a second, and was replaced almost instantaneously by the enraged visage of Krassrr, who was standing before the thronelike command chair that formed the nucleus of his vessel's bustling bridge.

"Rry'kurr!" rumbled the Gorn captain, his barely contained rage challenging the limits of the universal translator's capabilities. *"It is clear now that you cannot be bargained*

with in a civilized fashion. I hesitate to destroy you outright only because my legal counsel requires me first to take a thorough and accurate inventory of Tie-tan's *many crimes to enable the Gorn Hegemony to seek reparations against your Federrazsh'n."*

At last Riker thought he was beginning to understand the method behind Krassrr's madness. He hadn't necessarily misjudged the Gorn military mind; he may have instead failed to place it in its proper context within the larger whole of Gorn society.

Sometimes the lawyer caste trumps the military caste, he thought, suppressing an ironic grin. *And maybe more frequently than just sometimes.* He wondered if the Gorn Hegemony's present transition from an independent power to a member of a galactic confederation had triggered a hitherto-unnoticed power struggle between the military and legal castes.

Unfortunately Krassrr didn't appear to be in the mood to shed any light on the matter. *"I hold you personally responsible for the destruction of the Gorn Hegemony reconnaissance vessel* Zzrorss, *and for the deaths of its crew.*

Riker shook his head in disbelief. "Captain, it was *your* ship that attacked *my* shuttlecraft. My people acted in self-defense. If anyone has committed any crimes of aggression here, it's the captain of that vessel and *you.*"

After roaring something that utterly defeated the UT, Krassrr said, *"Our attack on your auxiliary vessel was precipitated by your insistence upon returning to this planet after we had warned you to leave on two previous occasions. Or do you claim not to have understood our unambiguous warnings?"*

"We understood you well enough, Krassrr. We just don't recognize your authority to arbitrarily chase us away. *Titan* has as much right to be here as your vessels do."

"This system is a territorial annex of the Gorn Hegemony, Rry'kurr. A Typhon Pact fleet will arrive shortly to enforce that lawful claim."

Riker reflected yet again that this entire mess would have to be resolved before then, one way or the other.

"And by harboring that creature," Krassrr continued, stabbing a lethal-looking claw in S'syrixx's direction, *"you have committed a crime of sedition against the Gorn Hegemony. He is a legally condemned saboteur whose execution has been duly ordered."*

Not to mention royally botched, Riker thought. Aloud, he said, "Mister S'syrixx is under the protection of the United Federation of Planets. I must regard any attempt to remove him or deprive him of his rights and liberties under Federation law as an act of war."

Krassrr flashed a startling array of teeth in what might have been a grin intended to convey a *bring-it-on* sentiment.

"Lastly," the Gorn commander said, continuing as though Riker hadn't even spoken, *"you stand accused of stealing vitally needed food and other supplies from a Gorn Hegemony military vessel. No doubt you relied on the assistance of our condemned saboteur to undertake that vile act of theft."*

Riker's mouth fell open involuntarily; a charge of petty theft was the last thing he expected to hear. "Frankly, Captain, I'm not at all sure what to say to that one."

"Captain Riker, if I may?" Tuvok said.

Riker turned toward the starboard tactical station,

behind which the Vulcan stood. Gesturing toward the main viewer, he said, "By all means, Commander." *When all else fails, why not apply a little pure logic?*

Tuvok stepped around his station and into the command well, coming to a stop at Riker's immediate right.

"Captain Krassrr, according to our most up-to-date intelligence about your people, the Gorn warrior's diet consists entirely of live, non-humanoid-compatible food."

Krassrr growled. *"Intelligence that you no doubt reviewed with your new Gorn saboteur-in-residence."*

Though he raised an eyebrow, Tuvok avoided addressing the comment directly. "Be that as it may, was my assumption regarding Gorn dietary requirements in error?"

"No, mammal. You are correct."

Riker wasn't sure how Krassrr could be so certain about the dietary requirements of humanoids. But he could guess. He had heard the rumors over the years, scuttlebutt that had circulated quietly in Starfleet's cadet and junior-officer circles for over a century, that some of the casualties of the first Starfleet-Gorn encounters hadn't been neatly vaporized by Gorn weaponry as James Kirk's logs had reported. It wasn't that anybody believed that Kirk or anyone else had falsified their reports. But the stories suggested that some of the officers involved may have mistaken the effects of an unfamiliar type of transporter beam for those of a long-range disintegration weapon.

According to one of the stories, a pair of *Enterprise* tactical officers—their names were Lang and O'Herlihy, if Riker could trust his memory—had become the prisoners and lab rats of Gorn experimentalists after apparently dying by disintegration on Cestus III. The Gorn had kept the two men alive for years, or perhaps even for decades, maintaining a perpetual suicide watch as the Gorn clinicians cold-bloodedly learned everything they could about humanity and its vulnerabilities through a seemingly endless series of painful and torturous experiments.

If there was any truth at all to the stories, Riker fervently hoped that Lang and O'Herlihy's torments had been brief.

Tuvok slowly paced across the front of the command well, like an attorney deliberately constructing his case before a fair-minded, disinterested jury. "Captain Krassrr," he said, "if any of *Titan*'s personnel had wished to deplete your stores of live food, then why would the guilty parties not simply have *killed* the food animals and left them behind? Why would we incur the additional cost of stealing such supplies, or anything else that we know to be useless to us?"

"You are being disingenuous, Vulcan-mammal, which is curious. Your people are said to be incapable of lying."

Tuvok again raised an eyebrow. "How have I been untruthful with you?"

"You have conveniently failed to mention the many nonhumanoids that serve aboard your vessel. Some reptiloids number among these." Krassrr pointed a claw toward Lieutenant Qontallium, who stood near the turbolift, ready to react should S'syrixx make any attempt to reprise his sickbay hostage standoff here on the bridge.

"All right," Riker said, rising from his command chair. "My chief medical officer is a reptiloid. A Pahkwa-thanh, to be precise. He's probably at least as big a carnivore as you are. Do you seriously believe I'd commit an act of piracy—

arguably an act of war against the Gorn Hegemony—just to get Doctor Ree some extra calories?"

"I came here to level charges against you, Rry'kurr, not to try your case," Krassrr said. *"Your guilt is a certainty. I have every confidence that the law-casters will vindicate me—after I have blown you out of Hranrar's sky."*

With that, Krassrr's image vanished from the screen, to be replaced by the menacing image of his vessel, the glow of its forward tubes quickly intensifying.

"I'm picking up two more incoming bogeys, Captain," Rager said. "Closing fast, roughly equidistant from the planet's eastern and western limbs."

"Gorn vessels, both originating at about equatorial latitude," Tuvok said.

"Their weapons read hot," Rager said. "As do Krassrr's."

Fresh from guarding Brahma-Shiva, Riker thought as he retook his command chair. "Evasive maneuvers, Lieutenant Lavena. And keep those shields up, Mister Tuvok. Both of you coordinate with engineering to execute the Archer maneuver as soon as we achieve the optimal ionization effects on the hull."

We're only going to get one shot at this, he thought as *Titan*'s bridge rocked seismically beneath his boots.

GORN HEGEMONY RECONNAISSANCE VESSEL *SSEVARRH*

Given what he knew of the battle prowess Rry'kurr had displayed during the Black Crest warrior's coup attempt several suncircuits ago, Captain Krassrr was genuinely surprised by the mammal commander's failure to put up more of a fight—or at least by his decision not to make a more sensible attempt at flight. He had expected the Federrazsh'n commander to repeat what he had evidently done at the conclusion of both of their previous encounters, which was to flee into the system's far fringe, whose icy vastness would offer the best chance of concealment.

What he *hadn't* expected was for *Tie-tan* to initiate a rolling dive straight down, directly into the atmosphere of the planet Hranrar itself. It was an act of suicide, as the *Ssevarrh*'s sensors, as well as those of both of the other two recon ships Krassrr had temporarily repurposed from their duties safeguarding the ecosculptor, would confirm soon enough.

Krassrr, however, was disinclined to leave an enemy's future to blind chance if he had an alternative. At his order, the *Ssevarrh* and her two support vessels launched full barrages of both particle beams and explosive missiles at the retreating mammal ship.

With the addition of the spectacular bow shocks and deflector-shield backlash that Krassrr's multiple weapons hits had generated, the plume of debris from Rry'kurr's vessel as it burned and disintegrated during its ballistic terminal descent through the atmosphere was something to behold, a thing of beauty that evoked Krassrr's youthful memories of the Rrrargran meteor displays of Gornar Farsouth, and the unpredictable firerains from Volcano Zzaren in the high northern steppes, where he had taken his basic training.

Krassrr ordered a cease-fire as *Tie-tan* descended further, since the thicker layers of the planet's lower atmosphere would have served to spoil the gunners' aim. Besides, Krassrr had no intention of jeopardizing any of his remaining vessels by ordering hot pursuit so deep within the planet's atmosphere. Even in the absence of further weapons strikes, *Tie-tan*'s ionized debris trail continued expanding in both length and girth, its coruscating reds and oranges multiplied by more than an order of magnitude by the auroral effects of the northern magnetic field. Now the display brought to mind the ostentatious tail-feather displays of Gornar's wingbeasts, creatures whose plumage extended to more than four times the creatures' normal overall body length during their time of rut.

And like the rutting wingbeast, Tie-tan *can no longer fly,* Krassrr thought as his compound eyes followed the long ellipse his adversary's meteoric drop traced across his main forward viewer. *But even the wingbeast will reclaim the skies if nothing eats him while he is confined to the ground.*

Krassrr reminded himself that this Rry'kurr was a tricky one. Rry'kurr had misled him before, and that made Krassrr chary about taking any chances with this wily mammal and his casteless, mongrel crew.

Loping toward the sensor station, Krassrr growled to get the attention of a slight young tech-caster. The technician was monitoring *Tie-tan*'s fall on a display that also generated multiple columns of swiftly-shifting figures.

"Follow that debris all the way down to the surface so that we will not have to struggle against Hranrar's magnetic field in order to find it later," Krassrr said. "I want to see hard proof that the Sst'rfleet ship is no more."

U.S.S. TITAN

The forward viewer displayed a confusing, distortion-dappled mishmash: the icy white curve of Hranrar's northernmost reaches, as seen from a high but suborbital altitude; a low, horizon-bound needle of light tended by a pair of slowly moving stars, which Riker immediately recognized as Brahma-Shiva, seen from Hranrar's figurative roof; and a trio of indistinct but clearly retreating metallic shapes, which could only be Krassrr's ship and those of his reptilian wingmen.

"All three attackers are moving off," Tuvok said, shortly after the descent had ended and the inertial dampers had restored the terra firma sanity of up-and-down to the bridge. "I believe the Gorn fleet is satisfied that we were destroyed during an uncontrolled atmospheric entry and descent."

Riker was relieved to hear Tuvok confirm what the viewscreen, such as it was at the moment, had already told him. Still, he hoped that Krassrr wouldn't ultimately prove too sophisticated to believe the evidence of his own buglike eyes. He looked around the bridge, from Rager and Lavena at the forward consoles to Tuvok, who stood at aft starboard. S'syrixx, still flanked by Keru and Qontallium, appeared somewhat unsteady but otherwise none the worse for wear.

Facing front once again, Riker said, "Position report."

"We're keeping station in the boundary layer between the upper troposphere and the lower stratosphere," Lieutenant Lavena said as she worked the flight control console. The bridge shuddered slightly, like an atmospheric aircraft encountering a pocket of turbulence. "Our structural integrity field is compensating for the atmospheric hull stresses, and our thrusters are compensating for the prevailing winds, keeping us 'anchored.' "

"Good," Riker said. "Maintain position. With any luck,

being 'at anchor' here, almost directly over Hranrar's northern magnetic pole, will keep the Gorn from seeing us."

"If Krassrr can find no reason to disbelieve what you have shown him, Captain," S'syrixx said, "then he has no reason to continue looking."

"I hope you're right."

"I still feel quite uncomfortable among you mammals. I may never get used to the shedding fur and the flaking epidermis. However, I must confess to having developed a certain admiration for your cleverness."

"Thank you," Riker said, though the compliment sounded ever so slightly backhanded. *That was a little like being told, "for a fat kid you don't sweat much."*

"Tell me, Captain," S'syrixx said, "how did you formulate such a creative stratagem?"

"I . . . dabble a little bit in history," Riker said after pausing briefly to consider how much he ought to tell him about his occasional hobby of running holodeck reenactments of pivotal moments in the history of Earth and Starfleet. He had participated in faithfully rendered holoprograms such as James Kirk's initial confrontation with a Gorn starship captain, and stinkers like the wildly inaccurate holoaccount of *Enterprise* NX-01's adventures on the eve of the signing of the Federation Charter. "More than two centuries ago, the first Earth starship named *Enterprise* was damaged by microsingularities. The damage caused pieces of her hull to end up in an asteroid field between Coridan and Theta Ursae Majoris. The markings on those hull fragments were enough to convince a couple of *Enterprise* crewmembers in a passing shuttle that the ship had been destroyed during their absence."

"An historical accident plus a little showmanship," Keru said, "equals a valid tactical plan."

"Only for as long as the other guy buys what you're trying to sell him, Mister Keru," Riker said. Facing forward, he said, "Lieutenant Rager, can you contact the away team from our current position?"

Rager tapped a swift series of commands into her board before shaking her head in evident disappointment. "No, sir. There's too much ionization and interference coming from the local magnetic field."

"Get Torvig and White-Blue busy creating a workaround," Riker said. "We've got to punch through that static somehow. We need to reach the away team and find a way to get them back aboard—without compromising our hiding place."

"Aye, sir," Rager said as she set about her tasks.

Riker tapped his combadge. "Riker to engineering. Status report."

"Ra-Havreii here, Captain," said the harried-sounding chief engineer. *"I hope we won't need to try that again any time soon. My supply of spare prefabricated hull plates is completely exhausted."*

"No promises. Report."

"I'm afraid we sustained more damage than I initially thought during the first Gorn salvo—the one that overloaded the primary EPS relays. We have no warp capability at the moment."

Riker's throat went dry. "How long before you can get the warp drive back up and running, Commander?"

"I'm still assessing the damage, Captain, so it's too early for me to formulate a precise estimate. But I can say one thing

authoritatively at this point: this ship won't be going anywhere except on impulse until some time after the Typhon Pact fleet arrives."

Titan would have to hide, and continue hiding, at least for the foreseeable future. *And maybe with ringside seats to the end of a world,* Riker thought.

He gazed at the forward screen, his eyes straining to pierce the chaotic vale of static and distortion that caused the distant, apparently tiny Brahma-Shiva artifact to ripple and shift as it orbited. The thing hung like a judgment over the world its wielders would so casually doom.

He contemplated the prospect of watching impotently while the object's cold-blooded masters ended the existence of his wife, his executive officer, his away team, and an entire civilization.

17

GORN HEGEMONY WARSHIP *S'ALATH*

"Has *Tie-tan* detected our presence yet?" Gog'resssh asked.

Turning away momentarily from her communications console in order to face Gog'resssh—the First Myrmidon had already made it abundantly clear, sometimes with the back of his manus, that he did not enjoy being addressed obliquely—Z'shezhira replied in the negative.

"The mammal vessel is merely holding its orientation over this planet's northernmost magneto-intensive region, just as we are," she said, all the while carefully avoiding making sustained contact with the war-caster's multifaceted silver eyes. "They seem to be expending a great deal of power to maintain position in a more rarefied atmospheric layer than the one we occupy."

"No doubt because their ship is so much less robust than ours is," said Zegrroz'rh.

Tie-tan *was evidently robust enough to transform one of Krassrr's best-armed vessels into a huge ball of burning plasma,* Z'shezhira thought. She kept the observation to herself, however, not wishing to provoke either of her principal captors. She found she needed Zegrroz'rh's goodwill, such as it was, now more than ever before; though the second myrmidon remained as repellently charmless as ever, Z'shezhira found she was glad for his ever-watchful presence now that Gog'resssh was making no secret of his unnatural designs on her. Zegrroz'rh's chilling, cyclopean insect's stare now made him an acceptably effective chaperone.

"But why have they come here at all?" Gog'resssh hissed. "If the mammals wish to evade Krassrr, why did they not skitter away and flee this system altogether?"

"Maybe their engines have suffered damage," Z'shezhira ventured. "Perhaps they no longer have the option of making a hasty exit."

"And they just happened not to see us as they entered the atmosphere over this world's north polar region," Gog'resssh said with a skeptical growl.

"Consider all the ionization and auroral effects the mammal vessel created on its way in, First Myrmidon," Z'shezhira said. "It is not difficult to believe that their sensors were sufficiently obscured during their descent for them to have failed to detect our presence so near to them."

"Their hull is no longer ionized, and only tens of thousands of manus now separate our two vessels," Gog'resssh said. "They should no longer be blind to us."

Z'shezhira spread her claws in a gesture of incomplete knowledge. "It is possible that some of their instruments were blinded permanently during their harsh descent. But we must also take into account the fact that we are significantly deeper in Hranrar's atmosphere than *Tie-tan* is. We therefore receive more of the combined shielding effects of both the atmosphere and the planetary magnetic field."

Z'shezhira wasn't entirely sure yet whether *Tie-tan*'s apparent lingering blindness was a good thing or a bad thing. She rejoiced, however, in the human vessel's presence, as well as in its relatively intact condition.

Which, of course, suggested that S'syrixx had remained intact as well.

"So they may be sightless," said Gog'resssh. "I wonder if they are also mute. Listen for any transmissions from *Tie-tan*. Perhaps they will reveal the real reason for their presence here."

"At once, First Myrmidon," Z'shezhira said, taking his command as permission to turn away from him and return her full attention to the communications console. She was surprised and pleased to be rewarded with some immediate results. "I am picking up some subspace beamscatter from a highly directional transmission. They appear to be attempting to hail someone."

"Another hidden ship?" Gog'resssh asked.

"Not unless that ship is located somewhere on the surface of the planet's northern hemisphere," said Z'shezhira.

"So they have already placed personnel on the ground," Gog'resssh said, sounding impressed. "And *Tie-tan* is checking in with them."

Z'shezhira again made the manus-gesture of incomplete knowledge. "Or at least they are making an attempt. The hail is repeating, over and over, but I see no indication as yet of any response."

"It may be that Rry'kurr came here for the same reason we did," Zegrroz'rh said. "To seek refuge and await the most propitious moment to mount a surprise attack against Krassrr."

"Then we may have a common cause with *Tie-tan,*" Z'shezhira said.

Moving menacingly toward her, Zegrroz'rh hissed his disapproval.

"Hear her out," Gog'resssh rumbled at his second, holding up a manus in a gesture of warning that froze his second in his tracks. Leaning so that his face came uncomfortably close to Z'shezhira's, the first myrmidon said, "Explain."

Z'shezhira paused long enough to ask silently that the Egg Bringer S'Yahazah guide her tongue and prevent her words from further endangering her beloved. "*Tie-tan*'s commander can only be here because he values the ecosculptor as much as Krassrr does. As much as *we* do." She knew it was critical now to reinforce in Gog'resssh's raddled mind the notion that she shared his interests.

Zegrroz'rh's incredulity came as no surprise. "*Of course* the mammals would love to get their paws on the ecosculptor. They would not hesitate to use it both as a weapon against us and as a means of remaking the worlds of the Gorn Hegemony for use by their own kind."

"Agreed," Z'shezhira said. "But working alone against Krassrr, they have no more chance than we do of taking the ecosculptor away from him before he uses it on this world. However, if we were to join forces with *Tie-tan,* work in tandem with the mammals, then we might succeed in—"

"Why in the name of all the grazerbeasts of Gornar should we want to take the ecosculptor *before* Krassrr tests it?" Zegrroz'rh said, interrupting. "I thought the plan was to gather our strength, restock our supplies—as we have just done—and then wait until Krassrr finishes ecosculpting this planet. The next step would be to take the ecosculptor and its first fruits as the birthright of our new warrior caste."

"The Typhon Pact fleet will probably arrive before any such test can occur," Gog'resssh said. "We would have to take the ecosculptor before that—and take it to some new world that it can reshape into the crècheworld of the new warrior caste we will found."

Madness, Z'shezhira thought, marveling at how little these rad-poisoned war-casters evidently understood of the realities of genetic diversity. Although Gog'resssh's surviving cadre of war-caster refugees from the destroyed Sazssgrerrn crècheworld contained individuals of both genders, its gene pool was neither broad enough nor deep enough to sustain an entirely new caste. The abortive mutiny had only further thinned out the war-caster ranks. And then there was the very real possibility that the radiation injuries the Sazssgrerrn catastrophe had visited upon the present slate of survivors had left most or all of them permanently sterile, their reproductive systems damaged beyond even the prodigious regenerative capacities of the hardiest members of the warrior caste. Whenever she contemplated her likely future with Gog'resssh, Z'shezhira could only pray that he numbered among the sterile.

And then there was the evident willingness—even eagerness—of both Gog'resssh and Zegrroz'rh to allow an entire world, millions of sentients who were far less repugnantly alien than the crew of *Tie-tan,* to be extirpated in pursuit of their futile plan.

Both steeled and shamed by her failure of nerve during the ill-fated mutiny attempt, Z'shezhira knew she couldn't simply sit back and allow any of this to come to pass.

"Well, tech-caster?" Zegrroz'rh snarled, evidently losing patience with her. "Is Krassrr not here to remake this planet to suit the needs of the warrior caste?"

Z'shezhira tipped her cranial crests forward to concede the second myrmidon's point. "So he is." Turning away from Zegrroz'rh so that she faced Gog'resssh squarely—making it crystal clear that she was addressing him and him alone—she continued. "But can you trust him to remake this planet to suit the new warrior caste *you* would build?"

Gog'resssh displayed his teeth, as well as a good deal of the interior of whatever creature he had eaten live during his most recent meal. Tracing the line of her left cranial crest with a single long claw, he said, "You mean the new warrior caste that *we* would build, together."

"Of course," she said calmly though she was now thoroughly nauseated. It wasn't just her captor's touch; it was also the realization that his understanding of gene-pool viability encompassed the necessity of severely bending Gorn society's ingrained cross-caste miscegenation taboo in order to build the future he envisioned.

Using the most persuasive tone of Voice she could muster, Z'shezhira continued. "If you wait . . . If *we* wait for Krassrr to complete his mission before we move to take Hranrar and the ecosculptor that will re-create it, then all we will have done is rebuild the same warrior caste that judged all of Sazssgrerrn's war-caster survivors to be unworthy of continued care and life after their rescue from the dead crèche's ashes."

"You really wish to make common cause with the Federrazsh'n mammals?" said Zegrroz'rh, incredulous. "Not even the weaklings in the political caste believe in such foolishness."

Gog'resssh said nothing. He had retreated inward, evidently evaluating what he was hearing. Z'shezhira knew from experience that this was when the first myrmidon was at his most dangerous. He would emerge from his meditations either with a calm acceptance of whatever suggestion had been made, or else with a stern—and usually physical—rebuke for any notion he deemed worthy of rejection.

Ignoring the second myrmidon, Z'shezhira continued working on Gog'resssh, layering her Voice in every overtone of trust she knew how to create. "I know you haven't forgotten how the war-casters who once commanded this ship—your own caste-peers—tried to euthanize you and all the other survivors of your garrison after we took you aboard and treated your wounds. They said it was 'for the greater good of the caste.' "

"Yessss," Gog'resssh said, his facial scales contorting into a fury that nearly made Z'shezhira flinch away.

"I implore you, First Myrmidon," she said, standing her ground against him. "Do something for the greater good of your caste now. Join forces with the mammals against Krassrr—at least until it is no longer convenient."

She prayed she'd get the chance to recover S'syrixx from the mammals' clutches before Gog'resssh's inevitable betrayal of *Tie-tan*'s commander and crew.

Heartbeat after heartbeat passed in silence as both Z'shezhira and Zegrroz'rh awaited the first myrmidon's decision.

"Hail *Tie-tan,*" Gog'resssh said finally. "Use a tight beam to prevent Krassrr from listening in."

Z'shezhira could scarcely contain her relief. "Immediately, First Myrmidon."

"This is unwise, First Myrmidon!" Zegrroz'rh exclaimed.

Gog'resssh flashed into motion with surprising speed. Moments later, Zegrroz'rh lay insensate on the deck. Z'shezhira's heart raced.

"Get me Rry'kurr," Gog'resssh said in a calm tone as cold as space.

HIGH ABOVE HRANRAR

The ancient thinker took in the sweeping blue curve of the world below with a feeling akin to awe. Having such rich raw material for its work was a vanishingly rare privilege. If only it could muster the power to do something with it. Unfortunately, time and entropy had long ago robbed it of this capability. For long eons, all the ancient thinker could do was listen to the voices of the small creatures who occasionally crossed the dark reaches in order to touch its body and organs with their energy pulses and their insignificantly tiny physical forms. Or watch with half-blind subspace eyes as its brethren succumbed one by one to the very same time and entropy that awaited everything that thought and lived, should it think and live long enough to experience it.

It had been ages since the ancient thinker had experienced the presence of so many smallminds at one time. And it was the first time it had experienced the simultaneous presence of two distinct groups. What a conundrum both groups presented, at turns unified and contentious, variegated and homogeneous, both within their respective groups and across whatever gulf of difference separated them one from another. Though the two groups were clearly mutually hostile, they were also more alike than either group realized. How long would it take, the ancient thinker wondered, before either or both groups understood that?

As a self-protective precaution, the ancient thinker extended a semipermeable subspace bubble around them, making it large enough so that the hundreds of smallminds on their various conveyances could communicate with one another when in close proximity, and yet small enough to prevent them from too easily summoning legions of other troublesome smallminds.

Unfortunately, that barrier could only delay the inevitable; already, the ancient thinker could sense the approach of a great armada of smallmind conveyances, all aligned with the most numerous of the two groups, coming in quickly from the Great Outer Darkness.

With one small portion of its vast but sedentary consciousness, the ancient thinker heard a new thread of cross-talk, something so far unprecedented: a dialogue between the two groups that did not appear to be the immediate precursor of either a fear-threat display or a violent conflict.

The ancient thinker settled in to listen. . . .

18

U.S.S. TITAN

"His name is Gog'resssh, Captain," Rager said as she examined the incoming hail. "He says his ship is not part of Krassrr's fleet."

Riker scowled as he leaned forward in his command chair. "Ship? What ship?"

Rager tapped a command into her console. "Sensors confirm the presence of his vessel, about a dozen klicks below us."

"Why didn't we detect his ship before now?"

"Look where we are, Captain," the senior ops officer said. "We're caught smack in a firehose of electromagnetic lines of force. We can barely see our hands in front of our faces, so to speak. My best guess is that we didn't see him earlier because he didn't want us to."

"Fair enough," Riker said. "What does he want?"

"He's asking to parley on a secure visual channel. He says Krassrr can't crack it."

"Pipe it into my ready room, Lieutenant," Riker said as he rose to his feet.

"I must advise caution, Captain," Tuvok said from the main tactical station. "The Gorn have a well known penchant for deception, going all the way back to the Cestus III massacre. I could also cite far more recent events."

Riker nodded, understanding that Tuvok was referencing S'syrixx's recent attempt to steal a shuttlecraft and escape from *Titan*—an action that Riker himself had thwarted with an act of pure guile. He felt reasonably confident in his ability to hold his own against whatever tricks this Gog'resssh might have up his sleeve. Still, he wished more than ever that Deanna could be at his side now to help him evaluate the veracity of this Gorn's words.

Pushing aside the ache of his wife's continued absence, he said, "Believe me, Commander, I'm fully aware of the risks of dealing with the Gorn. That's why I've got Commander Keru personally shadowing S'syrixx's every move." The Gorn tech-caster had complained of feeling unsettled shortly after *Titan*'s bumpy descent into Hranrar's atmosphere, so Riker had allowed him to return to Lieutenant Qontallium's borrowed crew quarters—under the close supervision of both Qontallium and Commander Keru, of course.

"But that Typhon Pact fleet is only about six hours away now," Riker continued. "We might not have warp capability for at least twice that long. Our away team is still out of touch and out of reach, despite every out-of-the-box technical trick Commander Pazlar, Torvig, and White-Blue have tried so far. And that artifact out there"—Riker gestured toward the distant, hazy image of Brahma-Shiva that hung on the forward viewscreen, nearly at horizon level—"could sweep every living thing on Hranrar into oblivion with almost no notice, thanks to our good friend Krassrr. I'd say that being overly cautious is a luxury we can't afford any longer."

Tuvok nodded, though his veneer of Vulcan calm seemed to have worn very thin indeed. "It is difficult to know how to proceed under circumstances such as these."

"Agreed. That's why I want you listening in on the conversation I'm about to have with this Gog'resssh. I'm going to need Mister S'syrixx's perspective as well. Just keep him out of sight when you bring him into the ready room."

The Vulcan nodded. "I will see to it, Captain."

Making haste to his private office off the bridge's forward starboard section, Riker sat alone at his desk and activated the computer that sat atop it. Within moments, a nightmarish visage—crocodilian except for its anomalously buggish eyes—appeared in the monitor's center. Partially healed burns and battle scars pocked and lined the creature's facial and cranial scales, forming roadmaps of pain, connecting craters and fissures that brought to mind the surfaces of ancient asteroids.

Definitely not a member of the Gorn Hegemony's lace-doily-knitting caste, Riker thought, making a mental note never to let his guard down around this one. Despite the reptiloid's obvious fierceness, this Gog'resssh didn't strike Riker as regular military. He also appeared singularly untrustworthy, in a way that somehow transcended Riker's own acknowledged visceral biological bias against sentient reptiles; right or wrong, he was certain he'd never invite Gog'resssh to *Titan*'s weekly officers' poker game.

"I'm Captain William T. Riker, commander of the Federation *Starship Titan,*" Riker said, opting for the strong, confident opening that often best concealed a weak hand. "To whom am I speaking?"

"I am First Myrmidon Gog'resssh, lately in command of

the Gorn Hegemony warship S'alath," growled the all but unreadable face on the screen. *"I believe that you and I can be of considerable help to one another, Captain."*

Riker nodded, impressed both by the creature's directness and the apparent sincerity of his overture. He was keenly aware, of course, that sincerity could be replicated at least as readily as most other commodities in the universe. "I hope that's true, First Myrmidon. Provided we both can find a way toward mutual trust."

"I can understand your reticence, Rry'kurr," Gog'resssh said. *"Our two peoples have had a long history of misunderstandings. My nation's recent decision to recall its envoys to your Federrazsh'n and co-found the Typhon Pact has no doubt greatly widened the breach that already separated us. It is hard to believe that only a suncircuit ago our fleets assisted your Sst'rfleet in opposing the incursions of the machine-mammals."*

The Borg.

Riker dipped his head forward in acknowledgment. "I salute your people's sacrifices."

"Would that I could have shared in them. Unfortunately, my duties at the time took me elsewhere."

A small amber light appeared at the bottom of Riker's screen, indicating that his ready-room door chime—which he had set to silent operation for the duration of this conversation—had been activated. He maintained eye contact with Gog'resssh as he touched a control on his desktop keypad, entering the override command that allowed the door to open with a quiet but appropriately serpentine hiss.

With a momentary upward glance, Riker noted that Tuvok had returned, and that he had S'syrixx, Keru, and Qontallium in tow. Per the orders he had given Tuvok, the quartet stood quietly just inside the ready room, their backs to the now-closed doors as they listened to the conversation and watched the reptilian face that was being relayed to the monitor on the ready-room visitor's table. Riker was the only person in the line of sight of the visual pickup.

Taking advantage of the Gorn commander's ostensible openness, Riker made an overture of his own. "I understand your frustration, First Myrmidon. During the Dominion War, I served aboard the *Enterprise*."

"The Federation's flagship. It bears a name as distinguished and freighted with history as that of the S'alath.*"*

Although his attention was largely focused on Gog'resssh, a stray movement from S'syrixx's direction momentarily caught Riker's eye. The Gorn technology expert seemed to have flinched, or at least tensed, at the mention of the name "S'alath." He mentally filed the observation away.

Focusing his entire attention back upon Gog'resssh, Riker said, "'S'alath.' I recognize that name. S'alath was the Gorn commander the Metrons pitted against Captain James Kirk right after the Cestus III massacre."

"The very same. At the Battle for Inner Eliar, S'alath was the warrior who thwarted a Met'rr'onz death sentence by defeating your K'irrk, despite his treacherous mammalian tricks."

Riker decided that the present moment might not be the best time to correct the rather large liberties Gog'resssh was taking with the history of Federation-Gorn relations. Instead, he said, "Kirk commanded an earlier era's *Enterprise*. As I was saying before, there were many times during the Dominion War when I wished my *Enterprise* had been more involved in the fighting."

"Then perhaps we are more alike than we are unalike, Captain," Gog'resssh said. *"We may even want the same thing from this planet."*

Though Riker was almost certain he already knew the answer, the question was worth asking. "What's that?"

"The ecosculptor."

Brahma-Shiva. "You're right about that, First Myrmidon. If that device really can rebuild entire planetary ecosystems to order, it would be tremendously useful for both the Gorn Hegemony and the Federation."

"Then let us work together," Gog'resssh said, *"to jointly acquire it."*

Riker held up a hand. "Let's discuss the issue of trust first. How do I know you're not secretly working with Krassrr?"

The relatively inflexible, bug-eyed visage displayed an expression that Riker could only interpret as disappointment. *"I know that Krassrr sought to destroy you, Rry'kurr. As far as I can tell, he believes he has already done so."*

"Krassrr holds us responsible for the destruction of one his ships," Riker said with a nod. "He's also accused us of stealing some of his fleet's food supplies."

Gog'resssh tipped his head forward so that his cranial crests seemed to make an ironic-looking salute. *"My apologies for Krassrr's error, Rry'kurr. The supplies in question now reside in the* S'alath's *hold."*

Riker realized that his first impression had been correct. Gog'resssh *wasn't* regular military.

He was a *pirate.*

"It was an act of treachery on my part, some would say," Gog'resssh continued. *"But were I possessed of a* truly *treach-*

erous frame of mind, I might have informed Krassrr of your real condition, as well as your present position. I have done neither."

Of course you haven't, Riker thought as his picture of the rogue Gorn's true agenda became clearer. *But that's only because you don't want Krassrr to know* your *whereabouts any more than I want him to know* mine.

He decided he could afford to believe what Gog'resssh had told him so far, though he still had other concerns. "Then perhaps we *can* work together, First Myrmidon Gog'resssh. By operating in tandem, the two of us might accomplish what neither of us could achieve separately."

"I am glad to see you are capable of making decisions quickly, Rry'kurr," Gog'resssh said around a formidable arsenal of newly revealed teeth. *"For little time remains for us to do what must be done. You must be aware that a Typhon Pact fleet is coming."*

Riker nodded. "Once those ships arrive, there will be no way for either of us to prevent Krassrr from using the ecosculptor to wipe out the Hranrarii."

Gog'resssh tipped his head to the side, as though he were pondering something puzzling. Even without the benefit of Deanna's empathic abilities, Riker could tell right away from the Gorn pirate's protracted silence that the fate of the Hranrarii had never even numbered among his lowest-priority considerations. He simply wanted to get his claws wrapped around a potent new technology as quickly as possible—without even allowing that technology's current possessors a chance to test it for him first.

"I know that your entire caste may soon face extinction without the intervention of the ecosculptor that Krassrr's crew is busy repairing right now," Riker said.

"Your Federrazsh'n intelligence gatherers are to be commended, Rry'kurr," Gog'resssh growled.

"Our subspace astronomers deserve some of the credit as well. A coronal mass ejection on the scale of the one that destroyed the warrior-caste crècheworld of Sazssgrerrn was bound to get noticed sooner or later."

Gog'resssh's multifaceted eyes narrowed slightly beneath the weight of his bony reptilian brow. *"Sazssgrerrn. I once thought I was destined to die there, unobserved and unmourned. I am gratified to hear that someone was watching, even if the watchers were only mammals."*

Riker ignored the Gorn's newest casual, almost pro forma slur. "Now the way I understand it, Krassrr intends to test the device on Hranrar. His plan seems to be to turn the planet into a replacement for Sazssgrerrn. Won't that benefit your entire caste? Why would you want to help me stop him from doing that?"

Gog'resssh snorted in evident derision. His usually unfathomable insectile eyes now seemed to glow with an eerie inner light. *"Krassrr would redesign this world to nurture the warrior caste as it* was. *Not as it is* destined *to be."*

Under your *benevolent rule, you mean,* Riker thought. *Piracy and paranoia, stir-fried with a healthy dollop of badly healed wounds and megalomania. Wonderful.*

Riker had no doubt that Gog'resssh would stab him in the back the moment the first myrmidon's objective was firmly in his scaly grasp.

He had only one question left. "Suppose destroying the ecosculptor turns out to be our only option?"

The Gorn pirate barely had to pause to consider his answer. *"It would not be my first choice, Rry'kurr. But that option would at least prevent Krassrr and those like him from achieving an irresistible advantage over my new warrior caste. I believe I could live with that eventuality, should it prove unavoidable."*

"Mister Gog'resssh, I think you and I may be able to do business together," Riker said.

"Then confer with your officers, Rry'kurr. I will call again in one of your hours to discuss specific plans. Gog'resssh out."

And with that the fearsome, scale-covered visage vanished from the screen, replaced by a neutral blue UFP emblem.

Riker pushed his chair back from his desk and favored the others with an expectant look. "Well?"

"I do not trust him, Captain," Tuvok said. "However, cooperating with him may enable us to take positive action on behalf of the Hranrarii—provided that action is concluded well before the arrival of the Typhon Pact fleet."

"I agree on both counts," Riker said. "Mister Keru?"

The big Trill scowled thoughtfully. "I can't argue with any of that, but I have to bring up one critical additional fact: we still don't have warp drive. If we try to save the Hranrarii by, say, blowing up Brahma-Shiva, then we'd better make sure we have our warp engines back online before we make the attempt. Otherwise we're talking about a suicide mission, pure and simple, whether the Typhon Pact fleet is here by then or not."

Riker's combadge interrupted the silence that reigned following Keru's simple but trenchant observation. *"Rager to Captain Riker."*

"Please tell me you have some good news, Lieutenant," Riker said with a sigh.

"I'm afraid I have both kinds of news, sir. It's about the away team."

"Give me the good news first," Riker said, steeling himself for the worst.

HIGH ABOVE HRANRAR

The ancient thinker was both surprised and puzzled. The two groups, each confined to a single conveyance, were simply . . . talking. *And more, they seemed to be working together toward a common cause. They both seemed to be trying to pool their respective feeble subspace communications abilities for the purpose of communicating with other smallminds on the surface of the world that turned far below the ancient thinker.*

Pleased by this apparent amity, as well as curious about the eventual outcome, the ancient thinker decided to offer some unobtrusive assistance. . . .

HRANRAR

"Just keep cooperating with them, people," Vale said, paying particular attention to Lieutenant Sortollo.

The big Italian appeared to have had his fill already of being, almost literally, frogmarched through the Hranrarii city by the dozen or so identically tattooed amphibious locals who surrounded the away team. All of them wore harnesses that bristled with Hranrarii tools that probably filled every function from communications devices to scanners to weapons. Unfortunately, those harnesses also contained some far more familiar-looking objects in addition to the enigmatic local ones.

"I'd feel a lot more cooperative if we hadn't let them take our phasers, Commander," Sortollo said drily as he continued walking quickly down an eerily quiet street that suggested the away team was being conducted along a prearranged, cordoned-off route. Despite the relatively traffic-free conditions, there was no shortage of wide, lanternlike eyes peering out of windows and over the edges of rooftops, prompting Vale to wonder whether Troi was picking up more curiosity than fear, more wonder than judgment.

Keeping her tone even so as not to alarm or annoy their captors, Vale said, "Stand down, Lieutenant. If we'd handled this encounter your way, we probably would have had a running firefight on our hands. We were outnumbered, remember? Besides, they haven't tried to hurt us so far. Something tells me that won't change unless we start making trouble for them."

"So my empathic sense keeps telling me," Troi said quietly, leaning close to Vale to make herself heard as the group walked briskly through the forest of spires. "But I wonder how *you* can be so sure."

"Chalk it up to my pre-Starfleet law-enforcement career. I know cops when I see 'em, phylum notwithstanding."

"We've been taken into custody by the local constabulary?" asked Ensign Modan. She sounded nervous, as though worried about where she might find the bail money necessary to secure her release.

"I suppose things could be worse," Ensign Evesh said acerbically as she struggled to match the fairly quick pace the away team's captors obviously desired. "We could have fallen into the hands—er, claws—of a squad of Gorn troopers."

Vale nodded. "We can be thankful that Hranrar's gendarmes seem to be a bit gentler than some other policefolk I could name. They haven't seen fit to stun us or restrain us. All they did was take our weapons."

"But I presume they also confiscated all the supplies we beamed down with when we bailed out of the *Beiderbecke,*" said Ensign Dakal.

"Probably," Vale said.

"So why didn't they take our tricorders or combadges as well?" Troi asked.

Vale shrugged. "I was hoping you could tell *me* that, Deanna."

The diplomatic officer brushed a stray hank of dark hair from in front of her face. Her dark eyes took on a strange, distant cast as she spoke. "I'm empathic, Chris. Not omniscient."

Vale turned her head in time to notice that Dakal seemed to be expending a lot of effort to touch his combadge without making a great show of doing so. A moment later he scowled and shook his head as he walked. "They might as well have taken the combadges along with the phasers, Commander. Something is still preventing us from contacting *Titan.* It's probably because of some sort of comm-dampening devices our hosts are carrying. Maybe if we still had the big portable transceiver with us . . ." Dakal allowed the thought to trail off, incomplete yet completely understood.

And even if you could *raise* Titan *right now,* Vale thought with a glumness she worked hard to conceal, *she probably couldn't beam us out of here through all the atmospheric craziness anyway.*

"I hope it doesn't have anything to do with *that,*" Modan said as she momentarily broke her stride, and thus that of the entire group. She was pointing toward a narrow swatch of the purpling, late-afternoon northern sky framed in the gap between two of the Hranrarii city's mighty towers.

Stopping along with the entire group, Vale watched in silence as something traced a silent, elliptical line of fire near the horizon, throwing off gouts of plasma and debris as it finished its ballistic descent.

"Oh, shit," said Sortollo.

Vale turned toward Troi, silently asking her what she knew had to be on everyone's mind.

"I can still feel my connection to Will and Natasha," Troi said at length.

Thank God, Vale thought, though she realized she was holding in her breath. Pointing at the pyrotechnics, she said, "Now please tell me that isn't *Titan.*"

Troi said nothing. As the Hranrarii police gently nudged the group back into motion, her face looked like a study in fear and uncertainty.

19

U.S.S. TITAN

S'syrixx found that he was growing not to mind Lieutenant Qontallium's company. Perhaps the respective losses they had suffered had forged something of a bond between them. This quiet collegiality made the fact that S'syrixx was always being watched closely at least somewhat bearable. Between the presence of Qontallium, the hulking mammal Keru, or one of *Tie-tan*'s other armed security personnel, S'syrixx was never left entirely alone, whether he was walking the ship's corridors, visiting a recreation area, eating an inadequate (and sadly nonliving) replicated meal, or even seeing to his personal hygiene.

That utter lack of solitude made what he had to do difficult, but not impossible. As he sat on the edge of the bed in Qontallium's quarters, his long, clawed fingers working the controls of a Sst'rfleet padd, he silently thanked Great S'Yahazah that there seemed to be limits to the extent of his guard-cum-companion's vigilance.

And for the fact that in the correct manus, a Sst'rfleet padd could be used to gain remote access to other systems aboard *Tie-tan*. . . .

GORN HEGEMONY WARSHIP *S'ALATH*

Ever since her initial engineering training as a youngling in the Techademie, Z'shezhira's singular gift for pattern recognition had placed her near the top of her training cohort. This talent enabled her to perceive patterns where others did not. Sometimes those patterns went undetected by her peers because of their own relative obtuseness. Other times, those patterns were merely products of her own overactive imagination, artifacts of her innate but constant desire to impose order upon chaos.

The moment she noticed the repetitious regularity of the infrared pulsations coming from *Tie-tan*'s impulse exhaust manifold, she was convinced they were not a by-product of the other vessel's engines.

Feverishly working her console on the command deck, she isolated and amplified the patterns, parsing them. She paused and looked about the command deck, where a pair of Gog'resssh's junior officers were examining their own consoles in desultory fashion.

Both war-casters looked listless, as though the radiation exposure they had suffered at Sazssgrerrn were finally about to catch up with them in terminal fashion.

Z'shezhira knew she couldn't count on any such luck. But she was more willing to accept a smaller particle of good fortune: the fact that neither war-caster seemed to have noticed the careful modulations that someone had so cleverly hidden beneath the surface chaos of *Tie-tan*'s waste-heat emission stream.

Someone who was using a Techademie pulse-code that

any sufficiently adept Gorn tech-caster could easily translate to, say, *Z'shezhira, I am safe here among the mammals. What is your condition?*

How should she reply? Tapping into the *S'alath*'s waste engine heat in the manner S'syrixx had evidently done aboard *Tie-tan* might prove both time-consuming and dangerous, since it would force her to risk rousing suspicion by accessing secure engineering systems. Instead, she opted to reply by flashing several of the running lights on the side of the *S'alath*'s hull that faced *Tie-tan.*

I am safe for the moment, beloved S'syrixx, she keyed, speaking with her right manus, one coded linguicharacter at a time. *But I cannot be certain how long I will remain so. Be strong. We will be reunit—*

"Do you believe me to be a *fool*?" thundered an enraged male war-caster directly behind her. His breath was nearly as evil as his temperament.

Her heart tried to rise through her jaws to flee her body as she turned to face the voice's owner. How could she have let herself be so unforgivably absentminded as to fail to hear—or smell—Gog'resssh's approach?

The war-caster's first blow landed before she even saw it coming.

20

HRANRAR

Now that the away team was finally standing before someone who obviously had more authority than the arresting officers who had brought them to the courtyard at the top of the tower, it occurred to Vale that she had finally received the opportunity to use the line she'd wanted to try since she'd first joined Starfleet:

"Please take me to your leader."

Vale was gratified to note that each member of the away team stood at attention, and that nearly everyone had adopted a poker face. The only exception was Lieutenant Sortollo, who was working visibly to suppress a grin.

The froglike, grasshopper-legged being into whose presence the constables had conducted the away team regarded its prisoners with wide, curious eyes. Unlike the local cops—as Vale had come to think of them since they'd confiscated the away team's gear, including the storage modules they had filled with Hranrarii data—this creature wore a sort of shawl made of a dark material whose texture looked to be somewhere between sharkskin and seaweed. Vale figured the shawl for a badge of office of some kind, though the "office" into which the away team had been herded more closely resembled a marshy meadow whose limits seemed to be the same as the tower-roof upon which it had been constructed. As the afternoon slumped into evening, those unfenced boundaries—and the kilometer-long drop that lay beyond them in every direction—seemed to be creeping inexorably inward, coming uncomfortably close.

"It is too soon in the criminal adjudication process for you to appeal to the higher levels of Hranrarii government," the creature said evenly, making Vale thankful that the away team's universal translators, at least, could be relied upon. "I am Senior Watcher Ereb, in charge of maintaining order in the Ghoziv Connurbation."

"Commander Christine Vale," Vale said, keeping her hands at her sides since the Hranrarii magistrate was making no move to employ any sort of greeting involving physical touch. "Executive officer of the Federation *Starship Titan.*"

Senior Watcher Ereb tipped its head almost sideways in apparent curiosity. "Federation?"

"The United Federation of Planets," Troi said. "We are a galactic civilization whose capital resides on a world more than three thousand light-years from here. The Federation consists of more than one hundred fifty member worlds, all working together for the common good."

"That sounds very noble. But your story so far does not comport with the sabotage charges of which you stand accused."

"Sabotage?" Vale said, confused.

"Our biometric recorders have positively identified members of your group," Ereb said, pausing while gesturing toward Ensigns Dakal and Evesh, "as being responsible for destroying Outer Information Node Nine Nineteen Green."

Since the local surveillance technology had evidently trumped the team's holographic disguises, Vale decided it was pointless to deny what had happened. It would make more sense, and probably curry more favor, to point out the mitigating circumstances. "Believe me, Senior Watcher, we had no intention of destroying anything."

"Yet destroy you did. Your unauthorized datatap killed Node Nine Nineteen Green's caretaker."

A sick feeling seized the pit of Vale's stomach. Dakal had mentioned the presence of organic components in the data hub. Evidently the organic mass that had governed the information hub's data traffic had been a good deal more complex than a mere gel pack. Perhaps it had even been a sentient being.

"When a Node falls, all of Hranrar is poorer for it. The damage will be reversed as soon as is practical, of course. But we cannot make the node operational again until we breed another caretaker."

"I had no idea," Dakal said.

"We intended no harm," said Evesh, sounding offended, as though the magistrate had unjustly impugned her motivations.

"Belay that, both of you," Vale snapped at the ensigns. Addressing Ereb, she said, "Whatever harm resulted from the team's actions is *my* responsibility. I ask that you save whatever penalties or punishments you have to mete out for me, and me alone."

"An interesting philosophical sally," Ereb said in tones the translator rendered as mild and contemplative. "But we Hranrarii believe in self-responsibility for each sentient creature. We do not regard responsibility as a transferable function."

"Well, I suppose I can't do anything about that," Vale said. "But we didn't come here to commit crimes, or to plead them out in your judicial system."

Ereb began walking in silence before the Starfleet officers, who had arranged themselves in a shoulder to shoulder line, like cadets being reviewed by a fleet admiral. At last the magistrate came to a stop directly in front of Vale, upon whom she focused two golden, owlish eyes. Several of the nearby cops edged closer, like outfielders approaching the baseball diamond in anticipation of a weak batter.

We must be the most exciting thing to come across this burg's police blotter in years, Vale thought.

"All of you do indeed appear to be something other than Hranrarii," Ereb said.

"We're human, Tellarite, Cardassian, Betazoid, and Selenean," Troi said. "As such we represent only a small sampling of the diversity that comprises the Federation."

Vale scowled at the diplomatic officer; now was probably not the best time to make a hard-sell Federation membership pitch.

"Very well," Ereb said. "If you have not come to destroy, then why *have* you come?"

"We're explorers," Vale said. "Our vessel's principal mission is to gather knowledge. In carrying out that mission we have learned that your world is in grave danger."

"Danger. I assume you refer to a danger other than a mortal threat to our global information network."

As badly as she felt about that, Vale was beginning to

tire of the subject. After all, if Captain Krassrr and the Gorn fleet carried out their plans, the global information network would very soon be the least of the Hranrarii's worries.

"There is a huge alien object orbiting your world," Vale said, looking up to the darkening sky. She wished she could see it and point it out for emphasis, but she knew that the object was keeping station somewhere over Hranrar's opposite side. "This object contains extremely dangerous energies. As we speak, members of a species called the Gorn are trying to release those energies. If they succeed, your planet will be scoured of every living thing. And the Gorn will simply move in and take what was once yours."

Though Ereb had listened with apparent patience, she—Vale had arbitrarily decided that the senior watcher was a she—did not seem convinced.

"I have seen the object that you speak of," Ereb said. "It is visible from the ground, even without a farseer. But it hasn't yet given anyone a reason to fear it."

"Trust me," Sortollo said. "When it *does* give you a reason, your people probably won't have *time* to be afraid."

"So you say," Ereb said. "And who created this . . . fearsome object? Surely not your benevolent Federation."

Vale gritted her teeth. "Of course not. All we want to do is learn as much as we can about it. And make sure it isn't misused as a weapon against the Hranrarii or anybody else."

"Ah. Hence your urgent need to speak to our planetary leaders."

She's not gonna buy what I'm selling, Vale thought. "Yes.

One of the things we learned from your info… work is that your world is already capable of blowing t… threat out of your sky. I want to encourage your government to do exactly that."

Ereb stood for a long moment in thoughtful silence, her huge amphibian eyes giving an air of cool appraisal. Or was Vale seeing the disdainful stare of an avowed pacifist who had just been told there was no alternative to fighting?

If these people really are *pacifists, that might help explain why they never applied their matter-antimatter technology to the purpose of space flight,* she thought. After all, alien contact all too often had the unfortunate consequence of alien conflict.

Vale watched as Ereb turned toward the cops. "Leave the prisoners locked up here overnight," the senior watcher said. "I will decide what is to be done about them by the time the morning arrives."

Moments later, a small grassy hill extruded upward from the otherwise flat meadowland of the tower's roof. A divot in the grass opened and grew until it became large enough to accommodate Senior Watcher Ereb and the entire group of constables, all of whom entered it. Then the divot sealed itself and the resulting greenery-covered mound of earth quickly settled down until it was once again flush with the rest of the meadow.

"Wow," Vale said into the ensuing silence of the rapidly approaching night. "I think this may be the first time I've ever seen a building with a grass elevator."

Now that they were unaccompanied for the first time since their capture by the Hranrarii, the away team broke formation. Tricorders came out and scans commenced as team members moved this way and that from what Vale judged to be roughly the center of the meadow.

"Don't get too close to the edge, people," Vale called out to the entire group as Sortollo and Troi approached her. "That first step down to street level is a lulu."

"I thought the justice of the peace said something about locking us up," Sortollo said. "Where are the bars?"

"Do you see any way off of this rooftop that doesn't involve accelerating to terminal velocity?" Vale snarked, though she understood how difficult it could be to square the team's present bucolic surroundings with the fact that they were really standing atop one of the tallest buildings in the Hranrarii city. They were therefore confined no less than they would be at the penal colony in New Zealand, or in the dilithium mines of icy Rura Penthe.

"Good point," Sortollo said. "I suppose installing bars would just be gilding the lily."

"At least it's pretty up here," Troi said. "I wonder how cold it's going to get, though. Assuming we're here all night, that is."

Noting a slight cooling and acceleration in the breeze, Vale wondered why the local gendarmes couldn't at least have brought their thermal provisions along. "Let's hope we're not stuck here long enough to find out."

Acting out of habit, she tapped her combadge and said, "Vale to *Titan*."

She expected to be greeted, yet again, with static-laced silence, to be followed by feelings of foreboding as she wondered what had become of the starship. Could *Titan* really have burned up in the atmosphere? Or was her captain merely employing the time-honored tactic of "playing dead" for the time being?

Instead, she received a surprise that nearly made her leap off the roof. "Titan *here, Commander,"* Will Riker said. *"Give me a sit rep."*

U.S.S. TITAN

"Somehow we've managed to pierce the ship-to-shore interference," Riker said, delighted that he was once again hearing the voices of his away team—and his *Imzadi*. "We're on a tight beam, so there's not much chance of Krassrr intercepting this. But that's only the good news."

"We can take it, Captain," said Christine Vale. *"What's the bad news?"*

Relaying the very information that Lieutenant Rager had just given him after his ready-room conversation with Gog'resssh, Riker said, "We still can't establish a transporter lock. Considering the fact that we're hiding out in the most geomagnetically active zone in this planet's atmosphere, we shouldn't be able to establish audio contact either. But I'll take whatever I can get."

"If the same thing should happen with the transporter, then we'll all take that, too," Deanna said.

"Believe me, Counselor, if that should happen you'll all be beamed up so fast it'll make you dizzy." Though he kept his tone light, being so paradoxically near to yet far from his wife caused him an almost physical sensation of pain, deep in his gut. "In the meantime, let's hope your instincts about Hranrarii pacifism are on target. Deanna, are you and Chris on the same page about that?"

"I believe so, Will."

"At least it means you'll probably be safe down there until we can find a way to retrieve you."

"There's that," Vale said. *"Still, I have to wonder how the Hranrarii's apparent aversion to violence squares with a need for armed cops."*

"Even the pacifist society on Halka creates enough low-level troublemakers to need a small police force, Chris."

"Point taken. But if these people are true pacifists, then convincing them that they have a better option than just letting the Gorn blow their ecosphere to quarks could be a much tougher sell. Unless these people are secretly superbeings like the Organians, they're about to be royally screwed."

As unfortunate as it was, such was the fate that all too often befell pacifists—as well as those unfortunate enough to be caught in their midst whenever somebody more aggressive decided to let slip the dogs of war.

"I swear I'll get all of you out of there before the Gorn have their way with the place," he said. "I could send a shuttlecraft out now. You're on a rooftop."

"I wouldn't do it, Captain," Vale said. *"Not unless Brahma-Shiva is showing signs of imminent Ragnarok, if you'll pardon my mixed pantheons. There's still a chance we might persuade these people to act on their own behalf. We start flying evac missions, then we'd not only be putting our theories about Hranrarii pacifism to the test, we'd also be tipping our hand to Krassrr."*

"Krassrr's not the only Gorn commander I'm concerned about," Riker said, and then filled his exec in on the conversation he'd just had with the rogue Gorn skipper about making a joint effort to neutralize Brahma-Shiva before its final activation.

"Please don't tell me you're going to trust *him, Captain,"* Vale said.

Riker grinned. "Let's just say I trust him to act in what he perceives to be his own self-interest. Don't worry, Chris—I won't be sticking my head in his jaws."

"That's a sound policy regarding the Gorn, sir. Very prudent."

Riker chuckled. "Keep me apprised of any changes, Commander. I'll do likewise. *Titan* out."

Rager turned from her console to face Riker. Her dark features were folded into a puzzled frown. "Captain, I'm picking up some unauthorized use of the external comm-system protocols. According to the comm logs, the transmissions were sent via the impulse exhaust manifolds."

"Sent where?" If somebody in Krassrr's fleet had received a "posthumous" message from *Titan,* then life was about to get an order of magnitude more complicated for everyone on board—not to mention for the away team that was still trapped on Hranrar's surface.

After consulting her console for a moment, Rager said, "The message was transmitted to Gog'resssh's ship. The *S'alath.*"

Having nearly been burned badly once already, the name of only one possible culprit sprang to mind. "S'syrixx." Riker rose from his chair and strode toward the turbolift. "Mister Gibruch, you have the bridge."

The human came storming unexpectedly into Qontallium's quarters, his entrance briefly seeming to startle the Gnalish Fejimaera security officer as much as it did S'syrixx. S'syrixx had never before seen Rry'kurr appear so angry.

"You haven't been honest with us, Mister S'syrixx," the

mammal said with a snarl that would have done credit to Captain Krassrr himself.

"I . . . do not know what you mean," S'syrixx said, though his protestation sounded weak even to himself.

Rry'kurr stopped after his furry mammalian face had gotten to within the width of a youngling's manus of S'syrixx's broad snout. "Fortunately for me, my executive officer can match you high-tech trick for high-tech trick—and she's at least twice as suspicious as I am. She thought you might try something like this after your little meltdown in sickbay."

S'syrixx took an involuntary step backward, toward the window that displayed the planet's frozen polar reaches and their auroral fireworks. The shelf below the window still supported the holopicture of Qontallium and his slain mate. S'syrixx's mind reeled; he'd been clumsy and stupid in tripping over an overzealous Federrazsh'n officer's security protocols.

"I know you're communicating with somebody aboard the *S'alath,*" Rry'kurr continued, advancing relentlessly as S'syrixx retreated. "Are you working with Gog'resssh?"

S'syrixx tried not to cower, but he couldn't bear to let the mammal get any closer to him. "No, Rry'kurr. I do not . . . work well with war-casters. Krassrr, for example."

"All right. Then who were you talking to aboard the *S'alath*?"

At length, S'syrixx said, "Z'shezhira was serving aboard the *S'alath* when Gog'resssh seized command over a suncircuit ago."

"Z'shezhira?" Rry'kurr demanded.

"My . . . betrothed. She is caught in Gog'resssh's claws, Rry'kurr."

The human lapsed into silence. He backed away a few paces, and seemed to calm somewhat as he processed what S'syrixx had told him. S'syrixx knew that Rry'kurr was separated from his own mate at the moment; perhaps he could even understand something of what S'syrixx was experiencing.

But was any mammal, however clever, *really* capable of empathy?

"So *that's* what you've been holding back," Rry'kurr said at length, his tone now far milder than when he had entered.

"It can be difficult to learn to trust, Rry'kurr," S'syrixx said.

"It's not any easier for me, Mister Ssy'rixx. Which is why I'm confining you to these quarters until that changes. And that means no access to padds or computers until further notice."

S'syrixx favored the mammal with a good-natured snort. "That's far better treatment than I received from Krassrr. Rry'kurr, is there anything you can do to free her from Gog'resssh?"

The mammal looked at him quietly for a lengthy moment with those disconcertingly tiny eyes. "I don't know, S'syrixx. But I'll do whatever I can. Provided you aren't withholding any *other* important information."

"I've told you everything," S'syrixx lied. There were some secrets so deep that they were beyond the ken of even the most cunning of mammals. "All I ask is that you continue to allow me to help you in your efforts to save the Hranrarii."

Rry'kurr began moving toward the door. "Mister S'syrixx," he said, "I think I'm going to need all the help I can get."

GORN HEGEMONY WARSHIP *S'ALATH*

Z'shezhira gradually became aware that a metal grillwork was pressing against her face, biting into the delicate scales near her right eye. Feeling, which consisted predominantly of pain, returned to her body, which she discovered was in a prone position. She hooked her claws into the deck grille, and the muscles in her arms burned as she pushed herself up into a sitting position.

Amid the gray starkness of what she immediately recognized as a warrior-grade detention cell, Second Myrmidon Zegrroz'rh towered over her, his body hunched in a taut, battle-ready crouch.

"You would be dead now if the decision were mine to make," he snarled. "I would have spaced you after your first act of betrayal."

She offered him only silence. *I cannot betray that toward which I feel no loyalty.*

The blue forcefield that protected the hatch threshold behind Zegrroz'rh suddenly flashed, then vanished altogether to admit First Myrmidon Gog'resssh. The commander stepped into the chamber, and the security screen returned with an ozone-tinged crackle a moment later.

"Then it is fortunate indeed that this vessel runs on my authority rather than yours, *Second* Myrmidon," Gog'resssh said. "Get to your station."

With a muttered grumble, the second myrmidon acceded, exiting the cramped cell.

Z'shezhira quietly studied Gog'resssh as Zegrroz'rh lumbered past. Although the first myrmidon appeared as authoritative and steady as ever, his facial and cranial scales seemed to be growing discolored, graying slightly around the edges as though he were finally beginning to succumb to the radiation exposure that he and his troopers had experienced at Sazssgrerrn. She wondered how long it had been since he had consented to a radiation treatment?

Perhaps, if we are all fortunate, his own fear of being poisoned by an infirmary medic will soon become his undoing, she thought.

"I have seen the message you received from *Tie-tan,*" Gog'resssh said. "I know you have a confederate aboard the mammal vessel. "If I did not need your genes to establish a new, more intelligent warrior caste, I would have left you to Zegrroz'rh's tender mercies a good deal longer."

Still seated on the hard deck, she rotated her shoulders slightly and winced at the pain the small movement generated. "It feels as though the time-interval was more than adequate."

Gog'resssh's chest resonated with a guttural, chuffing laugh as he reached down, grabbed her left cranial crest, and pulled her painfully to her feet. "There is a price for acting in bad faith, little egg bringer. But as I said, I need your wisdom to help shape the future." He released her cranial crest and turned toward the cell's sole entrance.

Z'shezhira struggled to maintain control over her breathing. "What future?"

He came to a stop less than a claw's width from the blue forcefield, which crackled and snapped as though driven to hunger by the nearness of Gorn flesh. "Why, the future that you yourself helped me visualize. A future in which a new

Gorn warrior caste, a hybrid of my lineage and yours, takes control of the entire Gorn Hegemony."

She nodded, understanding to the marrow of her bones that it would be extremely unwise to do anything other than humor him. "Yes, First Myrmidon."

"The ranks of my warriors are badly depleted," he said, deactivating the forcefield with an almost casual flick of his claws against the large, blunt keypad on the gray wall beside him. "As are your own caste's numbers here aboard the *S'alath*."

"I know," she said, feeling no small amount of regret. How many tech-caste lives might she have saved had her will to resist Gog'resssh not broken?

"I need you on the command deck, at your post," he said, stepping out into the narrow, semidarkened corridor. "To help me take the first step into the new warrior caste's future, just as you suggested."

Not at all certain she was experiencing either eagerness or reluctance, she followed him. "What exactly would this . . . first step involve?"

He paused in his march toward the command-deck lift and regarded her with his eerie insectoid gaze, his eyes refulgent with their own internal light. "We will destroy the ecosculptor before Krassrr can use it to annex this world for his old-order warriors—and before the mammals try to steal it for themselves. Before this dayturn ends, I will have set the old warrior caste back on its heels, frustrated the ambitions of the Federrazsh'n mammals, and even taken one of their most advanced vessels as part of a fleet of my own."

He turned and strode quickly toward the lift, leaving Z'shezhira to trot behind him. Though she was as disgusted as ever by the notion of sharing her genes with a mad war-caster—and it was surely nothing short of madness to entertain such ambitious plans of conquest when a Typhon Pact fleet would soon arrive to weigh in on much of Gog'resssh's agenda—she allowed herself to feel some relief as well; after all, a successful sneak attack on the ecosculptor would generate the decidedly nontrivial side effect of survival for millions of Hranrarii, unless certain Gorn or Typhon Pact decision-makers took the unlikely step of holding Hranrar responsible for the deed, rather than Gog'resssh.

As she once again contemplated the monster who would use her as a broodmother, she thought, *I wonder if the Hranrarii crossed Gog'resssh's mind even once.*

U.S.S. TITAN

Lacking access to any part of *Tie-tan* other than Lieutenant Qontallium's quarters—to say nothing of access to any device capable of interfacing with shipboard computer systems—S'syrixx had little to do but stare contemplatively through the window at the curvature of northern Hranrar. When he wasn't doing that, he was either gazing at the holophoto of the late Senior CPO Sar Antillea, or engaging her widowed mate in desultory conversation.

S'syrixx carefully avoided mentioning Antillea, however, so as not to remind himself of the peril his own beloved still faced.

The door chime sounded, prompting Qontallium to say, "Enter."

The tall, broad, and very hirsute mammal known as Ranul Keru entered, ducking slightly as he crossed the low threshold. He exchanged nods with Qontallium before approaching S'syrixx closely.

"The captain has made a change of plans," Keru said. "Because he still relies on your input, he wanted you to be informed."

"I am grateful to be taken into consideration," S'syrixx said, completely sincere. "What plan has changed?"

"With the Typhon Pact fleet only a little more than five hours out, the chances of successfully snatching the terraforming device away from Krassrr look to be about nil," Keru said. "Captain Riker has decided that our only option is to mount a sneak attack and destroy the thing outright. It's a shame, but it's the only way to prevent Krassrr from wiping out the Hranrarii. The captain just thought you ought to know while he's busy going over the tactical plans."

No, S'syrixx thought. *No, no, no,* no*!*

Feigning calmness, he said, "I need to speak with Rry'kurr immediately. He is not in possession of all the facts."

21

The damned thing is a sentient life-form, Riker thought as he made for Lieutenant Qontallium's quarters at a dead run. *God* damn.

Once he got inside, he lit into the Gorn without any preamble. "Why the hell didn't you tell me about this the *last* time you were allegedly leveling with me?"

"Because I was protecting something that many in my caste regard as holy," S'syrixx said.

"Holy? You're telling me that an ancient machine intelligence of some sort runs and maintains Brahma-Shiva—and that it's now somehow part of the Gorn religion as well?"

"I have come to believe that the mind that resides in that machine is nothing less than S'Yahazah Herself."

"S'Yahazah?"

"The Great Egg Bringer of Gorn prehistory. Our culture is extremely old, Rry'kurr, on the order of a million or more suncircuits. S'Yahazah, the progenitor of all the present-day castes, is the wielder of the awesome power of creation."

"And you believe this . . . S'Yahazah lives inside the artifact."

"It is the belief that has caused me to jeopardize both

my career and my very life in order to protect an entire planet—even as I acted to safeguard the life and integrity of the intelligence that inhabits the ecosculptor. When I initially disabled the device, Rry'kurr, I could have simply planted explosives on board, or forced it to deorbit and burn up in Hranrar's atmosphere. Haven't you wondered why I did neither of those things?"

In truth, he hadn't; time for reflective thought had not been in great abundance since his first encounter with Krassrr. "I suppose I assumed you were only trying to slow down Krassrr's mission—not destroy it."

"I was, but for reasons I could not reveal to you. Not without speaking of the ineffable before nonbelievers."

Riker folded his arms across his chest. "Well, you don't seem to have any problem doing that now—and in front of a lowly mammal, no less."

S'syrixx sat on the edge of Qontallium's hard bed and wrapped his arms across his chest, mirroring Riker's body language. "It was either that or see S'Yahazah destroyed by those same lowly mammals, Rry'kurr. No offense intended."

"None taken, Mister S'syrixx. I *like* being a mammal. Now why should I believe there's an AI living aboard that device, let alone a figure out of Gorn theology?"

S'syrixx leaned forward, his cranial crests moving slightly up and down as though driven by some wheel that turned within the reptiloid's great head. "When I was working aboard Krassrr's fleet I measured its thought-output—that which your Doctor Ree might describe as 'brainwave patterns.' We have seen this thought-output—the will of the entity that dwells inside the ecosculptor, regardless of whether or not one believes it to be S'Yahazah's own—manifest itself on many occasions."

Riker felt his brow furrow. "Manifest how?"

"I believe that the large-scale subspace communications interference *Tie-tan* has encountered all across this system to be S'Yahazah's handiwork, as well as the fortuitous instances of our breaking through it."

"You seem to be saying that a ghost in the machine—"

"A goddess," S'syrixx corrected, interrupting.

"—a goddess in the machine is arbitrarily deciding which comm signals we can send and receive, and which ones we can't."

"There is nothing arbitrary about it, Rry'kurr. S'Yahazah always follows a plan, even if its purpose is obscure to us. I believe that She is encouraging us to parley with our adversaries rather than fight them, and vice versa. That is why she has allowed us to speak with Krassrr and Gog'resssh, all the while barring our subspace signals from getting past the system's periphery."

Riker nodded, though he wasn't sanguine about accepting S'syrixx's story just yet. "Which would explain why we had to send our shuttlecraft pretty far outside the system to establish contact with Starfleet. I suppose *Titan* would have to travel a comparable distance to get beyond the reach of . . ." He trailed off.

"Of a goddess," S'syrixx said with no evident embarrassment. "Krassrr doubtless had much the same difficulty in summoning the Typhon Pact fleet that now approaches."

"So I have to weigh a global civilization of millions against a single AI," Riker said. Stated that way, the math still looked pretty straightforward. A simple case of the needs of the many outweighing the needs of the few.

But thoughts of another machine intelligence haunted him. The ghost of his late friend Data, a sentient being whose life had been no less valuable than that of any of Riker's other friends or colleagues, wouldn't let the captain resolve the conflict so simply.

"I hope what I have told you causes you to revise your plan of attack," S'syrixx said.

"It will," Riker said. "But I can't sacrifice millions just to save one. And I won't knowingly kill an intelligent being—even a machine intelligence—to save those millions."

"But what if you cannot rescue both? What will you do then?"

"I'll just have to find a way to split the difference," Riker said. He felt a gentle smile tugging at the corners of his mouth. "Come with me, Mister S'syrixx."

Xin Ra-Havreii took his seat at the conference table along with the rest of his away team, Lieutenant Commander Pazlar, the captain, and *Titan*'s Gorn guest. He stopped trying to conceal his annoyance at the last-minute, unplanned gathering.

"We're more than ready for this away mission, Captain," the chief engineer said with an impatient scowl. "I don't think this meeting is strictly necessary, especially with the Typhon Pact fleet coming in just over five hours. We still have a terraforming platform to raid and disable, and there is such a thing as overpreparing."

The captain spoke with a calmness that belied the gravity of the moment. "Believe me, Commander, the last thing

I want to do is hinder the mission. But some new information has just come to light, and your entire team needs to be brought up to speed."

Ra-Havreii listened with an escalating sense of incredulity as the captain and the Gorn began speaking in tandem, taking turns to spin a tale that seemed half ancient Gorn legend and half high-tech ghost story.

Ra-Havreii shook his head after they had finished. "So all we have to do is find a way to neutralize Brahma-Shiva's destructive capacity while sparing the existence of the AI that our guest claims dwells within it."

"That's essentially it," the captain said.

"That's assuming, of course, that there really *is* an intelligence of any sort aboard Brahma-Shiva," Ra-Havreii said. "At the moment, the only evidence for this is the entirely subjective opinion of Mister S'syrixx."

"I speak only S'Yahazah's plain truth," growled the Gorn, who leaned forward slightly over the conference table in Ra-Havreii's direction. Ra-Havreii saw that Lieutenant Qontallium, who was standing nearby, had tensed visibly, and hoped that he hadn't flinched involuntarily himself.

"Easy there," Keru said.

S'syrixx sat back in his chair, folding his long-clawed hands before him in a surprisingly graceful gesture. Then the Gorn lapsed into a silence that nevertheless seemed almost truculent.

"Perhaps other empirical evidence of Mister S'syrixx's assertion exists," said SecondGen White-Blue, who hovered a short distance from the table at about eye level, courtesy of his elegant array of antigravs and pneumatic thrusters.

"Explain," Captain Riker said.

"Mister Torvig and I noted a curious, nonrepeating anomalous reading on the subspace sensors," said the beachball-sized artificial intelligence.

Riker's brows knitted. "Why didn't either of you report this? We might have discovered this . . . intelligence a bit sooner."

"At the time we could not rule out our own instrumentality as the cause of our readings, Captain," White-Blue said, obviously unfazed by the captain's chiding tone. "Except when viewed in retrospect—and in juxtaposition with other information of better provenance—such rogue data points cannot be regarded as indicative of anything. Did we err?"

"I'll review *Titan*'s data-reporting protocols with you and Mister Torvig later," Melora told the AI.

"Of course, Commander."

"Putting this cybergoddess business to one side for a moment," Keru said, "I have to question whether it's wise to send Commander Ra-Havreii off the ship right now. Our warp drive is still down, and we're going to have a severe need for speed at about the time the Typhon Pact fleet arrives."

"If I thought there was anything that my engineering staff wasn't already doing to speed up the engine repairs," Ra-Havreii said, "then you'd need three wild *sehlat* and a couple of *mugato* to chase me out of that engine room. Don't worry, Commander. When *Titan* needs to roll, she'll be ready.

"Now back to the AI. How could its alleged presence affect the mission we're about to undertake?"

Melora spoke up. "Ideally, we'd find a way to communicate with this intelligence. If we could enlist its cooperation in saving the Hranrarii, the AI could prove to be a huge asset. It might even make the destruction of Brahma-Shiva entirely unnecessary."

"That's assuming we can trust the thing to consider us the good guys and Krassrr's people the bad guys," Keru said. "In terms of the immediate safety of the Hranrarii and the Federation's long-term security, that could be just as risky as deciding to do nothing at all."

"So we're still following the basic outline of the original plan," Ra-Havreii said. "We sneak a shuttlecraft to within transporter range of Brahma-Shiva, now that our good friend Gog'resssh has demonstrated that Krassrr's fleet appears to be blind to small, stealthy craft on certain inbound trajectories. Then we beam aboard with Mister S'syrixx's guidance, copy out all the data we can from Brahma-Shiva's onboard systems, set our timed charges, and get the hell out."

"That's right," Riker said.

"The possible presence of a machine intelligence complicates things a bit, Captain," Melora said. "A functioning AI is a lot more than the sum of its files. Consciousness as we understand it is an emergent property of complex networks of neural connections, or reasonable analogs thereof. As such, the 'essence' or 'soul' of a conscious entity can't always just be copied as though it were merely a holodeck program."

"Really?" Riker said. "Copies of Starfleet's early-model Emergency Medical Holograms are routinely passing the Turing Test. Some of them are even demanding full civil rights under the guarantees of the Federation Constitution. There's nothing 'mere' about that."

"I can serve as a vessel to contain such a cybernetic consciousness," White-Blue said. "At least on a temporary basis, my function would be similar to the holographic systems that house the sentience of Starfleet's Emergency Medical Holograms."

"Maybe," Melora said. "But we can't be sure it will work. Certain artificial consciousness matrices seem to resist being copied, the way latinum resists a replicator. For example, the Daystrom Institute has been trying to recover the mind of Lieutenant Commander Data for almost three years now, with nothing to show for it so far."

Ra-Havreii winced slightly. He was aware that the captain and Data had been close friends, so the shadow of sadness that passed across Riker's face didn't surprise him nearly as much as Melora's surprising insensitivity in bringing the subject up.

Still, he couldn't argue with her point. She was right.

"Indeed," Commander Tuvok said. "This aspect of the mission may be academic. *Titan*'s main computer still contains all the information it did after White-Blue accidentally caused it to achieve sentience. Since the time *Titan*'s emergent consciousness opted to sacrifice itself to save the ship, every attempt to recover that consciousness has met with failure."

Riker acknowledged the difficulties with a melancholic nod. "If anything inside that artifact is conscious," he said at length, "then we have to at least try to save it."

Tuvok said, "The needs of the many, Captain—"

"I know, Commander," the captain said, interrupting. "That's why you're still going on this mission. I'm not about to let Krassrr wipe out millions of lives, and neither are any of you." Then he stood, signaling that the meeting was at an end.

Ra-Havreii stood, following Riker's lead, as did everyone else save the hovering White-Blue. "We're ready, Captain."

From his command chair on the bridge, Riker watched an aft view of *Titan,* framed by the length of the starship's nacelles, beyond which lay a brilliant pink and amber aurora and the dim curve of the planet's cold northern reaches. The aftmost portion of *Titan*'s secondary hull, at the bottom of the central viewer, disgorged a small bright object that quickly dwindled in size until it was lost in the radiant taffy pull of local geomagnetic forces.

The shuttlecraft *Gillespie* was under way.

"Lieutenant Rager," he said. "Any sign that the *S'alath* has noticed the launch?"

"Not as yet, Captain," replied the senior ops officer.

"Time until the Typhon Pact fleet arrives?"

"Approximately five hours and five minutes, Captain," Rager said, sounding justifiably uncomfortable at the prospect of cutting things so fine. "Give or take."

What the heck am I supposed to do with all this excess time? Riker thought wryly as he settled in and awaited Gog'resssh's next scheduled call.

"The *S'alath* is hailing us, Captain," Rager reported a scant three minutes later.

Gog'resssh is nothing if not punctual, Riker thought. "Put it up, Lieutenant."

The frosty planetary vista on the main viewer abruptly vanished, replaced by a leering, lizardlike countenance that bore only a passing resemblance to that of the Gorn technologist who had accompanied the just-departed second away team.

"The S'alath *now stands ready to commit to a joint assault on the ecosculptor, Rry'kurr,"* Gog'resssh rumbled. *"We will leave immediately after your arrival aboard my vessel."*

"Come again?" Riker said.

"Have we not already agreed to act as partners in this venture?" said the Gorn warrior, whose gray, diseased-looking facial scales gave him a decidedly sinister appearance—even for a razor-toothed, insect-eyed reptiloid.

Riker felt a cavern of dread open up deep in his guts. "Thank you for the invitation, First Myrmidon Gog'resssh. But I'd be a more effective partner running *Titan* from here."

"You will beam aboard the S'alath, *Rry'kurr,"* the reptiloid said, his gray-green lips pulling back to display a veritable dental abattoir. *"Unless, of course, you wish Captain Krassrr to become aware of your fortuitous survival."*

Riker paused for a moment to do the math, and almost immediately realized he had no good alternatives—at least not without all but guaranteeing the deaths of millions of innocent people. To say nothing of the likely destruction of *Titan.*

"Send us the exact transporter coordinates," he said. "I'll beam over in a few minutes."

The Gorn's grin widened, and Riker resisted an impulse to shudder only through a sheer act of will. *"Excellent,"* Gog'resssh hissed an instant before he vanished from the screen.

Riker turned toward the main engineering console,

behind which the gamma-shift officer of the watch was looking askance at him. "Mister Gibruch, you have the bridge."

"Sir, you can't be serious about this," said Lieutenant Commander Tamen Gibruch. A native of the nonaligned planet Chand Aad, his bassoonlike voice was an amalgam of the sounds generated by the columns of air contained in the trunks—they were sometimes described as "tails"—that dangled loosely from his cranium.

"If I refuse, he'll tip our hand early to Krassrr before the *Gillespie* team has a chance to do its job on the terraforming device."

"He's got to be bluffing, Captain. He knows that if he contacts Krassrr he'll be placing his own ship in harm's way as well."

"Stand down, Commander," Riker said, sharpening his tone to indicate that the matter wasn't open to debate. "I've dealt with the Gorn during a couple of previous diplomatic crises. They're big on bluster, but they also value courage and trust. If I refuse Gog'resssh's . . . request, he'll interpret it as bad faith on my part."

Sounding somewhat chastened, Gibruch said, "Sorry, sir. It's just that his 'request' sounded more like a non-negotiable demand to me. And I'm not sure he's really crazy enough to risk revealing his own hiding place to Captain Krassrr."

Riker couldn't argue with any of that. But that didn't necessarily matter, given the particulars of the situation. "Maybe he is, and maybe he isn't. But the stakes are too high to risk calling his bluff. I'm not playing for poker chips, Commander. The stakes are millions of lives."

"But you'll be walking into a trap!"

"Very likely." The captain began moving toward the turbolift. "But I don't appear to have a better alternative."

"You'll be Gog'resssh's hostage!" Gibruch fluted, the pitch of his bellows-driven voice rising again, moving in lockstep with his emotions.

Riker paused momentarily on the turbolift's threshold and looked over his shoulder back at Gibruch. "No, I won't, Commander—because in that eventuality, I expect you to blow the *S'alath* out of the sky."

After the shimmering light-curtain of *Titan*'s transporter beam enfolded him, Riker felt as though he had just embarked on the longest transport of his life.

In point of fact, he had; so intense were the twisting, tangling lines of local geomagnetic interference that using the transporters of both *Titan* and the *S'alath* in tandem had turned out to be the only way—other than using a shuttlecraft—to safely traverse the few kilometers that separated the two vessels. He was conscious during his passage through the matter stream, like an orbital skydiver leaping through a turbulent storm system. The transit brought to mind recollections of a similar travail experienced by his *Enterprise* colleague Reginald Barclay, as well as a holodeck program in which he had spent a harrowing ninety seconds passing through a simulation of the mid-twenty-second-century prototype transporter that Dr. Emory Erickson had built with his own hands.

Then, with an abruptness that drew most of the air from his lungs, the combined Federation-Gorn transporter effect released him. He found himself standing on a bare metal stage, facing the glowing walls of a semicircular chamber that bore only a vague resemblance to *Titan*'s transporter room.

Something seized his shoulder roughly, spinning him one hundred and eighty degrees about.

Gog'resssh, flanked by a pair of armed and apparently hair-trigger-ready Gorn warriors, stood on the transporter stage facing him. Riker could see now that the stage was set inside a larger chamber, which included a freestanding control console. Gripping him by both shoulders hard enough to leave bruises, Gog'resssh presented Riker with a grin that was as foul-smelling as it was terrifying.

Whatever condition was afflicting Gog'resssh, from the gray coloration and wrinkled texture of his facial scales to the peculiar glow of his insectlike eyes, Riker decided that *Titan*'s main viewer hadn't done it justice. The rogue Gorn warrior was clearly unwell, perhaps even dying.

It came to Riker in a rush that Gog'resssh might be too desperate to behave rationally—and that in any such "nothing left to lose" scenario, Riker's assessment of the risks of beaming aboard the *S'alath* would almost certainly be way off the mark.

"You understand our traditions well, Rry'kurr," Gog'resssh's said. "Appearing in our midst with your back to us does us honor."

Thanks to his prior experiences with Gog'resssh's people, Riker understood that members of the Gorn warrior and political castes regarded any face-to-face transporter materialization as gravely offensive, a sign of unwarranted aggression.

"Just trying to be polite, First Myrmidon," Riker said, trying not to show any discomfiture at the rough handling—at least by human standards—that he was receiving in the first myrmidon's grasp. "Permission to come aboard the *S'alath*?"

"I would have you nowhere else, Rry'kurr," Gog'resssh said in sepulchral tones. The Gorn's thicket of razor-sharp teeth suddenly drew closer, as though he had summarily decided to bite Riker's head off. Then the transporter stage seemed to shift beneath Riker's feet, going abruptly perpendicular as it catapulted him into the air.

Riker landed on his back on the deck, beside the transporter console, his head intact; though disoriented, he realized he had come to rest precisely where Gog'resssh had thrown him.

Gog'resssh's armed toadies lumbered toward him, vicious-looking disruptor pistols gripped in scaly, clawed fingers that looked as strong as steel cables. Like their leader, these troopers also appeared unwell; they vaguely reminded Riker of the decomposing, flesh-eating ghouls that had been one of the mainstays of flatvid horror movies about four centuries ago.

"Rry'kurr!" Gog'resssh said. "You are now a prisoner of the new warrior caste of the Gorn Hegemony."

Before Riker had left *Titan,* he had heard protests not only from Lieutenant Commander Gibruch, but also from Dr. Ree. The latter had gone so far as to threaten to use his authority as CMO to relieve him of command. Only the sheer brute force of a command browbeating had caused Ree to back off, however reluctantly.

Now, as one of the troopers hauled him roughly to his feet and placed his weapon at his temple, Riker wished that his chief surgeon had been more persistent.

The other trooper searched him cursorily for weapons, but found nothing.

"'New warrior caste'?" Riker asked, focusing on Gog'resssh and ignoring his underlings as much as possible.

"Those of us who were charged with the protection of the crècheworld of Sazssgrerrn when the Egg Bringer S'Yahazah withdrew her protection from it," Gog'resssh said.

Things were beginning to make sense. "You and your people were on Sazssgrerrn when the . . . disaster struck."

Gog'ressh growled with barely contained anger. "We are the only survivors, Rry'kurr. Survivors that my own caste-brethren tried to euthanize. We take our continued survival as a sign from S'Yahazah that we are destined to supplant those brethren and build a new warrior caste of our own—a warrior caste with a mandate to rule all the other castes, and a destiny that will never again leave us vulnerable to the whims of fate."

"You want to control your destiny," Riker said. "There's nothing wrong with that. But what does that have to do with trying to blow up the terraforming device—the ecosculptor, as you call it? And what does it have to do with capturing me?"

"The ecosculptor is merely a symbol of the old warrior caste. It must be destroyed."

"Gog'resssh, I'm all for destroying the thing if that means saving the Hranrarii. But what I don't understand is why you'd destroy something that could create a hatchery world for your new caste."

"Our new caste will be strong enough to prosper anywhere, and without such tricks as an ecosculptor. We may even use this very world, Hranrar, for our hatchery."

"Putting the ecosculptor to one side, it's still just you and a few of your subordinates against the entire social order of the Gorn Hegemony," Riker said. "And not only that—you'll be going up against the entire Typhon Pact: the Breen, the Tzenkethi, the Kinshaya, the Tholians, and the Romulans."

"That is why you are invaluable to me, Rry'kurr," Gog'resssh said, now almost purring as he reveled in his vision. "Once the entirety of the Typhon Pact learns that we have struck a decisive blow against the old warrior caste, it will discover that we have also taken the commander of *Tie-tan,* along with his ship."

"Aren't you getting a little bit ahead of yourself, Gog'resssh? You not only don't have control of *Titan,* you have no way to stop her crew from following their orders."

"What orders?" Gog'resssh growled.

"Orders to destroy the *S'alath* in the event of my capture."

Gog'resssh loped toward him again, quickly closing to within kissing distance. Riker could feel his most recent meal trying to flee his body. "Why should your crew believe any such thing has occurred, Rry'kurr? Once I have your command codes, one of my tech-casters will see to their reassurance that all is well—using your voice, of course."

Riker shook his head and released a nervous chuckle that he hoped Gog'resssh would interpret as confident. "Go climb your thumb," he said.

"I have seen this mammal before, First Myrmidon," the trooper to Riker's left said, stepping on whatever response

Gog'resssh might have been about to make. "He came to Gornar aboard the *Ent'rr'priszz,* to put down the rebellion of the Black Crest warriors against the political caste."

"Yessss," Gog'resssh said. "A battle he waged on behalf of an old order that would just as soon extinguish us all."

At a gesture from Gog'resssh, the troopers seized him, each taking an arm. The rogue commander grabbed Riker's combadge and pulled it from his chest, along with shreds of black and gray fabric from his uniform tunic. Riker watched with as much impassivity as he could muster as Gog'resssh crushed the combadge as though it were an insect. Then the troopers half-carried, half-dragged him out of the chamber and down a length of grim, gray corridor before depositing him ungently into a cold, bare holding cell.

22

As seen from the forward section of the shuttlecraft *Gillespie,* Brahma-Shiva presented the aspect of a small but swiftly expanding disc, alone in the cosmic darkness but for the handful of smaller, nearby lights that surrounded it. Those lesser lights were all that could be seen of the five vessels that presently constituted Captain Krassrr's terraforming fleet. Like a coterie of solicitous servants, they appeared to be tending Brahma-Shiva.

Or perhaps, Xin Ra-Havreii thought, they were cajoling and scolding it like officious slave masters.

"Any indication that Krassrr's fleet has seen us yet?" the chief engineer asked as he leaned into the darkened cockpit to get a better view of the approaching artifact's ventral-most section.

"So far, so good," Ranul Keru said from the left chair, the pilot's seat. "We know that Gog'resssh used the same kind of 'bottom-up' approach vector to sneak up on these guys and exit before they figured out he was even there."

Seated in the right chair, Tuvok checked a sensor reading on the copilot's console. "We should not become complacent, Commander. Krassrr may have reassessed his security protocols since Gog'resssh's act of theft. The so-called blind spots that Gog'resssh exploited may no longer exist."

"I suppose there's only one way to make an empirical determination," Ra-Havreii said. Though battle tactics and strategy had never been his strong suit, he recalled something some military luminary or other had said about contingency planning—words to the effect that generals always plan for the next war using the already-outdated theories of the previous conflict.

Ra-Havreii heard a deep hissing sound coming from behind the cockpit section; it made him start with a starship engineer's ingrained vigilance against sudden decompression—until he realized it was merely the sound of *Titan*'s latest guest speaking.

"Krassrr is very exacting in his duties, but he does not excel at generalizing," said S'syrixx, who sat on the floor between the *Gillespie*'s seats while Lieutenant Qontallium and SecondGen White-Blue hovered nearby, the former figuratively, the latter literally.

"Meaning what, exactly?" Ra-Havreii asked, raising a snow-white eyebrow.

"Meaning that because Gog'resssh stole from the fleet's food stores, that will be the focus of any of Krassrr's tactical upgrades," S'syrixx said. "Not necessarily the security of the ecosculptor. Gog'resssh doesn't seem to have tried to disable it, or even approach it."

"Perhaps," Ra-Havreii said, turning to face the Gorn technician. "But if anyone focused Krassrr's attention on enhancing the artifact's security, it would have been *you,* Mister S'syrixx—the *first* time you messed with it."

"I cannot dispute that," S'syrixx said. "Nor can you dispute that I now share with you whatever risk might flow from that decision."

"I recommend that everyone focus on the mission at hand," Tuvok said.

A few seconds later the frantic beeping of an alarm began a duet with the urgent flashing of a light on Tuvok's console. For a few moments Ra-Havreii thought his heart had stopped.

"Krassrr must have seen us," he said.

"Calm yourself, Commander," Tuvok said. "The alarm merely indicates that we have reached optimal transporter range."

"All stop," Keru said. "Keeping station. There's still no sign that Krassrr knows we're here."

As the away team began to mount the *Gillespie*'s small transporter stage, Ra-Havreii found himself standing uncomfortably close to S'syrixx. "I hope the transporter coordinates you gave us were accurate," he told the Gorn. "As well as your assessment of the life-support conditions inside the artifact." *Not to mention,* he added silently, *the optimal transporter frequencies and confinement-beam settings necessary to get us inside that thing without merging our molecules permanently with it.*

"I share your hopes," S'syrixx said, speaking around a display of teeth that might have frightened fear itself. "But be comforted. If I have miscalculated, whatever may happen to you because of my carelessness will also happen to me."

Ra-Havreii felt reassured not in the least as the transporter's curtain of light took him.

GORN HEGEMONY WARSHIP *S'ALATH*

A snorting grunt of surprise from the forward section of the command deck drew Z'shezhira's attention to the central viewer, which continued to display the planet's frigid northern curvature.

Along with something new. A light, which one of Gog'resssh's junior troopers was watching with intent curiosity and no small amount of confusion. Within a few moments, Second Myrmidon Zegrroz'rh began to show an interest, his one good compound eye widening either with wonder or fear or both.

No, she realized after a moment's study. *It's not new at all.*

It was the ecosculptor, visible, if only barely, through the distortion of Hranrar's relentless northern auroral effects. It hung in its usual spot, just above the horizon line.

But its formerly passive, reflected-sunlight glow had escalated at least tenfold, making it more brilliant than any of Hranrar's natural satellites. It was as though the object had suddenly become charged with enormous internal energies, as one might expect were it about to release sufficient energy to remake an entire world.

Forbid this, Great S'Yahazah, she thought, imagining the millions of Hranrarii lives that would probably be extinguished very soon, perhaps right before her eyes.

The worst was finally happening. There was no longer any time to stall or temporize. Her limited slate of options suddenly narrowed to a single fateful choice. Taking advantage of the rapt attention the war-casters were paying to the beautiful and terrible image on the main screen, Z'shezhira began working quickly and quietly, entering a string of well-rehearsed commands into her station's console.

A moment before she could bring her task to completion, a voice behind her froze the blood in her veins.

"What are you doing?" bellowed Zegrroz'rh.

Determined never to hesitate again in the face of a war-caster's challenge, she slammed her left manus into the console as she hastened to enter the EXECUTE command.

Zegrroz'rh bellowed, charging toward her with outstretched claws even as the transporter beam began to make his body glow and shimmer. . . .

23

Slumped against one of the bare metal walls of the holding cell, Riker made a glum assessment of his present circumstances.

Gog'resssh must be on his bridge by now, giving orders, Riker thought. Having always had a gift for interpreting the "feel" of a ship, he felt he was a good judge of when a vessel was in motion, be it at warp or at impulse. But that gift didn't necessarily apply, he realized, to Gorn ships; at the moment he couldn't tell if the *S'alath* was still keeping station inside a geomagnetic hotspot over Hranrar's north pole, or if it was already under way, en route to Brahma-Shiva.

If Gog'resssh goes straight for Brahma-Shiva, then there's a good chance he'll destroy it before the crew of the Gillespie *can get to safety,* he thought, cursing himself for having so badly underestimated Gog'resssh's craziness quotient.

He gazed through the blue forcefield barrier that prevented him from walking into the corridor to confront the lone guard who was standing sentry, his broad back facing in Riker's direction. *And even if I* do *get out of here, this fine fellow must be itching for the least little excuse to rip my head clean off my shoulders.*

Deciding there was no point in keeping his minder waiting, he reached into the top of his boot and withdrew the palm-size "cricket" phaser he'd secreted there just before disembarking from *Titan.* He adjusted the beam to a tight focus at an intensity of "disrupt," and aimed it at what appeared to be a sealed circuit panel on the wall beside the energy screen.

He pressed the fire button, and the small but powerful weapon's bright red beam immediately began tearing into the wall. The acrid smell of ozone quickly spread through the cell as the blue energy screen across the doorway sparked, sputtered, and finally vanished.

A hulking form turned in the corridor beyond, its reptilian face displaying a mixture of incredulity and rage as a pair of compound eyes focused on Riker. Pausing to click the phaser to a less lethal setting, Riker aimed the weapon and opened fire.

The Gorn guard took the shot full in the chest, but lumbered forward after only a moment's hesitation.

Riker fired again. The Gorn took a stumbling half-step backward after taking a second direct hit to the center of its body mass, then resumed its advance. Riker swung his thumb onto the setting controls, re-set the weapon, and took aim again—

—but failed to click the "fire" button again before the Gorn had drawn close enough to slap his arm away, sending the weapon clattering to the deck. Though he tried to roll with the blow, claws raked Riker's sleeve, shredding it thoroughly enough to make him certain he was already bleeding as he dived to the deck.

Riker rolled to his feet, gathering himself immediately into a battle-ready crouch. Not only was the phaser nowhere in sight, the Gorn soldier was already coming for him again, leaving no time for the recovery of a weapon. Evidently more than aware that it had him overmatched, the creature hadn't even bothered to draw the wicked-looking sidearm it wore on its hip.

I'm getting too goddamned old for this, Riker thought.

Although Z'shezhira had taken great pains over a considerable interval of time to perfect her escape plan, she remained plagued by two gnawing questions: one, had the ideal time to execute the plan really arrived? And would the plan work when she finally summoned sufficient courage to carry it out?

She began to suspect that she wouldn't like the answer to either question as she worked in a space far more cramped than the command deck, using a wall-mounted console to resume her remote control of the transporter systems.

Despite her current difficulties, she was grateful for one important initial success; because of it, Zegrroz'rh would no longer pose a problem. But for reasons she could not yet fathom, that same success seemed to elude her in attaining her next objective. The targeting sensors were balking at establishing a transporter lock on what should have been a conspicuous and therefore easy target: the bio-signs of the only higher mammalian life form currently aboard the *S'alath*.

Something was interfering with the annular confinement beam. It was as though another bio-sign was getting in the way, scrambling her lock.

One of Gog'resssh's troopers must be with him, Z'shezhira realized. *Maybe interrogating him, or perhaps doing something worse.*

The need for haste and stealth having left her with little alternative, she broadened the confinement beam and keyed in the ENERGIZE command.

The hissing, growling reptiloid advanced again, but this time his body began to glow and distort, as though Riker was watching the creature's image being projected onto an ancient funhouse mirror.

When Riker raised his fists into a defensive posture, he saw that this strange effect wasn't limited to the Gorn.

Here we go again, he thought as the matter stream enveloped him.

Unlike his initial beam-over to the *S'alath,* however, this transit seemed to span only a few seconds. Within the space of several heartbeats, the cheerless metal walls of a Gorn brig seemed to have curved and constricted, giving him a momentary sensation of claustrophobia.

Unfortunately, the Gorn soldier was still charging him, either unaware of or apathetic toward the sudden unexplained change of scenery.

Riker let the Gorn charge, feinted right, then spun to the left at the last possible instant. He kicked the reptiloid solidly in the head as it lunged past, but to little apparent effect.

He turned as quickly as the little chamber's tight confines allowed, and heard a scream coming from his assailant's direction.

Now Riker could see that there was a *second* Gorn in this new chamber. The Gorn soldier had evidently forgotten about Riker as soon as he'd seen the other Gorn. This was a smaller, slighter creature, and the soldier was raising it from the deck using the single set of claws he had wrapped around the other reptiloid's throat.

"You!" the Gorn soldier said. "*You* are responsible for this!"

The creature in the soldier's iron grasp made incoherent sounds of distress as it strangled. Looking past the rapidly asphyxiating creature, Riker spied a window through which the white curvature of Hranrar's north polar region was clearly visible. *At least Gog'resssh isn't under way yet for Brahma-Shiva,* Riker noted with some relief, hoping that he'd rematerialized in an escape pod of some sort.

"Why did you bring me and this mammal here?" the soldier demanded. Riker could see on the smaller Gorn's facial scales evidence of more than one recent, only partially-healed beating. Evidently someone had used this smaller, weaker being as a punching bag.

Riker now understood that he probably owed an enormous debt of thanks to the underdog in this Gorn-on-Gorn encounter. *And there's only one way to repay that debt,* he thought as he crept up behind the angry soldier.

Spots swam before Z'shezhira's eyes. The universe had begun to contract around her as consciousness became increasingly problematic for her. Her feet kicked ineffectually at the air as the angry war-caster shouted questions whose answers he seemed unwilling to hear.

She wasn't surprised by this turn of events; the odds had always been very much against any attempt at mutiny or escape. She merely felt an intense sorrow at the prospect of dying with this killing machine's image burned upon her retinas and into her brain. She had always hoped to die in some far-flung future, her final vision filled with grandchildren, children, and her intended, S'syrixx. Now, all she could see, ringed as it was in darkness, was the face of her killer.

It was a face that suddenly displayed an emotion she had never associated with members of the warrior caste: intense surprise.

The manus at her throat squeezed her once, hard, nearly shattering her neck bones, then abruptly slackened. Then, like a burned-out eldertree in Gornar's southern forests, her tormentor swayed briefly before beginning an unceremonious terminal descent through a cloud of ozone-scented smoke. Z'shezhira would have fallen with him had she not managed to steady herself along the edge of one of the viewing ports.

Catching her breath, she saw that the mammal she had targeted was standing directly behind the insensate war-caster. In its pink claws it clutched an unwieldy war-caster matter-disruption pistol.

"He left his holster unfastened," the mammal said, nodding toward the fallen war-caster. "Gog'resssh's discipline must be getting sloppy."

"Rry'kurr," Z'shezhira croaked, rubbing her injured throat with both manus.

"I'm afraid you have me at a disadvantage," the mammal said, still holding the weapon in a manner that made Z'shezhira wonder if he might be contemplating using it again.

"You saved my life," she said.

Rry'kurr displayed his tiny white teeth, which emerged from a small jungle of mammal-fur. "I suppose we're even, then. Now unless I miss my guess, we're aboard one of the *S'alath*'s escape pods."

Z'shezhira could feel her disorientation beginning to fade. "Exactly," she said. Noting that feeling was returning to her limbs, she moved toward the main control panel and began inputting the launch-command sequence. "We must get under way before Gog'resssh discovers what I have done."

"You'll get no objection from me," Rry'kurr said, bracing himself against the pod's sudden burst of acceleration during the launch. The acceleration quickly leveled out, stabilized by the internal grav system. The silence of space ruled the pod's interior as Z'shezhira checked the instruments for signs of scanning beams from the *S'alath,* all the while taking pains to avoid looking at the war-caster corpse that lay near the forward viewing port.

"What should I call you?" the mammal said.

"I am called Z'shezhira," she said.

The display of fur-bracketed teeth returned, making her shudder involuntarily. "I believe we have a mutual friend back aboard my ship," he said. "A fellow named S'syrixx."

"S'syrixx is aboard your vessel presently?"

"Actually, no," Rry'kurr said.

Z'shezhira hissed in bitter disappointment. "You are saying he has died."

"Let's not get ahead of ourselves, Z'shezhira. At the moment, he's assisting some of my people on a mission away from my vessel."

She reached toward him reflexively, and she startled when he recoiled from her, apparently just as reflexively.

"Watch those claws, lady," Rry'kurr said.

Lowering her claws, she took a deep breath in an effort

to smooth her ruffled, vasodilated scales. "My apologies, Rry'kurr. Where have you sent S'syrixx?"

"To the terraforming platform," he said as he glanced at what appeared to be a chronometer, which he kept wrapped around the narrow stalk that connected one pink manus to the rest of his arm. "The ecosculptor. The team should be boarding it any minute now, if they're not inside it already."

"Why go inside it?"

"To access its internal computers. To learn everything we can about it."

Her heart sank as she realized what a fool's errand her beloved had undertaken. "The Gorn fleet from which the *S'alath* has hidden will find your team and kill them. And S'syrixx along with them."

"If I believed that, I never would have authorized the mission," Rry'kurr said.

Before she could reply, the escape pod shook as though from a sharp impact. "Gog'resssh has found us," she said as she steadied herself against the pod's rudimentary flight console.

"I'm not so sure about that," Rry'kurr said. He gestured with one scaleless, pink paw toward the viewing port.

Turning, Z'shezhira saw the bloated face of Second Myrmidon Zegrroz'rh pressed up against the viewing aperture. Despite the oxygen deficiencies of Hranrar's upper atmosphere, his one functioning eye focused upon her, radiating a hostility that was still very much alive.

"Friend of yours?" Rry'kurr asked.

"An impediment, and a slaver," she said, involuntarily allowing her own teeth to emerge in a long-suppressed expression of hostility as she used the maneuvering thrusters to dislodge the hated second myrmidon. With the viewing port now clear, the belly of the Federrazsh'n ship, *Tie-tan,* was swiftly growing nearer in the rarefied reaches of the upper atmosphere. "He was Gog'resssh's second in command."

Though she feared offending the sensibilities of Great S'Yahazah, she rejoiced in the prospect of Zegrroz'rh's impending final agonies. She hoped he would meet death while still conscious of its jaws enclosing him, horrifically aware of its venomous fangs as they pierced his hard-scaled, radiation-seared flesh.

Rry'kurr seemed to recoil slightly at her change in mood, and Z'shezhira couldn't say that she blamed him. She had caused several deaths today, directly or indirectly; was she not now as brutal as any war-caster?

"Remind me never to piss you off," Rry'kurr said.

"Zegrroz'rh!" Gog'resssh bellowed as he stomped onto the command deck.

Empty. No one so much as minding any of the instruments, let alone making preparations for the assault upon Krassrr's precious ecosculptor.

He stalked over to the abandoned communications console and literally punched a channel open, bending the panel's thick metal in the process. "Z'shezhira! Why have you left your post?" When he received no response he resumed calling for Zegrroz'rh, but achieved the same result as before.

Moving to another console that had not yet been the recipient of his rage, Gog'resssh checked the ship's internal sensors.

Neither his second myrmidon nor Z'shezhira were anywhere aboard the *S'alath.* Nor was his Federrazsh'n prisoner, Rry'kurr.

With a roar of inchoate rage, he checked the *S'alath*'s inventory of escape pods, though he was already certain that he knew what he would find. Once he'd confirmed that one of the pods was missing, he switched on the external sensors.

He grinned when he saw the initial scan results. Even with the fearsome electromagnetic hash from the planet's dynamic interior cloaking it, it was a simple matter to find the duranium pod as it arced higher in the atmosphere, following an elliptical trajectory toward the mammal vessel—a prize that he still meant to possess. It was a pity he lacked the expertise to attempt to beam back the pod's occupants, especially Z'shezhira, whose genes were destined to help him build his new master caste. Rry'kurr's escape would pose a problem as well, since Gog'resssh had had no opportunity as yet to wring from the mammal commander the authorization codes necessary to allow him to seize *Titan.*

But maybe Rry'kurr's escape would not matter.

Gog'resssh's grin broadened as he opened a channel to *Tie-tan.*

U.S.S. TITAN

Never before in his Starfleet career had Gibruch felt quite so powerless as he did right now, as he stood before the conn facing the main viewscreen.

Before him was a computer-enhanced image of

Brahma-Shiva, which not only still lingered like a malignant cloud over the equatorial region of the ringed planet, but had also just taken on a baleful, blue-green glow. Lieutenant Rager's scans had confirmed Gibruch's initial impression that the thing's ominous brilliance was steadily increasing. Obviously, the object was finally powering up, building toward an eventual release of the cataclysmic, world-destroying energies that it had quietly contained for untold eons.

"Incoming bogey!" Rager announced.

Gibruch turned away from the screen so that he faced the senior ops officer. "Another ship?"

Rager paused momentarily to consult her console displays. Shaking her head, she said, "Negative, Commander. It's a small metal object, originating from the *S'alath.*"

"Red Alert!" Gibruch said.

"Shields and weapons locks aren't reliable this deep in Hranrar's geomagnetic field," Lieutenant Lavena said.

"Then prepare to initiate evasive maneuvers," Gibruch said. "And I want to know what's inside that thing. If there's any sign of life in there, I want it beamed aboard."

After a few additional tense moments—during which the object drew inexorably closer to *Titan*'s unprotected belly—Rager shook her head again. "Internal bio scans are inconclusive, with all the local geomagnetism."

Gibruch's cranial tails released a fluted diminished chord that betrayed his tension and frustration. *That thing could be delivering a boarding party, a charge of antimatter, or another asylum-seeking refugee,* he thought as he craned his neck to get a better look at the sensor profile on Rager's console. *There's just no way to tell from here.*

"I've compensated for the interference enough to establish a limited phaser lock," Rager said.

Something about the object's sensor profile didn't look right—it simply didn't appear "torpedo-like" enough to justify shooting first and asking questions later.

But what if I'm wrong? he thought. Aloud, he said, "What's the status of the *S'alath*'s weapons?"

"They read as cold," Rager said, sounding surprised. "Belay that—they're beginning to power up now."

"Hold your fire, Lieutenant. Tractor that thing into hangar bay two and send a security team to greet it."

"Sir?" Rager said, her forehead wrinkling nearly as much as that of a Klingon.

"You heard me, Lieutenant." Gibruch did his best to sound confident, even though the only thing he felt completely certain about at the moment was that he would either be commended for his astute reasoning, or else he'd be singled out by future Starfleet Academy tactical studies instructors as the author of one of the worst on-the-fly decisions in Federation history.

"Gog'resssh is hailing us, Captain," Rager said.

Gibruch didn't mind the standard practice of being addressed as "captain" when he ran the bridge during *Titan*'s wee hours. But hearing it now, with Captain Riker, Commander Vale, and Commander Tuvok all off the ship simultaneously, was quite another thing.

"Let's buy some time by putting him on the screen," Gibruch said, working hard to prevent his postcranial airways from causing his air-column-generated voice from shaking and fluttering.

Though his image was being distorted by the polar

region's ambient geomagnetism, Gog'resssh's state of mind was clearly evident—the Gorn commander was beside himself with anger.

"Surrender Tie-tan's *command codes, mammal,"* Gog'resssh said, *"or your captain will become the main course in our galley."*

"Where is Captain Riker?" Gibruch demanded. "Show him to me."

Gog'resssh merely stared fixedly from the screen, his multifaceted eyes narrowing with fury. Then the image broke up in a flurry of static, and was replaced a moment later by the approaching *S'alath,* its weapons tubes glowing balefully as the vessel plied Hranrar's tenuous upper atmosphere.

A smaller, oblong shape tumbled in the foreground, substantially closer to *Titan* now, but no less enigmatic.

"Get that thing aboard, ASAP," Gibruch said, hoping he hadn't just enabled Gog'resssh to sneak a devastating weapon aboard *Titan* during his watch.

24

HRANRAR

Just after nightfall, Vale ordered the remainder of the team to get some rest. Sitting cross-legged at the base of a Hranrarii tree, she shared the first watch with Lieutenant Sortollo.

Of course, there wasn't all that much to watch when one was confined in an open-air jail that consisted primarily of a gently sloping rooftop meadow. Two of Hranrar's five moons, both in crescent phase, cast a wan light from high in the clear sky, doing little to compete with the multitudinous pinpoints of distant starlight. Toward the horizon, the dark lawn's distant edges were suffused with the faint glow of the Hranrarii city that lay far, far below, giving everyone on the away team a clear incentive not to venture far from the roof's center.

There, in what Vale's tricorder had declared the exact geographical center of the team's prison in the sky, lay Troi, Bolaji, Modan, Evesh, and Dakal. With the exception of Evesh, who was already on her back and snoring loudly, each team member not on watch had laid down to rest, if not to achieve an actual state of sleep.

Vale watched as Dakal lifted his head to cast a disgusted look at Evesh. "How in the name of Ailam's ashen arse can anybody sleep through *that*? The Dominion wasn't this noisy when they bombed Lakarian City."

"Consider getting some rest just another challenge, Ensign," Vale said. "When life hands you *rokassa*s, you learn to make *rokassa* juice."

"Commander, I might as well be trying to get to sleep on top of an overloading warp core," Dakal said. "If I had some *rokassa*s right now, I'd stick them in my ears."

"And if *I* had one right now, I'd be sorely tempted to make a ball gag out of it," Bolaji said blearily, remaining on her back, her eyes closed. "I always thought that Cardassians were supposed to be good at enduring hardship in silence."

"Settle down, people," rumbled Lieutenant Sortollo. For an absurd moment Vale wished she still had the option of threatening to turn the shuttlecraft *Beiderbecke* around and taking her straight back to *Titan,* addressing the away team in the manner of a parent dealing with unruly children.

All at once she felt the lawn rumble slightly beneath her, as though something just under the surface were causing the immediate area to vibrate. "People, I think we're about to have company," she said as a portion of the lawn several meters away distended and opened, just as had occurred only a short while ago.

Moments later, half a dozen armed Hranrarii cops were stepping in orderly ranks from one of their lift mechanisms, which appeared to have come from one of the tower-jail's lower levels. Emerging behind the cops was Senior Watcher Ereb, the official who had consigned the away team to this place.

Sortollo raised his hands to demonstrate that he was still unarmed. "Let's keep the local police-folk as calm as possible," he said. Vale did likewise, nodding to the rest of the team to get them to fall in line as well. Under Dakal's gentle ministrations, Evesh came awake with a series of sputtering snorts.

While the entire away team rose and fell in, Vale watched as Ereb pointed a handheld electronic device of some sort at the lawn about five meters away from the lift, which was already beginning to disappear back into the turf; soon the rent in the sod would vanish, making the lawn as seamless as it had been before the lift's arrival.

On the section of lawn at which the senior watcher had pointed, a glowing, golden disc appeared, an artifact with roughly twice the diameter of one of the personnel transporter stages aboard *Titan.*

"You're early," Vale said, feeling her endocrine system disabling the "safety" setting for her fight-or-flight response. "You said you'd be back in the morning. Something important must have happened in the meantime." *Or else,* she thought, *somebody has made a hasty decision to dispose of us.*

"Please stand upon the conveyance," Ereb said, affect-free in both face and voice as far as Vale could tell. "All of you, if you please."

"You first," Sortollo said.

Ereb released a breath in a manner that sounded remarkably like a sigh of frustration. "Yours is a most contentious species, Commander Vale."

"Confinement doesn't usually bring out the best in us," Vale said.

"You asked for a hearing with Hranrar's senior planetary leaders," Ereb said, sounding puzzled. "I believe your exact words were, 'Take me to your leader.' With this device we will fulfill your request."

A choice of phrase that I'm sure I will never live down, she thought.

Pointing at the still-glowing disc that Ereb had just conjured up on the lawn, Vale said, "How can we be certain that thing isn't some novel form of capital punishment?"

Ereb blinked in evident confusion. "Capital . . . punishment?"

"Execution," Vale said. "You know, state-sanctioned killing."

She felt a hand on her shoulder; startled, she spun toward the hand's owner, only to find that she was facing Deanna Troi.

"Relax, Christine. Ereb is appalled at the very idea of executions. I think we can trust that her disc is some sort of transporter, and not a matter-disintegrator of some kind."

Vale nodded, then turned back to face Ereb. Gesturing grandly toward the disc, she said, "In that case, Ereb—after you."

With a movement reminiscent of a shrug, Ereb sprang on grasshopper legs to the middle of the stage, to be followed by her six police escorts. Vale stepped up next, to be followed moments later by Sortollo, Troi, and the remaining four members of the team.

Vale had never been a fan of non-Starfleet transporters; in fact, if she'd had her druthers, she'd probably avoid entirely the process of having her body disassembled and reassembled. As she began to brace herself for whatever peculiar effects this alien transporter technology might have in store for her, she noticed that the sky had abruptly shifted.

In less than an eyeblink, the night sky had vanished, giving way instantaneously to mid-day. Nothing else seemed to have changed, from the Hranrarii transporter beneath her boots, to the fellow crewmembers and Hranrarii natives with whom she shared it, to the flat green meadow that surrounded the transport disc.

Despite the brightness of Hranrar's primary star, a brilliantly glowing object was clearly visible in the azure sky: Brahma-Shiva, Vale realized, since she knew it to be located on the opposite side—the day side, at the moment—of Hranrar. They must have instantaneously transported to some virtually identical glade atop an urban tower that she'd never be able to distinguish from the one she'd just left.

Vale looked up, using her hands to shield her eyes against Hranrar's fierce central star. Almost directly overhead, the disk of the lower portion of Brahma-Shiva, together with an oblique view of the object's long, vertical spire, hung over Hranrar like a luminous sword of Damocles.

"Commander!" Sortollo cried.

Vale looked away from the glowing apparition in the sky in time to see another lift begin to emerge from beneath the short, manicured grass. The sight of the sod ripping open from beneath disconcerted her, reminding her of the horror vids she had spent far too much of her youth watching.

Putting aside her mental images of caskets opening and ravening, flesh-eating zombies rising from fresh graves, she watched as the lift finished emerging and opened.

An august-looking, yellow-robe-bedecked Hranrarii

emerged, flanked by a pair of dour-looking, standard cops or bodyguards. The amphibious eminence wasted no time striding onto the transport platform. As though in possession of empathic or intuitive instincts to rival Troi's, the creature strode unceremoniously past the bowing First Watcher Ereb and approached Vale. The newly arrived creature met the commander's gaze head-on with an intense, yellow-eyed stare.

"I am Sethne Naq, Speaker for the Great Syndic of the Global Moeity of Hranrar," the creature said in tones rendered mellifluous by the universal translators. "I am told that you claim to be able to explain the new light in our sky."

"Someone must have called ahead to make sure the lights would be on," Ra-Havreii said moments after the transporter beam released its hold on the team assigned to board Brahma-Shiva. "I detest beaming into darkened spaces."

"That might not be far from the truth," said Lieutenant Commander Keru as he made a circular visual sweep of the brightly illuminated chamber, his phaser at the ready, mirroring the motions of Lieutenant Qur Qontallium.

"My sensor sweep indicates that the lights became active only a few of your minutes ago," said SecondGen White-Blue, who hovered nearby to form the third point of an equilateral triangle in conjunction with Keru and Qontallium. "A humanoid-compatible nitrogen-oxygen atmosphere heated to twenty-one point eight degrees Celsius seems to have preceded the lights by a lengthy interval."

"How lengthy?" Ra-Havreii said, sniffing the air; it carried a vaguely stale, musty smell, but was otherwise acceptable.

A reptiloid voice behind Ra-Havreii interrupted. "Long enough to allow Krassrr's engineering and tactical teams to install antipersonnel explosives without having to use pressure suits."

Ra-Havreii supposed the Gorn must have a natural aversion to pressure suits, at least as Starfleet personnel understood them; with claws like those the Gorn possessed, incidents of accidental explosive decompression must have been endemic.

"Why would Krassrr want to plant explosives in here?" Ra-Havreii asked. "He'd be placing his one chance to make this planet into a new Gorn warrior hatchery in jeopardy."

"He reasoned that such an outcome would be better than allowing an enemy to turn Great S'Yahazah's formidable power against the Gorn Hegemony."

"I wouldn't put it past Krassrr to try to bluff us," Qontallium said. "How do we know he's really installed any explosives?"

"I know they are here because I helped install them," S'syrixx said.

Both Keru and Qontallium appeared convinced. "Where?" said the security chief.

"Follow me," said the Gorn, who wasted no time leading the security contingent and Blue-White toward one of the nearby walls, where Keru and Qontallium began assisting S'syrixx in the painstaking removal of the series of small, palm-sized metal objects they found magnetized there amidst a busy, cramped filigree of complex markings that strongly resembled a written language.

Content to leave the task of looking out for further booby traps for the security contingent and the floating AI, Ra-Havreii devoted his entire attention to the room itself. Built into the center of Brahma-Shiva's base, the oval chamber extended some forty meters across at its widest point, while the ceiling stretched more than twenty meters overhead. Every surface of the gently curving walls was festooned with the same small, intricate shapes that had concealed the explosive charges S'syrixx and the security contingent were now busy removing and disarming. Ra-Havreii's engineering tricorder read the markings as primarily trypolymerized composites of silicon, molybdenum, and cobalt. Although the shapes on the walls strongly resembled writing, their composition led him to think they might be something far more subtle. He took his time studying them, discovering along the way that they weren't merely markings etched onto the walls—they were more like components stamped onto a substrate, analogous to integrated circuits imprinted onto old-fashioned duotronic or multitronic microprocessors, or even the microtranstators that were grown into the matrices of modern isolinear chips.

Looks a little bit like a heuristic matrix, he thought, awed as much by the complexity as by the evident age of this find. *Not too different from what you might expect to find imprinted on the positronic brain of a Soong-type android, or something similar.*

Evidently having completed the task of disarming Krassrr's explosives, S'syrixx approached Ra-Havreii and spoke in strangely low, reserved tones. "You may be looking upon the sublime thoughts of S'Yahazah, the Great Egg Bringer."

Ra-Havreii somehow found the Gorn's growling, hissing whisper more unnerving than the guttural rumble of his ordinary speaking voice, perhaps in part because of the alienness of their present surroundings. At least aboard *Titan*—an environment Ra-Havreii had essentially designed—he was surrounded by enough familiar touchstones not to be overly bothered by the Gorn's presence. But here, however . . .

"I don't suppose you can tell what she might be thinking about," Ra-Havreii said.

"I can only surmise, Commander," S'syrixx said. "But I imagine she wouldn't wander far from the usual topics. Life. Death. And the cycle that endlessly iterates them both."

"I recommend against making any further active scans while we are aboard, unless absolutely necessary," said Commander Tuvok as he consulted his own tricorder, which he was presumably running in a passive-scan mode.

"Yesss," S'syrixx said. "This place may conceal any number of additional surprises for us."

"I agree," Ra-Havreii said with a nod.

As he opened up the small case that carried the team's cache of antimatter charges, Keru spoke up quietly, pitching his voice low in an apparent effort to make himself audible only to his Starfleet colleagues. "Speaking of surprises, I can't help but wonder why Captain Krassrr hasn't posted any guards in here."

Ra-Havreii had no answer to that, other than one he didn't like very much—the possibility that the away team had just beamed into a carefully laid trap that Krassrr could spring shut on them at any moment.

"Krassrr claims to revere the Egg Bringer as much as any member of the technological or religious castes does," S'syrixx said, either unaware or unoffended by Keru's attempt to exclude him from the conversation. "He is no exemplar of piety, of course, or he would not be endangering the Hranrarii. But he may be disinclined to court S'Yahazah's displeasure by quartering his troopers in Her sanctum."

That made sense to Ra-Havreii, if such superstitions could be said to make sense on any level. *Perhaps the reverence for the Ur-mother of Gorn mythology that S'syrixx exhibits—along with a predilection for identifying it with this ancient technological artifact—also exists in Krassrr's caste, where it manifests as a general disinclination to risk the displeasure of an alleged god-thing by approaching it too closely.*

Tuvok spoke, distracting Ra-Havreii from his musings. "Now that we have finished disabling Krassrr's antipersonnel ordnance," the Vulcan said, addressing the entire away team, "I suggest we make finding an active computer interface our top priority. We do not know how much time we have to accomplish that task, nor do we know how long it will take to download whatever data this structure might contain. I trust that I need not remind anyone that the shuttlecraft *Gillespie* could be discovered and destroyed at any moment."

If anything were to happen to the *Gillespie,* the away team's chances of escaping from Brahma-Shiva before Keru's antimatter charges blew it to oblivion wouldn't be worth computing.

With a nod to Tuvok, Ra-Havreii adjusted the scan radius of his tricorder and busied himself taking additional scans.

25

U.S.S. TITAN

Riker felt the teeth-rattling impact a moment after the tractor beam released the escape pod and allowed it to settle onto the hangar deck.

"Your tractor beam is badly out of adjustment, Rry'kurr," Z'shezhira said as Riker began frantically working the hatch controls.

"I don't think our tractor beam had anything to do with that," he said as the ship rocked and rumbled again.

The hatch irised open with a hiss that sounded vaguely reptilian in Riker's ears, and the captain bounded out of the small vessel, nearly bowling over Chief Petty Officer Densisar and Ensign Hriss, the nearest members of the security detail that had come to greet the *S'alath*'s escape pod.

"Take my guest up to the bridge," he told the surprised Orion security man, then headed for the nearest turbolift at a dead run.

"Return fire!" Gibruch said as he seized the arms of the command chair in a death grip. The bridge vibrated as the phasers stabbed into Hranrar's atmosphere.

"Sorry, Captain," Rager said. "With all this geomagnetic interference, I can't maintain a weapons lock. I can't tell if I'm hitting anything or not."

When the port-side turbolift doors issued their signature pneumatic hiss, Gibruch turned his head briefly to determine the cause. A disheveled, slightly out-of-breath William Riker stepped across the threshold. The relief that the gamma-shift watch officer felt at the sight of his CO was so palpable and intense that he only barely restrained his cranial tails from fluting a triumphal major chord.

The tones burst forth nevertheless as a joyous, singsong "Captain on the bridge!"

As Gibruch stepped aside from the command well in the bridge's center to make way for Riker, *Titan* rocked from yet another salvo from the *S'alath.*

"Proximity alert!" Rager shouted as a klaxon blared.

On the main viewer, the *S'alath* could be seen approaching rapidly; since the Gorn warship had been keeping station inside Hranrar's atmosphere at a depth greater than *Titan*'s, it was obvious that she was now gaining altitude rapidly. The hostile vessel's forward tubes flared with eye-searing brilliance as it hurtled relentlessly upward, filling the screen.

"Evasive maneuvers!" Riker shouted as the bridge rocked and bucked, the lights dimming as the *S'alath*'s weapons conspired with the planetary magnetic field to tax *Titan*'s shield generators to their limits. Gibruch half-fell and half-sat in the empty seat to Riker's left, since the inertial dampers were under no less strain than were the shields.

Gibruch did not resume his regular breathing pattern until several seconds had elapsed—when it became clear that *Titan* had miraculously avoided what had looked like a certain collision.

The port turbolift doors hissed open once more. Gibruch was surprised again, but not altogether pleasantly; a Gorn he had never seen before stepped onto the bridge, flanked by Dennisar and Hriss from security.

"The shields took a hell of a pounding from that last salvo, Captain," Rager said, intent on her console. "Judging from the *S'alath*'s firing pattern, it looks like Gog'resssh wanted to knock out our engines as he passed us."

Riker rubbed his beard contemplatively as he turned and acknowledged the new arrivals. "Gog'resssh doesn't want us following him."

"He expects to claim *Tie-tan* and its technology as his own," the Gorn said in a voice that sang with low growls and soft sibilances. "Just as he expects to claim me as the brood mother of his new warrior caste. He can't very well achieve either aim if he destroys this vessel outright."

"Good point," Riker said. Addressing ops, he asked, "How much damage did he do to us?"

"Nothing serious, Captain," Rager said. "The magnetic field spoiled the *S'alath*'s aim for the most part. Our shields did the rest, even though this isn't their optimal working environment. Warp drive is still down, but I don't think the Gorn ship made life any harder down in the engine room than it was already."

Gibruch still couldn't believe how lucky they had been. "I thought for a moment Gog'resssh meant to ram us," he said, addressing no one in particular. "I wonder if he's really crazy enough to do something like that."

"I just dealt with him up close and personal," Riker

said. "He might know better than to ram *Titan,* but I think he's crazy enough to run headfirst into *something.*"

"The ecosculptor," said the Gorn female.

"Lay in a pursuit course, Mister Lavena."

Although the Pacifican hastened to comply with the order, she said, "Once we leave this magnetic hot spot, we'll be exposed to anything Captain Krassrr decides to throw at us."

"I think we lost the option of anonymity the moment Gog'resssh started that firefight," Riker said. "Engage."

Gibruch felt the ship lurch very slightly during the instant it took the inertial dampers to catch up with *Titan*'s forward acceleration. It occurred to him that this was the most excitement he had experienced on the bridge in over a year, since the Droplet affair last year.

The sound of the captain's voice interrupted his reverie. "Commander, I'd like to ask you a question, if you don't mind."

"Sir?"

The captain hiked a thumb toward the female Gorn who still stood a few meters behind him. "When Z'shezhira and I slipped away from the *S'alath,* it was probably a little bit difficult to tell our escape pod apart from a torpedo casing."

Gibruch nodded. "Given all the geomagnetism-related difficulties we've been having, I couldn't distinguish two such objects using only sensor profile data."

With a furrowed brow, Riker said, "Are you telling me that my escape pod *might* have been a photon torpedo as far as you could tell?"

"No, sir. Only that your sensor profile was inadequate to make the determination. I used other means instead."

"You guessed."

Gibruch felt his cranial tails filling involuntarily with air, which he began releasing in as quiet and controlled a fashion as possible, given his escalating nervousness. "Yes, Captain. But my guess was based on the fact that the *S'alath*'s weapons tubes were all cold at the time we detected your escape pod."

The captain's frown quickly smoothed itself over, and a wide grin split his face. "Commander, Miz Z'shezhira and I are both lucky that you have such a good eye for detail."

"Thank you, sir," Gibruch said.

Embarrassed by the praise, he looked forward, into the main viewer, which showed Hranrar's rarefied upper atmosphere giving way to the blackness of space. The planet's deceptively delicate-looking ring system hove swiftly into view, suffused in one spot by a weird, ghostly glow. The bright red emissions of the *S'alath*'s impulse engines appeared next as *Titan* began to close with the Gorn vessel rushing headlong toward the ring's hazy luminescence.

As the ring plane seemed to grow relative to *Titan*, Brahma-Shiva appeared over the horizon. The artifact shone like an incipient supernova.

That can't be a good thing, Gibruch thought.

HRANRAR

"Total, absolute annihilation: That's the kind of danger your world is facing, Honored Speaker," Troi said, a tone of genuine pleading in her voice.

Vale did not consider that a good sign at all: it told her that the diplomatic officer could sense that she was failing to persuade her audience.

"You don't need to take our word for it, Honored Speaker," Vale said, stepping forward while taking care not to alarm the Hranrarii leader's extremely tense-looking bodyguards. "Look into your own sky."

She pointed upward at the angry cross of fire that rent the heavens almost directly overhead. The speaker did as she was bid, as did about half of her bodyguards and nearly all of the Hranrarii government functionaries who had accumulated in the tower-top meadow around the planet's highest-ranking leader.

"If you let this object carry out its function," Vale said, "then your world as you've known it will end forever. I know you possess the power and the technology necessary to destroy or disable that thing."

Sethne Naq, Speaker for the Great Syndic of the Global Moeity of Hranrar, averted her eyes from the sky and focused her gaze upon Vale. "If the object really is of extra-Hranrarii origin, as you say, then we would prefer to have an opportunity to study it before any destructive energies are directed against it."

Mumbles of assent circulated among the Speaker's nest of aides and assistants.

Gods save us from the meek and lowly, and the pure and holy, Vale thought in exasperation.

Aloud, she said, "I'm afraid you don't have that kind of time, Speaker. This device—this *weapon*—could go off at any moment, killing everyone on this planet. That includes all of *us*, by the way."

"Good, balanced decisions are never made in haste," Sethne Naq said.

"Sometimes there's no survivable alternative to haste,"

Troi said. "I respectfully submit that this is one of those times."

"You claim the . . . object . . . is from another world," the Speaker said, waving her hand airily at the angry omen in the sky. "From another solar system, in fact."

"Yes," Vale said.

"According to our histories, a similar object appeared in our skies long ago. Our people demolished it when it failed to answer our initial calls."

"Your ancestors must have been very wise," Vale said. It occurred to her then that the Speaker's story seemed to square neatly with the metal fragments *Titan* had encountered elsewhere in the Hranrar system.

"We feel now that our forebears may have acted prematurely," the Speaker said. "We do not wish to repeat their error. We will demonstrate more patience than they did."

"With respect, Honored Speaker, too much patience will lead to a catastrophe," said Troi.

"As will an excess of panic. We do not even know for certain as yet that the object in question really is of alien origin. The preponderance of our most prominent Elder Knowers has concluded that intelligent life—life of the kind that Knows and Builds—can exist nowhere but on Hranrar."

Vale wished vainly that she could access a little of the Speaker's overabundant patience. "What about *us,* Speaker?"

Sethne Naq's froggy eyes blinked in slow perplexity. "I do not understand the question."

"As one of my people's great thinkers might have said, 'Are you gonna believe your planet's Elder Knowers, or your own lyin' eyes?' "

The Speaker's evident bemusement only deepened as Troi glowered silently in Vale's direction. *All right. Maybe misquoting Groucho Marx during a tense first-contact situation isn't playing quite according to Hoyle. But I've got to find* some *way to drill through this thick amphibian skull.*

"What I mean is this, Honored Speaker," Vale said. "It's pretty obvious that neither I nor any of my people are Hranrarii."

"That much seems clear," the speaker said.

Vale nodded. "So if non-Hranrarii intelligence really is as impossible as your scientific consensus says it is, then how do you account for *us*?"

Sethne Naq, Speaker for the Great Syndic of the Global Moeity of Hranrar, lapsed into a troubled silence. Her eyes seemed focused upon her flipperlike feet for what felt like a full minute before she craned her gaze skyward again.

"Perhaps the universe is a larger place than we had imagined," said the speaker.

Vale hoped that meant she was finally achieving some intellectual traction here. "It's all waiting out there for you to explore. The universe could be at your fingertips in a matter of months, via technology that you already have. You can venture into it as peacefully as you like. In fact, there's only one thing the universe *won't* let you do."

"And what is that?"

Vale pointed up at the pyrotechnic apparition burning overhead. "The universe won't let you get away with ignoring it."

26

GORN HEGEMONY WARSHIP *S'ALATH*

To make certain that every critical flight and combat function was at least minimally covered, Gog'resssh had deployed his most able remaining warriors on the command deck, leaving the remaining tech-casters confined in the security area. With the loss of Zegrroz'rh now silently acknowledged by everyone aboard the *S'alath*—the second myrmidon could no longer enforce discipline merely by virtue of his menacing presence as the first myrmidon's good right manus—the troopers had already begun to become slack and unruly.

But breaking K'zgarr's neck, and then twisting his head off, right out on the command deck and in full sight of Great S'Yahazah, had immediately gone a long way toward instilling a renewed sense of order among Gog'resssh's ragtag ranks.

Gog'resssh was about to ask for a tactical update when the forward viewer told him everything he needed to know: as the *S'alath* glided toward the relatively small ventral side of the orbiting ecosculptor, using Hranrar's ring system in an attempt to hide its approach, several starlike lights swooped into view from the ecosculptor's opposite side.

"Krassrr has prepared a welcome for us," Gog'resssh rumbled. "Narrzsesh, you fool! You have given away our approach!"

Narrzsesh turned from the helm station to face Gog'resssh, his rad-scarred facial and cranial scales arrayed in a posture of fear/respect/obeisance. "No, First Myrmidon, I promise you!"

Gog'resssh leaped from his thronelike chair and drew the helmrunner into a bone-grinding hold.

Azagrern spoke up from the main sensor console. "Narrzsesh might not be at fault, First Myrmidon. Something else may be responsible."

"And what would that be?" Gog'resssh said, poised upon the brink of disposing of yet another recalcitrant crewmember.

"Look!" Azagrern cried, pointing at the main viewer, which displayed a greatly magnified image of a small spacecraft that was keeping station near the ecosculptor's base.

Gog'resssh allowed an ivory forest of serrated teeth to emerge from his mouth, accompanied by an involuntary lacing of saliva. "A mammal spacecraft, launched from *Tietan,* no doubt."

"Power readings are minimal," said Hressh, the armory officer.

Which makes it likelier that it was the S'alath *that drew Krassrr's attention,* Gog'resssh thought. But this was no time to rehash that.

"Life signs?" he said.

"None aboard," said Azagrern. "However, I read intermittent, confused bio-signatures coming from *inside* the ecosculptor."

Rry'kurr's mammals. "That small vessel is the escape route for the humans who have boarded the ecosculptor. Arm a torpedo and close off that escape route."

"At once, First Myrmidon," said Hressh as his talons clacked against his board. The command deck vibrated, signaling that the forward torpedo tube had disgorged its deadly cargo. Moments later an expanding orb of fire replaced the little mammalship.

"Give me a tactical plot of Krassrr's fleet!" Gog'resssh bellowed, eager to face larger foes.

The image of the immolated mammalship vanished, replaced by a split screen. On the left side were five moving lights, which already looked more like ships than the distant background stars that lay beyond the ecosculptor's immensity. The screen's right side displayed five corresponding red icons that represented Krassrr's vessels, and a single green one that stood for the *S'alath,* which approached Krassrr's fleet head-on; in between these opposing forces was a graphic of the ecosculptor, as unmoving and serene as a mountain on Gornar.

"Will we engage Krassrr's fleet all at once, First Myrmidon?"

"That depends on how many of his captains are foolish enough to get in our way, Helmrunner," Gog'resssh said, leaning forward like a predator ready to strike. "Ready the weapons and take us to the ecosculptor's core. Maximum impulse."

If anyone is to remake this world for the future of my caste, it will be me, Gog'resssh thought. *And I will do it with my own two manus, not by hurling fire from the skies.*

A proximity alarm sounded, abruptly snapping the first myrmidon out of his musings. "What?"

"Incoming vessel!" Azagrern roared. "She's opening fire!"

Then something struck the *S'alath*'s hull with a ferocity that Gog'resssh imagined might have rivaled the flames that had consumed Sazssgrerrn.

U.S.S. TITAN

"Fire!" Riker said.

Now that *Titan* was free of the magnetic interference of Hranrar's northern polar region, Lieutenant Rager's aim was true. Riker watched as great gouts of hot plasma and vented atmosphere commingled in the sections of the *S'alath*'s dorsal hull that had taken the brunt of the phaser barrage.

That last one's for the Gillespie, Riker thought. He was thankful at least that no one appeared to have been aboard the shuttlecraft when Gog'resssh had blown it out of the sky.

"It helps to know precisely where to aim your particle weapons, does it not, Rry'kurr?" Z'shezhira said, displaying her teeth in what Riker charitably interpreted as the Gorn equivalent of a convivial smile. A few paces behind her stood Lieutenant Pava Ek'Noor sh'Aqabaa from security, her Andorian antennae angled vigilantly forward. Nearby stood the huge green Orion, Dennisar, also from security and every bit as vigilant.

"Once again, I am in your debt," Riker said. Rising from his command chair to take a better look at the ops console, he said, "What's the status of the *S'alath*'s weapons?"

"Disabled," Rager said. "Shields are failing as well. He still has impulse power, but other than that he's dead in the water."

"Maintain Red Alert," Riker cautioned. "And don't

make the mistake of counting Gog'resssh out just yet. He can still do a hell of a lot of damage."

"Yesss," Z'shezhira said. "He is committed to destroying the ecosculptor. Nothing short of death will stop him."

Riker nodded. "I know. Blowing up the platform is a subject he seems to enjoy monologuing about. Trouble is, he doesn't mean to let our away team finish their business there before he does it."

"You will stop him, Rry'kurr." The reptiloid's yellow, vertically-pupiled eyes grew moist with unshed tears. His compassion took an involuntary leap across phylum boundaries; with his own *Imzadi* still in harm's way on the surface of Hranrar—not to mention a second team that he couldn't beam safely away from Brahma-Shiva under the present circumstances—he realized he understood precisely how Z'shezhira felt.

"It's my top priority," he said, managing not to flinch as he placed a hand gently upon her cold, scale-covered shoulder. "Aside from keeping this ship in one piece, that is."

"Speaking of which," Lieutenant Lavena said, "it looks like Captain Krassrr is sending his regards. Incoming!"

"Evasive maneuvers, Aili!" Riker cried as the bridge shook and shimmied beneath him yet again.

"Aye, sir."

"And take us right up to within spitting distance of Brahma-Shiva, no matter what Krassrr or Gog'resssh do next. I want to get a transporter lock on the boarding team, ASAP."

GORN HEGEMONY WARSHIP *S'ALATH*

"Weapons systems are down," said Hressh, the armory officer. "Forward torpedo launchers have taken direct hits."

No, Gog'resssh thought. *I cannot come this close only to be denied.*

"There has to be one good tube left aboard this ship!" he roared. "Drag the tech-casters out of confinement and put them to work on the main disruptor array and at least one of the aft launchers. I want you to deploy the torpedoes using your own two manus if you have to."

"At once, First Myrmidon," Hressh said. Though his voice resonated with doubt, he wasted no time exiting the command deck.

Gog'resssh reflected that it was good to have troopers who feared their commander more than they feared the wrath of a balky torpedo tube.

"Qontallium and I just set the last of the antimatter charges along the chamber's perimeter," Keru said as he approached the circuitry-laden wall where the most technical phase of the mission was being conducted.

"Good work, Commander," Tuvok said, carefully concealing his relief at hearing that the tactical personnel, at least, had met with some immediate success.

Tuvok heard a growl behind him, and turned to face its source.

"I cannot support any plan to destroy the ecosculptor," S'syrixx said, his tone low and dangerous. "I came here to help preserve the vessel of the Great Egg Bringer S'Yahazah."

Tuvok stood his ground. "You agreed to help us prevent this artifact from slaughtering millions of innocent Hranrarii. And *we* agreed to do everything possible to preserve whatever information is stored here—which may or may not include the essence of your Egg Bringer. If such an entity actually exists, then surely it is beyond the ability of any of us to do it harm."

S'syrixx stood in silence for a lengthy time, clenching and unclenching his three-fingered hands as he weighed Tuvok's logic.

"Very well," he said at length. "For all the millions who would otherwise die to please Krassrr, I will cooperate with this. I can only pray for S'Yahazah's forgiveness after the fact."

"Good," said Commander Ra-Havreii. "The sooner we get this done, the sooner we can key in the delayed detonation command and beam back to the *Gillespie.*"

A cloud of dread settled over Tuvok as he contemplated the shuttlecraft, which the away team had left expending only enough energy to maintain a constant relative position about fifty klicks below Brahma-Shiva relative to Hranrar. There it remained, powered down and defenseless as it awaited the team's return. Tuvok knew that Krassrr's fleet was unlikely to detect the shuttle's presence, both because of its darkened power profile and because it was positioned along one of the best stealth-approach, blind-spot trajectories connecting Hranrar to Brahma-Shiva's base. But if Krassrr *had* somehow noticed the *Gillespie,* the team would have lost the option of surviving the destruction of the terraforming device—and whatever information they might retrieve here would be lost as well.

"You *can* still beam us back to the shuttle . . . right, Commander Keru?" the chief engineer asked, apparently giving voice to Tuvok's own private misgivings.

"Don't worry," Keru said. "I just received the regular check-in signal from the *Gillespie*'s computer about a minute ago."

Scowling, the engineer tapped his combadge. "Ra-Havreii to the *Gillespie.* Check transporter lock on away team."

Silence replaced the reassuringly affect-free voice of the shuttlecraft's computer. Two more combadge hails, one from Tuvok and another from Keru, met with the same nonresponse.

"Maybe it's just a temporary glitch," Keru said.

"And maybe Krassrr found the *Gillespie* and destroyed her," said Ra-Havreii.

"There is no logic in speculating," Tuvok said. "We still have a mission to complete."

"I am detecting EM pulses from space that are consistent with the firing of certain particle weapons," Second-Gen White-Blue said.

"That is by no means conclusive evidence of anything," Tuvok said.

"Except, perhaps, of S'Yahazah's displeasure," S'syrixx said.

Ra-Havreii muttered something under his breath that sounded like a curse. "We're dead."

Keru closed his eyes and rubbed at the spots on his temples as though they were causing him pain. "Let's all try to stay on topic, just in case the cavalry arrives in time to pick us up after all. Have any of you guys had any luck yet finding a working computer interface?"

Ra-Havreii shrugged. "I hate to have to admit this out loud, but I'm beginning to wonder if we might be out of our depth here."

"You're giving up?" Keru asked, incredulous.

"Not at all," Tuvok said. "However, we cannot minimize the fact that we are dealing with a highly advanced alien technology that appears to be at least half a million years old."

Ra-Havreii nodded. "And that's to say nothing about its many humanoid-unfriendly features. How can anyone expect to decipher it in the space of a few minutes?"

"I get it now. You're trying to manage the team's expectations," Keru said, smiling in an apparent display of what humans sometimes described as "gallows humor."

"I'm merely trying to put my latest technological miracle into its proper context," Ra-Havreii said.

"*Our* technological miracle," S'syrixx said in an uncanny approximation of the engineer's voice. The Gorn pointed a single sharp claw at one particular segment of the raised, metallic techno-hieroglyphs on the chamber wall. "Based on our best analysis and White-Blue's scans, this should be our interface."

"'Should be?'" Keru asked. "You still aren't sure? A little while ago you gave us the impression that you knew this place inside and out."

"And so I do," S'syrixx said, his voice returning to its regular register while also conveying a mild timbre of warning. "But I am . . . I *was* . . . merely one member of a team of technologists. No one member of the team could know every aspect of a thing such as this."

"Do you believe it is safe to proceed, Commander?" Tuvok said, addressing Ra-Havreii.

The engineer smiled crookedly. "What do we have to lose by trying?"

27

GORN HEGEMONY WARSHIP *S'ALATH*

"*One disruptor emitter and one torpedo tube are now restored to operation,*" Hressh reported over the intraship comm.

The ecosculptor, the very symbol of the dominion of the old warrior-caste, loomed on the main viewer, almost close enough to reach out and touch.

Determined to do a good deal more than that, Gog'resssh grinned broadly.

"Open fire."

GORN HEGEMONY RECONNAISSANCE VESSEL *SSEVARRH*

"The warship *S'alath* is ignoring our hails," said Grezzsz, Krassrr's Second.

Missing for longer than a suncircuit, only to return piloted by ghosts, Captain Krassrr thought unhappily as he watched the ship's approach on his command deck's central viewer. *Or by pirates.*

He was loath to fire upon a ship of the line of the Gorn Hegemony. But this was a restricted volume of space, and the *S'alath* had transmitted no clearance codes of any kind.

And she continued drawing ever nearer to the ecosculptor.

"Lock disruptors on target," Krassrr said.

"The *S'alath* is locking weapons on the ecosculptor!"

Krassrr released a growl born of deep frustration. He had worked hard to restore the ecosculptor to operational status; realizing its abundant promise, both for his own caste and career and for the Hegemony in general, had been Krassrr's responsibility.

Now he could only watch helplessly while that promise was forever snatched away.

"Sir!" the science tech-caster Trr'reriss roared. "Another vessel approaches the ecosculptor as well, at high impulse."

Within the span of heartbeats, the second ship became discernible on the viewer. A moment later, as it interposed itself between the *S'alath* and the ecocaster, it became recognizable.

Krassrr's heavy lower jaw swung slackly over his sternum. *The mammals,* he thought.

"Tie-tan," he said as the Federrazsh'n vessel's bright blue particle beams raked the *S'alath* even as the latter ship fired a torpedo at the ecosculptor.

"Target both vessels!" Krassrr snarled.

The Vulcan tactical officer knelt briefly as he removed a newly fabricated custom ODN cable from the team's portable industrial replicator. After he rose and handed one end of the cable to the engineer, Tuvok plugged the cable into a high-capacity data module while Ra-Havreii affixed his end into the ancient slot whose location S'syrixx was pointing out with his claw. SecondGen White-Blue hovered quietly nearby, apparently content merely to observe.

"No explosions," Keru said. "So far, so good."

Tuvok watched the displays on the data module for several uneventful seconds. Nothing appeared to be happening as the time stretched. Tuvok knew that the team probably couldn't spare the time to make many more attempts at this. With or without an escape route, either for the team or for the data stored inside this ancient construct, the antimatter charges would have to be detonated soon to ensure the safety of Hranrar.

The data module suddenly came to life. Alien symbols raced across the displays, each appearing for a minuscule duration, like images of playing cards being shuffled with impossible speed.

"The data module is definitely recording data of some kind," Tuvok said as he continued studying the external display.

S'syrixx approached closely, drawing near enough to make Tuvok wary of a religiously motivated attack. But he immediately noted that the Gorn was only watching the ultraquick spooling of alien data.

"The immortal essence of Egg Bringer S'Yahazah," the Gorn said in a reverent whisper that sent a chill up the Vulcan's back, as though he were once again studying with the *Kolinahr* Masters on the Plains of Gol; he hadn't thought a cold-blooded being like S'syrixx capable of such an impassioned expression of devotion.

Suddenly the floor beneath Tuvok's boots shook violently. The lights overhead flickered and dimmed, and sparks flew from the data module, which slipped out of his grasp.

As the module plummeted toward the hard floor, the Vulcan noted that S'Yahazah's immortal essence seemed to have gone abruptly dark.

GORN HEGEMONY WARSHIP *S'ALATH*

Gog'resssh watched incredulously as *Tie-tan* raced toward the ecosculptor on what at first appeared to be a ramming trajectory. Then the mammal vessel came about, the weapons arrays on its dorsal hull glowing nearly as brightly as the gigantic artifact that now lay behind it.

"Torpedo away," said Azagrern as twin beams of cobalt-colored force lanced out from *Tie-tan,* smashing into the *S'alath* nearly hard enough to loosen some of Gog'resssh's back teeth. The lights dimmed as instruments overhead and behind sprayed sparks, fire, and acrid smoke. Flakes of hot metal seared his neck scales, but he ignored the pain.

He watched as the torpedo Hressh had just launched arced toward the ecosculptor. With a little luck, Rry'kurr would fail to lock his own weapons on the missile before—

Contact.

A nimbus of fire erupted at the impact point, almost dead center at the ecosculptor's base—which was, incidentally, the source of the bio readings of *Tie-tan*'s boarding party. Gog'resssh continued watching as the conflagration dissipated.

And left behind no evidence of a weapon strike of any kind. A full charge of contraterrene matter had expended itself against the ecosculptor's weirdly glowing hull, to no apparent effect.

That glow, Gog'resssh thought. *Perhaps it is the soul of the Egg Bringer.*

Whatever it was, he could afford to treat it as nothing less than a force that was determined to thwart his will.

"Ship status!" Gog'resssh demanded.

"We cannot take another such hit," Narrzsesh reported from the helmrunner's console. "Weapons systems have failed again. The torpedo bay Hressh was running manually has depressurized."

"*Tie-tan* is hailing us, Captain," Narrzsesh said.

Azagrern sounded alarmed. "The Federrazsh'n vessel is powering up weapons for another salvo."

Gog'resssh considered his options for a moment. He decided that only one remained.

"Narrzsesh, set a course for the base of the ecosculptor," he said. "Ramming speed."

Tuvok handed the singed, acrid-smelling piece of equipment to Ra-Havreii and braced himself for the bad news. Brahma-Shiva's interior lighting remained dimmed and reddened.

"I'm afraid the data module is completely fried, Commander," the chief engineer said with an unhappy shake of his head.

"We must find another option," S'syrixx said.

"Our tricorders aren't anything like those big modules in terms of storage capacity," Keru said. "Looks like we don't have a lot of options available to us."

Something moving at about eye level in Tuvok's peripheral vision attracted his attention. "Perhaps we have an alternative that none of you has considered as yet," said

Second-Gen White-Blue a moment after coming to a hovering stop in the midst of the team.

"What do you have in mind?"

"I have a substantial data storage capacity," the little AI said. "I would estimate it as at least two orders of magnitude greater than your largest data module."

Ra-Havreii raised his hands in a gesture of apparent impatience. "Wait a minute. Isn't most of that capacity in use at the moment, occupied with the business of . . . well, of being White-Blue?"

"I am capable of executing extreme data-compression regimes when necessary," White-Blue said. Bobbing in Tuvok's direction in a gesture that strongly resembled a humanoid's nod, the AI added, "Besides, there is too much at stake here to allow me to forgo whatever personal risk my plan might entail. For the millions on Hranrar whose survival is in doubt, and the billions across your Federation who stand to benefit, I ask you to plug me in to the dataport."

Tuvok raised an eyebrow, profoundly impressed. Still, he needed to make certain that this creature, artificial though its intelligence might be, was fully cognizant of the risks it was choosing to face. "You may cease to exist as a consequence of this action," he said.

"I understand, Commander Tuvok," White-Blue said. "But it is the only rational choice under the present circumstances."

"Good," Ra-Havreii said. "Let's do it. We don't have a lot of better alternatives. Or time, for that matter."

Although he wasn't entirely convinced, Tuvok nodded and reached for a fresh length of ODN cable.

28

U.S.S. TITAN

"The *S'alath* is just . . . *waiting* out there," Rager said.

"Gog'resssh must have seen for himself just how much effect his weapons had on Brahma-Shiva," Riker said, sitting on the edge of his command chair.

"Well, as far as I can tell, he won't get another chance to fire," Lavena said. "It looks as though his weapons systems have finally gasped their last. Same with his shields."

We thought he was down and out before, Riker thought. *And he still managed to surprise us.* He was determined not to let that happen again if he could help it.

Still standing on the bridge under the watchful eyes of both Lieutenant sh'Aqabaa and Chief Dennisar, Z'shezhira said, "Gog'resssh should never be underestimated."

"That ship-class is supposed to have some pretty tough weaponry," Rager said. "I sure hope that Brahma-Shiva was taking good care of the boarding team when the *S'alath*'s torpedo hit it."

"Until we can raise the team on the comm, all we can do is hope," Riker said.

Gibruch, who was now running one of the tactical

stations, spoke up. "There's something here I don't understand, Captain."

"What's that, Commander?"

"According to the telemetry signals from the *Gillespie,* the boarding team beamed aboard Brahma-Shiva from about fifty kilometers away without any trouble," Gibruch said in tones that reminded Riker of an orchestral woodwind section. "But an ordinary comm signal is a lot less complex than a transporter beam. You'd think we wouldn't have any trouble raising them at such relatively short range."

Riker nodded. Gesturing toward the main viewer's depiction of the steadily intensifying blue glow of the terraforming platform, he said, "My guess is that they beamed inside just before *that* happened."

"Maybe their beam-in woke something up," Lavena said.

Rager made a weary face. "If that's true, let's hope it's not grumpy first thing in the morning." Turning toward Riker, she said, "Phasers are still charged and ready, sir."

"Stand down from Red Alert, Lieutenant. But keep the phasers warm. I don't want to kill Gog'resssh or destroy his ship unless he forces me to. I'd rather see Krassrr arrest him."

Even as he voiced the wish he knew it had precious little chance of becoming reality; however distinguished his military record might have been before the Sazssgrerrn catastrophe unhinged him, Gog'resssh was now no longer the sort of person who would bend willingly to authority.

He could feel in his bones that the rogue Gorn would never permit himself to be taken alive.

Just as he knew he couldn't content himself with waiting

any longer to take action to pull the boarding team back from the terraforming platform, regardless of any mysterious forces that might be protecting it at the moment.

"Lieutenant Lavena, nudge us to within ten klicks of Brahma-Shiva's base," he said. "Mister Gibruch, ready the transporter, and hail the boarding team. I'm gambling that we can get *some* kind of signal through if we get close enough. We'll press our ears up against their windows if we have to."

"Aye, sir," his officers chorused.

No sooner had he felt the subtle but unmistakable "velocity-change tell" of the deck beneath his boots than an amber light began flashing on Rager's console.

"Krassrr's hailing us, Captain. His rant appears to be already in progress."

Riker sighed. "What a delight. Put him on audio, Lieutenant."

"—eem to have acted to protect the ecosculptor, Rry'kurr, which is the only reason I have chosen not to blow your vessel to quarks," said the commander of the Gorn terraforming fleet.

"I thank you, Captain Krassrr," Riker said. "Now what can I do for you?"

"Withdraw from this world and this system, Rry'kurr. Your only alternative is destruction."

Riker made a throat-slashing gesture, prompting Rager to mute the comm system's pickup. "Mister Gibruch, any luck contacting the boarding team?"

The Chandir shook his head sadly, causing his cranial tails to sway from side to side. As they moved, the tails made a noise that reminded Riker of an Australian aborigine's didgeridoo. "Nothing yet, sir. And that . . . energy field surrounding Brahma-Shiva is thoroughly confusing the transporter scanners. I'm going to try boosting the gain."

"Lieutenant Rager, what do you suppose Krassrr concluded from Gog'resssh's attack on Brahma-Shiva?" Riker asked.

"One of two things, sir," Rager said. "He either thinks that Brahma-Shiva is invulnerable now, or else he's assumed that Gog'resssh's torpedo somehow misfired before it reached its target."

Riker nodded. "My thoughts exactly. In my experience, Gorn warriors tend to be fairly conservative creatures. So I'm going to bet on choice number two—that Krassrr won't risk taking a shot that might hit his ecosculptor.

"Take us in closer, Lieutenant. A *lot* closer."

"Keep speaking to us as the download proceeds," Tuvok said to the quietly hovering SecondGen White-Blue as Ra-Havreii, Keru, Qontallium, and S'syrixx looked on. "That may enable us to disconnect you in time to prevent irreparable damage should anything go wrong."

"I shall comply," White-Blue said. "Download process is initiating. Copying incoming datastream to central storage core. Working. Working."

As the AI droned on, floating all the while at the end of an ODN-cable tether, White-Blue reminded Tuvok of a walk he had taken in San Francisco's Golden Gate Park during his most recent tenure as an instructor at Starfleet Academy. He had passed a human family who had been out enjoying the clear, warm spring day; one of the children had held a length of string pulled taut by an airborne polymer bladder filled nearly to bursting with a lighter-than-air gas, presumably helium. Attached to whatever ancient knowledge (or consciousness?) might yet dwell within the information systems of this ancient artifact, White-Blue now bore an absurd resemblance to that children's toy.

"Working," White-Blue said as the seconds slowly passed. "Working. Working. Work—" A coruscating nimbus of electric energy engulfed the AI, bringing its constant but repetitive commentary to an instantaneous halt.

White-Blue plummeted toward the floor, so much dead weight now. Keru dived to catch the AI as Tuvok grabbed the ODN cable and disconnected it from Brahma-Shiva's interface with a single hard tug.

Keru set White-Blue down gently on the hard metal floor while Ra-Havreii scanned the AI with his tricorder.

"Did he just fry like the data module?" Keru asked.

Ra-Havreii shook his head, a gesture that made his snowy mane and his long white mustachios wag from side to side. "I don't think so. My guess is he's gone into some sort of 'safe' mode. He seems to be using nearly all of his resources to perform self-diagnostic and self-repair subroutines."

"Then we're out of options, at least as far as salvaging anything here goes," Keru said. "I know you're in charge of this mission, Tuvok, but I would strongly advise you to cut bait at this point—we really should start the countdown on the antimatter charges and get away from here."

Once again, Tuvok wasn't entirely sure. "Perhaps," he said.

"S'Yahazah may not permit that," S'syrrix said. "Any more than she has permitted you to record her most unfathomable, unknowable thoughts."

"I'd prefer to concentrate on the practical issues," Ra-

Havreii said. "Such as finding out for sure whether or not we can get out of here."

"Logical," Tuvok said. Tapping his combadge, he once again hailed the *Gillespie,* although he strongly suspected the shuttlecraft's computer wouldn't be able to answer.

Exactly as before, he received only silence and static in response.

So it has come down, at last, to this, Tuvok thought. *The lives of the boarding party against the millions who will die should Captain Krassrr release Brahma-Shiva's energies on the surface of Hranrar.*

His combadge chirruped, startling him so much that he almost jumped in a decidedly non-Vulcan manner. "—itan *to boarding tea—Boarding team, d—you read?"*

Despite the wash of static that competed with the comm signal, Captain Riker's voice was clearly recognizable. Tuvok maintained his studied air of Vulcan sobriety only with the greatest effort as he replied.

"Commander Tuvok here, Captain. The boarding team is safe. Can you establish a transporter lock?"

An uncomfortably static-filled interval passed before the answer arrived. *"—firmative, Commande—"*

"Please stand by to beam us out at our next signal, Captain. We still have to activate the delayed-detonation sequence."

"Why the hell can't we do that remotely, once we're all back aboard *Titan*?" Keru said to Ra-Havreii in an almost conspiratorial tone as he busied himself entering the detonation parameters into a control padd.

The engineer shrugged. Sotto voce, he said, "Mostly because the 'kaboom' signal might not get through. As much as I'd like to do this thing by pushing a button a quarter-billion klicks away from here, we can't risk letting a stupid malfunction bring down a whole civilization."

*"—cknowledged, Commande—Finish up—s quickly as—ou can. —*itan *will stand by—as long as Krassrr will—et us."*

Scant moments later, Keru looked up from the displays on his detonator padd. "Ready, Commander Tuvok. In sixty seconds, this whole place will be just more raw material for Hranrar's ring system."

Tuvok nodded. He was about to tap his combadge again when a sibilant growl from behind him interrupted the motion.

He turned away from the wall, facing the cavernous main room's formerly empty center.

The space was empty no longer. Hovering about three meters off the floor was a red-orange sphere approximately twice the diameter of a typical humanoid's head. It seemed both solid and insubstantial, both real and unreal, a thing of ethereal dreams and rock-hard reality all at once. Intermittent, ephemeral flares of energy orbited the thing as it steadily grew, nearly doubling in size in the span of just a few seconds. Lightninglike flashes encircled it, popping in and out of existence like pairs of virtual subatomic particles, or the short-lived electrical discharges that bridged the progressively widening gap in the primitive device known on Vulcan as a T'Klaas's Ascent, or on Earth as a Jacob's Ladder.

"It would appear that the Great Egg Bringer has decided to alter the plan," S'syrixx said, his tone at once fearful and awestruck. "S'Yahazah comes!"

"Time until detonation?" Tuvok said, ignoring the Gorn's displays of fear and reverence.

"Damned timer stopped at fifty-two seconds," Keru said after glancing at his detonator padd.

Tuvok acknowledged the security chief's observation with a nod as the glowing, energetic apparition in the middle of the chamber continued to swell and grow. The ruddy sphere already filled the room's center, nearly touching both floor and ceiling.

"I'm afraid that's not all," Ra-Havreii said.

Tuvok braced himself for still more bad news. "Go ahead, Commander."

"The antimatter in the explosive charges has somehow been . . . neutralized."

Tuvok's left eyebrow involuntarily lofted toward the ceiling. " 'Neutralized?' "

"Rendered inert somehow. I've never seen anything like it, so I'm afraid I don't have any better way of explaining it. Whatever caused it, here's the bottom line: those charges now have all the destructive power of so much Kaferian apple butter."

"There is only one cause for everything in all the universe," S'syrixx said, staring worshipfully into the expanding energy sphere. "S'Yahazah, the cosmic mother."

Visibly losing control of his temper, Keru turned his large frame toward the Gorn and said, "Will you please shut up about your precious—"

"Commander Keru," Tuvok said, interrupting. "Regardless of its possible religious significance to the Gorn, this manifestation is undoubtedly the source of our current . . . technical problems."

"It could be some sort of internal defense system," Ra-Havreii said with a nod.

"Indeed. It may even exhibit at least a rudimentary intelligence, just as Mister S'syrixx alleges."

"Real sentience?" Ra-Havreii sounded skeptical. "Forgive me for saying this bluntly, Commander, but I think that may be something of a stretch."

Tuvok couldn't blame Ra-Havreii for adopting such a skeptical perspective; ordinarily, he was no more sanguine about what the humans called "hunches" than was the engineer. On this occasion, however, a sensation—a *feeling*—of near certainty plagued him, refusing to relinquish its hold over his imagination.

"This . . . *object,*" Tuvok said, pointing toward the still-growing sphere, "recognized the active ingredient in our munitions and neutralized it. It could have employed any number of more lethal methods against us. Yet it acted with apparent deliberation in taking a more moderate approach."

"I think 'apparent' is the operative word, Commander," Ra-Havreii said, still clearly unconvinced.

"Outside the context of some manner of direct telepathic contact," Tuvok said, "all sentience is mere appearance—even sentience capable of passing the Turing test."

"So what are you proposing, Commander?" Keru said, gesturing toward the glowing, expanding orb. The object now seemed well on its way to pushing the boarding party into the walls. "That we try to *reason* with this thing?"

"That is *precisely* what I am suggesting, Mister Keru. Since destroying it is no longer an option, establishing communication with it may be the only way to save the

Hranrarii from obliteration." *To say nothing of the boarding party,* Tuvok added silently.

"Tuvok, exactly how do you propose to do that?" Keru said.

"I will initiate a mind-meld."

Ra-Havreii shook his head. "You saw what happened both times we tried to download a little data, Commander." He gestured toward the section of the floor where White-Blue's inert metal-clad body lay beside a burned-out data module. "What makes you think you'll fare any better?"

Tuvok could see that Keru, Ra-Havreii, and Qontallium were all looking askance at him. He ignored their obvious disapproval.

"Beam back to *Titan,* all of you. Take White-Blue with you."

"What about you, Commander?" Keru said.

"Have *Titan* maintain a lock on me for as long as possible," Tuvok said. "Await my signal. I do not want to risk beaming back to *Titan* until we are certain that Brahma-Shiva has been neutralized."

"And if you end up just like White-Blue?" Ra-Havreii said with a scowl.

"In that event, please inform T'Pel that I merely did what logic demanded," Tuvok said. "And that my last thoughts were of her."

With that, he turned and approached the ragged edge of the spreading globular nimbus of coruscating energies. He felt the hairs on his neck and arms stand on end as he spread both hands and slowly extended them toward the object's sparking, flashing boundary layer.

29

U.S.S. TITAN

Xin Ra-Havreii held his breath as the transporter took him. During the few seconds he spent disembodied in the matter stream, as the arcane hieroglyphics of the alien artifact's interior gave way to the minimalist blue color scheme of one of *Titan*'s transporter rooms, he conceived a ridiculous hope.

Once the materialization process was complete, he noted with no small amount of disappointment that the transporter had reassembled the guilt he carried, along with the rest of his mind and body. The guilt, of course, had been well earned—he had agreed, along with the rest of the boarding team, to leave Commander Tuvok to face a deadly danger by himself.

"Where's Commander Tuvok?" said Lieutenant Bowan Radowski, who was running the transporter console. "And your Gorn, um, guest?"

Still standing on the transporter stage, Ra-Havreii turned to look at his teammates. He quickly noted that only Keru and Qontallium stood with him, with the insensate metal form of SecondGen White-Blue and the dead data module each lying on one of the stage's rear pads.

"Our friend Mister S'syrixx hopped out of the way of the beam at the last moment," Qontallium said. "I saw him move but I didn't want to risk . . ." The Gnalish security officer trailed off in apparent shame.

"Nothing to be embarrassed about, Qur," Keru said. "Trying to dodge an active transporter beam is a good way to get yourself sliced in half. If S'syrixx is still alive he can count himself as damned lucky."

"Okay," Radowski said, looking troubled, as though the unilateral decisions of two members of the boarding team to remain behind signified a personal failure on his part. "That accounts for *one* of the missing transportees. Why did Commander Tuvok insist on staying behind?"

"He had to take care of some . . . unfinished business," Ra-Havreii said as he helped Keru and Qontallium carry White-Blue from the transporter stage.

Radowski's combadge interrupted the proceedings. *"Bridge to transporter room two,"* Captain Riker said, his signal refreshingly static-free. *"Report."*

"Most of the boarding team is back aboard, Captain," Radowski said sheepishly. "Commander Tuvok and our Gorn guest are still aboard Brahma-Shiva."

While Radowski and Keru quickly brought the captain up to speed, Ra-Havreii walked to the console that tied in with the main bridge viewer and activated it; having just witnessed the rather startling changes the artifact's interior had undergone, he wanted to see what, if anything, was happening to the thing's ancient, meteoroid-pitted exterior.

What appeared on the screen startled him. From its squat base to the kilometers-long needle-like structure that comprised the bulk of the object's length, Brahma-Shiva was now nearly blindingly refulgent with an internally generated, bluish brilliance. Judging from the rate at which the illumination seemed to be increasing, it wouldn't be long before no one aboard *Titan* could safely look at the thing without the intervention of filters and digital image enhancements.

"I hope the ghost in this machine isn't an obsessive conversationalist," Ra-Havreii said. "There's no way this thing's internal power buildup can be sustained for much longer."

Ra-Havreii could foresee only one ending—a massive energy discharge directed at the surface of Hranrar. And the gods only knew what close proximity to such an enormous release of power would do to anyone foolish enough to be aboard Brahma-Shiva at the time.

"I've just established new transporter locks on both Commander Tuvok and Mister S'syrixx," Radowski said, a note of triumph in his voice. "Don't know how long they'll last, though, considering the rise in Brahma-Shiva's energy output."

"Tell them you're beaming them back, Bowan," Ra-Havreii said to the transporter engineer.

Radowski nodded, his nimble fingers quickly opening a channel to what remained of the boarding team. "*Titan* to Commander Tuvok. Stand by for immediate beam-out."

"Negative, Lieutenant," Tuvok responded, his preternaturally calm voice bursting through the curtain of static being generated by Brahma-Shiva's immense internal power buildup. *"Mister S'syrixx and I are not yet ready to leave."*

Keru's brow crumpled. "Are you communicating with S'syrixx's AI?"

"We have reached a . . . critical juncture," the Vulcan said enigmatically. *"Please stand by."*

Radowski threw his hands in the air.

"We'd better get the captain to settle this one," Keru said, tapping his combadge.

Ra-Havreii had to agree. "I'll be in engineering."

GORN HEGEMONY WARSHIP *S'ALATH*

Gazing around the command deck with ever-increasing rage and frustration, Gog'resssh could see that the tattered remnants of his crew had all but turned to stone. They had balked at his order. The first myrmidon neither knew nor cared whether this reticence was born of a desire to save their own lives, or superstitious dread of some Gorn fertility goddess, or misgivings about the fate of the new warrior caste he still dreamed of building even now.

But he knew that what *should* matter to a Gorn warrior was the fulfillment of his orders; the will of a warrior's superiors, once articulated, was to be carried out, and could be contravened only by death itself—a death that could later be extended to an entire family line should that warrior's death turn out to be the result of his own cowardice, error, or some other malfeasance.

Gog'resssh reached Narrzsesh in two long paces. The diffident helmrunner lay sprawled on the deck, neck-broken and twitching, before he'd even realized what was happening to him. Before anyone else present could react, Gog'resssh entered all the necessary course and speed changes into the helm console with his own two steady manus.

The glow of the ecosculptor increased to nearly blinding intensity as it rushed toward the *S'alath,* swiftly filling the entirety of the forward viewer as the warship began its final headlong dash.

U.S.S. *TITAN*

Z'shezhira ignored the two armed mammals hovering nearby as she stood near Rry'kurr's chair and studied the main forward viewer; it displayed the squat lower portion of the ecosculptor, and the night-darkened immensity of Hranrar far below it.

"It seems we're on the same side of the planet as our surface away team now," Rry'kurr said. "Lieutenant Rager, can we get a transporter lock?"

The mammal Rry'kurr had addressed shook her head. "Not with all the energy emanating from the artifact at the moment, Captain. There's way too much interference to lock onto anything on the planet's surface. I can barely get a comm signal through right now. We're lucky to maintain a transporter lock with Brahma-Shiva."

None of that came as a surprise to Z'shezhira, and she doubted it was news to Rry'kurr either; he was merely exploring every conceivable option in a bad situation.

"That's not the only obstacle in our way," he said, apparently addressing no one in particular.

"You refer to Captain Krassrr's fleet," Z'shezhira said. "And the Typhon Pact reinforcements that are on their way."

"There's more on top of that. The Hranrarii took our surface team into custody inside one of their cities. They're advanced enough to have put any number of antitransporter measures in place."

Z'shezhira used her left manus to gesture toward the portion of the screen that showed both the *S'alath*—motionless in relation to the ecosculptor—and a pair of Captain Krassrr's recon vessels, which appeared to be slowly moving away.

"The news is not all bad, Rry'kurr," she said. "You at least appear to have achieved a stalemate with Captain Krassrr, in a manner of speaking."

"Maybe," he allowed. "At least for the moment."

"Call it what you will. But none of Captain Krassrr's vessels have opened fire on *Tie-tan* as yet. And the *S'alath* is merely holding station near the ecosculptor—as though Gog'resssh has become indecisive."

"We both know from experience that Gog'resssh has no trouble making snap decisions. This is only the calm before the storm."

"Captain," the mammal named Rager said, "Krassrr's five ships are spreading out into a roughly globular formation surrounding Brahma-Shiva, the *S'alath*—and us."

Z'shezhira's forked tongue darted across her teeth and lips several times rapidly, a mark of her frustration. "That is certain to complicate any effort you might make to leave the immediate vicinity of the ecosculptor, Rry'kurr."

The mammal captain displayed his tiny teeth. "Don't worry. I have no intention of going anywhere until after Commander Tuvok persuades Brahma-Shiva to spare the Hranrarii."

Focusing her narrowed gaze on him, she said, "Assuming that such a thing is even possible."

"S'syrixx believes that the artifact carries the essence of a Gorn elder goddess. Can't your deities be swayed by prayer?"

"Appealing to gods can be like bargaining with a supernova," she said. "S'syrixx's faith has always been stronger than mine. I always meant to tell him that he entered the wrong subcaste—that he should have taken religious orders."

The mammal captain was watching her intently with those strange blue eyes. "You'll have the chance to do that, Z'shezhira. I promise."

An involuntary growl started up, directly behind her sternum. "How, Rry'kurr? Captain Krassrr has you backed into a corner, forcing you to use the ecosculptor as a shield. What can you do with a set of options that bad?"

The mild expression—the *smile*—returned, but without the display of tiny teeth. "What I can do is wait until a better set of options presents itself. I can—"

"The *S'alath* is moving again, Captain," Rager reported, interrupting the conversation. "High impulse." She turned from her console to face her captain. "He's going to ram Brahma-Shiva!"

I wonder what took him so long, Z'shezhira thought. She supposed some of his crew might have rejected a suicide order after having listened to Gog'resssh's fire-breathing rhetoric about being destined to found a new warrior caste.

"Get a tractor beam on that ship!" Rry'kurr shouted, leaping to his feet.

Tie-tan shook slightly under Z'shezhira as Rager complied. On the screen, a golden shaft of light seemed to impale the *S'alath* as though it were lakeprey struggling on the end of a spear.

"Got him," Rager said. "He's still on a heading directly for Brahma-Shiva, and trying to accelerate."

"Pull him back, Lieutenant," said Rry'kurr. "Lieutenant Lavena, hold station here. Keep us steady."

"Aye, sir," said the helmeted fishmammal pilot.

"The *S'alath* is doubling down on her engine output, Captain," Rager said.

An angry-sounding voice issued from the comm system. *"Ra-Havreii to bridge!"*

"Bridge here," Rry'kurr said.

"Captain, this ship is still healing from the last couple of poundings it's received from the Gorn. We can't sustain such high-power tractor-beam contact for much longer."

"Sorry for the inconvenience, Commander," Rry'kurr said. "But I'm afraid your team may have to play hurt just a little while longer. Keep up that beam intensity, at least until we can retrieve Tuvok and S'syrixx."

"Make it soon, please, Captain. Engineering out."

Z'shezhira regarded the human who stood watching the *S'alath*'s image with a growing sense of wonder. *He is beset on all sides by enemies. And yet he remains willing to risk his ship and his crew on the unlikeliest of prospects—calming the proverbial supernova, dissipating its destructive energies with persuasion as his only tool.*

Of all the specimens of alien life she had either encountered or studied, Rry'kurr was either the bravest or the most foolish.

Tie-tan's aquatic helmrunner turned her chair so that she faced Rry'kurr. "We really can't run the tractor beam at this intensity for much longer, Captain."

"How much time do we have?" Rry'kurr said.

"Ten minutes. Maybe twelve at the outside. Unless the *S'alath* generates too much kinetic energy for her exhaust manifolds to cope with and vaporizes herself first."

Rry'kurr made an expressive exhalation. "Then we keep at it for the next ten or twelve minutes. In the meantime, stay alert for any signals from Tuvok. Mister Gibruch, maintain the transporter locks and watch for any sudden changes in Brahma-Shiva's power output. If that happens, I want Tuvok and S'syrixx beamed back here *immediately.*"

"Aye, sir," said the mammal with the bizarre, dangling cranial appendages.

"I'm receiving an incoming signal," Rager said.

"Commander Tuvok?" Rry'kurr asked.

"No, sir. It's Krassrr."

"On audio, Lieutenant."

Z'shezhira was relieved that Rry'kurr had again opted not to open a visual channel; he must have thought, as she did, that the presence of a Gorn on *Tie-tan*'s command deck might complicate Captain Krassrr's mood unpredictably.

"Rry'kurr!" rumbled Krassrr's guttural voice over the comm speakers.

"Good to hear from you, Krassrr," Rry'kurr said. "I'd love to chat, but I'm a little busy at the moment trying to stop a member of your own warrior caste from making a suicide run at your ecosculptor."

"So I can see. I also see that your power grid is overloading from the effort. My ship is approaching yours. I will direct its tractor beam to reinforce Tie-tan's."

"Thank you, Krassrr. I appreciate the help. *Titan* out."

Z'shezhira watched the screen. Another beam of force,

this one a mixture of gold and green, lanced toward the *S'alath,* converging with *Tie-tan*'s beam amidships.

"Is this the new set of options you were waiting for?" she asked.

Rry'kurr's lips again curled upward. "We're about to find out."

"Ra-Havreii to bridge!" It was the voice of the chief engineer, though much more shrill than before. *"What's going on up there, Captain?"*

"Krassrr has added his tractor beam to ours," Rry'kurr said. "To take some of the weight off our shoulders."

"Well, tell him to stop! Our beam is losing power fast. Krassrr's beam operates at a power frequency that creates interference rather than reinforcement. We're trying to compensate down here, but we're putting every power relay we have at risk to do it. If our beam fails, that ship will slam into Brahma-Shiva at nearly warp one."

"Understood, Commander," Rry'kurr said. "Lieutenant Rager, get me Krassrr."

Within a matter of moments, *Tie-tan* was down to a single struggling tractor beam.

"Perhaps several of Krassrr's ships can operate their tractors in tandem," Z'shezhira said. "Then *Tie-tan* could power down its tractor beam."

"There wouldn't be any margin for error during the handoff," the helmrunner said. "Our beam would have to remain on until theirs established contact and began to reinforce one another. But our beam would also tend to affect theirs the way theirs affects ours."

"Couldn't we recalibrate our tractor beam to reinforce Krassrr's?" Rager said.

"Not in under half an hour," said the being with the cranial appendages. "Commander Ra-Havreii is in contact with Krassrr's chief engineer right now, probably going over all of this and more."

"Then why not have Krassrr's fleet blow up the *S'alath* while we're holding it in our tractor?" said the fishmammal.

Rager shook her head. "For the same reason it's a bad idea for Krassrr to take any potshots at *us*—the proximity of Brahma-Shiva."

"All right then, what about beaming a boarding team over to the *S'alath*?" the helmrunner said. "We could take control of Gog'resssh's helm."

"And free my caste-mates as well," Z'shezhira said. "But I would not advise any such attempt. Gog'resssh would have been a fool not to deploy transport scramblers since your captain and I escaped from the *S'alath*. He may be insane, but he has never been *stupid*."

"So in other words it's up to *Titan* to save the day," Rry'kurr said with evident weariness. "What else is new?"

The hiss of one of the turbolift doors momentarily drew Z'shezhira's attention; she turned and observed the approach of a black-haired, dark-complexioned female mammal whose pinnae tapered to delicate points at their upper ends.

As she stepped to the side of Rry'kurr's command chair, the mammal captain noticed her as well.

"T'Pel. Is everything all right in the nursery?"

"Yes. Natasha is fine. But I haven't come to discuss the children. I am here to speak about my husband."

Rry'kurr nodded, though he appeared troubled. "I know you must be very concerned about his safety. I am as well. In fact, I have to beam him back to *Titan* now, whether his mission is completed or not. When the tractor beam fails—"

"No, Captain," the mate of Tuvok said, interrupting. "I understand his mission."

Rry'kurr's brow wrinkled. "Funny. I don't recall seeing you at the briefing."

"Vulcans share a telepathic bond with their mates. Ours is particularly strong."

The striations on Rry'kurr's brow suddenly went smooth. "I understand."

"Obviously, I do not know the mission details. However, I am aware that he is currently engaged in a form of . . . debate. And that he is very close to achieving a successful resolution."

Z'shezhira was too hardheaded a scientist to put much faith in such things as telepathic mating bonds. Rry'kurr, surprisingly, appeared to have no such qualms, either because of his own personal experiences or some primitive mammalian superstition.

Of course, she knew that some of her own people might scoff at the spectacularly unlikely circumstances that had conspired to separate her from her beloved, only to bring them close to a reunion more than a suncircuit later.

"All right," Rry'kurr said at length. "I'll wait a little longer. But not until the tractor beam fails."

"I thank you, Captain," said the pointed-eared mammal. She withdrew from the center of the command deck, but made no move to exit.

"Perhaps," Z'shezhira whispered as she leaned toward Rry'kurr, "yet *another* set of options will present itself before that time."

• • •

"We can only hope," Riker told Z'shezhira.

Then he settled into his chair, continually checking on the status of Lieutenant Radowski's short-range transporter locks, the tractor beam, and the concomitant power drain it was causing in many other shipboard systems.

Everything was beginning to focus to a single point, and that point had little to do with the safety of his away teams, his ship, his family, or even the likely fate of millions upon millions of innocent Hranrarii.

Riker knew he had a military duty to the Federation that transcended any concerns about what might become of either Hranrar or *Titan*—he could not risk allowing Brahma-Shiva to remain under the Gorn Hegemony's control.

There was a simple, expedient way to reach a desirable outcome—order Lieutenant Rager to shut down the tractor beam, thereby instantly turning the *S'alath* into a high-impulse projectile that would more than likely transform Brahma-Shiva into rubble in a matter of seconds.

The main problem would be the likely reaction of the Gorn. Krassrr seemed to regard *Titan*'s present course of action as evidence of good faith; it was all but certain that he would take a far dimmer view of any action that resulted in Brahma-Shiva's sudden obliteration.

"Tuvok has succeeded," said T'Pel, who had somehow glided back over to his command chair without his having noticed her approach. He almost did a double-take when he noticed a single tear rolling down her cheek. "The effort has been costly, but he has rendered the Brahma-Shiva artifact benign."

"You're certain?"

She nodded.

Riker tapped his combadge. "Bridge to transporter room two. Beam Commander Tuvok and Mister S'syrixx aboard immediately." Recalling what T'Pel had said about the mission's cost, he added, "Send them both straight to sickbay."

"Aye, Captain," Radowski said over the comm. Moments later, the transporter engineer appended, *"They're both back aboard, safe and sound in sickbay."*

"Doctor Ree," Riker said, tapping the combadge again. "You have two new arrivals. What's their condition?"

"Comatose, from what I can tell so far, Captain," said the Pahkwa-thanh surgeon. *"Their lives do not appear to be in any immediate danger. However, I must run some tests to make a diagnosis. I will inform you as soon as I know anything definitive."*

"If you'll excuse me," T'Pel said.

At Riker's nod, she walked quickly but gracefully to the turbolift, obviously bound for sickbay.

Turning to face Z'shezhira, Riker asked, "Would you like to visit sickbay as well?"

"Yes." Her eyes grew cold. "But later. S'syrixx is not conscious at the moment. And I have yet to watch Gog'resssh die."

"Gog'resssh won't be the only one to die, Z'shezhira. I saw other members of your caste when I was aboard the *S'alath*. Their lives are at stake as well."

"Unless Gog'resssh voluntarily shuts down his engines, those lives are lost already. Unless you can spare the power to beam them to safety."

Riker looked toward Gibruch for an answer to Z'shezhira's question.

The facial brow the Chandir used as his speaking mouth turned downward in apparent sadness as he slowly shook his head. "Sorry, Captain. We not only can't spare the power, we wouldn't know which life signs to lock on to."

Z'shezhira acknowledged Gibruch with a nod. "Then releasing Gog'resssh's ship is the only way to free them from bondage. The duty of informing their families of how they lived their lives this past suncircuit—and how each of them made their return journeys to Great S'Yahazah—will fall upon my shoulders."

As will the guilt of being the lone survivor among them, Riker thought.

Aloud, he said, "All right. You're welcome to stay on the bridge and observe."

"Thank you," Z'shezhira said with an almost courtly nod.

"Captain!" Gibruch exclaimed in oboe tones. "I'm reading a small decline in both external luminosity and internal energy generation. Brahma-Shiva seems to be powering down."

T'Pel was right, he thought. Though he shared a similar link with his *Imzadi,* he wished he could feel as much certainty about the success of Deanna's mission, or at least her well-being. Then he recalled the tear he had seen on T'Pel's cheek. Her bond with Tuvok must have been powerful indeed to provoke such an intense emotional reaction in a Vulcan; perhaps having such an intimate connection could be a mixed blessing.

Gibruch continued: "The power drop is marginal, Captain. But if it continues . . ." Though the gamma-shift watch officer trailed off, his meaning was crystal clear.

If it continues, Riker thought, *then the Hranrarii are out of immediate danger—and my reason for blowing the damned thing up could start looking a whole lot less morally defensible.*

But what other option did he have?

He arrived at a decision. Opening another comm channel, he said, "Riker to Ra-Havreii."

"Engineering," replied the Efrosian chief engineer. *"Please tell me you're done burning out my power couplings."*

"Almost, Xin. First, I need you to make sure that the main tractor beam power coupling fails."

"That'll interrupt the tractor beam, Captain. And send the S'alath *into Brahma-Shiva like a projectile."*

"That's the point."

"Why not just shut off the tractor beam on the bridge?"

"Because I have to assume that Krassrr is keeping as close a multifaceted eye as possible on everything we're doing right now. And a component failure might make it harder for him to argue that I deliberately allowed Gog'resssh to blow up his terraforming toy. When can you be ready?"

"Just a moment, Captain," Ra-Havreii said. *"Stand by."*

"You speak as though you expect Krassrr to put you on trial, Rry'kurr," Z'shezhira said.

Riker suddenly felt an unpleasant certainty that the Gorn Hegemony's military justice system would make Klingon criminal jurisprudence look like a little girl's tea party.

"I expect," he said at length, "to have a little bit of difficulty getting out of here once all the dust settles."

"Everything's ready, Captain," Ra-Havreii announced. *"One main tractor beam power coupling failure, coming right up."*

GORN HEGEMONY RECONNAISSANCE VESSEL *SSEVARRH*

Captain Krassrr stood in an alert warrior's crouch on his command deck. Since his engineering tech-casters had explained the necessity of his inaction, there was little else he could do other than watch the *S'alath,* as it remained in the precarious grasp of the mammalship *Tie-tan.*

So he watched.

Until all at once the golden energy beam, the last narrow tether that was preventing mad, cursed Gog'resssh from enforcing his anarchic will upon the entire warrior caste, abruptly vanished.

Within the space of that selfsame heartbeat, the Gorn Hegemony warship *S'alath* vanished from sight as all the pent-up energy generated by the vessel's powerful impulse engines was converted from heat back into pure kinetic energy.

The result was a virtually instantaneous impact of warship and ecosculptor at a substantial fraction of lightspeed (as the tech-casters belowdecks explained).

The conflagration began at the ecosculptor's base, then quickly spread all along the length of the narrower upper portion. The sight was spectacular in its intensity and color, though Krassrr didn't care to comment on the aesthetics of it. It reminded him of a funeral pyre, and perhaps it was—a torch to mark the passing of an entire Gorn caste.

Once we had warriors, they will say of us, Krassrr thought as he watched the unthinkable unfold before his silver eyes. *Now we must rely on the weaker, lesser castes for our protection.*

And soon, we shall be extinct, Typhon Pact or no Typhon Pact.

He realized a moment later that he couldn't even take solace in the hope that *Tie-tan* had been immolated as well. There was the Federrazsh'n mammalship, battered and seared but still able to limp out of and away from the expanding cloud of pulverized debris, which was already spreading out across Hranrar's darkened limb, probably already well on its way to placing an additional ring in the planet's sky.

But four of Krassrr's ships were still in formation. *Tie-tan* needn't go anywhere if Krassrr wished otherwise.

Did Rry'kurr just deliver a malicious attack against a Gorn technological and military asset? Or had he merely failed in a good-faith effort to prevent another—a member of the Hegemony's own revered warrior caste, no less—from doing exactly that?

"Grezzsz, tell the fleet to detain *Tie-tan,*" Krassrr said. "Trr'reriss, inform *Tie-tan* that I would speak with Rry'kurr here, aboard the *Ssevarrh*—immediately."

U.S.S. TITAN

Very slowly, consciousness began to return to S'syrixx.

It began with a vision of a ball of brilliance that turned out to be a light fixture mounted on a light-blue ceiling. As his eyes came fully open and he realized he was in an infirmary of some sort, a sense of repetition—the feeling that he had already experienced these very circumstances before, perhaps many times—rushed over him.

Ridiculous, he thought, closing his eyes. Now he heard a rhythmic beeping. *I have merely been dreaming.*

When he opened his eyes again, he saw living proof that much of what was in his head at the moment was merely the aftereffect of a strange fantasy, or perhaps even an hallucination.

Z'shezhira.

"You've been with me all along," he said. His throat felt parched, just as it had after *Tie-tan*'s crew had rescued him from the vacuum.

No. That was only a dream.

"Shhhhh," Z'shezhira hissed. "Be still and quiet. "Doctor Ree says you must heal. You appear to have suffered a degree of neurolytic shock."

Ree? Do I know a Ree, other than the one I met in the dream?

No. Ree was but a phantasm. Like the Temple of the Egg Bringer, where he had spoken to the Great Mother S'Yahazah herself.

Like the Federrazsh'n mammals, who were nothing like I had expected them to be.

A creature strode into the room. Pale, pinkish flesh. Cranial fur. Prominent mammalian characteristics concealed only superficially by a blue tunic.

"He seems . . . confused, Nurssse Alysssa," Z'shezhira said to the creature.

"It'll pass." The mammal could *speak*! "The neurolytic shock he suffered was relatively mild. It could have been far worse—he wasn't in direct contact with . . . with whatever it was Commander Tuvok encountered. Excuse me, please. I need to tend to him."

S'syrixx craned his neck to watch the mammal walk to the other side of the infirmary, toward another bed like the one on which S'syrixx now lay. A dark-skinned mammal with tapered eartips lay unconscious upon it.

Tuvok, S'syrixx thought. *I didn't dream* you, *either?*

He turned back toward Z'shezhira, saw that her delicate manus lay in his. He squeezed it gently between the three fingers of his own manus. Together again, after such a long absence. It seemed impossible. And yet here they were, wherever *here* was.

As memory slowly came back to him, much to the relief of S'syrixx's confused consciousness, he began to wonder what sort of opposing dreams and realities the slumbering Tuvok might have to contend with right now. . . .

30

HRANRAR

Christine Vale experienced a sensation of intense relief as she looked up at the fireworks display that lit up the Hranrarii firmament, covering nearly half the sky.

"It's beautiful," said Deanna Troi, who stood to Vale's immediate left on the rooftop meadow amid the loose cluster of craned necks that was the rest of the away team.

To Vale's right, Sethne Naq, Speaker for the Great Syndic of the Global Moeity of Hranrar, stood every bit as spellbound as everybody else present, including her ever-present retinue of attendants; Vale stole a glance directly at the speaker, whose huge, golden amphibian's eyes were locked on the spectacular tableau unfolding overhead.

"Something tells me this thing is done threatening your world," Vale said at a decibel-level just short of her "XO shout" to ensure that the speaker could hear her.

"Creation and destruction, all one thing," Sethne Naq said reverently, as though quoting some revered work of Hranrarii literature, or perhaps a sacred text.

"Here's to hoping we can all concentrate more on creation than destruction from here on in," said Vale as a terrible thought occurred to her—a vision of *Titan* making a last, desperate ramming flight as the only way to save the lives of millions. Quickly approaching the upward-gazing Troi, she said, "Please tell me Will wasn't forced to light that candle the hard way."

The senior counselor tipped her head slightly to one side, as though straining her ears to hear distant voices. The look of awe she had displayed while gazing up into the luminescent sky gave way to a poker face borne of concentration.

Then her mouth slowly spread itself into a beatific smile. "I can feel Natasha. And Will."

Vale was having a hard time sharing completely in the other woman's joy. *That might just mean they were lucky enough to make it to the escape pods.*

"I sense tension, recently released," Troi continued. "Great relief, as from a crisis just passed."

"*Titan* is safe," Vale said with a sigh.

"Yes. But I sense Will is still worried."

Vale grinned. "He's the captain. It's his job to worry. Besides, who can blame him? The last time I checked, the sky was crawling with Gorn, and a Typhon Pact fleet was on its way."

At that moment, someone tapped her on the shoulder. Vale turned and saw that Ensigns Modan and Evesh were pointing to a location directly behind her.

Turning completely about, Vale found herself standing almost nose-to-nose with Sethne Naq.

"Honored Speaker," she said, bowing her head momentarily after suppressing an absurd urge to curtsy.

"I assume you will wish to leave us now," the speaker said.

Vale nodded. "We will need to get back to our ship as quickly as possible. Enemies of ours are on their way to this system."

The speaker's eyes widened in apparent alarm. "Do they pose a danger to Hranrar?"

"With the destruction of the . . . artifact," Troi said, gesturing toward the still-expanding fireball overhead, "they would have to resort to far more laborious means. If they don't think we are hiding among you, they will have no reason to move against you."

"Besides," Vale said, "with your technological capabilities, you don't have to let anybody else impose their will on you."

The speaker's eyes now seemed to radiate a deep sadness. "We Hranrarii have not employed war-violence for eons, since our recorded history began. How tragic that our first acquaintance with extra-Hranrarii life should also reacquaint us with bloodshed. Our forebears were wise to keep us isolated."

"Judging from the beauty of your cities and the harmony the Hranrarii have forged between your civilization and the natural world, I believe your species values knowledge as much as it values peace," Troi said. "You can only profit from greater knowledge of the outside universe—even if some of that knowledge proves unpleasant."

"Perhaps," Sethne Naq said. "Either way, we appear to have little choice in the matter."

"When it comes to our adversaries—the Gorn and the other Typhon Pact states—that may be true," Troi said. "But whether or not Hranrar receives any further visits from the United Federation of Planets is entirely up to you."

"If we requested that you leave, and never return," the speaker said, "you would honor that?"

"I'll make a deal with you," Vale said. "One of the items your police force confiscated from us is a portable subspace transceiver."

"It will be returned to you immediately."

She momentarily considered asking the speaker to let her keep the data the away team had taken from the global information network, but decided against it. Holding up a hand, she said, "Thank you, Honored Speaker, but no. Please accept the transceiver as a gift. The unit should be powerful enough to reach the nearest Federation subspace relay station."

Vale paused to look toward Ensign Dakal, who had been listening attentively; the young Cardassian stayed silent as he made a *comme-ci comme-ça* hand gesture.

"Use the device to call us, Honored Speaker, whenever you feel the time is right for another Federation visit," Vale said. "We'll stay away until we hear from you, or one of your successors."

Sethne Naq, Speaker for the Great Syndic of the Global Moeity of Hranrar, appeared to take her time weighing Vale's proposal.

"That is acceptable," the speaker said at length, raising her webbed right hand as though in benediction. "May all of you have gentle winds and sweet water."

Vale copied the speaker's gesture as best she could; Troi did so as well, moving with a fluid grace that Vale could only envy.

Tapping her combadge, Vale said, "Away team to *Titan.*"

"Titan *here,*" responded a voice that she recognized

as belonging to Lieutenant Rager. The standard ship-to-shore channel had already cleared up almost completely, no doubt because of the still-ongoing destruction of the orbiting artifact.

"Hi, Sariel. Seven very tired people would like to beam up now."

U.S.S. TITAN

It wasn't until she stepped down from the stage that Vale noticed the personnel change that had occurred behind the control console in transporter room two. Once the away team had mostly departed and the population of the room had declined to a total of three, Vale favored Captain Riker with a wry grin. "We've talked about this before, Captain. You've really got to learn how to delegate."

"I missed you, too, Chris," he said as he glanced toward Troi, who stood beside him behind the console, reflecting and amplifying the relieved grins of both her husband and his executive officer.

Vale was no Betazoid—or even a half-Betazoid—but she could sense how badly the captain and the counselor wanted to be alone together at the moment. Circumstances being what they were, of course, that just wasn't in the cards.

"Seriously, Will," Vale said, planting her elbows on the side of the console opposite from him, "unless Captain Krassrr and his fleet have just high-tailed it from the system, don't you think at least *one* of us belongs on the bridge right now?"

His expression grew suddenly sober, as did Troi's.

"You're right, Chris," he said. "That's why the bridge is yours until further notice."

Vale scowled. "Going someplace?"

"Nowhere special," he said with a nod. "I just have a little meeting coming up with Krassrr aboard his flagship."

"That's not very damned funny, Will," Vale said as she watched Troi's facial expression take a decidedly unhappy turn. Addressing the counselor, she said, "Wait a minute. He's not kidding, is he?"

"No, he's not." Facing her husband, Troi said, "Are you really sure this is such a good idea?"

"For me, personally?" He shrugged. "Maybe not. On the other hand, I wasn't in a very good position to refuse. Commander Ra-Havreii is still trying to get the warp drive back online, and we're outnumbered and outgunned by a terraforming fleet that just lost its one chance at terraforming. *Titan* needs Krassrr's goodwill."

"I can't believe you just used 'Krassrr' and 'goodwill' in the same sentence," Vale said, shaking her head.

"Krassrr isn't Gog'resssh," Riker said. "Besides, I'm the only one who stands a chance of convincing Krassrr that Brahma-Shiva's destruction was entirely Gog'resssh's doing. It's *Titan*'s only chance of getting out of this relatively unscathed."

"As *Titan*'s senior diplomatic officer, I'll try not to take that assessment personally," Troi said, her violet eyes pleading. "But I could go in your place just as easily."

"She's right, Captain," Vale said. *Unless you're experiencing an irresistible impulse to protect your wife from the nasty lizard-people.*

The captain was shaking his head as he entered a command into the console, apparently checking a set of preprogrammed coordinates—information that must have been transmitted straight from Krassrr's lead vessel. Vale noticed only now the dark semicircles of orange-peel flesh beneath his eyes.

"No," he said, looking at his wife. "You can't. *I'm* the one that has to convince Krassrr that Gog'resssh blew up Brahma-Shiva on his own—and that all I did was try to stop him."

The doors to the transporter room swished open, admitting a pair of Gorn, followed by Lieutenants Qontallium and sh'Aqabaa from security, and Dr. Ree. The larger of the two Gorn Vale recognized immediately as S'syrixx; the smaller one she had never seen before.

"Commander Vale, Commander Troi," Riker said, "meet Z'shezhira, Mister S'syrixx's . . . significant other."

"Hello," rumbled the lady lizard.

Troi bowed and said something enviably diplomatic.

"Ah. Glad to meet you," Vale said. She hoped that the biological and cultural gulf that separated them would disguise the awkwardness in her voice; for a fleeting moment, the simultaneous presence of so many reptiloids flashed her back to her early childhood, and her first visit to the reptile house in the New Seattle Zoo back on Izar.

"This is *not* a good idea, Captain," said Ree, his forked tongue flicking in and out of his mouth.

"Not you, too," Riker said. "I'm sorry this makes you uncomfortable, Doctor, but Krassrr made it damned clear that this meeting was anything but optional."

The CMO slashed a razor-sharp claw through the air, as though waving away the captain's words. "I understand that, Captain. I am referring to my patient. I don't think Mister S'syrixx should be leaving sickbay yet."

"I understand. But Krassrr wasn't willing to bend on that point, either."

Riker walked around the console and mounted the steps to the transporter stage, followed by the two Gorn.

Vale circled the console so that she stood beside Troi; they faced the transporter stage together, shoulder to shoulder.

"This might take a little time, Chris," Riker said. "So I need you to *let* it take time. Krassrr probably won't take it very well if you go off half-cocked trying to rescue me if this . . . discussion ends up taking a little longer than you think it should. Keep *Titan* safe."

"All right. But I presume the Typhon Pact fleet is still on its way. What if you're still . . . enjoying Krassrr's hospitality when they get here?"

He grinned. "I guess that would mean I haven't done my job very well." His demeanor once more growing serious as he focused on Vale, he added, "You need to let this thing run its course, Commander. An outside interruption from my own XO at the wrong time can only make things more tense between the Federation and the Gorn Hegemony. Understood?"

Vale frowned. "Understood, Captain."

"And don't start measuring my ready room for new carpeting," he said, his insouciant grin returning. "I expect to be home in time for dinner."

Nodding, Vale thought, *I swear, if you make me cry, I will kick your ass.* "Godspeed."

Riker turned to face the Gorn couple. "You'll be facing

an unserved death sentence, Mister S'syrixx. Krassrr's ship isn't exactly a safe place for you. But you're still under my protection, for whatever that's worth."

"Thank you, Rry'kurr. However, Krassrr was emphatic about requiring my presence alongside yours."

"He tried to execute you once," Riker said. "What makes you think he won't try again?"

S'syrixx's lips parted, displaying a palisade of jagged ivory. "*Tie-tan* is wounded and surrounded. Why would you believe me to be any safer from death here than in Krassrr's custody?"

"And where S'syrixx goes, I go," Z'shezhira said.

Riker nodded. "All right, then."

Then he turned to face the rear of the transporter stage, per Gorn warrior-caste protocols, as did S'syrixx and Z'shezhira.

"Energize," he said.

"Wait a minute, Will," Vale said, her right hand pausing over the slide control's touch interface. "You still haven't explained why *you* are the only one capable of convincing Krassrr that we've been the good guys here."

"The reason," he said, "is that it isn't entirely true."

A little more than two hours had passed since the beam-out. There was nothing to do but wait. And in Vale's opinion, there was no better place to wait than on *Titan*'s bridge.

As the XO sat in the command chair, with Counselor Troi seated in her customary place at the big chair's immediate left, the starship's nerve center seemed preternaturally quiet. The background susurrus of the various duty stations, the very pulse of the bridge, sounded somehow muted, as though *Titan* herself were holding her breath until Captain Riker's safe return.

Vale realized only then that she had been holding her own breath as well.

"He's off to see the lizard," she said very quietly, just to break the deafening silence.

"Excuse me?" Troi said.

"I said, 'What could the captain and Krassrr be doing over there?'" Vale said, her eyes facing front. The main viewer showed Hranrar in all its ringed glory, including the slender new ring that Brahma-Shiva's explosive death throes had left behind. Also visible were three of Krassrr's five vessels, the most that could be seen simultaneously from any single vantage point, thanks to their current formation; Krassrr had positioned them around *Titan* to discourage any escape attempt.

"I don't yet sense any reason for worry," Troi said.

Other than the fact that our captain is all alone at the moment among a large number of bloodthirsty, cold-blooded members of the Typhon Pact, thought Vale. *And for the second time in the same day, I'm told.*

"There's an inbound Typhon Pact fleet maybe an hour away," she said. "A little ahead of schedule. I think *that's* a damned fine cause for worry."

Vale's combadge suddenly sounded, speaking in Commander Ra-Havreii's voice. *"Engine room to Commander Vale."*

"I hope you're calling with good news, Commander," Vale said.

"Is a functioning warp drive good enough news for you?"

Vale barely restrained herself from letting fly an exuberant war-whoop. "Ahead of schedule—and ahead of the Typhon Pact fleet to boot. I'm impressed."

"It's what I do."

"If I didn't know how much it would upset Melora, I'd kiss you right on the mouth. Keep that warp drive warm for me, Xin. We're gonna need every last millicochrane you can generate, and soon."

"Understood. Engineering out."

"That's certainly a game-changer," Troi said. "Those Typhon Pact ships won't be able to catch us."

"Assuming we don't cut our departure time too fine—and that we can run broken-field past Krassrr's squadron without taking any serious damage."

Lieutenant Lavena turned from her flight-control console so quickly that her hydration suit sloshed audibly. "There's only *five* of them. That means I'll only have to evade maybe two of them in the direction of travel, and then pour on the speed. Just give the word, Captain, and I'll make it happen."

"Very good, Lieutenant," Vale said. "Stay ready. And you can call me 'Commander,' naval tradition notwithstanding."

"Aye, Commander," Lavena said, sounding somewhat abashed.

Vale didn't consider herself superstitious, but at the moment she had no use for the ancient practice of addressing a ship's ranking officer as "captain" regardless of that officer's actual rank; she supposed that on some level she feared "jinxing" Will's safe return.

"I sense that Will is working very hard to persuade

Krassrr on more than one issue," Troi said. "There's a lot of general outrage coming from Krassrr and his senior staff over Brahma-Shiva's destruction, of course. But so far they don't seem to be directing it against Will—or against *Titan*."

Even though Titan *seems to have had a wee bit more to do with bringing Brahma-Shiva down than Krassrr knows,* Vale thought as she nodded her acknowledgment to Troi.

"And I even sense that Will is gaining some traction in the discussions," Troi said. "I believe he's dealing with members of the Gorn legal caste, as well as Krassrr himself."

Lawyers, Vale thought. *Well, that explains a lot.*

"I hope you're right," she said, wondering if even an empath as gifted as Deanna might be deceived by her own wishful thinking.

Still, judging the Gorn by what she'd seen so far, negotiating with them was akin to haggling with the Grim Reaper. She was unpleasantly aware that Krassrr could be cynically running out the clock until the arrival of the Typhon Pact fleet as a ploy to capture *Titan*.

Reality struck her like a gut punch: *Titan* would have to be on its way before that time, whether Riker was back on board by then or not. From the stricken reaction she saw on Troi's face, the counselor had just done the same math, or was tuned in to Vale's own emotional reactions.

"Lieutenant Rager, open a channel to the *Ssevarrh,*" she said.

"Aye, Commander," said the senior ops officer.

Within moments, a growling, hostile-sounding voice

rumbled from the bridge's audio speakers. *"What do you want, mammal?"*

"This is Commander Christine Vale," she said. "I'd like to speak to my captain for a moment."

"Your captain is in a meeting with our *captain,"* came the roaring, hissing response. *"Captain Krassrr has ordered no interruptions."*

"I understand, bu—"

"Ssevarrh *out."* The channel went dead.

"I don't believe this," Vale said with a hard scowl. "Bastard hung up on me. Mister Dakal, scan for the captain's life signs. Get a transporter lock."

"Aye, Commander," the youthful Cardassian said as he set about his task. "In the midst of all those reptiles, one human bio-sign shouldn't be all that difficult to find. I just have to make sure I don't confuse his signal with any of the live food animals they're carrying."

"Chris," Troi said quietly, an unmistakable note of warning in her voice. "Will specifically ordered—"

"As long as Will's off the ship, Counselor, *I'm* in command," Vale snapped. She instantly regretted the harsh tone she'd taken, and deliberately softened it. "He can put me in the brig later."

"Found him, Commander," Dakal reported. "Lock established. Should I engage the transporter?"

Vale was sorely tempted, but she decided to abide a bit longer; she had her orders, after all.

"Maintain the lock for now, Ensign. And stand by."

"Aye, Capt—" Dakal said, halting himself mid-word. "Commander."

Either ignoring or failing to notice Dakal's awkward

slipup, Troi leaned close to Vale. "Waiting makes sense, Chris. I'm not sensing any secret agendas on the part of the Gorn—at least not yet."

Of course being secret—and staying secret, even in the presence of people whose business was to ferret out secrets—was part of the fundamental nature of any secret agenda.

"And for what it's worth," Troi continued, "in your place, I'd do exactly what you're doing."

That made Vale feel better about what the present circumstances were about to force her to do—but only a little.

Ensign Dakal's voice sounded enviably calm in Vale's ears.

"Long-range scanners indicate the Typhon Pact fleet's lead ships will enter the system's Kuiper belt in approximately thirty minutes."

If they don't wrap this damned meeting up in the next couple of minutes, Vale thought, *then I'm gonna have to wrap it up* for *'em, orders or no.*

"Status of transporter lock?" she said.

Dakal paused to check a readout on his console. "Transporter lock positive."

Time to call it a career, she thought, taking a single deep breath; whatever diplomatic brownie points her captain might have earned with the Gorn Hegemony today could be scattered to the winds. *But at least he'll be alive to testify at my court-martial.*

Aloud, she said, "Energi—"

"Belay that, Ensign!" Troi cried from the adjacent seat.

"What the hell?" Vale said. "That's not something *you* get to say, Counselor. That's something *I* get to say."

The diplomatic officer was flashing a high-wattage smile, as though she'd just received some extraordinarily good news. "Just hold on for another couple of—"

Lieutenant Rager executed a half-turn in her chair. "I'm receiving a hail from the *Ssevarrh*." She paused momentarily, giving Vale the urge to fidget. "It's the captain!"

Relief flooded Vale like a desert rainstorm. "Put the captain on audio."

A moment later, the comm speakers filled the bridge with a familiar voice. *"Riker to* Titan. *Sorry to cut things so fine."*

"It's all right, Captain," Vale said. "It's good to hear your voice again."

"You sound surprised, Commander."

"Not at all, Captain. It's just that there's this new carpeting I have to pull up in the ready room. But that can wait, I suppose." Rising from her chair, she added, "See you in transporter room two."

Vale narrowly beat Troi in a quick race to the starboard turbolift.

31

Vale operated the transporter console herself while Troi and Radowski looked on.

Which was why she didn't notice until just after the materialization process was complete that *Titan* had not only recovered its captain, S'syrixx, and Z'shezhira, it had also acquired a *third* Gorn.

Vale couldn't have been more surprised if Will's first words had been, "He followed me home, Mom. Can I keep him?"

Troi wasted no time crossing to the transporter stage. It was obvious even without the benefit of Betazoid empathy that it was all the counselor could do not to leap into her husband's arms. For the captain's part, the feeling was obviously mutual.

"Welcome aboard, Captain," Vale said with a grin as her colleagues recovered their composure. "Are you going to introduce us to your new, um, little friend?"

The unfamiliar third Gorn had backed up from his transporter pad so that his back was up against the glowing plasteel of the rear wall. Though his yellow, vertically-pupilled eyes and dexterous-looking, three-fingered hands marked him as another member of the technological caste, this creature looked somewhat older and less robust than either S'syrixx or Z'shezhira.

But like S'syrixx, this new Gorn visitor seemed extremely uncomfortable in the presence of humans and humanoids—almost cowering, in fact, whenever he made eye contact.

"There is nothing to fear, Doctor," S'syrixx said as he followed Riker and Z'shezhira down the transporter stage's steps to the room's main deck.

"I could never make a home for myself aboard this . . . *mammalship,*" the newcomer said, his growling tones dripping with disgust, or perhaps fear.

"Nor could either S'syrixx or myself," Z'shezhira said.

Vale tried to stifle a scowl, an effort that met with only indifferent success. *That's just fine by me,* she thought. *Between Doctor Ree, Lieutenant Qontallium, Ensign Rynaph, and Chief Urkral, our officers' mess is already serving all the vivicarnivores it can handle, thank you very much.*

"Fortunately for us all, that is not the plan the lawcaster tribunal imposed upon the three of us," S'syrixx said.

"Okay, color me confused," Vale said.

Troi nodded. "Me, too. Didn't you ask us for sanctuary, Mister S'syrixx?"

"I withdrew the request," S'syrixx said, "in exchange for a judgment of banishment from the tribunal."

Vale shook her head. "I don't get it. You got a formal judgment that forbids you from returning to your homeworld—and you're throwing away an opportunity to live in the Federation, or even to stay aboard *Titan*?"

"The only alternative was to submit to a second summary execution," Z'shezhira said. "Which almost certainly would have succeeded this time."

S'syrixx dipped his long skull forward, momentarily

displaying the vibrantly iridescent blue-gold highlights of the tops of his cranial ridges. "Of that I have no doubt, because Krassrr would have prevented one of my oldest friends from again coming to my aid." He waved a three-fingered hand toward the third Gorn.

Riker made the formal introductions. "Commander Vale, Commander Troi, meet Doctor R'rerrgran. The doctor secretly gave S'syrixx the drug that enabled him to survive vacuum-exposure long enough for us to rescue him."

"Unfortunately," R'rerrgran said in a slightly higher-pitched growl than that of S'syrixx, "Captain Krassrr is very skilled at discovering secrets."

He just can't quite match Will Riker's poker skills, Vale thought.

"So Krassrr gave you the options of exile," she said, "or walking the plank."

"Coming here seemed a better option than learning to breathe the airless void," R'rerrgran said in apparent bemusement. Although it was hard to read reptilian emotions solely on the basis of facial expression and body language, Vale couldn't help but wonder if the doctor hadn't already come to regret his decision.

Riker nodded. "Once Krassrr was convinced that we weren't trying to destroy Brahma-Shiva, he was willing to listen to my testimony on behalf of S'syrixx—who was of considerable help to *us.* The tribunal apparently took all of that into account when they handed down their decision."

"Still," Vale said. "Banishment. That's pretty harsh."

"Another tribunal might see fit to lift the sentence someday," said S'syrixx. "Under the appropriate circumstances."

"Such as?" said Troi.

Z'shezhira intertwined her claws with those of S'syrixx. "Such as developing a viable replacement for the Sazssgrerrn crècheworld—without the benefit of the ecosculptor. Captain Krassrr has already agreed to supply the three of us with the basic research equipment necessary to begin such a project."

"Where would you go to do this?" Troi asked, saving Vale the trouble.

"The planet Hranrar already possesses the gross characteristics necessary to be a crècheworld," R'rerrgran said. "Because the Hranrarii's technological imprint on their world is relatively small, much of the planet's land surface is unoccupied."

"Wait a minute," Vale said. "I thought the warrior caste hatcheries were extremely rare birds—hence the need for terraforming technology."

"Such worlds are indeed rare," Z'shezhira said. "But perhaps they need not be—not if we alter the warrior caste itself slightly, even as we attempt to restore it."

R'rerrgran's head bobbed in a nodlike gesture. "Small genomic modifications. Just enough to enable eggs and hatchlings to fit the available environments. It is more sensible than continuing to try in vain to re-create that which no longer is, and perhaps never can be again."

Why carpet the world, Vale thought, *when you can just put on some slippers?*

"In a way, it resembles what Gog'resssh wanted," said Z'shezhira. "He wanted to mate with me, to bring new genes into the new ruling warrior caste he dreamed of creating." She paused, seeming almost to shudder at memories that could have been nothing other than highly unpleasant. "He would have tried to use the very planet below us, Hranrar, for that purpose—assuming, of course, he had survived his own campaign to destroy an ecosculptor that he believed was a weapon intended to defeat his plans."

S'syrixx's claws entwined more tightly with those of Z'shezhira. "It did not escape our notice that we might implement a portion of Gog'resssh's plan for Hranrar ourselves. Allow some good to come of his misguided evil."

Vale saw a worried frown appear on Troi's forehead. "There's at least one fairly major problem with your idea. The Hranrarii government would have to give its permission before you could try anything like this."

"Beam us down," S'syrixx said. "We will make all the necessary queries ourselves."

"I'm afraid it isn't quite that simple," Troi said. "We've already agreed not to send anyone down without advance authorization."

S'syrixx suddenly let go of Z'shezhira's hand and sat heavily on the edge of the transporter stage. His eyes widened as he spread his claws out before him, making him look utterly bereft.

"It is hopeless then," he said. "We have taken a road that leads nowhere."

"Stay with us," said the captain. "You can work with the Federation's best scientists on a solution to the hatchery problem. I owe you at least that much."

But Vale could see from the Gorn trio's collective reaction that this simply wasn't in the cards. Despite Starfleet's oft-stated dedication to diversity and respect for the Other, there was only so far such an ethos could reach; its success ultimately depended on the Other's willingness and ability to reach back.

Damn, she thought. *This was starting to sound like one of those offbeat Will Riker–style solutions that always ends up saving the day.*

It was too good an idea not to at least *try* to find a way to make it work.

"Hold on a minute, S'syrixx," she said. "Don't give up just yet. I might have a little bit of pull with somebody in the Hranrarii government."

Riker's eyebrows climbed as though accelerating into opposite escape trajectories. "I'm really looking forward to reading your after-action report, Commander."

His back and upper body still aching after his brief physical ordeal aboard the *S'alath*—not to mention the considerably longer legal one he'd just experienced aboard the *Ssevarrh*—Riker hoisted little Natasha up onto his shoulders.

"Pretty!" she said, reaching past his head to touch the observation lounge's panoramic transparent aluminum window.

"Yes it is," said Deanna, who stood at his side, smiling at them both. "Very pretty."

Riker looked out over Hranrar's spectacular ring plane, perhaps for the last time. Lying just outside the faintest of the planet's age-old rings was a brand-new annulus composed of the pulverized remains of Brahma-Shiva.

Pretty, yes, he thought. *But it's also a damned shame.*

"Brahma-Shiva is spilled milk now, *Imzadi,*" Deanna said gently.

Tell that to Tuvok, he thought. *Or T'Pel.* It pained him to think that the woman who had been forced to endure a seven-year separation from her husband now might have to bear a far more open-ended parting.

"That's not fair, Will. You know I wasn't trying to trivialize Commander Tuvok and White-Blue's condition."

"I know you weren't, Deanna," he said, bouncing slightly in response to the spurring of Natasha's sock-clad feet. "But I can't help thinking about it. Not just what happened to Tuvok and White-Blue, but the artifact itself—the missed opportunity it represents. Now we'll never know how much good the technology Brahma-Shiva carried might have done back in the Federation. If only we'd managed to take even a little of it home with us. Beyond S'syrixx's notes, I mean."

"That technology could have been misused as a weapon just as easily," she said. "I don't need to remind you about Project Genesis."

"You're right, Deanna. But still . . ."

He trailed off, lost in contemplation. Looking beyond the majestic rings and the limb of the planet, he could see a handful of moving lights—Krassrr's ships, still maintaining their vigil over Hranrar. His plan was to keep *Titan* in orbit until the Hranrarii government answered the formal request of the three Gorn exiles—unless the imminent arrival of Typhon Pact reinforcements forced an early departure.

His combadge suddenly began to speak in a slightly tinny rendition of Lieutenant Lavena's aqueous voice. *"Conn to Captain Riker."*

"Riker here. Go ahead, Lieutenant."

"Ensign Dakal reports that the lead ships of the Typhon

Pact fleet are expected to reach Hranrar orbit in approximately twelve minutes, sir."

"Thank you, Lieutenant. Stand by."

"Our course is laid in, Captain. Ready to warp out. More *than ready, in fact. Sir."*

Getting nervous, are we? he thought as the door behind him hissed open, then closed again. Handing Natasha off to Deanna, he turned toward the sound.

Christine Vale was approaching him, a weary but thoughtful expression on her face.

"Don't worry, Aili," he said into his combadge. "I think we'll be able to weigh anchor in a couple of minutes, tops. Riker out."

"Well?" Troi asked, stepping toward Vale. "What's the word from Hranrar?"

Judging from the small smiles he saw on both women's faces, he suspected that Vale's diplomatic gambit had succeeded, at least partially.

"First of all, Deanna, I wish you'd been the one making this request instead of me."

"I'm sure you did fine, Chris," Deanna said as she moved Natasha from one arm to the other. "Besides, *you* are the one who pledged that we'd leave this world alone should the Speaker request that. That made you the best choice to make the request."

Vale pushed a strand of brown hair away from her eyes. "You just enjoy dragging me out of my comfort zone."

"I'll make a diplomat of you yet," Deanna said, grinning.

Riker frowned at them both. "So what the hell did the Hranrarii government *say*?"

"Right," said the exec before pausing to clear her throat. "Sethne Naq, Speaker for the Great Syndic of the Global Moeity of Hranrar, has given a provisional 'yes' to our three Gorn exiles. She's agreed to let them live on Hranrar as long as *they* will agree to abide by Hranrarii law."

Deanna's eyes widened. "That's quite a change. They've gone from believing they're alone in the universe to inviting parts of it to stay over as houseguests."

"And it seems to have happened literally overnight," Vale said with a nod, her face mirroring Deanna's surprise.

"But what about their plan to establish a Gorn hatchery?" Deanna asked.

Vale shrugged. "The Speaker says she'll at least hear their proposal. I just hope that the Gorn and the rest of the Typhon Pact will leave the Hranrarii in peace if the Speaker turns them down."

"From what we've seen so far," Riker said, "I think the Hranrarii have enough power and know-how to discourage outsiders from making trouble for them." The specialists in *Titan*'s science labs were still analyzing the exotic metal fragments that appeared to support that idea.

"As long as their leaders can muster up the will," said Vale.

Riker nodded. "Or their people can." Their destiny was their own. Although the Hranrarii were arguably first-contact-worthy peers of the Federation in terms of their sociotechnological development, Riker knew that didn't give him a license to interfere willy-nilly on their behalf.

"And if they find themselves besieged on all sides by

Typhon Pact aggressors?" Deanna said. "Breen, Tzenkethi, Romulans, Kinshaya, Tholians . . . *and* Gorn?"

"Then the Gorn might find themselves as badly in need of help as the Hranrarii," Riker said. "The Hegemony is very territorial, especially when it comes to their breeding colonies. If the Typhon Pact values the Gorn as members, they won't step on a raw nerve like that. And we can't dismiss the possibility that our three Gorn friends will talk the Speaker into letting the new warrior caste incubate a few eggs here."

Deanna nodded. "Z'shezhira must have some genuine talent for persuasion—after all, she managed to survive as one of Gog'resssh's hostages for more than a year."

"By the way, do we have time to bid our Gorn guests farewell?" Riker asked.

Vale shook her head. "They wanted to see the Speaker immediately, so I went ahead and beamed them down. I didn't think you'd mind, since they don't seem to be big fans of long, drawn-out goodbyes."

"Or of mammalian humanoids," Deanna said.

Riker nodded. "There is that." *It's probably just as well,* he thought, *especially with the Typhon Pact cavalry due to arrive any minute.*

Vale's expression suddenly became grave. "We're leaving this society balancing on one hell of a sharp knife's edge, Captain."

"It's not a perfect solution," Riker admitted. "But it looks like the best one available, given this imperfect universe we all seem to be stuck with."

He tapped his combadge. "Riker to Lieutenant Lavena," he said.

"Yes, Captain," came the flight controller's breathless reply.

"Let's get going, Lieutenant. Take it away, from the top."

His XO and his wife, carrying their daughter, preceded him through the doorway. Once he reached it, he paused on the threshold for a backward glance at the planet and its ring system, just in time to watch the infinite darkness swallow them both. He experienced another pang of regret that he hadn't found a way to extract anything usable from Brahma-Shiva.

Then he pushed the matter aside and left the room, bound for the bridge.

Epilogue

U.S.S. TITAN
Stardate 59663.4

The sound of the door chime nearly startled Ensign Torvig Bu-Kar-Nguv into letting the coil spanner slip out of the grip of his prehensile tail.

"Come in," he said, composing himself as his twin bionic arms set his tools back on the worktable beside the junkyard-still, multilimbed metal body.

The door whisked open to admit his engineering colleague, Ensign Mordecai Crandall, who wasted no time assessing what Torvig was doing.

"Still trying to get White-Blue jump-started? Torvig, it's been nearly four days since he was . . ."

"Injured," Torvig ventured after his friend trailed off.

"All right, injured. And you haven't rested for a minute since then, have you?"

"SecondGen White-Blue is my friend. I owe him my best efforts."

"You keep this up much longer, Torv, and *nobody's* going to get your efforts, best or otherwise."

Torvig noticed that his tail was beginning to move back and forth in a pattern of agitation; he stifled its motion with an act of will. "I believe I am close to restoring White-Blue to full functionality."

Crandall looked at the still metal form on the table and shook his head. "Could have fooled me." The human engineer focused his attention back upon the little Choblik. "Look, Torvig, take a day away from this, at least. Please. Don't force me to speak to Commander Ra-Havreii about this. He'd probably make you sit through a few abusive sessions with that Tellarite counselor, Haaj."

"But . . ." Torvig said, realizing he had no good options—and that his friend had a point. "Very well. I will initiate a rest interval. After you leave. It is late for you humans to be up and about, as well."

Crandall frowned at him in a way that Torvig had learned to characterize as skepticism, or perhaps even suspicion. "All right, Torv. You wouldn't lie to me, would you?"

"I would not know how, Mordecai. There is a good reason why my people tend to go into science and engineering rather than politics."

Crandall exited with a small smile and a chuckle, apparently satisfied.

Torvig looked across his quarters and contemplated his rest chamber. He ambulated toward it.

Then he walked back to the worktable and grasped tools in each of his three manipulative limbs.

The "operational" light located on the AI's carapace near its "brain" suddenly switched on.

"Finally," Torvig said, speaking as much to himself as to his friend, "the nightmare is over."

"No," White-Blue said. "It may just be beginning."

• • •

T'Pel maintained her patient vigil at her husband's bedside, just as she had done for the entirety of the three previous days and the four previous nights.

A soft voice spoke from directly behind her. "You need to eat or drink *something,* T'Pel."

T'Pel turned to face Counselor Troi. "Thank you, Counselor. But I am not experiencing any difficulties at the moment."

Troi's dark eyes narrowed as she folded her arms across her chest in a gesture of gentle challenge. "Remember who you're talking to, T'Pel. I know what a dedicated caregiver you have always been for Natasha and Totyarguil Bolaji and Noah Powell."

"I regret that I have had to ask others to take over those duties for the duration," T'Pel said.

"I haven't come to drag you back to work, T'Pel. I came because I'm worried about *you.* You've become so used to taking care of those around you that you forget to take care of yourself. I'd like you to get some rest."

"I am a Vulcan. I require very little rest."

Troi sighed, apparently willing to accept T'Pel's word, at least for the moment. "All right. Just think about what I said. How is Tuvok?"

"He remains in a coma. Doctor Ree can find no physiological reason for it. Still, the cause can only be the prodigious amount of data to which his brain was exposed when he attempted to meld with the . . . entity that Mister S'syrixx believed was living inside Brahma-Shiva's computer system."

"I sense . . . a great deal of activity in the commander's

brain," Troi said. "I apologize. I didn't mean to intrude."

"Not at all. Vulcan thoughts and emotions can be difficult for esper species to avoid sensing."

T'Pel suddenly noticed a change on the overhead biomonitor. Her husband's life signs had abruptly strengthened.

"She . . . is correct, my wife," Tuvok said, his voice sounding as dry as Vulcan's Forge, his eyes still closed. "You must take better care of yourself."

Apparently alerted by the changed bioreadings, Nurse Ogawa and Dr. Ree rushed into the room, their medical tricorders already deployed and scanning. Despite her desire to extend her hand toward her husband, T'Pel retreated several paces to allow the medical professionals to work unobstructed.

"Do not be concerned about me, my husband. You should concentrate instead upon your recovery."

"Pulse, respiration, EEG," Ogawa said. "All life signs have strengthened. But they are also growing less stable."

"Twenty ccs inaprovaline," Ree said.

Ogawa nodded, then picked up a hypospray and began to set it.

"I prefer the . . . traditional Vulcan method of regaining consciousness," Tuvok said, his eyes still tightly closed. "My wife, please attend me."

Ogawa and Ree exchanged confused looks for a moment, then stepped aside to clear a path for T'Pel.

T'Pel silently crossed to the biobed, pulled Tuvok's shoulders until he had reached a slouched sitting position, and then methodically, unemotionally began to deliver a series of hard slaps across his face. Forehand. Backhand.

Forehand. Backhand. She repeated the process as her husband absorbed the punishment with as much apparent equanimity as T'Pel delivered it.

Suddenly both his inner and outer eyelids opened, and his combat trained hands moved swiftly to immobilize T'Pel's.

She remained at his side, gazing into his dark eyes as Ree and Ogawa scanned him. Her right index and middle fingers became her only point of physical contact with him, touching the same two fingers on Tuvok's left hand.

"I believe you may finally be on the way to recovery, Commander," Ree said at length. "Though I'm not sure I can explain it any better than I can account for what happened to you in the first place. I still don't like the look of some of your brainwave readings, but we'll keep an eye on those—perhaps they'll settle down in time."

Tuvok nodded in acknowledgment to everyone present. "Thank you, Doctor. Nurse. Counselor. If you don't mind, I should like to speak with my wife."

"Right," Ree said good-naturedly. "Nothing to see here. Move along, everybody."

Within moments, T'Pel was alone with her husband.

"How long have I been unconscious, T'Pel?"

"Four days, one hour, thirteen minutes," she said. "I did not take note of the seconds." She wondered if the counselor's dire assessment of her condition might not have been correct. "What do you remember, Tuvok?"

Emotional strain of some kind striated his forehead slightly as he broke their tenuous physical contact. "My thoughts . . . remain rather jumbled. But I remember being aboard the Brahma-Shiva artifact."

"You were beamed away from it shortly before its destruction. *Titan* left the Vela OB2–404 system not long afterward."

"I see." He straightened, squaring his shoulders, though he remained seated on the edge of the biobed.

"What do you remember of the mission?" T'Pel asked.

The striations on his forehead deepened as he forced himself to remember. "The away team made two attempts to access and download the contents of the device's computer. Both attempts failed. We were running out of both time and alternatives."

She was beginning to understand. "So you attempted to mind-meld with Brahma-Shiva's computer system."

"Yes. If that is indeed all that it was."

"Do you believe you were in contact with a sentient entity?"

"I do not know. Whatever it was, it seemed capable of taking certain volitional actions to protect itself, such as jamming our out-system communications."

"Surely it could have taken less circuitous action—such as preventing the Gorn from seizing control of it."

"Perhaps. But it seemed . . . injured. Incomplete. Or perhaps it was simply very old, and finally beginning to succumb to the inevitability of entropy." His eyes now seemed very large and earnest, as though the Brahma-Shiva artifact's passing had greatly affected him. She had seen such intense emotions burning within him on only a few previous occasions, such as during the *pon farr,* the time of mating. Or more recently, during his ongoing meditations on the grief occasioned by the deaths of their son Elieth and their daughter-in-law Ione Kitain, both of whom perished while working as first responders during last year's Borg attack on Deneva.

She realized that his intensity frightened her, making it a challenge to keep her emotions under the expected degree of control.

Suddenly as certain of herself as she had ever been, she said, "Something came back with you from Brahma-Shiva." She reached toward his face with outstretched fingers.

Once again, he caught her hand, this time more roughly than before. "No. I do not know if it is safe for me to share my thoughts with you. Or with *anyone.*"

Her certainty began to evaporate, sublimating away like a chunk of polar ice dropped onto the Plains of Gol. "Why?"

"Because I can see so *much* now, so clearly. Diagrams. Specifications. Materials lattices. Energy vectors."

"Terraforming knowledge," she whispered.

He nodded. "Perhaps enough to reconstruct the device with which I melded. Perhaps not. I do not know."

"Just like Genesis."

"Like Genesis, such knowledge has undeniable potential to do good," he said. "Particularly on Federation worlds that are still recovering from the damage the Borg invasion inflicted."

Worlds like Deneva, she thought. She felt tears welling up, but willed them to stop with a brutal determination.

Aloud, calmly, she said, "And it could just as easily be misused. Even with the best of intentions, terrible consequences can eventuate from the use of such power. I am sure I do not need to reacquaint you with what happened at Eurymede VI."

She carefully avoided using the phrase that some had used, unfairly in her estimation, to describe the incident: the Eurymede VI Massacre.

Tuvok stared straight ahead silently, obviously weighing each item on a very small slate of alternatives.

"Will you tell the captain?" she asked.

"I don't know. As you say, there would be terrible risks."

She considered what she knew of the chain of events that had led him from Eurymede VI to their marriage, their child-rearing years together, and finally his return to Starfleet, this time as a middle-aged, loss-averse security and tactical specialist rather than as the callow young scientist he once had been.

Touching his hand with two fingers, she said, "I shall support whatever decision you reach, my husband."

He reciprocated the hand gesture. "I am grateful, my wife."

"I merely ask you to keep in mind what happened the last time circumstance thrust such a decision upon you," she said. "And that you remember S'vec's dictum that one man can summon the future."

"I have never been more aware of that proverb than I am at this moment, my wife," Tuvok said, his inner torment now clearly on display. He held creation in one hand, destruction in the other. "But how can I determine *which* future I will summon?"

Appendix

Who's Who Aboard *Titan* in *Seize the Fire*

Captain William T. Riker
(human male) commanding officer

Commander Christine Vale
(human female) first officer/executive officer

Commander Tuvok
(Vulcan male) second officer/tactical officer

Commander Deanna Troi
(Betazoid-human female) diplomatic officer/senior counselor

Commander Xin Ra-Havreii
(Efrosian male) chief engineer

Lieutenant Commander Shenti Yisec Eres Ree
(Pahkwa-thanh male) chief medical officer

Lieutenant Commander Ranul Keru
(unjoined Trill male) chief of security

Lieutenant Commander Melora Pazlar
(Elaysian female) senior science officer

Lieutenant Sariel Rager
(Human female) senior operations officer

Lieutenant Commander Tamen Gibruch
(Chandir male) gamma-shift bridge commander

Chief Axel Bolaji
(human male) gamma-shift flight controller

Lieutenant Commander Onnta
(Balosneean male) assistant chief medical officer

Lieutenant Alyssa Ogawa
(human female) head nurse

Lieutenant Eviku Ndashelef
(Arkenite male) xenobiologist

Lieutenant Chamish
(Kazarite male) ecologist

Lieutenant Huilan Sen'kara
(S'ti'ach male) junior counselor

Pral glasch Haaj
(Tellarite male) junior counselor

Lieutenant Pava Ek'Noor sh'Aqabaa
(Andorian *shen*) security officer; gamma-shift tactical officer

Lieutenant Aili Lavena
(Pacifican "Selkie" female) senior flight controller

Ensign Torvig Bu-Kar-Nguv
(Choblik male) engineer

Ensign Mordecai Crandall
(human male) engineer

Lieutenant Bowan Radowski
(human male) transporter engineer

Ensign Tasanee Panyarachun
(human female) engineer

Chief Garem Urkral
(Saurian female) engineer

Ensign Peya Fell
(Deltan female) relief science officer

Dr. Se'al Cethente Qas
(Syrath male) senior astrophysicist

Ensign Y'lira Modan
(Selenean female) cryptolinguist

Ensign Zurin Dakal
(Cardassian male) sensor analyst

Ensign Evesh
(Tellarite female) sensor technician

Ensign Olivia Bolaji
(human female) shuttle pilot

Ensign Waen
(Bolian female) shuttle pilot

Ensign Kuu'iut
(Betelgeusian male) relief tactical officer

Chief Petty Officer Dennisar
(Orion male) security officer

Lieutenant Gian Sortollo
(human male) security officer

Ensign Hriss
(Caitian female) security officer

Lieutenant Qur Qontallium
(Male Gnalish Fejimaera) security officer

Chief Petty Officer Bralik
(Ferengi female) geologist

Ensign Ot Rynaph
(Kasheetan male) airponics lab technician

Lieutenant Savalek
(Vulcan male) botanist

Crewman Ellec Krotine
(Boslic female) security guard

T'Pel
(Vulcan female) civilian child-care specialist

Noah Powell
(human male) civilian child, son of Alyssa Ogawa

Totyarguil Bolaji
(human male) toddler, son of Axel and Olivia Bolaji

Natasha Miana Riker-Troi
(human-Betazoid female) infant, daughter of Will Riker and Deanna Troi

SecondGen White-Blue
(artificial intelligence) guest

Acknowledgments

The author must recognize the contributions of the legions who enriched the contents of these pages, most especially: my editors, the patient and long-suffering Jaime Costas and Margaret Clark; Marco Palmieri and Keith R.A. DeCandido for coming up with the Typhon Pact in *A Singular Destiny*; my Typhon Pact colleagues (Dayton Ward, David R. George III, and most especially, David Mack, who demonstrated forbearance above and beyond the call of Starfleet duty); Andy Mangels, who coauthored the first two *Titan* novels (*Taking Wing* and *The Red King*) with me, and all the *Titan* novelists who have followed (Christopher L. Bennett, Geoffrey Thorne, James Swallow, and David Mack [again], whose astonishing *Destiny* trilogy has shaken the *Star Trek* universe to its foundations, thereby making this volume possible, and whose earlier TNG novels *A Time to Kill* and *A Time to Heal* were instrumental in getting Will Riker's captaincy off the ground); Marco Palmieri (again), for laying the keel of the *U.S.S. Titan* in the first place, thereby allowing *Taking Wing* to take wing; the kind and indulgent folks at the New Deal Café (née the Daily Market and Café), where much of this volume was written; John Van Citters at CBS Consumer Products, for signing off on all the havoc I have wrought in these pages; the entire

Star Trek internet community, those tireless wiki-compilers whose multitudinous and serried ranks defy enumeration here; Michael Jan Friedman, for lessons in Gorn protocol in his TNG novel *Requiem* and for introducing the Gnalish species in his earlier TNG novel *Reunion;* Geoffrey Mandel, for his ever-useful *Star Trek Star Charts,* which kept me from getting lost in the galactic hinterlands on countless occasions and added some color to Christine Vale's Izarian background; Kevin J. Anderson, for conceiving the failed Gorn warrior coup of 2374, as detailed in Wildstorm's *The Gorn Crisis* graphic novel; Judith and Garfield Reeves-Stevens, for chapter 24's oblique reference to the myth of the first Cardassians (Ailam and Neroon), initially presented in their *Deep Space 9: Millennium* novel, *Inferno;* Robert J. Sawyer, whose outstanding s-f novel *www:wake* (Ace Books, 2009) piqued my interest in Zipf plots as they relate to languages and information theory; Michael and Denise Okuda and Debbie Mirek, whose *Star Trek Encyclopedia: A Reference Guide to the Future* (1999 edition) remains indispensable even in this modern age of ubiquitous wikis; Shane Johnson, whose *Star Trek: The Worlds of the Federation* yielded valuable information about Tau Lacertae IX (the Gorn homeworld) and its inhabitants; the brain trust at Interplay Games, whose *Starfleet Command* video game was the source of my references to the Egg Bringer S'Yahazah of Gorn mythology; Dan Abnett and Ian Edginton, for christening the original Gorn captain (played by Bobby Clark and Gary Coombs in the TOS episode "Arena") "S'alath" in the premiere issue of Marvel Comics' *Star Trek Unlimited* ("Dying of the Light," November, 1996); Diane

Carey, who originated "Eliar" as a Gorn name for a planet in the Cestus system in her TOS novel *Dreadnought;* John Vornholt, for his explorations of the pitfalls of terraforming technology in his *Genesis Wave* and *Genesis Force* novels; L. A. Graf, whose story "Reflections" in *The Lives of Dax* anthology begat the Trill *mreker*; Kenneth Hite, Ross A. Isaacs, Evan Jamieson, Steven S. Long, Christian Moore, Ree Soesbee, Gareth Michael Skarka, John Snead, and John Wick for creating the ancient Vulcan philosopher S'vec, who I culled from their 1998 Last Unicorn Games RPG module *The Way of Kolinahr;* Pocket's own Emilia Pisani, who was hugely helpful during the copyediting and proofing phases of this *Titan* voyage; all the performers, show runners, and behind-the-camera talent who brought *Star Trek* to screens large and small over the past four-plus decades; every actor whose character participated in this volume's events, beginning with Jonathan Frakes, Marina Sirtis, and Tim Russ; Gene Roddenberry (1921–1991), for originating the universe in which I get to spend so much time playing; and lastly, though never leastly, my wife, Jenny, and our sons, James and William, for their long-suffering patience and unending inspiration.

About the Author

Michael A. Martin's short fiction has appeared in *The Magazine of Fantasy & Science Fiction,* and he is the author of *Star Trek Online: The Needs of the Many* and *Star Trek: Enterprise: The Romulan War—Beneath the Raptor's Wing,* as well as its forthcoming (2011) sequel, *Star Trek: Enterprise: The Romulan War—in Shariel's Jaws.* He has also coauthored (with Andy Mangels) several *Star Trek* comics for Marvel and Wildstorm as well as numerous other works of *Star Trek* prose fiction, including: *Enterprise: Kobayashi Maru; Excelsior: Forged in Fire; Enterprise: The Good That Men Do;* the *USA Today* bestseller *Titan: Taking Wing; Titan: The Red King; Enterprise: Last Full Measure;* the Sy Fy Genre Award–winning *Worlds of Deep Space 9 Volume Two: Trill—Unjoined; The Lost Era 2298: The Sundered; Deep Space 9 Mission: Gamma Book Three—Cathedral; The Next Generation: Section 31—Rogue; Starfleet Corps of Engineers* #30 and #31 ("Ishtar Rising" Books 1 and 2, re-presented in *Aftermath,* the eighth volume of the *S.C.E.* paperback series); stories in the *Prophecy and Change, Tales of the Dominion War,* and *Tales from the Captain's Table* anthologies; and three novels based on the *Roswell* television series. Other publishers of Martin's work include Atlas Editions (producers of the *Star Trek Universe* subscription card series), Gareth Stevens, Inc., Grolier Books, Moonstone Books, *The Oregonian,* Sharpe Reference, Facts on File, *Star Trek Magazine,* and Visible Ink Press. He lives with his wife, Jenny, and their sons, James and William, in Portland, Oregon.